Praise for Jessica I

'Jessica Dettmann has an eye for the ...., ... and inspirations of life which coupled with a truly original turn of phrase and great way with a gag makes for sparkling and heartwarming reading' Ben Elton

'Has a natural knack for humour' Better Reading

This Has Been Absolutely Lovely

'Brilliantly observed, Jessica Dettmann's portrayal of messy, modern family life is packed with delicious humour and balanced with moments of real poignancy. Her knack for writing sharp, witty dialogue makes for a hugely entertaining read. I adored it' Joanna Nell, author of *The Single Ladies of Jacaranda Retirement Village*

'With humour and heart, Dettmann weaves an unforgettable tale about the lives we choose, and the lives that choose us. Dettmann nails the funny, sad and bizarre nuances of family life in this gripping novel that will appeal to fans of Liane Moriarty, Jojo Moyes and Marian Keyes. I expect to see this everywhere this summer' Sally Hepworth, author of *The Mother-in-Law*

How to Be Second Best

'Hilarious and heartwarming ... Part Marian Keyes page-turner, part Holly Wainwright local brilliance, this book is all too relatable for those who have found themselves at the supermarket or school drop-off wondering why they can't quite get it together. Ultimate summer read' *Herald Sun*

Jessica Dettmann is a Sydney-based writer and performer. Her blog, *Life With Gusto*, turns a sharp but affectionate eye on modern parenthood. She has performed her work several times at Giant Dwarf's Story Club, and has appeared on their podcast.

After a decade working as an editor for Random House Australia and HarperCollins publishers she made the transition to writing after two small children rendered her housebound. She once appeared as the City of Sydney Christmas Angel and sat on top of the Town Hall in a frock that reached the street.

Also by Jessica Dettmann

How to Be Second Best

This Has Been Absolutely Lovely

JESSICA DETTMANN

HarperCollins*Publishers*

HarperCollins*Publishers*
Australia • Brazil • Canada • France • Germany • Holland • Hungary
India • Italy • Japan • Mexico • New Zealand • Poland • Spain • Sweden
Switzerland • United Kingdom • United States of America

First published in Australia in 2021
by HarperCollins*Publishers* Australia Pty Limited
Level 13, 201 Elizabeth Street, Sydney NSW 2000
ABN 36 009 913 517
harpercollins.com.au

A catalogue record for this book is available from the National Library of Australia.

ISBN 978 1 4607 5598 3 (paperback)
ISBN 978 1 4607 1001 2 (ebook)

The quote Annie thinks of on page 135 is taken from *Enemies of Promise*
(George Routledge & Sons: 1938) by Cyril Connolly.
Cover design by Hazel Lam, HarperCollins Design Studio
Cover images by shutterstock.com
Author photograph by Sally Flegg
Typeset in Baskerville by Kelli Lonergan
Printed and bound in Australia by McPherson's Printing Group. The papers used by
HarperCollins in the manufacture of this book are a natural, recyclable product made from
wood grown in sustainable plantation forests. The fibre source and manufacturing processes
meet recognised international environmental standards, and carry certification.

For Drew, with all my love.
You see? Sometimes I can just say something nice.

Home is where I leave you,
where you feed me, where I grieve you,
where you need me, where I don't need you.
Home is where the truth lies,
where your heart breaks, where our youth dies.
Home is where we'll never be again.

'Home Is Where Your Heart Is',
Great Britain's Eurovision entry, 1983

Chapter 1

The most successful song Annie Jones ever wrote had been stuck in her head for the best part of forty years, and it would only be a slight overstatement to say she hadn't had a moment's peace from it in that time.

So it had been too much to hope that her father's funeral that morning would have been enough to mute the self-inflicted soundtrack jangling inside her head. She wondered if this made her some sort of sociopath.

She'd managed to ignore it during her eulogy. She'd stood at the front of the blond wood crematorium chapel and paid tribute to the man who had always been in her corner — her most unwavering supporter, always ready to admire a lyric or fund a new instrument.

You'd have thought that grief would have dissolved or muffled the tune, but no. Not even the clanking old Anglican dirges her father had stipulated by turning down pages in his hymn book could drown it out. There the song remained. Sometimes the volume went down a bit, so she could, for example, hear people in the church singing along to 'Immortal, Invisible, God Only Wise' and later, back at the house, telling her how proud he had been of her; that he'd had a good innings.

She couldn't understand why her dad had wanted 'Immortal, Invisible'. It sounded the way carrying too many bags of groceries home from the shops felt. 'Tell Out, My Soul' was his other choice, which was slightly better — like something cut from a lesser Andrew Lloyd Webber musical because it didn't move the plot forward.

But neither managed to properly dislodge 'Home Is Where Your Heart Is', which was, if not the best song she'd written, certainly the one with the greatest impact on how her life had turned out. That song was supposed to have been the beginning of something big, and it almost was.

Back when she wrote it, she'd imagined one day telling journalists what the song meant to her. They'd sit together at quiet tables in exclusive London or New York hotels, or in a cottage in Laurel Canyon, and the subsequent magazine profiles would celebrate her down-to-earth sensibility, her refreshing candour and her charm. They would describe her lack of makeup and her fresh-faced beauty, and mention that she ordered tea and not coffee. How could someone so brilliant and successful be so warm and unguarded? the journalists would write. The interviews would range over her young life growing up in a beachside Sydney suburb, to meeting Paul and Brian, forming the band, Love Triangle, with them, then their move to London, and the story of how they worked their way up, tiny gig by tiny gig. The journalist would obviously want to focus on Love Triangle's big break, Eurovision 1983, which should have been the moment the world fell in love with 'Home Is Where Your Heart Is' and with Annie.

She hadn't expected the song to take on this other life, as a personal form of permanent musical tinnitus. She had never dreamed no one would interview her.

There had been lots of moments in her life when she thought the 'Home' earworm might finally give up and fade away. The moment another singer performed it at Eurovision. The break-up of her band. The births of her three children. Her divorce. Her mother's death. The moment the previous Friday morning when her father closed his eyes and became just a body on a bed. But none of them had done the trick.

Now at her father's wake, in the house where she had grown up, Annie opened the oven to check the cheese and spinach triangles and a burst of hot air rushed out and curled her eyelashes back. For just a second the song was shocked into silence, and she had her first inkling in thirty-five years that she might be free. It was mid-December in Sydney, in an already stifling kitchen, and the extra blast of heat was enough to singe off the last of her feelings of obligation.

When she stood back up — the triangles were still pale and needed three more minutes — everything had changed. It was a delayed reaction, of course. Her father had died five days earlier, and her mother four years before that. Her children had been adults for a while, in the eyes of the law at least. She let out an involuntary squeak of elation, and her daughter Naomi looked up with concern from washing a sink full of teacups.

'Did you burn yourself?'

'No, no. Nothing like that.'

Naomi rubbed a frosted lipstick mark from the rim of a cup. 'Are you sad?'

Annie shook her head. 'No,' she said. 'Surprisingly. I should be. But no.'

Naomi shrugged gently. 'There's no "should" with grief. We feel how we feel. No emotion or response is right or wrong. Don't fight the feelings, or judge them. I know you don't believe in auras, but yours is cloudy right now and bluer than it normally is too. That usually suggests some fear around the future, or a lack of self-trust.'

Annie pressed her lips together to stifle a smile. Her middle child was an actual mad hippie. So different from the other two. There was no explaining Naomi.

'There's a lot of power in the house at the moment,' Naomi went on. 'The more of us who gather, the stronger the energy becomes. The family will be whole when Dad and Brian get here. How are you feeling about them coming back? Combining energies — re-forming the triangle?'

What a way to put it. Annie was actually looking forward to seeing Paul and Brian. The other two members of Love Triangle were somewhere over the Middle East right about now, on their way from London for their first Christmas Day together in years, and, despite all that had happened between the three of them, they were her oldest friends. But they weren't a triangle any more.

Annie could remember being five and drawing a picture of her family: Mummy, Daddy, Annie. Or maybe she only remembered the picture itself, because her father had kept it taped to the wall in his study for decades. It was in crayon, on a lined sheet of paper torn from a pad held together with gummy red glue. In the picture her dad was at the top, drawn with a brown crayon, his shirt and trousers the same colour. His shoes, though, were red, in a fit of childish exaggeration on Annie's part, and he held a cake. Her father would no sooner have worn red shoes than made a cake and posed for a portrait holding it.

Below him to the right was her mother. Smaller, yellow-haired and wearing a blue dress. Her shoes were not coloured in. Annie had drawn herself the same size as her mother, in the opposite corner. She'd drawn lines connecting the three figures and realised they formed a triangle. Her father had been impressed by that. She could remember him, possibly then but certainly many more times over the years, reminding her that they were a triangle, and that triangles were the strongest shape. She'd always been happy with their triangle, though quite frankly a sibling or two might have been a lot of help during her parents' last years.

Anyway, now those years were over, and her three children — another triangle, though one in which each corner was outward-looking, only sneaking glances over their shoulders to make sure the others weren't receiving preferential treatment — were leading their own lives. Maybe she was actually, finally, wonderfully, alone in the world.

She needed to examine the situation properly. Surely it couldn't be that she was no longer beholden to anyone. There had to be something to tether her. 'Home Is Where Your Heart Is' started up again in her head, but it was quieter and less obtrusive than usual, like an iPhone playing accidentally in a handbag.

'Mum?'

Annie realised she hadn't answered Naomi. 'Sorry, darling, what was the question?'

Naomi smiled. 'Nothing. I'll watch the oven. You go get some air.'

Annie kissed Naomi's cheek as she passed by to open the back door and step out onto the patio. At once, from around the corner in the driveway, came the soundtrack of the past twenty-something years: her eldest and youngest children, bickering. The voices grew louder as Simon and Molly approached the patio.

'I don't see why I have to go. I got exactly as much beer and wine as Mum said, and it isn't my fault those old boozehounds want whisky.' He tossed a set of car keys at Molly, who caught them without thinking.

'Simon, you have to go because Mum said you have to go. You're unbelievably selfish — this is her father's funeral. It really shouldn't be that big an ask to drive one kilometre to the shops.'

She threw the keys back at him, but he kept his hands clamped by his sides like one of the queen's guards and they clattered to the ground.

'You go,' he told her. 'You're not even drinking. I'm halfway through my second beer. Possibly my third. I might be over the limit.'

'I'm a thousand weeks pregnant and my back is killing me. You're not over the limit. You're just lazy. Mum, tell him he has to go to the bottle shop.' Molly crouched awkwardly down, her bump preventing a bend, picked up the keys and shoved them down the back of Simon's shirt.

'Oh shit, Molly. You're so fucking immature — pardon my French, Mum.'

Annie frowned at them. It was half an hour since she'd asked Molly to source a bottle of whisky for the aged great-aunts. 'Have you two been arguing about this since I asked? For goodness' sake, I'll do it myself.'

Molly glared at her brother. 'You're making Mum leave her dad's wake? Really?'

'Mum,' whined Simon. 'Why can't Molly go? You never make her do anything.'

Annie sighed deeply and looked past them to the garden. Her two grandchildren were out there somewhere, swallowed up by the rambling garden on the oversized suburban block. You could usually hear kids out there but you couldn't see them, which were the ideal conditions for children between the ages of two and twenty — or maybe fifty, she thought now. It was after four but the sun was still high and hot above the patio.

She couldn't be bothered with Simon and Molly any more. She saw them look uncertainly at her. They didn't know how to end arguments without maternal intervention: they never had.

She waved a hand dismissively. 'Do whatever you want. Get the whisky, don't get the whisky.' She dragged a heavy iron-lace chair off the paving and onto the grass, which was rudely green and lush thanks to her diligent dawn and dusk watering regimen.

Simon untucked his shirt, pulled the keys from the waistband of his trousers and stalked off in the direction of the car. Molly lingered for a moment, the winner of quite a hollow victory, before muttering something about low blood sugar and heading inside.

Annie sank onto the chair. The evergreen wildness of the garden pleased her. That had been her father's work. It took a lot of effort to make a garden look untamed, without it actually being overtaken by weeds. He had encouraged the tangled greenery, the creepers and vines, but he'd never let them encroach on the lawn. Her mother had been a different sort of gardener, preferring to cultivate a few roses, happy to wait through the long periods of the year when they were just bare sticks to be rewarded with the unfurling of tiny bright green leaves in the spring, followed by a few months of blooms. Most of the rose bushes back here were barely visible now, overcome by the bolshy spread of geraniums and the great drooping buddleias.

Sitting out in the garden was one of Annie's habits now. For the past two years, almost every afternoon, while her weakening father's dinner was cooking and before she would bathe him and help him to bed, she had come out to the lawn, just to be in the air and breathe the smell of medicine and disinfectant out of her lungs. She'd played songs she loved on the little Bluetooth speaker perched on the kitchen window, facing out. The songs were good for drowning out her earworm.

She rested her hands in her lap. Now. This was when the grief would come. Her friends had warned her. She'd be all right until the funeral was done, they'd said. They'd all turned into versions of Naomi on this subject, to varying degrees. Apparently she had to allow her loss to flow through her.

Closing her eyes, Annie tried to observe her feelings. Grief can take many forms, she told herself. What am I feeling? Hot. And pretty itchy in the only black dress she owned. Were hot and itchy common manifestations of grief?

A sudden urge to laugh overcame her. Hysteria, she thought at first, but as she sat and let it bubble up through her chest, she remembered when she had felt it before: long ago, on another turning-point day. It was the feeling that had swept through her as she walked out of the assembly hall after handing in her final exam of the HSC, an Ancient History paper on the Peloponnesian Wars. It was the feeling of having a future.

'Fuck,' she said to the garden. A flood of euphoria swept over her and she let out a loud 'Ha!' A magpie pecking around at pastry crumbs on the patio paused and cocked its head at her. In the absence of anyone else to tell, she leaned down and, laughing, said to the bird, 'Little mate, I think I've done it. I think I've escaped.'

Still smiling, she sat back and mentally turned to the checklist that had existed in her head for thirty-five years, since the birth of Simon: the list of Who Needs Looking After And What Precisely They Require And When.

Simon's had been the first name on the list. He shouldn't have still needed looking after but, although he did, he was now in the capable hands of his German wife, Diana. She was a logistics co-ordinator for Ikea, unflappable and slightly severe. One of those women who seemed effortlessly fit, she had smooth olive skin and wore her dark hair in a spiky crop that Annie hadn't seen on anyone else in real life since the Berlin Wall came down. Their life ran smoothly, and Simon was well fed on a combination of grain-heavy breads and plum-based cakes. He could stand to take more exercise, but he'd figure that out when he turned forty. For the past decade he'd been gainfully employed in a managerial role by a construction company in Berlin, they had enough money to visit Sydney every two years, and their only child, Felix, at six years old was a delight. Annie had no cause to worry about Simon.

Next was Naomi. On paper, Naomi should have been a worry. She was thirty-three, the single mother of a daughter, Sunny, also aged six, and she lived what Annie could only describe as a hand-to-mouth existence as a freelance masseuse in Byron Bay. Annie was only mostly sure that wasn't a euphemism for sex work. Recently she'd started selling paintings of people's auras, too, after years of telling everyone she could see colours around them. Naomi's life seemed to involve a lot of swapping vegetables, and while Sunny apparently possessed a pair of shoes, she was rarely seen wearing them. Annie might worry about her daughter's myriad piercings getting infected, but Naomi was a sensible-level hippy — though she did believe apple cider vinegar to be the panacea for all ills, Sunny was nonetheless fully vaccinated.

Annie turned her mind to her youngest, Molly, and felt a growl of anxiety. It seemed uncharitable to use the expression 'a fly in the ointment' to describe her own offspring, but she couldn't help thinking it. Molly was twenty-seven and pregnant. She was married to Jack, happily enough, it seemed. Jack was pretty nice. Neither short nor tall, fat nor thin, he had blondish brownish hair and the sort of face that was difficult to remember — usually it was easier to describe him by his bushy beard — but, once reminded, people usually recalled him fondly. He was much more sensible than Molly: he had two jobs, neither of which was really a career as Annie understood it, though the definition of careers had changed since she was young. He mixed cocktails in a city bar that sold one hundred and six kinds of gin and tended to present them under a smoky cloche, and he was a sales rep for a type of dried cat food that cost more per week than Annie had had in her budget to feed three kids.

Annie had once said she thought their pairing was like a draughthorse had taken up with a poorly trained racehorse, but Paul, Molly's father, had said that in such an equine metaphor he saw Molly less as a racehorse and more as two enemies trapped in a pantomime horse suit. Annie was pleased she and Paul could still talk like that, because there was only one person who you should laugh at your children with, and that was their other parent.

Paul was right about Molly: she was a mass of contradictions, which made her a lot of fun, but certainly slowed her progress through life. She was forever changing her mind about what she wanted to do, which everyone said was just the millennial way, but Annie thought Molly would have been a dilettante no matter when she'd been born.

Half of Molly's problem was her beauty. She got that from her father. They were both blessed — if that was how you chose to see it — with fine features, large eyes, thick, wavy golden hair that did whatever was fashionable, high cheekbones and generous, naturally pouting mouths that made them look like they spoke French. People had always turned to stare at their willowy frames and their dazzling smiles. After watching people fall at Paul's feet for forty years, Annie wasn't sure it was necessarily to Molly's benefit that she moved through the world like that too, but there wasn't anything she could do about it.

Annie wondered if Molly's baby would look like its mother and grandfather, or if it might have Jack's broader, slightly doughier features. She felt pretty sure it would be one or the other, as it was with her own children. The beautiful genes didn't seem to mix. Annie's first two children looked like her: attractive by ordinary standards — regular features, one chin each — but not when compared to the dazzling perfection of Molly and Paul.

Regardless of what the child looked like, the idea of Molly as a mother didn't sit easily with Annie. Molly had a tendency to get bored with things.

She'd been very enthusiastic about the three different university degrees she had begun. Her podcast was clever and well liked — for the four episodes she released before she moved on to a volunteer position with a refugee aid organisation. Her interior design phase had followed that, and the small inner-city flat Molly and Jack had bought with a gigantic mortgage had almost been beautifully decorated, until Molly fell in love with stand-up comedy for six weeks. She could play the piano pretty well, and sing, like both her parents, but she'd never liked doing either for an audience.

Her latest passion was home organising, and she had been putting sticky labels on people's jars of dried kidney beans and consolidating all their open packets of Nurofen for a year, which was almost record-breaking for a Molly job. Annie wondered how close they were to the end of that phase.

Annie chided herself: that was a silly way to think. Molly wouldn't treat her baby like one of her jobs or hobbies, something to tire of like she had of her sewing machine, stand-up paddleboard and sourdough starter. Motherhood was different. It taught you to sustain interest. Just because Molly hadn't chosen a solid career path didn't mean she wouldn't be a terrific mum.

Honestly, Annie was a little surprised that Molly was happy to be pregnant at all, given that she had seemed almost violently unmaternal since the unfortunate afternoon when, at the age of six, she accidentally witnessed a classmate's mother giving birth on the laundry floor. Annie remembered that like it was yesterday and she hadn't even been there. Poor little Molly and her friend Catherine had watched in terror as Catherine's baby brother entered the world as if shot out of a cannon onto a pile of freshly washed soccer shirts in a plastic clothes basket. The girls had called an ambulance, but it was all over well before the paramedics came.

It had been a surprise, then, when, in winter, Jack and Molly had announced they were going to be parents. They were too young, by today's middle-class standards. They'd only got married a year back, and none of their friends had even got that far. Annie supposed Jack had talked Molly into it. Or it wasn't planned. Molly's fear of missing out, her love of new adventures, would have overridden her fears of carrying on with the pregnancy.

As always, Molly had been unsustainably enthusiastic to begin with. Blessed with a nausea-free first trimester, for the first twenty weeks she had taken daily photographs of her profile and stitched them together into a time lapse. She'd downloaded three baby growth apps on her phone and could and did tell you at any moment how many weeks and days pregnant she was.

But nine months was a long time, and by the end of the second trimester the shine was off the pregnancy and Molly was just annoyed by all the things she wasn't allowed to eat. Or do. Only the week before, she'd raged to Annie that tuna and tooth-whitening were forbidden.

'Your teeth are white already,' Annie had said, bemused. 'And you hate tuna. You used to call it trick chicken when I gave it to you on sandwiches.'

'You're missing the point,' Molly told her, but Annie wasn't sure Molly knew what her point was. 'It's like no one even remembers mothers are people too. Suddenly I'm just a vessel for a child. It's obscene. What if I decided I did like tuna? Then what?'

Annie hadn't been able to summon a satisfactory answer. There was no point trying, really — when Molly got her knickers in a twist like this the best thing to do was nod and stand well back.

She'd always been like that. Well, not always, Annie admitted to herself. Only since her dad left. Annie had heard once, or read, that sometimes when a young person has something monumental and catastrophic happen in their life, they remain emotionally the same age forever after. It sounded like nonsense, and obviously it was, but there was no denying that there was a touch of the eight year old, even now, about her daughter. Molly thought she had her whole life ahead of her, that the world owed her a happy ending, and that she could spend as much time and energy as she wanted making her own story just right. Becoming a parent would come as quite a shock.

Annie shook her head and told herself Molly would be fine. She was bound to figure out motherhood. People did. Babies changed you, mostly for the better. They gave you a sense of your place in the world, in the circle of life and all that.

In the warm evening air Annie breathed slowly and calmly. Her children were no longer her responsibility, her marriage had been over for nearly twenty years and now her parents were both gone. There really was a decent chance she was free.

She let out a delighted whoop, and the magpie flapped off in alarm.

Chapter 2

Molly looked at the plate of finger sandwiches on her grandparents'
dining room table. They'd been made in stacks and a serrated
knife had de-crusted them neatly before they'd been flipped on
their sides and transferred all at once to the plate. Why did being
at a funeral mean no one had to eat their crusts? The question
tickled her and she briefly thought about writing it down in the
notes app on her phone in case it was useful for something one
day, but the urge passed and she didn't bother.

No one had taken a sandwich yet. They were chicken and
mayonnaise on white bread, which was so compressed by the
stacking and de-crusting process that it was hard to see where
one sandwich ended and the next began. Maybe that was why
no one was eating them. There was a real risk of taking the side
of the next sandwich along with the one you wanted, leaving the
filling of the neighbouring sandwich open to the air, and then
no one would take that and the whole row of sandwiches would
be shunned. It was all a bit fraught and probably, on balance, it
would be better to have another piece of cake instead.

Not that the cake was particularly nice. Pa had been ninety
years old when he died, and Molly had attended enough funerals
to have observed the inverse correlation between the age of the
deceased and the quality of the food. Very old people meant very
dry squares of cake — and no good ever came from cake cut in

squares — and white-bread chicken sandwiches that always had bits of chopped cartilage in them.

When she was in Year Five, her friend Ellen's brother had died of leukaemia. He was only six. There had been little roast beef crostini at that funeral, and tiny chocolate eclairs. Caterers, she realised now. Ellen's mother probably wouldn't have been up to making sandwiches. A shudder ran through her. It was hard to tell if it originated in her shoulders or if the baby was shifting itself about in her abdomen. She hadn't heard anyone else mention getting the shivers when their baby kicked, but hers shocked her on a regular basis. Thirty-six weeks, that's how long her body had been getting used to this share-house situation, but it still wasn't feeling any less weird.

'All right, mate,' she said. 'It was only an observation about eclairs. I wasn't saying it isn't a very sad funeral. He was my grandfather.' She glanced around to see if anyone had noticed her talking to her own belly.

Seated on clusters of dining chairs, and some on the exhausted lounge suite in her grandparents' living room, were old people drinking cups of tea, wishing it was whisky. They came in varying shades of aged — some were her parents' vintage, sixty-ish, but a few were getting right up into their nineties. Not so many of the very old guard: hardly any of her grandfather's friends were still alive. Most of the ancients were women: old acquaintances or distant relatives of her late grandmother. At least half of them were named Pat.

One of the old women caught Molly's eye and smiled, beckoning her over.

Molly attempted to bend down to her, but there was nowhere for her belly in such a position, so she sat cross-legged on the floor instead.

The old woman took her hand. 'Now,' she said. 'You're the youngest one. The one with the lovely voice.'

'No,' Molly said. 'You're thinking of my mum, Annie. I'm Molly. I don't really sing.'

The old eyes were sharp and the grip on Molly's hand tightened. 'I know who you are. And you certainly do have a lovely voice. Whether or not you choose to sing.'

Molly looked around for someone to rescue her from whoever the creepy Macbethian creature was. She had to be one of Pa's cousins. Or Granny's. When had this woman heard her sing? Molly hadn't played or sung for years.

The only other person under sixty in the room, Naomi, was excellent at this sort of thing — sitting and talking to old people. Molly couldn't bear it. Very old ladies smelled like forgotten toast and she was always distracted by the wiry chin hairs poking out of their crumpled faces. But not Naomi. She seemed unbothered by their prickly kisses and the way they held you tightly with their claws, as if they feared Death would drag them away before they had bored you senseless with a story about a war, or some trams.

Naomi was holding a plate of delicious-smelling cheese triangles and Molly desperately wanted one, but not desperately enough to stay in this room with the contents of the municipal courtesy bus. She stood up and muttered something about the bathroom, pulling her hand free from the woman's clutches, and retreated back to the dining room, hiding behind the return where she couldn't be easily seen.

It was all right for Naomi. She probably had some witchy Byron Bay spell she could perform afterwards to slough off the pall of mortality Molly could feel descending on the room. Naomi probably liked being close to people who were almost dead.

She was always going on about what a privilege it was to be in the company of *community elders*.

'We have so much to learn from them, Molly,' she'd said that afternoon at the crematorium when she'd found her sister behind the hearse, hiding from two hobbling crones who wouldn't stop trying to touch her belly. 'Babies and the very elderly — they're on the threshold of another world. They inhabit a liminal space. That's a very sacred thing.' Molly also inhabited a liminal space — between being able and unable to cope with her sister's Northern Rivers pseudo-mystic bullshit.

Even Naomi's daughter, Sunny, seemed relaxed around old people and she was only six. Maybe because she was still young enough to be hanging out in this liminal space Naomi was so obsessed with. Earlier Molly had seen her standing patiently beside Great Aunt Enid, whom the child had never met before, as the old woman squeezed her hand and stroked her little face. If anyone tried that on Molly — today, let alone when she was six — she would kick them in their papery shins and be off on her bike before anyone could stop her.

Molly didn't know where Sunny was now. Probably in the garden with Felix. The cousins had only met a few times, but they'd hit it off. Simon had taken them out to the garden and shown them the old treehouse.

Molly looked out the back window and past her mother, who was sitting alone in a chair on the grass, which seemed an odd choice of activity for a person in the middle of hosting a wake. She saw the children's legs, dangling over the edge of the treehouse platform, swinging back and forth.

It was hard to believe the treehouse could still be safe, but her grandfather had been a build-it-once, build-it-very-slowly, build-it-properly type of man.

She and Naomi and Simon thought of the treehouse as their own, but it was there long before them. Pa built it for Annie, when she was a little girl. Pa had loved Annie like crazy, probably because she was his only child. Molly wondered if her dad would have felt like that about her, if Simon and Naomi hadn't been born first. Or at all.

Simon had been up the tree that morning to give it his developer's seal of approval, knocking away spiderwebs and stomping about on the floorboards, shaking the sides to see if they were likely to give way. The rope ladder needed replacing, but for now they were making do with the aluminium one from the garage.

When was the last time Molly had been up in the treehouse? Years and years back. You don't always notice the last time you do things. The treehouse was beautiful: a miniature cottage, with a sloping shingle roof, windows on two sides, and a balcony with a rail running around it. Certainly more to her taste than her grandparents' actual house. As a kid she had found this heavy Victorian style of architecture pleasing: it reminded her of the houses in the books she liked — *Anne of Green Gables*, *The Secret Garden*, *Callie's Castle* — but her taste had matured and it wasn't her thing at all now. The blood-coloured brick was ugly, the wide verandah — with all the frilly iron lace — on the front and the enclosed porch on one side kept the main rooms cool but very dark, and the furniture was unfashionably heavy wood, with turned legs and the sort of mahogany tinge her hair had taken on when she first tried to dye it at the age of fourteen. She'd been trying to look like Lindsay Lohan.

But she had to admit the feel of the house was precious. She hadn't ever lived there permanently, but every summer, as soon as school broke up for Christmas, her mum and dad had crammed children, suitcases, guitars, books, board games and bikes into the Mitsubishi Nimbus, handed over the keys to their cramped narrow Glebe terrace to whichever family of tourists had rented it through an analogue holiday rental service run by the local real estate agent, and headed up to Granny and Pa's.

The hour-long drive didn't take them terribly far, as the crow flies, but it was a world away from their inner-city life. Molly hated the idea of someone else sleeping in her bed, but being able to ride her bike to the beach at Granny and Pa's had been pretty consoling.

She and her siblings had effectively been handed off to their grandparents for the next six weeks while Annie and Paul ran school-holiday music workshops for eight- to sixteen-year-olds in the local bowling club. Once or twice the three of them had joined in, but ultimately the awkwardness of treating their parents with the same degree of respect they would show to a teacher proved too problematic — not to mention having to listen to them sing — and they elected instead to stay at home with their grandparents, doing whichever thousand-piece jigsaw puzzle had been selected for that summer, playing days-long Monopoly tournaments, watching the box set of *All Creatures Great and Small*, going to the beach, and arguing over the sole Game Boy.

Besides, the popularity of her parents' music workshops relied to an embarrassing degree on their fleeting moment of fame, back in the early 1980s. Their band, Love Triangle — even the name had made Molly cringe — had been sort of famous, briefly. If fame were on a spectrum from one to ten, one being a busker outside the supermarket in a country town with under a thousand inhabitants and ten being Taylor Swift, Molly reckoned Love Triangle had peaked at six: Trivial Pursuit answer level. It had been excruciating to watch parents dropping off their kids and trying to make them care that these middle-aged music teachers were once all the rage. Even their use of the term 'all the rage' had only served to give Molly, quite literally, all the rage.

The only part of her parents' previous life she was ever prepared to indulge was the existence of the third member of their band, Brian. Brian lived in England, but for a long time he had come back each Christmas and stayed with his old mother, who'd lived two streets from Pa's house on Baskerville Road, further from the beach than they were.

Back then, Molly had felt a bit sorry for Brian. He'd been the third wheel in the band after her parents coupled up, and he'd clearly still carried a torch for the old days. So many nights she had lain in her bed upstairs at her grandparents' house, drifting through the place between sleep and wake, and hearing the adults' laughter as they drank red wine out on the back patio. Brian was always trying to get her parents to move back to England, to give the band another shot.

Sometimes they would get their guitars out and play their old songs. Annie was always shushing Paul and Brian, telling them they'd wake the children. Molly didn't hate their old songs. They were horribly uncool, obviously, and the sort of stupid pop music she had absolutely never been into, but sometimes, in the dark of night, if Brian was playing along too, she'd let herself like them a tiny bit.

Brian was all right because he didn't hassle Molly about music. Her parents couldn't help themselves. They'd made her learn the piano until she was in Year Eight, which was fine — piano wasn't hard. But it wasn't fun. They seemed to think that just because she could do it she must like doing it and they couldn't have been more wrong. Molly could do it, she thought, because she was genetically predisposed to be able to play music and she'd been absorbing it her whole life. She had long fingers and a wide reach, and the structures and chords — the language of the piano — made inherent sense to her. What she didn't have was the slightest desire to be a musician. She didn't particularly care if people looked at her. She didn't burn with untold stories and unexpressed emotions. And she certainly didn't have the commitment.

Her parents mustn't have had it either: the drive to succeed in music. Otherwise they wouldn't have chucked it in as early in their career as they had. From what Molly could tell of her parents' musical past, the enthusiasm had belonged to her dad and Brian, and her mother had possessed the talent.

After all, once the band broke up, her dad became a teacher, whereas for a while her mum had still written some songs. Well, advertising jingles. The first had been an adaptation of one of their original songs. A dairy company had paid a small fortune to change the lyrics and play it in the background of a television commercial in which three women with shoulder pads demonstrated for thirty seconds that being a working woman meant eating a tub of low-fat yoghurt with a plastic spoon at your desk.

After that, Annie had written her first built-for-purpose jingle: a piano ditty that plinked merrily along on Australia's televisions as another working mother — this time popping into the back room of her flower shop — added boiling water to a cup containing the contents of a sachet of what appeared to be dehydrated vomit, then closed her eyes in rapture at the steamy aroma of the packet soup. The ads could still be seen on YouTube in a montage of commercials now considered sexist and daggy.

During the school year, her mum had worked in the office at a private school, so she only worked on her jingles in the Christmas holidays, when Granny was there to look after the kids, and Dad and Brian were there to act as co-writers — though how much they helped write the jingles and how much they were occupied with other pursuits, who could say.

The baby kicked again. It had an uncanny ability to jolt Molly whenever her thoughts wandered somewhere she'd rather they didn't.

Molly heard Naomi approaching. She made a soft tinkling sound as she moved — her personal fanfare a combination of the tiny bells embroidered onto her skirt and her many anklets and bracelets. She put down the now-empty cheese triangle plate. Molly eyed it with disappointment.

'It's wild being back here, all together,' Naomi said.

Molly glanced into the living room. There was barely any movement. 'Is wild the word?'

Naomi laughed. 'Not them, just us, you know? The three of us and Mum. Dad's back tomorrow. And Brian.'

'But not Pa or Granny.'

Naomi looked around knowingly. 'They're here. They haven't gone far.'

'You reckon?'

'For sure. Spirits don't go, not straight away. I can feel them both here today.'

'Why? What do they do? Just lurk around? Watch us? Put coasters under drinks?'

'Depends on the spirit, and whether they're still here because they're trapped, or because they're free and choose to visit.'

'Right. And which situation fits our grandparents?'

'I'm not sure. Sometimes spirits can't move on because there's someone still here who needs their help.'

'Oh, that'll be it. Granny probably wants to help me with the baby. Do you think I can get the childcare rebate if I leave my kid with a ghost when I go back to work?'

Naomi ignored her. 'Sometimes they stay because they have unfinished business. Something is holding them here. Or someone.'

Molly regarded her sister. 'You really are very weird. Do you know that? This might all be normal up in Byron. But objectively it's very weird to believe in ghosts.'

Naomi shrugged. 'You asked.' She took the plate of chicken sandwiches in to the old people.

Molly turned back to the window. In the back garden the jacaranda was reaching the end of its bloom: the lawn was carpeted prettily with the mauve flowers, but they were turning brown and slimy very quickly on the bricks of the patio. Her granny wouldn't have left them there to turn like that. If her spirit was really still around, Molly was sure it would have swept all those blossoms back onto the grass, like a spectral leaf-blower.

Molly and Jack's home had no garden. It was a one bedroom flat in a 1970s tower in Darlinghurst, with corridors that smelled like stewed chops. The building was named Maralinga, after the smaller 1930s red-brick block of flats it had replaced, and it had occurred to no one, apparently, that perhaps that name was no longer appropriate.

The flat, which looked okay now she'd painted most of it and updated the bathroom a bit, was not somewhere she wanted to stay for a long time. One day they hoped to buy a mid-century house. That would be much more her style. One of those northern beaches ones with windows that go almost to the floor. She would fill it with Danish furniture so slender and smooth it looked like it rode a bike everywhere and only ate smoked salmon. At the moment Molly's taste leaned towards things that were economic of form, delicate of line, and hefty of price tag.

She'd hoped they could buy a bigger place before they had a baby, but the pregnancy had happened sooner than planned.

Stupidly, she'd listened to Naomi the previous Christmas, when she'd told her getting pregnant wasn't as easy as the grownups had liked to make them think when they were teenagers. Apparently, it was quite common for it to take years, since there were actually only about four days a month when you *could* conceive. This was especially the case for someone who has been on The Pill, she stressed, which Molly had been since the age of sixteen. It could take ages for the body to regulate and the cycle to figure out what it was meant to be doing.

A couple of months later Molly had thrown her contraceptive pills in the bin, and Jack promised to buy condoms to use until they were ready for a baby. But before he remembered to do that, all it took was one night — well, one early morning, if she had her dates correct — and that was that. Up. The. Duff. At twenty-seven, which nowadays, in the circles she moved in, was basically equivalent to a teen pregnancy.

Jack was delighted. And what was done was done. It was just a few years earlier than she would have preferred. It probably wouldn't make much difference to her life in the long run.

Molly took a square of bad cake to nibble on and looked for somewhere to sit. Her grandfather's furniture, like the man himself, looked like it had never exercised, intentionally or incidentally. Pa must have moved — he'd been a golfer after retirement — but Molly couldn't picture him in motion. She mostly remembered him sitting: behind his mahogany desk with the red leather top, or in the wrought-iron patio chair in his sunny spot at the side of the house, or in the upright wingback chair in the sitting room, as he called it. That was where he read, with a lamp angled down, like he was interrogating his book rather than reading it, and where he watched the seven o'clock news every evening. He must have moved in a way that fit with every other aspect of his personality — calmly, without fuss, not so as you'd notice. He liked to stand in a doorway too, leaning against one side, one foot crossed over the other. He had a particular wry smile she had loved, like he was about to say something extremely clever and funny. He didn't often do that, but he frequently looked like he might.

Her grandmother had been different. Granny had never been still. She'd flitted. She'd moved after her husband like the wash after a ferry, never able to just sit. Her hands were always brushing things — crumbs off the table, her hair away from her face, imaginary lint off other people's shoulders.

Her mum, too, moved almost ceaselessly, but she wasn't as fidgety. She was more like a sapling in the breeze. Slim and constantly shifting. Though right now she was sitting still, in a garden chair on the grass, staring out at the garden. Molly wondered if she was all right.

She glanced back in to the living room, where all the lumpen chairs were still full of senior citizens. This lot were evidently of the stationary variety of oldies. It felt like a nursing home. There was too much dark woodwork, in her opinion — doorframes, windows, skirting boards. If Molly had her way it would all be covered over with a calming coat of white paint. Not absolutely white, of course, not like an asylum. An expensive white, with enough warmth not to look clinical but no discernible other hues in it. Whites like that weren't easy to find, she had discovered during her interior design phase, but they made such a difference and now she recommended them to most of her home-organisation clients.

Thinking about work the next day made Molly's heart sink. She hadn't mentioned it to anyone, least of all Jack, but to be honest she was getting bored by her job. She'd been a home organiser for the better part of a year now, and it wasn't holding her attention any more. Jack would be so disappointed if she quit. Maybe after the baby came she could just quietly not return to work.

Unfortunately the stupid huge mortgage on the ugly flat wouldn't pay itself. That would be a problem. She had to go back to work, once the baby was a few months old, at least part-time.

But the countdown to maternity leave was on: she was working till the Saturday before Christmas and then she'd have three weeks to herself before the baby was due. Not even a fortnight to go, thank fuck. Pre-Christmas was busy in her line of work. Her boss, Tien, had explained that people could sense the onslaught of gifts just over the horizon and the smart ones were getting in now and hiring Molly or Tien to come and clear out their accumulated guff before the tsunami of new shit hit.

Business had been booming lately, probably helped along by Tien's extreme Instagram proficiency and increasing physical resemblance to Marie Kondo. It wasn't something Molly would bring up, but it couldn't be a coincidence that since the Netflix show about throwing out anything that didn't spark joy had become such a hit, Tien had undergone a dramatic style makeover and eschewed her bright Gorman wardrobe in favour of pale cardigans and little cropped jackets, and had cut her formerly wild curls into a long bob with a fringe, which required ironing into place every morning and sometimes again in the afternoon if it was humid. A bit cynical, Molly thought — Tien wasn't even Japanese: she was Thai and Israeli — but fair play to her. Tien knew how to work a trend.

Molly was getting tired of getting rid of things rich people shouldn't have bought in the first place. She thought she might like to start her own business after the baby was born. Maybe making something to sell online. Or perhaps she'd have a nice little shop. A little shop would be cool. What she'd sell, she hadn't decided.

Something irresistible: a must-have. She'd figure it out. She'd start up a start-up of some description, although it was hard to think of something that people really needed, and which wouldn't just end up being thrown away by someone like Tien a few months later.

Annie would help with the baby. Obviously Molly wouldn't have any income for a bit, so paying for daycare would be hard on just Jack's earnings, but she was sure her mum would love to be involved. She was always saying how sad it was that Sunny and Felix lived so far away and she'd missed their babyhoods. This would be her chance. It would be brilliant. The baby could have the same close relationship with Mum that Molly'd had with her granny and pa. There was honestly nothing better for kids than their grandparents.

Through the window, Molly saw her mother's shoulders begin to shake. Shit, was she crying? But then she tipped her head back, and Molly could see she was laughing. So weird. There was no one with her. Her mum was smiling more this week, laughing at silly things — you honestly wouldn't guess her father had just died. Simon said he'd caught her dancing, on her own, in the laundry, to no music. Maybe it was having all the kids there for the funeral. Ever since Simon and Diana landed from Berlin on Monday with Felix, and Naomi's van crawled to a spluttering stop out the front on Tuesday morning, Annie had seemed to be floating. Molly hadn't seen her like that for years. She hoped she wasn't having some sort of breakdown. That would not be convenient at all.

Chapter 3

'What's so funny, you lunatic?' Annie's friend Jane appeared from around the side of the house, carrying a large glass of wine and bearing shards of filo pastry on the front of her blouse — evidence that the cheese triangles had been taken out of the oven and served.

'I honestly couldn't tell you,' said Annie, struggling to regain composure. 'Maybe I'm in shock. I just feel completely excellent.'

Jane sat down on the edge of the patio, her feet on the grass. 'You're not in shock,' she said. 'It's sheer fucking relief. I've seen it a million times before. No one likes to admit it, but sometimes it feels really bloody good when your parents are gone.'

'But I loved them.'

'Not saying you didn't, but to everything a season and all that.' Jane's bluntness still shocked Annie slightly, but it was one of the reasons she had felt so drawn to her. They'd met at the gym, and although they'd only been friends for less than a year, Annie felt like they understood each other. She hadn't had a friend like Jane in a long time.

'I suppose,' said Annie. Then she thought of something. 'I'm an orphan.'

'So you are. Orphan Annie.'

Annie sang the opening lines of 'Tomorrow', and Jane thumped her on the arm.

'Why don't you sing more? You have such a gorgeous voice.'

Annie thought about it. 'I don't know. Maybe I've sung all the songs that were mine to sing.'

'What's that from?'

'What's what from?'

'That line — what you just said. It sounds like something from a song. "Maybe I've sung all the songs that were mine to sing." A fucking depressing song, but still.'

'It's not from anything.' Annie smiled. 'It was just something I was thinking.'

'Well, I think it should be in a song,' said Jane, as if that was that. 'Write it down or you'll forget it.' Neither of them moved. 'When's your ex back?'

'First thing tomorrow.'

'Tell me again why? Why are you having them for Christmas? Why are you not hopping on a plane tonight to Bali and then lying very still in a bath of pina coladas until you run out of money?'

'It's almost Christmas. The kids are all here. And Brian and Paul are my oldest friends. They were my band. I can't wait to see them.'

'But — and forgive me if I have this story confused — but didn't the one you were married to —?'

'Paul.'

'Yes, Paul. Didn't he run off with the one you weren't married to?'

'Brian. They didn't actually run off. That's not what happened.'

'But they're a couple now, and you and Paul aren't.'

'Correct.'

'God. Imagine.'

'It wasn't as dramatic as all that. Paul and I had come to the end of our road, I suppose, and he walked on with Brian.'

'So you'd already split up.'

'Well, no,' Annie admitted. 'We were together until the day Paul told me he was in love with Brian. It was here, actually, after Christmas. We went to the corner shop to buy milk and he told me they were going to be together, and he was leaving me. I remember I had the door of the fridge open and I just stood there for ages, trying to take in what he'd said. The lady who ran the shop, Vicki, shouted at me to shut the fridge while I was deciding. And I remember feeling confused, because I wasn't deciding anything. It was all decided for me.'

'The absolute fucking nerve of the man,' said Jane, shaking her head. 'Leaving you to raise three kids. Did they pay child support?' Jane never shied away from asking questions other people might have considered indelicate.

'They were good. There wasn't much of a mortgage on our terrace, and they gave me money for the kids. I had my job at the school. We had enough. The boys stayed very involved. It was more like my kids gained an extra dad than lost one. Even though they moved back to London. Anyway, my big two were teenagers, and only Molly was still a kid, really.'

'And you never remarried? Ever get close?'

'No.' Annie shook her head. 'Never found anyone else I could stand for long enough. I'm pretty good on my own. The upside of being an only child, I suppose.'

* * *

Molly looked out again to see that her mother had been joined by that friend of hers, Jane. Molly wasn't sure about Jane: she didn't get the impression Jane liked her very much. When Molly saw Annie stand up and turn back towards the house, leaving Jane sitting on the patio, she steered her protruding belly between the wrinkled faces and into the kitchen. She felt like a ferry in an archipelago of liver-spotted islands.

Her grandparents' kitchen was truly something to behold. Molly couldn't think what the opposite of timeless was, but this kitchen embodied the concept. After inheriting the house from his father at the age of twenty-one, Pa had waited until 1970 to renovate. The cabinetry was all dark wood veneer, with metallic filigree handles that hooked themselves into passing beltloops like the fingers of a pre-#MeToo boss, and the lino floor tiles and Formica countertops were custard yellow. A brass rangehood loomed over the electric stove, and the matching brass splashback, which was easily marked by every droplet of water or splatter of fat it encountered, shone with the thousands of hours of resentful polishing her granny and, more recently, her mother had lavished on it. Her grandfather's long-running joke had been to come in after it was polished and say, 'You missed a spot.'

The kitchen was, by modern standards, a monstrosity, and the worst part was that an exact replica of it sat waiting in the garage for the day this one wore out. Her grandfather had bought two, for a fifteen per cent discount, back in 1970, having declared its design would never date.

Now that he was gone, surely this kitchen could be torn out, and its Dorian Gray counterpart sold to a television production company for the set of an ABC screen adaptation of some long-forgotten Australian novel.

Annie came back in from the garden, took another tray of bad sandwiches from the fridge, and began peeling off the layers of plastic wrap. She scrunched them quickly into the bin: so Naomi wouldn't spot them and fold them up for reuse, Molly assumed. Simon's wife, Diana, had appeared and was rinsing wine glasses at the sink.

Molly heaved herself up onto the counter and clasped her hands under her taut belly. 'When are they all going to leave?' she asked.

Annie looked up. 'In the next hour or so, I imagine.'

'But it's four thirty. Won't they miss their dinners?'

Diana looked around with a sympathetic smile. 'I think it's lovely that so many of your grandfather's friends have been able to make it today. It's a real tribute to him.'

'He didn't care about most of these people,' Molly continued, as if Diana hadn't spoken. It was the best way she had found to deal with her sister-in-law.

When it became clear that neither Diana nor her mother was going to agree with her about this, Molly changed the subject. 'Is there anything I can eat? Are there any more cheese triangles?'

'Nope, they were snaffled up by Pa's friends,' said Annie. 'Goodness knows what they feed them in their retirement homes.' She offered Molly the tray of sandwiches instead.

'I'm not supposed to eat premade things with mayonnaise in them. Or lettuce. Salmonella and listeria risk. Salmonella isn't so bad — that will just make me really ill, but listeria will straight out kill the baby.'

Annie opened the fridge again. 'There's not much to eat besides the food for today, love. I cleared out the fridge last night so we could fit all the platters of sandwiches. There's cake. Is that safe?'

Molly sighed. 'Yes, it's safe. But it might give me gestational diabetes.' Her mother didn't need to know she was too full of cake to eat any more cake.

'My goodness, Moll,' said Annie. 'These food restrictions are quite something. Sometimes it sounds like the safest thing would be to eat only hot chips!' She turned to Diana. 'Are they this strict with food during pregnancy in Germany? We didn't have to worry about any of it when I was having kids. We were just told not to drink so much that we crashed the car. Mine turned out all right.'

'It seemed like common sense for me,' said Diana with a shrug. 'I didn't feel like alcohol or coffee, and my body just told me what to eat.'

Molly wrinkled her nose at the back of Diana's spiky head. She was a pain in the arse. But then so was Simon. They deserved each other. Such a pair of know-it-alls. Molly took a lump of sandy almond cake from the box on the counter and went looking for her husband and the car keys. It was time to wrap this up. Sitting around there would only mean having her blood pressure driven sky-high by Diana's Teutonic nonchalance.

Simon was back from the shop. She knew the errand was a matter of five minutes' work. It was just like him to have argued with her for so long about something that ultimately took practically no time. Molly found him with Jack, sitting in the right of way beside the enclosed verandah on a garden bench they had dragged around from the backyard. They were drinking bottles of beer and idly watching the old man next door, Ray, through his kitchen window.

It was a strange set-up — Molly had always thought so. Her grandfather's garage was in the backyard, but his house ran the full width of the block, leaving no room for a driveway to access it. Somewhere in the dim distant past, an arrangement was made with the original owner of the house next door for Pa's house to have a right-of-way access down the side of the neighbour's block. It was enshrined in the deeds for both houses. Whoever lived in Pa's house was permitted to traverse the land to get to their own garage and back garden, but they weren't allowed to block it with anything. Like a garden bench. Where Jack and Simon were sitting was technically Ray's land.

Ray, who had lived next door for as long as Molly could remember, had always resented this situation.

'There's Right-of-Way Ray,' Pa used to say when he drove along the strip, past Ray's kitchen window and into the garage where he would park his old EH Holden beside the dust-sheeted replacement kitchen. 'Wave to Right-of-Way Ray, kids!' They'd all wave and Ray would scowl and turn away from the window.

Now Molly felt sorry for Ray. It was a pathetic thing to hold a grudge over. Imagine hating your neighbour that much because you didn't like sharing a tiny strip of land. He'd always seemed old and miserable. Her mum said he was married once, but his wife ran off, taking their baby son with her. The wife had been nice, apparently. Heather was her name. She'd been friends with Mum, although she was a few years older. And Pa and Granny and Mum hadn't realised anything was wrong until one day Heather and the baby were gone.

When pressed about why Heather might have left, Mum had only ever replied, 'You can never know what goes on in a marriage.'

Molly felt a sudden rush of fury towards Ray. How dare he have been so rude to Pa? Pa had never been anything but a good neighbour. And now Pa was gone and bloody Ray was still there. There was no justice.

'Hey hey, Molly Jones,' said Jack when he saw her. His smile was crooked, and she could tell from this and the particular pink of his face that he was on his third beer. He moved over to make room for her on the bench and she sat, pulling his arm around her like a shawl. The beer smell was strong, but she nestled into his shirt anyway. Somehow it was appealing.

Her brother raised his bottle in greeting. 'Arseface,' he said.

'Arseface,' she replied. 'What are you two doing?'

'Just having a drink to your pa,' said Jack.

'Yep,' said Simon. 'A farewell to him in his sunny spot.'

There wasn't any sun now, but each morning their grandfather had read the newspaper there in the company of one of his indistinguishable series of tabby cats named Richard. The Richards had ordinal suffixes, like Kings of England. When Pa died he was up to Richard V, outnumbering the real kings by two.

He'd dragged around a chair from the patio and set himself up with a cup of coffee and the newspaper, every morning, for half an hour after breakfast and before work. Once he retired it was after breakfast and before golf, or working in the garden.

'His sunny spot,' Molly remembered. 'It's not like it's the only sunny spot. Why did he like it here so much?'

'Probably because it was both a genuinely sunny spot, and because it pissed Ray off,' said Simon. 'He was such a shit-stirrer, Pa.'

'He didn't start it. Ray was always horrible to him.'

'Do you reckon old Right-of-Way Ray will be happier now your pa's gone?' said Jack.

'Probably. But maybe not. He might just be miserable forever. He'll probably hate the next owners just as much,' said Simon.

Molly looked sharply at him. 'What next owners? Mum is the next owner. Or us. But probably Mum. She's an only child. It's all got to be coming her way.'

'Well, yeah. But what would she want with a massive place like this? She's on her own. She's got her flat to go back to. She can kick out her tenants now. I reckon she'll sell the house.'

The baby did a backflip inside Molly.

Jack squeezed her shoulder. 'It's all right, Moll, nothing's going to happen straight away. I'm sure Annie will discuss her plans with you all before she makes any decisions.'

Molly nodded. She didn't trust herself to speak. It hadn't occurred to her that Mum might sell up. This house was their whole history. When she pictured having her baby, she imagined bringing it here. She'd known Pa wouldn't live long enough to meet her child, but the house wasn't going anywhere. It couldn't. Her mum wouldn't sell it. This was Annie's home.

'Did she ask you to come to the solicitor's tomorrow?' asked Simon.

Molly nodded.

'Do you reckon there's more in the estate than just the house?'

Molly had been wondering the same thing but it was crass of her brother to say it out loud. 'I've no idea,' she said haughtily. 'I imagine he might have had some super. But it's not really my business. I'm going tomorrow to support Mum. Not because I'm expecting a bequest.'

Simon looked her straight in the eye. 'That,' he said, 'is bullshit.'

Molly looked away from him, and watched Jack take another swig of his beer, then hold up the bottle and assess it. There was a warm inch left — had anyone in the history of bottled beer ever finished that last inch? — which he poured onto the gravel before offering Molly a hand up.

'Shall we head home? You look ready for an early night. Work tomorrow.'

'That's right,' said Simon. 'People's undies aren't going to fold themselves.'

'That isn't what I do,' Molly said.

'Have you given that up already? I thought you'd be about ready for a change.'

'No, I mean, it is still what I do, but that isn't *what I do*.'

'It is. Oh no, wait, my mistake — I've seen that show. You don't fold the undies, you roll the undies.'

'Well, it's better than working for Nazis.'

'They're the second biggest construction company in Germany. That doesn't make them Nazis.'

Molly was already walking towards the house, hand in hand with Jack, but she looked back to say, 'It actually probably does. When was the company founded again?'

'Nineteen twenty — oh fuck off, Molly.'

'*Gute Nacht, mein Bruder.*'

* * *

Annie and Diana were still in the kitchen, and the number of old people in the lounge room seemed unchanged. Sunny and Felix had come inside now, and were attempting to unpack the dishwasher, under Diana's supervision.

'Goodbye,' Molly said to her mother, leaning in to have her forehead kissed. She thought about her mum, moving in there to look after her sick parents. Five years she'd been back in the house, nursing them. Molly didn't think she'd be able to do that. It was a lot to ask of your kid. But her mother was an only child — there wasn't anyone she could share the burden with. As annoying as Molly's own siblings were, she was grateful they'd be equally responsible for dealing with their parents if they got sick. If that day ever came, her plan was stay very quiet and pretend to help from a distance. Naomi would be much better at the full-on bedpan-and-morphine end of things. Simon would stay in Germany being no help at all: that was pretty much a given.

'Will you be all right here, alone, without Pa?' she asked her mother.

'I'm not alone. Simon and Diana are staying, and Felix, and Naomi and Sunny.'

'The spoons all cuddle each other like that,' Diana told Felix, as he put the cutlery away. No one but Molly seemed to be watching Sunny add a sixth water glass to the already teetering stack she was holding. On discovering the tower was too tall to fit in the cupboard, she carefully laid it on its side and gently closed the door. Molly could see it would probably roll out and smash the next time anyone opened the cupboard, but she didn't say anything.

Jack nodded in the direction of the sitting room. 'Do any of them need dropping back to anywhere?'

Molly held her breath. Please say no. Please say no. She didn't want old people in her car, leaving it smelling like all the worst biscuits in a family assortment.

Annie patted Jack's cheek. 'You're a good boy. Simon and I can drive them back later, or put them in taxis. I'll let them stay as long as they want. They don't get out much. They love a good funeral.'

'See you tomorrow then, Mum,' Molly said, deeply relieved.

'The meeting with the solicitor is at nine thirty. I've texted you the address.'

'Right-o then,' said Jack. 'Hooroo, everyone.'

Diana looked confused. 'Hooroo?'

'It means goodbye,' explained Annie. 'It's quite old-fashioned.'

'I like it,' Molly said loyally, even though that was only true about half of the times Jack said it. He had grown up in the country, but, still, he wasn't eighty years old. Quite often it made her shrink with embarrassment when he cracked out a 'hooroo', but if Diana thought it was strange Molly was automatically prepared to defend it. 'It's important to maintain linguistic connections to our history.'

'Okay,' said Diana, and Molly left, feeling like somehow her sister-in-law had got the better of her in a competition neither of them was prepared to admit they were having.

Chapter 4

Annie carried the last box of empty wine bottles through the still night air out to the backyard and placed them quietly beside the recycling bin. Everyone else was asleep, but she wasn't tired. After the old people had finally finished drinking everything they could lay their hands on and gone home, she'd cleaned up and one by one her houseguests had retired to their rooms.

The light was still on in Ray's kitchen. It was the only window on that side of the house. A small panel of fence ran from the end of Ray's house on an angle to Pa's garage door, and continued down the boundary to the back fences. This part of the fence was neat and solid, but there were still broken palings in the section behind the garage. She used to slip through them to visit Heather.

She rarely thought of Heather any more. It felt like someone else had been friends with the young woman next door, but she could remember meeting Heather as if it were a book she'd read over and over for comfort.

* * *

Annie was seventeen when Heather moved in. Ray, who'd lived next door forever, would have been in his mid-thirties, a single man who worked long hours. Annie didn't know what his job was, but he wore a smart suit and his shoes were always shiny. He mostly kept to himself, but gave a cordial wave or a polite nod whenever Annie looked out of the enclosed verandah windows or happened along the right of way while he was at his kitchen sink. He wore pink washing-up gloves, a fact that in combination with his established bachelorhood and the care he lavished on his rose garden caused Annie's dad to class him firmly in the No Threat To My Womenfolk camp, and for a long time no one in the family gave him much thought.

One Friday evening, just before seven, Ray had rung the front doorbell. Jean was clearing away the dinner, scraping congealed tuna mornay into the bin before handing the plates to Annie, who was waiting in front of a sink of hot water.

'Will you please get that, Robert?' she called to her husband, who was in the front room, a glass of beer on a coaster beside his armchair, about to switch on the ABC news.

'If I must.'

Annie heard the door open; voices. A woman and a man.

Robert's head suddenly popped around the kitchen door. He raised one eyebrow. 'Ray's got a wife,' he said. 'He's come to show us.'

Annie and Jean dried their hands and followed him back to the front hall, where Ray and a young woman were standing, each looking as uncomfortable as the other.

Ray lifted one hand and placed it nervously on his new wife's right shoulder. Annie could see he was accidentally pulling on a tendril of the woman's long strawberry blonde hair, which was parted in the middle and smooth in a way Annie's never was. Annie thought she was the prettiest girl she'd ever seen.

'This,' Ray said proudly, 'is Heather. My wife, Heather. She's my new wife. We've just got married.' He beamed at them.

Heather offered a warm smile. 'Hello,' she said, and reached out to shake hands. Her skin was soft, but her grip was strong. 'It's really nice to meet you.'

Jean had been all dithery and overly welcoming. 'Hello, Heather love,' she'd said. 'Welcome. I'm Jean. It'll be lovely to have you as a neighbour. Pop in whenever you like. I'm always around. It's a pretty quiet street, mostly, but there's always a cup of tea to be had with me.'

Robert, who was leaning against the living room doorway, his arms folded, nodded in agreement. 'Always a cup of tea,' he echoed. 'And it's quiet enough, unless madam here and her band of minstrels are at it on the verandah.'

Heather turned to Annie. 'Oh, yes, Ray said you're in a band. How excellent. I can't wait to hear you play.' It was like a blessing from the sun. Annie felt herself blush, and she knew what came out of her mouth next would be nonsense.

'We're nothing really, not so much a band, more a musical collective, well, actually I guess that's just another word for a band, isn't it? We're probably not very good — we'd be better if we played other people's songs but we just like making up our own stuff. It's just me and my friends, Paul and Brian. Well, Brian's just my friend but Paul's my boyfriend. Now, at the moment, I mean.' When she finally made herself stop talking, Annie would have quite liked to die.

But Heather smiled at her again. 'Are you about my age, Annie? I'm twenty-two.'

'Well done, Ray,' said Robert, before Jean shot him a reproving glance.

'I'm only seventeen,' said Annie.

'You look older,' said Heather, setting a seal of approval on their friendship.

For a while there had been a quiet competition for Heather's affection. Jean made sustained overtures of friendship — offering recipes, tips on stain removal and the care of Ray's precious roses, and inviting her in for tea several times a week — but every time Heather popped round, Annie would wander in and before long the conversation would move to musicians Jean hadn't heard of and shops she never went into. Annie had much more in common with Heather than Jean did.

Eventually Jean stopped asking, and Heather just came over most afternoons anyway, to lie out on the grass with Annie, flipping through copies of *Juke* while Jean pushed her carpet sweeper over already clean rugs.

Annie knew she'd been victorious when her mother started making little comments about Heather. Jean wasn't given to snide remarks, but she nonetheless said occasionally that it was terrific how young women these days were able to do what they liked. And if that meant not wearing a bra then more power to them. If Heather didn't care that her nipples sometimes showed through her top, then why should Jean?

Annie and Heather giggled at Jean when she wasn't around. 'She wants you to have a baby so I'll settle down and do it too,' Annie told her new friend. 'She's dying for you to get pregnant.'

But Annie had other plans. She didn't think it should have been as much of a surprise as it obviously was when about a year later, the night after her last exam, she announced at dinner that Love Triangle was moving to London.

'London?' Her mother was aghast. 'What on earth for?'

'So we can become famous,' said Annie. She saw her mother look to Robert for support, but he was smiling at Annie. He had known about the plan for ages.

'Darling,' her mother said, 'I know you're very good. You've a lovely voice and you play the piano beautifully, and the boys with their guitars and everything ... but you don't know anyone in London. You don't have a manager or a ... what is it called, a recording thing.'

'A record contract,' said Annie. 'I know. But we won't get one hanging around here playing at the Police Boys' Club.'

'I think it's a great idea,' said Robert.

'Robert, you do not think it's a great idea. She's far too young.'

'When you're young is when you have to do these things,' he said.

'How will you afford it?' demanded Jean. 'You all spent all your money on that synthesiser.'

Annie gave her father a grateful smile. 'Dad said he'd help. With another investment.'

Robert reached out and took his daughter's hand and squeezed it. 'My money is safe as houses invested with Love Triangle. I am one hundred per cent confident of a tenfold return.'

Her mother had pleaded. 'Will you please at least defer your university place? Rather than rejecting it? Who knows, maybe you'll be famous enough in a year that you might want to come back and have a break from all the screaming fans by doing your arts degree, or a Dip. Ed.'

But in her head, Annie was already gone.

* * *

By the time Heather and Ray did have a baby, a couple of years later, Annie, Paul and Brian were happily ensconced in their new London life. Jean wrote to say she had offered to mind the baby, a long thin child they named Patrick, but Heather never took her up on it. They didn't seem happy together, Heather and Ray. She was too young for him, Jean said. Fifteen years was far too great an age gap.

There came more hints in the letters that all was not well next door. Sometimes there were loud arguments. Jean tried not to listen, she said, but even with the kitchen radio on she couldn't help hearing Heather shouting. Ray didn't seem to shout back, but who could say what was going on. And it was none of her business. Children could put a strain on relationships, and poor little Patrick was a particularly unsettled baby. Jean often heard him crying, lying in his pram out in the back garden.

Then one day Annie got a letter from her mother that said Heather was gone. Jean had realised, while unpacking the shopping, that she hadn't heard shouting for a while. She couldn't remember when it had stopped. She hadn't heard Patrick crying either. She popped round with a plate of Anzac biscuits, but no one answered her knock.

Later, she told Annie, she'd asked Robert to stop in when Ray was home from work, to see what was going on. Robert had initially refused, saying it was none of their business: a marriage was between two people only.

She'd insisted, though, and eventually he'd dragged on his tennis shoes and gone. Two minutes later he was back to report that Ray was drunk, had shouted at him to go away, and that, as suspected, Heather had shot through with the baby.

Jean had wondered if she should try to phone Heather. She asked Annie if she knew where Heather's mother lived, for surely that's where she had taken Patrick. But Annie didn't know. She wrote back to say she thought Heather had grown up on the south coast somewhere. Or maybe it was the north coast. They hadn't really talked about that sort of thing. Heather had written to her sometimes, and Annie promised to let Jean know if she heard from her again, but she never did.

Thinking back now, Annie had been too busy in London to miss Heather. Occasionally she'd thought of her, and hoped she was well, and felt a pang of guilt for not missing her more, or trying harder to find her. After all, they'd been such great friends for the year or so at home. A few times in recent years she'd googled Heather or looked for her on Facebook, but she hadn't found her. Maybe she'd changed her name.

Now Annie looked at the fence and wondered what would have happened if she had never gone to London. Would Heather have stayed? Annie probably would have ended up exactly where she was now: there really wasn't much to show for the promising start she'd had.

* * *

At first, things had gone better over in England than Annie could have dreamed. Unlike in Sydney, where if you didn't have a drummer no one thought you were a real band, in London there seemed to be room for everyone. If you looked hard enough and went to enough clubs, you could find your tribe, and Love Triangle's particular brand of songwriting was gaining popularity. It even had a name in London: they played synth-pop, albeit at the poppier end of the synth-pop spectrum.

After only a few months they had found a manager, a slight, bug-eyed Welshman called Dai, who never seemed to blink. Annie had found him an alarming presence, but he was good at his job, and Love Triangle started travelling the country playing in little clubs. They released an EP, and then an album, and joined other bands each summer for the festival season, touring Europe in a bus, playing in towns that would have really preferred ABBA but were grateful to have anyone.

The relief at escaping the surf-rock scene they'd grown up in made them giddy. 'We were oppressed and repressed back home,' Brian explained one night as they sat on the sofa in the one-bedroom flat they shared in Brixton, drinking cider and watching Wham on *Top of the Pops*. 'All good music comes from cultural oppression, and our middle-class suburban upbringing was oppressing us. And Sydney was oppressing us, just because we weren't Cold Chisel.'

Annie wasn't sure about that, but she suspected, a while before Brian reached the same conclusion, that he was actually talking about something else. She and Paul hadn't felt terribly hard done by back in Sydney, musically, so it made sense that Brian might actually have been talking about his preference for blokes rather than his taste in lightweight instrumentation and parallel thirds.

The triangle remained strong through those years in London. And their success helped. They weren't massive — they never made it onto *Top of the Pops* themselves — but they sold enough albums to still feel like they were a proper group. The real money was coming from the songs they were selling to other people. It was a truth none of them liked to talk about, but the material they wrote did a lot better when other people recorded it. One or two became actual bona fide chart-toppers. That was a slightly bitter pill to swallow, but they were able to wash it down with a bottle of vintage Champagne.

It was their fourth year in London when they almost made it really big. 'Home Is Where Your Heart Is' was on the shortlist for Britain's Eurovision song that year. They weren't famous yet, but they could see it from where they were sitting.

The only slight hitch in their plan for world domination was the boisterous child Annie was accidentally gestating. Simon, still four months from his birth, roiled and kicked so violently that even when disguised under a red crushed-velvet square-shaped dress, he caused the fabric to shake like a stagehand was ham-fistedly changing sets behind theatre curtains. Whenever Annie sang, her baby writhed. It was distracting to watch.

A band meeting was called, and after briefly considering the stipulation (made, naturally, by the middle-aged record company executives who ran things) that they replace only Annie for the Eurovision heat, the triangle stood strong and handed the song over entirely to an unknown English singer called Lorraine Darmody. Lorraine had a voice like golden syrup, hair so fluffy you could read the telephone book through it and a body that didn't bring to mind a scene from *Alien*.

It was then that Annie had suggested maybe it was time to go home. She had run out of puff. Paul, in no real position to argue, agreed, and they got married in the Chelsea and Kensington Register Office on a rainy January morning in 1983, with Brian and his latest squeeze Trevor as witnesses. The newlyweds flew back to Sydney the next day.

Brian, seeing no future for the triangle, stayed in London, where he tried to get work as a producer but ended up writing for a music magazine.

Lorraine Darmody had acquitted herself well in *A Song for Europe*. 'Home Is Where Your Heart Is' was selected to represent Britain, and in Munich in April she earned a respectable seventh place at Eurovision. She'd gone on to act a bit, playing the landlady in a long-running Yorkshire drama about a rural pub, and ended up marrying a chinless minor aristocrat —

Annie had gleaned all this from various magazines in dentists' waiting rooms over the years.

Annie watched the broadcast of Eurovision that year with Paul in the living room of their rented flat in Sydney, a newborn Simon asleep in a crochet bouncinette, which Paul nudged with his foot to the beat of someone else making a hit of their song. When Paul had grabbed her hand and squeezed it, she'd looked away so he wouldn't see the tears in her eyes.

* * *

Paul had taken on guitar students, and studied for his Diploma of Education at night. Once he had that, a private school employed him full-time as a music teacher.

Annie had thrown herself into her new life the way someone who has run out of other options might throw themselves into a cold dark lake. But as with a cold lake, once she got used to it and stopped feeling anything, she found motherhood was survivable. She met other mothers at the park, and the local playgroup. One or two old school friends lived nearby and they would gather to drink tea at one of their homes while their babies lay on rugs on the linoleum floors and yanked each other's hair.

The next Christmas, when Simon was starting to drag himself around and occasionally slept through the night, Annie and Paul sublet the flat, packed their guitars, the playpen and the nappy bucket, and moved back in with Robert and Jean for the month of January. On arrival Simon was handed to Jean, and they saw very little of him for the next four weeks. Annie slept a lot, and Paul gave guitar lessons in the enclosed verandah where they used to write their own songs. Brian came home to see his mother for

Christmas and in the evenings he came round to drink on the patio, but nothing was the same any more.

When the summer was over, Brian returned to England, Paul went back to work at the school, and Annie took a deep breath and squared herself to face motherhood again.

That pattern had continued for a decade and a half, and it was enough for Annie. When Simon was two, she had Naomi. Two children were plenty, Annie and Paul decided. But five years after Naomi was born, a gastro bug swept through the family, resulting in a permanently stained living room carpet and the failure of Annie's contraceptive pill, and nine months later Molly was born.

Having just reached the point of both her children being at school, and the possibility of thinking about what the future might hold, Annie found herself back in the newborn trenches.

But still the summers at Baskerville Road continued, and in the evenings they played their old songs, and Annie composed new ditties infused with the scent of jasmine on the night breeze that made people feel good, which advertisers soon discovered would make people buy cars and shampoo and wet-wipes. Even after Paul and Annie bought a house of their own they kept going to Baskerville Road. They could leave the kids to Jean, Robert would come home at the end of each day from the office and pour them cold beers — and the enclosed verandah, with the piano, and the sliding windows, that was where they could pretend to be starting out again.

Until the end of the seventeenth summer, and Annie and Paul's fateful trip to buy milk.

It hadn't come as a complete shock to Annie to learn Paul was in love with Brian, but the sadness that coursed through her was more than she'd been expecting. She was thirty-nine and heading into a new millennium. She would have to navigate it on her own, with a sixteen-year-old, a fourteen-year-old and an eight-year-old.

When they got back from the shop, Annie put the milk in the fridge and went out to the garden. Paul and Brian came and sat on either side of her on the bench under the jacaranda and they cried together.

'Will you go back to London with Brian?' Annie had asked the man who was suddenly no longer her husband.

'I don't know. What would be best for the kids?'

None of this, she'd thought. What would be best for the kids is if you preferred me to Brian. 'Can't you both live here?'

But by then Brian had moved from music journalism to ghostwriting memoirs for other, more successful musicians. The work wasn't really something he could do in the Sydney suburbs, where world-famous rock stars were fairly thin on the ground. He needed to be London-based, with all-expenses-paid sojourns in New York and Los Angeles when required. They would visit as much as possible, they said, and fly the kids to London whenever there was enough money.

The summers of writing together at the house had to end. Annie knew exactly what her father was going to make of the new development. Homosexuality was not on the list of things Robert approved of. He'd turned an aggressively blind eye to Brian's orientation for almost twenty years, asking him every summer when he was going to settle down and put all the ladies of London out of their misery. Annie wondered if she could run the holiday music camps on her own. She supposed she'd have to. They'd need to be smaller.

Love Triangle had faded away, like the end of one of their own songs. And tomorrow, thought Annie, we'll be back together.

Now that her father was dead and the coast was clear, her ex-husband and his boyfriend were coming to Baskerville Road for a family Christmas. Annie wished they weren't. Jane was right as usual. Annie wanted her future to begin, and that would be hard with her entire past in the house, filling her pockets like stones.

A bat flew overhead and landed in the fig tree in Ray's back garden. Naomi would say that it was Pa. It probably was.

Chapter 5

Molly lay in the bath, watching her stomach, risen from the water like a Polynesian volcano. She loved baths, and had turned the air conditioning right up on her return home so she would actually feel like submerging herself in hot water on a warm December evening. The water was really very hot, which Jack would tut-tut about if he came in and saw the steam. He'd read that hot baths increased your risk of miscarriage, and he'd suggested Molly sit in a tub of lukewarm water when she needed to relax. She reasoned that the increase in blood pressure from how utterly annoying and non-relaxing that would be would outweigh any possible dangers from a bit of hot water.

She ran through what she had to do the next day. She would get up at six. Prenatal yoga for an hour from the streaming subscription that had been aggressively marketed to her after she made the fatal error of buying a six-pack of maternity knickers online. She'd subscribed three months back but tomorrow was definitely the day she would begin her yoga practice. No more putting it off.

Ha. As if. She'd switch off the alarm at some point in the night, before it had a chance to go off. Jack would wake her in a panic just in time for her to get in the car and head into the city for the reading of her grandfather's will.

She didn't actually have to go to the solicitor's, but she could take a half-day off work for it so why not? Maternity leave honestly couldn't come soon enough. Home organisation had felt like a funny job for her to do at first: playing against type, going off-brand. Everyone knew her as impetuous, disorderly. What more unexpected line of work for her to take up than sorting other people's possessions into overpriced storage solutions? But it had become utterly mind-numbing, if truth be told, and it was drawing to a natural end.

The doorbell rang and she groaned. She called to Jack, 'If that's for me, tell them I'm dead.'

She heard him open the door, then he stuck his head into the bathroom.

'It's Suzanne,' he whispered.

'Fuck,' she muttered. Their neighbour and secretary of the building's strata committee was an incorrigible popper-in. 'What does she want?'

'I don't know. She looks like she's been crying.'

'Oh, for god's sake,' Molly said, and put her hand out for Jack's help. He pulled her up and water streamed off her body and onto the floor. 'You'd better ask her in.'

When Molly emerged into the living room Suzanne was hunched over on the sofa, nursing a cup of tea with both hands, like a witness to an accident. Jack was sitting beside her. Her eyes were red and her face was mottled. Suzanne looked up at Molly, once more burst into sobs, and dropped her head again.

'What's wrong, what is it?' asked Jack, putting his arm around her shaking shoulder.

'C-c-c-cancer,' she managed to get out in a high squeak before dissolving again.

'Oh my god, that's terrible,' Molly said. 'I'm so sorry. What sort? What treatment is there? You poor thing.'

'Not me,' said Suzanne. 'Maralinga.'

'Sorry,' said Jack. 'I'm not following.'

Suzanne put her mug down on the coffee table and turned on the sofa to look straight at him. 'Concrete cancer,' she said. 'Maralinga —' she paused '— has concrete cancer.'

'The block of flats has cancer? Not you?' confirmed Jack.

'It's serious. It's going to take a huge amount of work to cure it.'

'Do we say cure, when it's a building?' asked Jack. 'Not repair?'

Suzanne glared at him. 'To cure it.'

'How bad is it?' Molly asked.

'Stage three,' she said. 'It's spalling.'

'That does sound appalling. Are there more than three stages?'

'Not appalling. *Spalling*,' said Suzanne, as if she was speaking to a particularly dense child.

Molly looked at Jack, who shrugged. 'Sorry, Suzanne,' she said. 'I'm not familiar with that term. Spalling, is it?'

Suzanne took a deep breath and in a shaky voice explained that to treat the concrete cancer would be a huge undertaking and very expensive. 'We need to have an extraordinary meeting and raise a special levy,' she said. 'There's not enough in the sinking fund to even begin to cover it. It will be a long process to bring this building back to full health.'

As Molly listened, her mind wandered to what might have happened in Suzanne's life to make her care so much about a block of flats. She had heard a rumour — something the Irish schoolteacher downstairs claimed Suzanne had confided after about a bottle and a half of pinot grigio — that Suzanne had once lived on a houseboat that caught fire and sank, killing the man she lived with, but Molly wasn't sure that story was true. The Irish teacher listened to a lot of Leonard Cohen, and the tale seemed to slightly resemble the lyrics of the song 'Suzanne'. She tuned back in to Suzanne's quavering voice only when she heard the words 'six months'.

'Oh well, I suppose we'll cross that bridge when we come to it,' she said. 'Now, we must let you get back to your night. Thanks for letting us know about the repairs. Email us through the quotes?' She shifted her weight and took a deep breath — a movement she hoped would look like she was about to get up to show Suzanne and her out-of-proportion drama to the door.

Jack took the hint. 'I'll see you out,' he said and, putting his arm around Suzanne's still shuddering shoulders, he led her to the front door.

* * *

Molly and Jack sat down in front of the TV with plates of grilled salmon and sweet potato with broccoli. Again. At least four nights a week they ate the same thing. It had been Jack's idea when she got pregnant, to choose an optimally healthy meal and eat it often, to save themselves time planning meals each week, but it was getting both boring and expensive. Molly wasn't even sure it was as healthy as he thought. She'd seen a headline on an article in her newsfeed saying farmed salmon was inferior to wild, but she hadn't clicked on it because it had annoyed her so much. And she knew there was something about mercury and large fish that was bad but she couldn't decide if salmon counted as large. Why were the rules so unclear and ever-changing? It was too hard to keep up.

And, god, how much more would wild salmon cost? If they switched to that, they'd be living under a bridge by the time the baby came.

'Holy shit,' said Jack, looking at his phone.

'What?'

'Suzanne's just forwarded me those quotes for the repairs. It's going to be eighty grand per unit.'

'What? Show me.' She snatched his phone and scanned the email. Eighty thousand dollars. He hadn't read it wrong. Three quotes, all in the same ballpark. A fluttering began in her chest. And the six months she'd heard Suzanne mention: that wasn't when the work was going to start, it was how long the repairs would take.

How could they live with a newborn baby in the noise and dust of a construction site for six months? It was out of the question. Plus the money, the special levy — there was no way they could afford that on just Jack's income, not on top of their mortgage payments.

Molly put her hands on her belly for reassurance, but the baby didn't kick. It was probably paralysed with fear. Anyway, it wasn't the baby's job to reassure her. She was the grownup here.

'It's all right,' she said brightly, as though the baby could only hear her words, and wasn't in fact connected to the current of pure stress hormones that was coursing through her bloodstream, infusing its nervous system, laying down pathways of panic that would light up for the rest of its life. 'It's only money.'

Jack was still frowning at his phone. He'd opened up their online banking app. 'Where are we going to get another eighty thousand dollars? You're about to go on maternity leave.'

'We can borrow it. From the bank. Banks love lending money. We'll tack it onto the mortgage.'

'How will we pay it back?' He opened a loan calculator and started stabbing in figures.

'We're going to be fine, Jacko. Hey, maybe Pa left us some money. That might be why Mum wants me to come to the solicitor's office tomorrow. It might be eighty grand. This might all be fate.'

'Even if we do get some money we can't stay here. We can't live in a building site. Our baby will never sleep. It will breathe in asbestos and get lung cancer.' He was sounding panicky.

Molly put her hand on his cheek. 'There isn't any asbestos. That's not what's wrong with the building.'

'That's not what they know is wrong with the building. Once they start looking of course they'll find more things, and they will be worse than the concrete cancer. Why's it called concrete cancer anyway?'

'I don't even know what it is,' admitted Molly.

'It's where the metal that reinforces the concrete gets rusty and starts causing the concrete around it to crack. Which is more like osteoporosis than cancer.'

'That's not a very catchy name though is it: "concrete osteoporosis"? Not as alliterative.'

'No, I guess not.' Jack paused for a moment, before his eyes widened in fear again. 'Is it even safe for us to be in here now? What if the building cracks and the roof falls on us? While we're asleep?'

'We'll be entombed like Pompeiians,' replied Molly, but Jack didn't even smile. He looked around the room and his gaze lit on the spiderweb of cracks radiating from one corner of the living room ceiling. 'Is that new?'

'No,' said Molly. 'It was there when we bought the place. I remember painting over it.'

'I don't think it was that big. We have to go. We have to get out of here.'

As a person to whom things tended to come easily, Molly wasn't prone to panic, and she'd never really settled on a way to deal with Jack's moments of complete flap. Sometimes a joke did the trick. Sometimes she rolled with it, indulging his fears. Telling him to calm down had never once worked, and yet it was still the first thing she said each time he began to build up to a panic attack.

'Calm down. If you really don't want to be here with the building work going on, I understand that. We'll find somewhere else to go for a bit.'

He took a few deep breaths and squeezed her hand gratefully. 'We can go to my parents' place.'

'Well, no, we can't, because we haven't met the hell-freezing-over threshold for that yet. And they live two hours away. You can't commute that far.'

'They're not that bad,' said Jack. 'And I don't mind the drive.'

Molly said nothing.

'The dogs,' Jack said. 'I know you don't like the dogs.'

'It's not the dogs that are the problem. It's the way your mum and dad treat them like they are human.'

'They don't treat them like humans.'

'Jack, do you know which universities those dogs would go to if they weren't dogs?'

'Molly —'

'Do you?'

He closed his eyes. 'Yes. I do.'

'Well?'

'Toggle would go to Wollongong Uni and do International Relations and Law, because it's the closest to them and she gets homesick, and Fifi would go to ANU.'

'Yes. And that is insane. They are dogs. We aren't staying with your parents. A baby would not be safe in a house where the concept that dogs are inherently wild animals is just not an accepted fact. They won't care if their dogs eat our baby.'

'That's a bit rough.'

'Well, I'm sorry, but I really don't feel like that's an option. It's not out of the question that their dogs will bite our baby and we'll have to call the police and they'll refuse to get the dogs put down and we'll all end up in the *Daily Mail*, and all the commenters will be like, "Why on earth did those people move in with those crazy dog owners? Of course their baby got eaten." If we can't live here it would make more sense to move in with my mum. Especially if she's going to stay at Baskerville Road.'

'You really think your mum is going to want us and a crying newborn living there with her?'

'Why wouldn't she?' Molly was indignant. 'We're lovely and our baby isn't going to cry all the time. People just say they do to freak you out. And the house is massive.'

'I don't know,' said Jack. 'Besides, we don't know what the will says about the house. It might not even be in the family any more.'

'Do you reckon Pa has gone and left it to the RSPCA or something? Of course it will be left to Mum,' she said firmly. 'And she will love having us. It takes a village, you know? It'll be like forming a little village.'

Jack gave her a look, and she could tell he was wondering if that really qualified as building a village — or if it wasn't more like an invasion.

The ceiling didn't fall in on them that night. Molly felt Jack lie awake beside her for a long time, no doubt flipping through the catastrophe Rolodex in his head, while Molly heaved herself over every twenty minutes like a shoulder of pork trying to brown itself evenly in a pan.

Chapter 6

Walking through Darlinghurst the next morning, trying to remember where they'd managed to find a parking space the night before, Molly wondered why her grandfather, a suburban accountant whose own office had been above the fruit shop on the main street of the suburb he lived in his whole life, had bothered to use a firm of solicitors on the twenty-first floor of a tower in the city. His affairs weren't exactly complex. The man had owned one house. He might also have had cash savings and some other investments, maybe some super, Molly surmised, because he never received the pension, and hadn't seemed to want for money. It was most likely his will was straightforward.

It was probably just to make himself feel more important. Unless things weren't what she thought. She briefly entertained the idea that Pa had somehow amassed a fortune and invested it in a complicated series of trusts that meant a fleet of lawyers had been working away behind the scenes so after his death all could be revealed to his family and none of them would ever have to work again. That would be handy.

It wasn't completely out of the question. Maybe he'd been given a tip by a client fifty years back, and invested in McDonald's or Tampax. A private security firm. Something he would have been embarrassed to admit to but which made him a massive amount of money. Maybe that's what they were all being brought together to hear about.

Finding the car, she got in and sat for a moment, reminding herself of the route to the airport. Her father and Brian's flight from London, which was supposed to have arrived at six am, had been delayed, meaning Annie wouldn't have time to collect them. Now Molly had to get them and they'd need to tag along to the will reading.

Was it appropriate for them to come? Pa hadn't been what you would call supportive of their relationship. Perhaps she could leave them in a coffee shop.

She pulled off the expressway at the entrance to the international terminal, and as she approached the pick-up zone she could see them from fifty metres away. Both wore extremely loud Hawaiian shirts: Brian had teamed his with a pair of three-quarter length cargo pants, all pockets bulging, while her father's was tucked neatly into a pair of pleated cream linen trousers. They looked like an ageing Bart Simpson had taken James Bond to Barbados.

She never knew how to feel when she saw her dad. It was like knowing someone and not knowing them all at once. Was this how everyone felt around their father? Or just those whose dads had nicked off? He always acted like they had this normal strong father–child relationship, like he had with Naomi and Simon, but it felt fake to Molly. She didn't know him like she knew her mum. Sometimes she even felt closer to Brian. When she'd gone to stay with them in London as a child, Brian had been the one who made sure they did things that were fun for Molly, not just for the bigger two. Brian had taken her to see Buckingham Palace and Madame Tussauds when Naomi and Simon had said such things were too babyish. All they'd wanted to do was try to get into pubs and wander around Portobello Road market.

When she got out of the car, Paul started towards her and stopped short. He put his hand to his chest. 'Oh, my Molly-dolly,' he said, and his eyes filled with tears. 'Look at you.'

She looked down. 'Oh. Yes, this. You haven't seen me. Well, ta-da! Baby on board!' She gestured at her swollen front like a regional television spokesmodel trying to drum up interest in a diesel hedge-trimmer.

'I've been trying and trying to picture what you'd look like and I just couldn't. I couldn't see you pregnant. But now —' he waved both hands at her '— this. I just … So much like your mum.' He wrapped her in his arms.

Molly felt her chest tighten and her eyes sting. She smiled over her father's shoulder at Brian, and reached out her hand.

'Hi, Brian.'

'Hi, Molly. We're so glad to see you.' He squeezed her hand firmly and smiled at her.

Paul let her go. 'Now, Mum texted to say we're not to dilly-dally. Is your mother the only one who still says "dilly-dally"? Apparently you have to be in the city in half an hour for The Reading of the Will.' He said it like it would be taking place in the panelled study of a country house in an Agatha Christie book and might involve fainting, or murder with an antique pistol during a blackout.

'Yeah, sorry, I won't have time to take you to Pa's first. That's where you're staying, isn't it?'

'It is, but that's totally fine. We're at your disposal. We just want to be with you.'

Brian loaded their suitcases into the boot and climbed into the back seat. Paul sat beside Molly, and they set off.

Molly inserted the parking ticket into the machine at the exit and the boom gate lifted without asking for payment.

'Winning at life, as the young people say!' Paul crowed. 'Getting out of this airport for free is a rare and great achievement.'

She smiled. 'Pa thought that too.'

'Well, you know what they say,' said Paul. 'Women go for men like their fathers.'

'What about men?' Molly replied. 'Do men go for men like their fathers? Is Brian like your dad? Brian, is Dad like your father?'

'That's an excellent question,' said Paul. 'I don't remember my father — I was so little when he died — but my mum always liked Brian, so maybe he was a bit like him.'

Brian grinned at Molly in the mirror. 'Your dad is nothing like my dad was. My dad was a kind, thoughtful, lovely fellow. Never had a bad word for anyone. Only thought of others.'

'Fuck you,' Paul said happily.

'I rest my case,' Brian replied.

* * *

In the parking station nearest to the solicitor's office, Annie's ancient Volvo station wagon was blocking the entrance. Molly could see Simon gesticulating in the driver's seat. Five minutes passed as they sat quietly waiting. Simon stabbed the button on the ticket machine several times, and leaned out of the car to speak into the intercom.

Eventually Molly gave an exasperated growl, jerked on the handbrake and unclipped her seat belt.

'It's all right, love,' said Paul, putting his hand on her arm. 'Stay here. I'll go see what the problem is. Maybe the machine isn't working.' He got out and walked over. She rolled down her window to listen.

Paul rested one hand on the roof of his ex-wife's car.

'Hello, Simon,' he said.

'Hi, Dad.' The sliver of Simon's face that Molly could see from her vantage point was red. 'Good flight?'

'Fine, thanks. What's the hold-up?'

'This,' said Simon with a snort. 'This is the hold-up. This is an actual hold-up. They want thirty-six dollars for half an hour.'

'That's a lot,' agreed Paul. 'But it is the CBD. On a weekday.'

'That's outrageous,' said Simon. 'I'm not paying it.'

Molly stuck her head out her window, with difficulty, and shouted, 'Simon, just take a ticket. What's the big deal? You've used car parks before.'

'But it will cost us at least eighty bucks. To park the car.' Simon wouldn't be placated.

'Yes, it will,' Molly said.

'Well, I think that's —'

'No one cares what you think. You don't have a lot of choices here, Simon. Unless you can put the car in your pocket.' She settled back into her seat. 'Or stick it up your arse,' she muttered. Paul dashed back and got in.

Grudgingly Simon took the ticket and drove in. They spiralled around and around, down and down, through a double helix of no spaces. Molly could practically see the steam coming out of Simon's ears in the car ahead.

'Why does he get so upset about everything?' she remarked. 'And why's he such a skinflint?'

They all breathed a sigh of relief as Simon pulled into a space, and Molly found another three spots along.

'Simon was always frugal,' said Paul. 'He never used to buy anything with his pocket money. There were always things you and Naomi wanted — toys and stuff — so you'd save up and buy them. Just little things. But Simon never did. He just kept on putting it in his Dollarmites account. Maybe that's how he's ended up doing so well. They seem to have quite a nice life in Berlin. Their house is in a very smart part of town.'

'Well, hooray for Simon,' said Molly. 'It doesn't seem to have made him very happy. Or Diana. They're the grumpiest stressheads ever. Honestly, you'll see when we get back to Pa's. Maybe he's tormented by guilt for all the people pushed out of their homes by the developments he works on.' The narrative of her brother as a Big Bad Property Developer was one of Molly's favourites. It probably wasn't accurate — she didn't really understand his job — but she knew he was involved in gentrifying residential areas of Berlin and gentrification always meant lower-income city dwellers suffered, didn't it?

* * *

No one else thought Paul and Brian should wait in a coffee shop while the will was read. They were coming along to the meeting. The lift up to the solicitor's office went so fast it made Molly's ears pop. Her parents had greeted each other when they got out of the cars in the same way they always did after being apart for a year or two: as if they'd last seen each other the previous day. Paul hugged Annie, Annie hugged Brian, and they started chatting about a movie Brian and Paul had seen on the plane. There wasn't a hint of awkwardness.

Molly was perplexed by them. Sure, it was almost twenty years since they had split up, but how could it not be strange to see your husband and your oldest friend as a couple? Sometimes she wondered if perhaps her mother had never loved her dad. That was the only way she could see how someone might be okay with their husband leaving them for their friend.

If Jack realised he was gay, and took up with her best friend … but the analogy didn't work because the situation with Mum, Brian and Dad had been unusual even before Dad and Brian fell in love.

How much of her mother's acceptance of the situation was rooted in a twisted sort of romantic affirmative action? Molly didn't think everyone would have been nearly as supportive of her dad if he'd fallen in love with another woman. But because he left her mum for a man, no one was allowed to be pissed off about it. By coming out, her father had effectively immunised himself against criticism of his behaviour. He was seen as a hero for admitting his truth — even by the woman he had pledged to be with forever, and with whom he had three children.

Molly loved Brian, and her father, but still, such thoughts floated to the surface every now and then, and they weren't exactly okay to talk to people about.

Her grandfather had been the only other person in the family who wasn't all right with Brian and Dad becoming a couple. Since that January when Annie and Paul separated, Pa had refused to see or speak to either Paul or Brian. Molly had quietly approved of his stance: not the blatant homophobia, but definitely the loyalty. It had made Christmases awkward: since she was eight, whenever her dad and Brian came back to Australia for the festive season they would celebrate with them on Boxing Day, round at Brian's mum's place while she was alive and after that at whatever holiday house they were renting, after spending proper Christmas at Granny and Pa's.

On the twenty-first floor they were ushered into a boardroom, where the solicitor kept them waiting for ten minutes. Sitting on white leather chairs on little wheels, they gazed out at the million-dollar city views. The receptionist offered coffee, and Simon accepted almost before she had finished asking the question. Molly could see he was determined to get his money's worth, judging by the heaped spoonfuls of sugar he stirred in and the number of biscuits he managed to grab before the plate was offered to the other side of the table.

Molly declined coffee but took a biscuit. She was in no particular rush for the meeting to begin. The longer it took, the later she could start work. Work today was at a house in Vaucluse, rearranging the pantry of one of the laziest couples she'd come across. Every six weeks or so they called Molly in to tidy their kitchen cupboards and implement organisational systems. Every time they praised her to the heavens, said she was a wonder and that they would never need her again because this time they would put clearly labelled things back in the correct places on the clearly labelled shelves. But they didn't, and they always called her back. They were infuriating, but Tien's business would grind to a halt if people could actually change their ways. Their inherent slobbishness paid Molly's salary.

Simon was getting antsy. 'Why did Pa use these people? He didn't need a fancy firm like this. Is there something we don't know about him?'

Annie replied calmly, as she always did when Simon got the bit between his teeth about something. 'As I understand it, the local solicitor he used originally ended up moving to this firm. Years and years ago, though: he's long gone. Dad followed him here for estate planning because he liked him. There's no great conspiracy, Simon.'

'Hmph,' said Simon, and as he folded his arms and furrowed his brow, the boardroom door swung open and a woman about Molly's age marched in, wearing an elegant suit and the sort of stupidly expensive high heels Molly was used to seeing in her clients' wardrobes. She wondered idly if maybe she should have done law.

'Annie. I'm Cara Lee — good to meet you in person.' The woman put down her manila folder and held out her hand.

'Yes, hello, Cara,' said Annie. 'This is my son, Simon, my daughters, Molly and Naomi, my children's father, Paul, and his partner, Brian.'

Molly flinched at that explanation of their family, but Cara seemed unperturbed. She sat down. 'Shall we get started?'

'Yes, please,' said Annie.

'Firstly, let me say how sorry I am for your loss. I didn't have the pleasure of meeting Robert in person, but some of my older colleagues knew him and speak very highly of him.'

Molly saw Simon shift impatiently in his chair. Three minutes, that's how long Cara had been in there without actually getting down to business. If the parking prices were bothering Simon, the ten-minute billable increments for this woman's time would likely cause his head to explode.

Cara went on. 'Robert's estate was very straightforward. He left the house at 28 Baskerville Road and its contents to his only child, Annie Elizabeth Jones. Also the balance of his savings account — which was almost five thousand dollars — plus his small super fund.'

'And?' Simon couldn't handle the suspense.

'And?' Cara echoed.

'Yes, and what else? Presumably he left his grandchildren something?'

Cara was obviously used to this sort of reaction. Looking straight at Simon she said, 'No. That was all. He left everything to Annie.'

Everyone looked at Annie.

'I don't understand,' she said. 'Are you sure? About six months ago he had me drive him in here for a meeting. He said he was making some changes. He suggested it was about my kids, and leaving them a bequest. It was after he watched an episode of *Q+A* about how millennials in Sydney will never own homes.'

Cara leafed through the file. 'Yes, I see here that he did come in. But he didn't end up making any changes. He consulted one of our senior partners, Hamish Baxter, but ultimately he left the will as it was.'

'What did he consult him about?' demanded Simon. 'What did this Baxter person tell him?'

'I can't disclose that,' said Cara.

'Why the hell not?'

'Because you're not our client.'

'That is outrageous,' said Simon, his brow furrowed and his cheeks beginning to inflate. 'That doesn't make any sense. Where's this Baxter person? I'd like to speak to him. If he talked our grandfather out of making a change he wanted to make, then surely that's not legal. We'll sue him.'

'Simon,' said Annie sharply. 'Behave yourself. We will talk about this later. Let's not take up any more of Cara's time. Cara, can we take the paperwork with us to complete?'

Cara nodded and handed the folder to Annie.

With a snort, Simon pushed his chair back from the table and marched out to the lobby. One by one they followed and found him furiously jabbing the call button for the lift, breathing heavily and still puffing his cheeks out with rage.

'That doesn't make it come any faster,' Molly told him. She nudged Brian. 'Doesn't he look like the North Wind on that old map in Pa's dining room?'

Brian tried to hide his smile.

* * *

As soon as the lift doors closed, Simon erupted. 'I can't believe you dragged us all into town to hear that Pa left us nothing.'

'I didn't know he'd left you nothing. I wouldn't have asked you to come if I had,' said Annie, trying to calm him.

Simon was pacing on the spot and breathing like a horse who had been forced into a float. 'Why didn't he leave us anything? I don't understand. We're his grandchildren. We've been really good grandchildren. We deserve something. What do you need with a massive great house? You already own a flat.'

'Jesus Christ, Simon,' muttered Molly. 'You're not the only one this is affecting. You're fine. You own half of the bloody Rhineland. I'm the one who has a shitty mortgaged flat that's dying of concrete cancer.'

'What? What are you talking about? I don't live anywhere near the Rhineland.'

'Molly?' asked Annie gently. 'Is something the matter with your flat?'

'Yes, actually. It's completely busted and Jack and I have to pay eighty thousand dollars to fix it, that's all. So a bit of money from Pa would have been really game-changing for us. But you don't see me shouting about it in a lift, do you, Simon?'

The lift stopped and the doors opened. Simon started to leave but Paul grabbed his shoulder. 'Not our floor.'

Two men in suits entered, and they rode the rest of the way down in silence.

* * *

In the parking station Naomi took her mother's hand. 'It's all right, Mum. It wasn't your fault. It's only money.'

Annie marvelled at her daughter's thoughtfulness.

'It's all right for you,' said Simon. 'You can just pick fruit from the side of the road and live off that. Bet you don't even file a tax return.' He stuck his ticket into the payment machine. 'Fuck off. Seventy-two bucks. For thirty-five minutes of learning that now Mum owns a flat and a house.'

'You should be pleased our mother has somewhere nice to retire to, you shit,' said Molly.

'I am pleased. I just don't think I should be down seventy-two dollars for the privilege of knowing it.'

'Oh my god, would you shut up about the parking.' She opened her bag, pulled out her wallet and thrust two fifty-dollar notes at him. 'There. Parking. Paid for. You owe me twenty-eight bucks.' Simon took the money and she rewarded him with a look of pure disdain. 'I can't believe you accepted that. It was a gesture.'

'Then you're an idiot for offering it,' he replied.

'You're the idiot. For being born an idiot.'

Annie squeezed Paul's hand. 'Didn't we do a lovely job with Naomi?' she said to him.

'Oh yes,' Paul said. 'Naomi was a lovely child who has turned into a beautiful adult. I think we made such a good decision when we only had one child.' He put his arm around his middle child's waist and squeezed her. 'Naomi, you're a credit to your parents.'

Naomi leaned her head onto her father's shoulder.

Simon glared at them. 'That wasn't a funny joke when we were kids and it's especially not a funny joke now.'

Molly opened the boot of her car and began to heave out the suitcases. Brian rushed to help her. 'Mum, can you fit Dad and

Brian in your car?' She scowled at Simon. 'Some of us have jobs to go to.'

'Of course,' he said, scathingly. 'You go, fight the good fight in the War on Clutter.'

'Don't forget to …' she struggled to think of a suitable insult '… buy fifty different kinds of horrible boiled sausages on your way home. Don't want to piss off your hausfrau.' Hmm, she thought, not her finest work.

'That's just racist,' Simon called after her, but she slammed the door and started the car. She reversed out of the space, then paused and opened the window. 'Mum. Can Jack and I move into Pa's place for a bit? Jack's worried about asbestos.'

'You said it was concrete cancer,' said Simon.

'I'm asking Mum.'

'Sure, of course,' said Annie. 'You're always welcome. Come whenever.'

'We're a bit crowded, actually, aren't we?' Simon appealed to his mother.

'Did we not just establish it isn't your house?' retorted Molly.

'You can all stay,' said Annie. 'It's a huge house. There's plenty of room. We'll all have a good time,' she added, but her attempt to sound calming came off like a stage hypnotist faced with a room of unbelievers. 'It'll be absolutely lovely.'

Molly gave her the thumbs up and drove off, and Simon got into the back of Annie's car.

'Are you sure that's a good idea?' Paul asked Annie.

'The last time I was sure something was a good idea I was sixteen and I thought you and I should start going round together,' she told him. 'Look where that got us. Maybe I need to start embracing the bad ideas instead.'

Chapter 7

Annie stretched out on a towel she'd spread on the lawn behind the house. She listened to the currawongs in the tree and the distant hum of traffic. Scrunching her eyes shut she strained to hear what she always heard, but the wretched song was actually gone. Her own stupid song. It was remarkable. That was three days now that it hadn't been in her head. She couldn't believe how light she felt.

The sun warmed her face and she was grateful for the gift she'd given herself when she turned fifty-five: no more sunscreen. She'd grown up in a time before SPF, and the advent of 15+ had put a serious dampener on her life. As part of the first generation of parents who knew about skin cancer, Annie had spent every morning for years attempting to rub thick zinc creams into her furious children's soft pale skin, dragging it with her fingertips, beginning every day with a battle and stinging eyes.

Next had come the news that sun exposure was what caused premature aging of the skin, and Annie too had started wearing protective face creams, and putting on a hat when she was in the garden or at the beach. For thirty years she'd done what she was meant to, but it didn't matter what happened to her face any more. She had sailed past the years where premature aging was a concern. Any aging from here on was entirely right and correct. Besides, she thought smugly, she had genetics on her side. Her mother had always looked a good twenty years younger than her age, and Annie seemed to be following suit.

Moving back in to look after her parents had been confronting, but in a good way. Fear of turning into her mother — who, though she had a smooth face, was brittle of bone and mood, spent too much time in the house and was too dependent on her husband — had led Annie down to the local gym and into a beginners' Zumba class.

Zumba was a shock to her system, but except for the front row of sharp-eyed, long-necked hip swivellers, who wore branded Zumba shoes and copied the sex-faces the young Spanish instructor made during the slower songs, everyone in the class was shamelessly bad, mostly on the wrong beat and two or three steps behind. People laughed, crashed into each other, and on more than one occasion were sent outside by Ale-*hannnnndrrrrro* to calm down until they could take the class seriously again.

She'd told Simon about it when he'd arrived home for the funeral, and he'd frowned. 'Zumba's a gateway exercise,' he warned her. 'It happened to Diana's mum. They get women like you in with a bit of Zumba, because it's really just dancing. Then you'll start doing Barre and Pump and before you know it you'll be able to bench-press your own cars and then because you're bored you'll think you need to "find yourself" so you'll take up yoga. After that you'll retrain as a yoga teacher and want to move to India. It should be illegal. I should have thought walking on the beach was more in your wheelhouse.'

She'd laughed at him. 'Would that be so bad, if I moved to India to look up my own asana?'

'You can do yoga here, if you must. I don't know why you need to find yourself anyway.'

Annie hadn't mentioned finding herself. Or doing yoga, for that matter. She wondered why Simon was so prickly. His level of corporate jargon was off the charts this visit. Maybe he felt guilty about not having been there to help her with Pa. Probably not, though. Guilt wasn't really 'in his wheelhouse'.

Simon wouldn't have coped with watching his grandfather fall apart. Pa's eyesight had dimmed, he'd grown shorter day by day, and his flesh had seemed to melt off his once grand frame. His skin tore easily, his nails thickened and yellowed.

His mind had stayed sharp until almost the very end. That had been hard. It would make more sense if the body and the mind could give way at the same rate, Annie thought. It would be less cruel. It was almost a relief when, a few days before he died, her father stopped realising what was happening, as his heart grew weaker, his breath became more laboured, and his limbs swelled with the fluids his body no longer had the strength to process.

She was with him all the time. Her friends — mostly new friends from the gym — were so helpful. All through that last week someone had been in the house with them constantly. Just being present, making sandwiches for Annie, sitting with her father while she showered, keeping the dishes washed and the floor swept. There would have been a roster: she'd participated in a couple since she'd met them — once when Geraldine was treated for leukaemia, and once when Deborah's husband died quickly from aggressive bone cancer.

A bee tumbled past her head, flying low and unsteadily like the A380s that dragged themselves over the backyard so many times a day, and landed on the drooping head of a blood-coloured dahlia. There were more bees this year. On the advice of the *Gardening Australia* website, she'd put a water tray out for them with stones to land on, and planted more flowering herbs, lavender and alyssum. It seemed to have worked.

She wondered how long Molly and Jack would stay. Hopefully they'd move on after Christmas, once Jack realised that concrete cancer and asbestos weren't one and the same and they could safely head back to their flat.

Once everyone had left, things would be quiet, and she would be able to hear what she'd started listening for again since her stupid old song had gone: the music. Some new music. It occurred to her that maybe songs would come, if she found a space for them, made some room in her head and her life. She wasn't sure how to go about it. How did you attract inspiration? If she put a birdbath of vodka in the garden would the Ancient Greek muses come clambering over the fence like a trio of pissed back-up singers?

A single shriek came from the bottom of the garden. Annie shielded her eyes from the sun, trying to see her grandchildren. Sunny and Felix had been down the back all morning. Naomi had given them each a pair of secateurs and told them to try to cut their way into the tangled plumbago hedge. Naomi, Simon and Molly built a hideout in there when they were kids, and Naomi assured the grandchildren that they would find forgotten treasures within, if they could make it to the middle and cut themselves a clearing.

Silver teaspoons: that was what they might find. Annie remembered Jean mildly raging about the way, when Simon, Naomi and Molly were in summer residence, all the teaspoons went one way only — out of the kitchen, in jars of jam, pots of Nutella, or bowls of ice-cream, and into the plumbago cave, never to be seen again.

She'd only half-listened to her mother's complaints, before turning back to planning the next day's activities for the music workshops, or tinkering with a jingle she was writing, leaving her mother to supervise, feed and care for her kids once again, but now without any teaspoons.

Very gently, Annie lifted the corner of the box in her mind marked *Songs*. What if there was nothing there?

She wouldn't write jingles. Not any more. They weren't even fashionable in advertising nowadays. And they didn't interest her anyway. If she was going to do this again, it was going to be proper songs, for her to perform. She had been talented, in the beginning: she knew that now. For so long she had thought she needed Paul and Brian to be involved, for them to write together, but she felt now that that might not be true. There was only one way to find out. And for the first time in decades it felt like they were still there, the songs, bubbling away, breeding in her like a viral load. It was only a matter of time before she began to show symptoms.

The house could be rented out. That money, along with the income from her flat, and the interest from her father's small superannuation fund, would mean she could literally stick a pin in a map and go anywhere she wanted. If the interviewers ever came after all, they could say, 'Annie, who lives in a shack in Nashville' or 'Annie, who writes in an apartment in the 11th arrondissement of Paris' or 'Annie, whose music reflects her new home on Mykonos'.

After Christmas, she would go. She'd stay for the birth of Molly and Jack's baby, but then she'd sell most of her belongings, rent out the house and head off into the wide blue yonder. She played with the phrase: why were yonders only ever wide and blue? It was such a positive expression. Finally it felt true. For the first time since becoming a mother Annie felt like there really might be a wide blue yonder and that she might be in a position to explore it. For so long her yonder had been, if anything, biscuit-coloured and too small to swing a cat.

Sunny and Felix were just visible through the sticky mauve flowers of the plumbago. Annie loved kids at this age. They were independent and curious, past the rather dull point of wanting to show you every single leaf and stone they came across. Annie hadn't been displeased that her first two grandchildren were born in Germany and Byron Bay. She'd visited them every so often, and now they were six, and more like actual people with ideas and jokes and opinions, she enjoyed seeing them. She liked being an occasional presence in their life, rather than a default extra parent, the kind so many of her friends were finding themselves to be.

All these wonderful women, who had worked and raised families, supported husbands and each other and their own parents, now they were being asked to go back to work as unpaid nannies. And if they said no, they were made to feel like they didn't care about their kids. The unfairness made Annie's blood boil.

Her friend Elizabeth had been talking about it after Zumba only the week before. She had asked her son if he could start to look for a daycare place for his two-year-old twins, whom Elizabeth had been looking after three days a week since they were nine months old. Just for one day a week, she'd said. She was still prepared to do two days, but she thought that maybe now that they were walking and talking, daycare might be fun for them. Her son had said no. He wouldn't consider that until the twins were three.

'Why didn't you tell him to go jump in the fucking lake?' Jane had responded. That's what Jane would have done. Jane was brilliant like that. She could say no for Australia. If it was up to Jane, pretty much everyone would be in a fucking lake.

It was Jane who'd warned Annie to be careful about Molly's expectations of free childcare. Apparently that was what happened nowadays: girls expected their mothers to look after their kids so they could go back to work more easily. 'Nip it in the bud,' was Jane's advice.

But Molly hadn't even hinted at Annie looking after the baby, thank god. Annie hoped that it was indicative of her having quietly made other arrangements, but she worried that it was in fact lack of forethought. From the sounds of it, by this stage of pregnancy, Annie's friends' daughters had done an assortment of birth courses, installed car seats, set up baby monitors, painted the nursery, and booked daycare places and private schools. Molly was living in the moment, admiring her growing bump and revelling in her now ultra-thick hair.

Annie's relief was tempered with guilt, having had so much help from her own mother when her kids were small. For in addition to the summer holidays, Jean had always been prepared to drive down to Glebe at a moment's notice to mind the children for an hour or two, to give Annie a breather. The idea of being trapped at home again with a baby for a whole day was horrifying.

It wasn't a fashionable attitude, but for Annie there was nothing more boring than babies. Even her own babies had been boring. Simon and Naomi were only eighteen months apart and while of course she'd loved them, felt pride and delight when they'd rolled over and smiled, those days back before they had started school had been truly a kind of purgatory. It was proper soul-crushing, brain-shrivelling boredom.

When Molly was one, Annie went back to work, leaving her with a neighbour, Roz, who had a baby the same age. Moderate pop-stardom being the only thing on her resume, Annie had been grateful to secure a position in the office at the school where Paul worked. The work — basic admin and reception duties, with a sideline in playground injury first-aid and sick-bay triage — was not especially challenging or interesting, but she liked her colleagues, and it fit with the kids' school hours and left the holidays free.

Molly had somehow thrived as an almost entirely ignored third child. Although there was no baby book marking when she reached her milestones of infancy, she'd done everything she was supposed to with almost no help from her parents. She might have even done some things earlier than Naomi and Simon: it was hard to remember now. Annie couldn't, to her shame, recall teaching Molly anything. She'd started school and seemed to have picked up her ABCs from somewhere. She could ride a bike. Who raised her? Roz, mostly, and Jean, in the summers, but then who? It was a bit of a mystery. Annie and Paul's third child was much loved, but hardly noticed.

It had been a surprise when Molly took her parents' separation so badly. With the benefit of hindsight, it was clear that they'd asked too much of her. Simon and Naomi, at sixteen and fourteen, had seemed able to process the split in a more adult way — they'd accepted that their father had fallen in love, that his sexual orientation was undeniable. As far as they were concerned, it was a no-fault divorce. They were upset that he was moving to England, but mostly because they missed him. Annie didn't see much change in their behaviour.

Molly wasn't nearly as accepting. They'd all been in the firing line of her anger. She considered the three adults equally culpable in destroying the family. Annie remembered Molly's face, tear-stained and wild with fury, in the days after the separation. 'You let him go,' she'd wailed. 'You don't even care.'

Annie had tried to explain that it wasn't up to her, that she wanted Paul and Brian to be happy because she loved them both, but that made Molly even angrier.

'Why does he get to be happy and not us?'

Annie didn't have an answer for that back then, and she still found it a hard question. Maybe it was that Paul wanted it more. His feelings for Brian seemed to be stronger than her feelings for Paul. Also, life wasn't fair: there was that to be taken into consideration.

'He's still your dad,' she'd tried to tell Molly. 'Nothing will change that. He'll always be just a phone call away. You can ring him any time you want. I won't even make you wait for off-peak.'

Molly had refused to be placated. As far as she was concerned, Paul had not just left Annie, but all of them. She had predicted, quite accurately as it turned out, that the distance would matter: their relationship would change, for how could her father know or understand Molly or her life when it was reduced to what she would report in a phone call or write in an email? What she was doing, the netball games won and lost, the awards in assembly, the movies she had seen with her friends: they were just building blocks of her life. Paul knowing those facts didn't mean he knew her. In her Year Seven art class Molly saw a portrait of van Gogh, done in tiny dabs of colour. She'd explained to Annie that that's what it was like: her dad only saw the portrait from afar. He didn't see the dots.

You couldn't properly know someone, not without being there to hear them humming through the bathroom door, to see them laughing at Column 8 in the paper as they ate cereal in the morning, to make them a hot Milo to cheer them up when they lost their half-moon friendship necklace on the beach. Annie conceded that all those little things were what made Molly who she was, and that Paul couldn't know them once he had gone.

Truthfully, Annie wasn't utterly devastated and broken by the end of her marriage. It might have ended anyway, one way or another, she thought. After all, she and Paul had got together when they were practically children and over twenty years later they had been no longer the same people. She felt oddly pragmatic about it all.

Their love, she believed, had been the love of the very young. That sort of love wasn't meant to last forever. It was naive to think it would. Saying that to Molly wouldn't have helped, though. Molly had been eight and she'd wanted so much to believe her parents' love was true and everlasting.

After the split, Molly changed. Where some kids would have turned inwards, she became almost unnaturally confident. She got funnier and more outgoing. She aggressively collected friends, and each time she tried becoming a version of that friend: taking up the same pastimes and sports, listening to the music they were into and watching the same TV shows. She'd move on to a new friend just before her imitation became pathetic.

At fourteen she took up Having A Boyfriend as a serious hobby. They were all different, but they had in common the fact that if you plotted their attributes on Venn diagrams none would have overlapped with her father.

Each boyfriend she kept for three years, like a mobile phone, before upgrading to someone who was not yet worn out by her. Steve, Kyle and Tom came and went, before Molly met Jack when she was twenty-three. Jack had so far proven more durable than his predecessors.

Annie hoped Molly would stick with Jack more than she stuck with other parts of her life. The way Molly picked up and put down careers like they were earrings she was browsing in an expensive shop terrified Annie. Nowadays it was normal to move around between jobs, she did understand that, but not like Molly did, not like an easily bored pinball.

Naomi didn't own anything more valuable than her van. Only Simon was doing okay, financially. Annie felt a pang of guilt. She'd always tried to focus on the kids doing what made them happy. She should have put more thought into what would make them a reliable living.

Sunny popped out of the plumbago, brandishing a handful of dirty spoons. 'Annie!' she shouted. 'We found them!'

'Well done, Sunny. Do you want to come and wash them up?'

'No! We want to swap them for knives. We want to throw knives at the tree.'

Annie sat up and crossed her legs. 'What if I give you knives to throw at the ground? You can stand there, on the edge of the paving, and see who can throw their knife the furthest along the lawn, while getting it to stick into the ground. If it doesn't stab the ground, it doesn't get a point. Minus a hundred points for killing a cousin.'

Sunny ducked back out of sight, presumably conferring with Felix. They both emerged, Sunny's T-shirt smeared with dirt and the tutu Felix wore over his shorts covered with sticky purple plumbago flowers.

'Yes please, Annie,' said Felix, in his sweet strong accent. Annie was impressed by his English. He was perfectly bilingual. Simon seemed to have picked up almost no German in eight years of living there. He spoke only English and Corporate Guff. Annie knew Simon would be pleased to see Felix throwing knives: he would think it offset his son's tutu-wearing, which worried him.

She went inside to find some knives.

In the kitchen Naomi was cramming sliced cabbage into a jar. 'You just got a text from Molly.'

Annie picked up her phone and held it at arm's length to read the message, because her glasses had been missing for several days. They'd work their way to the top of a pile eventually. 'She says they're coming after work.' She put the phone down. 'It'll be a bit crowded.' Annie considered the logistics of adding two more people — soon to be three — to the household.

'A bit,' agreed Naomi. 'But you'll be in your room, Dad and Brian are in Pa's old room, I'm in the box room, Simon and Diana are in the guest room. So if we move Sunny and Felix out of the sunroom and put Sunny back with me and Felix back with his parents, Molly and Jack can have the sunroom.'

'Ten is a lot of people in one house. There are only two bathrooms.' Perhaps, Annie thought, I should go back to my flat and leave them all to it.

She hummed six notes. They'd been floating around her all day, those six notes. That was how her songs used to begin life, as a few notes that tickled away at her subconscious like the beginning of a cold. It would take a few days to realise they were there. If she acknowledged them too soon, they sometimes evaporated. She'd learned it was best to ignore them for as long as she could, until they bedded down and wouldn't leave her alone. But it was so many years since a decent song had done that. The notes were a tease, she knew. They'd be gone in the morning, and 'Home Is Where Your Heart Is' would have taken up its usual place, banging away on the piano in her mind, the obnoxious drunk friend who won't be told that no one else is up for a singalong.

Chapter 8

Diana was serving up goulash, potatoes and cabbage salad when Molly and Jack arrived. Jack carried bag after bag in from the car and dropped them in the sunroom, then came into the kitchen, sniffing the air like a bloodhound. Molly had sat down at the kitchen table, her legs spread wide to accommodate her belly.

'It's too hot for food like that,' she said, half-heartedly attempting to irritate her brother, who was gathering plates and forks, but her stomach rumbled disloyally.

'It's very hot in the dining room,' Annie said. 'Why don't we eat outside?'

In the garden, Paul and Brian sat on the iron chairs, the kids on the grass, and the others improvised with kitchen and dining room chairs they'd carried out to the patio.

'Isn't this fabulous?' said Paul, beaming around at them all. 'Together again! We haven't done this for ages.'

Annie's leg wouldn't stop jiggling. How rude would it be to ask how long they were all planning on staying? 'I hope you can all stay through Christmas,' she ventured. Was it implicit enough that as soon as they had turned the TV off after the beginning of the Sydney to Hobart she would like them all to go home?

'Are you "This has been absolutely lovely"-ing us already?' Molly replied, indignantly.

'What is "This has been absolutely lovely"-ing?' asked Diana.

'It's something our grandmother used to do,' said Naomi. 'When guests had outstayed their welcome she used to get up and say, "This has been absolutely lovely," and then just stand there until they got the hint.'

'I'm not doing that. I'm just … forward planning,' Annie said, trying to defend herself.

'It's all right,' said Paul, patting her on the shoulder. 'Our flight back is on New Year's Day. Brian's ghostwriting a new book. He's got two weeks of interviews lined up.'

'Anyone we'd have heard of?' asked Molly.

Brian glanced sidelong at Paul, then at Annie. 'Actually, it's Lorraine Darmody.'

'Oh,' said Simon. 'Massive awks.'

'I don't know who Lorraine Darmody is,' said Diana. 'Why is she massive awks?'

No one spoke.

Finally Annie said, 'She's a successful British performer. She got her big break when she performed a song at Eurovision. A song that we wrote — Brian and Paul and me.'

'Why didn't you perform it?'

'Mum was pregnant, and that meant she wasn't allowed to,' said Naomi. She stabbed at her plate of coleslaw crossly. 'The patriarchy at work.'

'What's a patriarchy?' asked Sunny.

'It's a situation where men are in charge of everything,' Naomi told her.

'What, all men? In charge of everything?'

Felix glanced at his father, and then at his mother. 'Is that a good idea?'

'It's how things were back then,' said Annie. 'I was about to have Simon and the powers that be decreed that seeing a pregnant woman on stage and on England's television screens would not be conducive to winning Eurovision.'

'It was a travesty,' added Paul. 'We should have fought harder. You were gorgeous.'

Annie scoffed at him. 'I wasn't. And you didn't fight for me at all. You both called me the *Fairstar*.'

'Dad, you didn't!' Naomi was appalled.

'What is a fairstar?' Diana squinted in confusion.

'It was a cruise ship,' Annie explained. Poor Diana. Annie had never realised quite how much of what they talked about would require explanation to a foreigner.

'Anyway,' said Brian, 'what goes around comes around, as they say, and I'm once again putting words in Lorraine's mouth.'

No one quite knew what to say after that. All conversational avenues seemed to lead down memory lanes littered with the used syringes of what might have been, and it seemed impolite to talk any more about the woman who had more or less stolen Annie's future.

Paul turned to his son. 'Simon? When do the German schools go back after New Year?'

Diana cleared her throat and looked at Simon.

'Actually,' he said, 'we're not sure how long we're staying. We're throwing around some ideas.'

'What's that supposed to mean?' demanded Molly.

'We're just exploring our options,' Diana said.

'That's what people say when they've been sacked. Simon, have you been sacked? Diana, have you?'

'Who needs another beer?' asked Simon, rising and marching back into the house as though his youngest sister hadn't spoken.

'Maybe let it go?' Jack put his hand on Molly's leg.

The unmistakable sound of a Champagne bottle being opened echoed across the fence from Ray's house and as one the family looked up in time to see a cork fly over the fence and land in the middle of the lawn. Sunny and Felix downed cutlery and dashed over to it, fighting for possession.

'That was unexpected,' said Brian. 'Do you think Ray's having a party?'

'Ray doesn't have parties. He never even has visitors,' Annie said. 'Honestly, since I've been staying, I don't think I've ever heard anyone else's voice from that house.'

The sound of a man's laughter drifted over: too young to be Ray.

'He has a very cheerful home invader then,' said Paul. 'I want to go look.'

'I'm coming,' Annie said. She put her plate down and padded across the lawn in her bare feet. Paul followed her around the garage.

The side fence was still half-rotten there. Over the years the nails had rusted away, leaving the wooden palings leaning against each other like disaffected teenagers smoking around the back of a toilet block.

Quietly, Paul and Annie peered through. Ray stood on his verandah with another man, both holding glasses of Champagne and looking out at the garden. Annie hadn't had a good look at the old bloke for years. He was thin, but still tall. He hadn't curved into a question mark like some thin old men do. His hair was white but thick. How old would he be? She tried to figure it out. He was about ten years younger than her dad. Somewhere in his late seventies, early eighties?

The evening sun glowed through the trees at the back of Ray's garden, and the other man on the verandah, the one holding the

Champagne bottle, raised his glass in salute to Ray, his back to Annie and Paul.

'Who do you reckon that is?' Paul asked quietly.

'No idea.'

'Didn't Ray have a kid?'

'He did, but I don't think they had a relationship. Heather left when he was a baby.'

They watched for a few moments longer, both pressed up against the fence, their arms touching. His arms felt strong and firm. Hers had grown thinner and softer, although the Zumba was making a difference. She remembered being behind this garage with him before, his whole body pushing hers up against the fence as they kissed each other with the desperation that only virginity brings.

They'd met at sixteen in a ballroom dancing class, she and Paul and Brian. They were the only students under fifty. Paul had caught her watching him during the first lesson, and pursed his lips into a funny little half smile. He'd made a beeline for her when Miss Laurel said it was time to choose a partner but Brian beat him to it.

Brian was definitely the better dancer. He had filled out the template of a man earlier than Paul, who still looked like all his joints belonged to his father. Paul's extreme handsomeness didn't become apparent for another year or two: back then any potential was masked by pimples and awkwardness. Brian was tall and strong already, with shoulder-length dark hair that Paul used to say made him look like Richard III. Annie thought it made him look like David Cassidy.

They'd bonded over their affection for uncool music. Their city was exploding with underground sounds of the burgeoning pub rock and punk scene, so finding two other teens also prepared to admit they loved ABBA and The Seekers was an unexpected relief and a delight.

As children of middle-class parents who, while not musical themselves, knew playing an instrument competently to be a life skill akin to possessing a decent game of tennis, between them they could more or less manage the piano, guitar and bass. After three dance lessons they'd stopped going, and instead began meeting in the enclosed verandah at Annie's parents' house each weekend.

That was where they wrote their first song, 'I See You Every Day', and where they decided one afternoon, while tipsy on Chateau Tanunda brandy Paul had stolen from his mum's drinks cabinet, that although it was tempting to call the group Brian, Paul and Annie, times were changing and the name Love Triangle might help them go further.

Annie had realised she had a knack with a lyrical melody and catchy hooks. Brian and Paul could add guitar and bass to whatever she came up with. All their songs had a minimum of two upward key changes and a bridge that could double as the opening theme to a sitcom. Once they pooled their pocket money savings, the funds from the sales of their three bikes and a not insignificant investment from Annie's dad, their compositions were transformed by the otherworldly sounds of a synthesiser.

Six months later, at the cinema one night, the group's dynamic had changed. Poor Brian, Annie thought. He'd turned away from *The Pink Panther Strikes Again* to find Paul tongue-deep in Annie's face, with one hand firmly up her jumper. Annie could still remember the shock in his eyes when they'd come up for air.

The next morning Brian had called a band meeting and they'd decided Annie could become Paul's girlfriend as long as it didn't threaten the existence of Love Triangle. It was big of Brian.

They were not children, they all agreed, and could be trusted to put the future of the band first. ABBA would be their model: sensible, strong relationships, but always putting the focus on the work. They would be having no Fleetwood Mac nonsense.

Annie's mum and dad weren't thrilled at the romantic development, but they still let the band use their enclosed verandah to practise. Probably, Annie now realised, so they could keep an eye on proceedings. She didn't think they had ever known how frequently she and Paul climbed out of the window and scurried along the right of way so they could pash behind the garage.

Love Triangle knew how lucky they were to have the Thornes' house to practise in. Jean baked them biscuits and always had cordial made up in a tall yellow plastic jug in the fridge, and Robert never seemed to mind their noise.

'Sorry, Mr Thorne,' Paul would say when he spotted Robert through the open windows, often spraying poison from a backpack onto the weeds springing up between the Besser bricks that lined the drive. 'We'll try to keep it down.'

Robert would smile back, and say, 'Don't give it another thought, young man. You just keep on making your music. It's not bothering anyone.'

It must have bothered Ray, Annie always thought. His house was just on the other side of the driveway, about six feet away.

Annie moved her arm a fraction away from Paul's. He didn't appear to notice. He had wanted her, back in those days. For sure. They'd had several years of perfectly fine sex before the kids gradually leached them of desire. After that it was Brian who Paul wanted, not Annie.

Annie straightened up and gestured with her head that they should go back to the patio. Paul caught her eye and looked away. She knew he remembered too, but it wasn't something they talked about. They hadn't then and they wouldn't now. It was easier that way.

'Well? What's happening over there?' asked Simon when they sat back down.

'Nothing very exciting,' said Paul, picking up his plate and refocussing his attention on his goulash. 'Ray's having a drink with someone.'

'Maybe he's celebrating Pa's death,' said Molly. 'He hated Pa as much as Pa hated him, right?'

'I don't think they hated each other,' Annie said. 'Hate's a very strong word. They just weren't friends.' She picked up her plate and held it in her lap. She couldn't face another mouthful.

Molly frowned, scraped the last forkful of food up and burped. 'Sorry,' she said. 'This food isn't really agreeing with me. It's a bit rich.'

* * *

'I'll do the washing up,' Annie said to Diana as they stacked the dinner plates on the kitchen counter. 'You cooked.'

'No, no,' said Diana. 'Let me help.'

'I'd rather do it on my own,' said Annie, realising too late her voice was too bright.

Diana looked up in patent alarm. Annie's eyes felt dry, but she knew she was grimacing the set smile of a woman who needed to be alone. Her daughter-in-law stepped back out into the garden and Annie blessed her unfussy kindness.

Methodically, she scraped the plates, rinsed them in a sink of hot water, and stacked them in the dishwasher. She decanted leftovers into the new glass containers Naomi had made her buy after declaring the ancient Tupperware both a health and an environmental hazard. She picked pieces of parsley out of the sink strainer and wondered if Paul had ever truly loved her, or if she'd merely been a placeholder until he was brave enough to love Brian.

Chapter 9

The slam of a car door woke Molly on Saturday morning. In her confused somnolent state, she couldn't immediately place where she was. She opened her eyes and looked up. Mattress-ticking wallpaper. On the ceiling. Pa's house.

Swinging her legs out of bed, she pushed herself into an upright position. Her body felt like it had been filled with custard. Bracing her lower back with one hand, she shuffled out of the sunroom and down the hall.

The bathroom door was closed and she could hear the shower running. She banged loudly. 'I need to pee.'

No response. She thumped the door again. 'I need to *pee!*' she shouted.

'The whole neighbourhood will be pleased to hear that,' said Diana, sticking her head out of the kitchen. She was holding a spatula.

'Who's in the bathroom?' Molly asked.

'Simon. I think the upstairs bathroom's free.'

Molly gave her a withering look. She would sooner wee in the gutter in front of the house than drag herself up all those stairs. 'I'm busting.' She opened the bathroom door and plunged into the cloud of steam.

'Hey!' Simon's shouts reverberated around the tiled room and he clutched the shower curtain around himself dramatically. 'Can't you knock? Ever heard of privacy?'

'I'm your sister. There is no one less interested in seeing you naked than me. I need to pee.' She sat down on the toilet. 'I thought Germans were meant to be relaxed about nudity. You're a pretty shit German.'

Simon turned off the shower and reached for his towel. He pulled it in behind the curtain and emerged, wrapped and furious. 'At least I have lived somewhere else. You haven't ever lived more than twenty kilometres from where you were born. You've got regional agoraphobia.'

'That's not a thing,' she shouted as he slammed the door behind him. She heard him stomp up the stairs overhead.

There was a knock on the bathroom door. 'Molly?' called Annie. 'Want to come to the gym?'

Molly got up, flushed the toilet and opened the door. 'What?'

'Do you want to come to the gym? I've got advanced Zumba, but you can sit on an exercise bike, or potter along on the treadmill. Or there's a yoga class on at the same time, and they can always modify the moves for pregnancy.'

'Can they modify it into not being a yoga class?'

Annie laughed. Molly wanted to go to yoga with her mother about as much as she wanted to see her brother naked, but still she dragged on leggings and a T-shirt of Jack's advertising SKYY vodka and climbed into Annie's car. How bad could one yoga class be?

* * *

Unspeakable. That's how bad one yoga class could be. The other eight students were ancient, seemed to have a working knowledge of Sanskrit, and were as flexible as willow. It was their last class before the Christmas break, so they were all dressed in green and red, and one woman had brought felt Santa hats for everyone. The enforced jollity made Molly's skin crawl. After fifteen minutes of Molly failing to get herself into any of the positions the instructor, Pascal, suggested, he took pity on her and told her to lie on her side in modified savasana. 'Just be still and feel,' he said, patting her shoulder gently.

Molly was embarrassed, but she lay in the recovery position as if she were the plastic model in a lifesaving demonstration while Pascal fetched more and more props from the cupboard at the back of the room: a rolled-up blanket between her knees to align her hips, a wedge beneath her stomach and another behind her lower back, a foam brick under her head. Finally he draped a heavy blanket over her body and legs.

Her stomach rumbled. The idea of a baguette pierced her consciousness like a crusty blunt javelin and lodged there. She tried to focus on her body, beginning at her toes, moving to her feet, ankles and up her legs. It worked as far as her knees. Then the baguette was back. A tiny bit sour, fresh and soft. A chewy crust, not the crumbly kind that shatters and leaves golden shrapnel in your lap. She would spread it with salted butter and sprinkle more salt onto the salted butter. There was a bakery in the same block as the yoga studio. How much longer was there to go?

Her eyes felt heavy and Pascal's voice droned softly. Beside her the other women moved through their poses, and she fell deeply asleep.

Another hand on her shoulder awakened her. Her mother. The others were gone, their mats rolled up and put away. How long had she slept? She wiped her mouth with her T-shirt. God, she'd been drooling.

'All right, darling?' asked Annie. 'How was the yoga? We're going to get a coffee. Coming?'

'Mmm, yes.' Molly was groggy. She'd been dreaming about a dance class. She'd had no shoes and had to borrow some from her mother. They were too big. Her dreams were always so embarrassingly literal. She never told anyone about them, partly because there is nothing more boring than hearing about anyone's dreams, but mostly because she felt there was nothing more boring than her own specific dreams. Not being able to fill her mother's shoes. How pedestrian.

Her mother helped her to her feet. The baby seemed to have shifted during the class and now it felt like there was an aggressive cement bowling ball lodged in her pelvis.

* * *

Annie and her friends were well known in the tiny cafe they repaired to after the class. There were only three small tables and they took all of them, after the two men sitting with newspapers took flight at the sight of so much grandmotherly activewear blustering into their space. It was like a murder of crows had muscled in on a couple of pigeons. The barista asked if they wanted the usual. Molly prided herself on not having a usual coffee order. Why would you? Life was too short to have the same thing over and over again. She asked, today, for a decaf skim latte.

'That's what we call a "Why Bother?",' remarked Jane, who was small and wiry, with cropped grey hair and eyelids that drooped down and rested on her eyelashes.

'I'm not supposed to have caffeine,' Molly told her.

'Are you excited? About the baby?'

Molly arranged her face to resemble that of someone who didn't feel like there was a chainsaw cutting through her undercarriage. 'Very excited.'

Jane looked her in the eyes. 'It's okay not to be. I felt like I was walking to the gallows before my first was born. It's very frightening, the prospect of entering a room as you and walking out as a mother.'

'I'm not frightened. I'll still be me. It'll be great. I'm doing a preparation program called Birth World. It teaches you to build an optimal environment of your own imagining around you while you give birth. That way whatever happens, you're protected in your own bubble of safety, where you remain in choice and power.'

There was general unsupportive tittering.

'Good for you,' said Jane. 'Whatever floats your boat. I opted for an epidural followed by a Caesarean, which I highly recommend. All the women I know who had their babies vaginally ended up ripped from here till Tuesday. Mark my words, if anything looks iffy, you want to get a man —'

'Or a woman,' said the one in fluorescent leopard-print leggings, who Molly thought might be called Lynn.

'Excuse me, or a woman, to chop that baby straight out with a scalpel.'

'And try to relax,' added probably-Lynn. 'When my Fiona had her first she was so stressed I thought the baby was going to come out her face.'

Molly wasn't planning a Caesarean, in as much as she wasn't planning the birth at all. She wasn't keen on injections, so voluntarily allowing someone to saw her in half like a magician's assistant was absolutely off the table.

But Jane's question brought up the undeniable fact that although she was planning to follow the Birth World method, it was, like the prenatal yoga, still no more than a plan. A few times she had gone to the laptop to sign up for one of the workshops, which came with an online program of videos and podcasts and an app that was scientifically proven to reduce Caesareans by up to forty per cent. It was just that each time she was about to put in her credit card details, she slammed the machine shut and opened up Words With Friends on her phone instead.

Chapter 10

Wafts of cinnamon and pepper greeted Annie and Molly on their return to Baskerville Road. 'What are they making now?' Molly muttered.

'It smells wonderful,' said her mum. 'Must be the pfeffernusse Diana was talking about. She said Simon makes them every year at Christmas.'

'Simon? Simon isn't even German. Other people have traditions too. They can't keep making us all eat German food all the time. They're so expansionist.'

'It's some seasonal bikkies, Moll, not a Reich. And you're welcome to cook too.'

'I would if the kitchen was ever free.'

Molly went into the sunroom and shut the door. She needed to get on with the Birth World business. The baby wasn't going to stay inside her forever, and she had very little idea about how to get it out. Having declined all the hospital-run birth classes, she was left with the online options or relying on her body's intrinsic biological ability to know how to birth a baby. The laptop seemed a safer bet.

She entered her credit card details into the website, pressed play on the introductory podcast, and lay on the bed.

Outside in the right of way, Felix and Sunny had tennis racquets and were hitting a ball against the side of Ray's house.

The rhythmic thwack pierced Molly's tenuous concentration. Her grandfather's study would be quieter. Having not really registered a word of the podcast so far, she sat up again and pressed the space bar to stop it.

Molly hadn't been into the study since Pa had died. She wondered if she would feel his presence in there. Probably not. She didn't feel his presence anywhere else in the house. Besides, she didn't believe in that sort of thing.

The study door was ajar. It was always left open so Richard V could get in and out. Since his master's death, Richard V had carried on with their shared daily routine. He still sat in the sun in the right of way each morning, scowling at Ray's kitchen window. It would be poignant, Molly thought, if he weren't such an unpleasant animal. By eleven o'clock most days he was curled into a comma, asleep on top of a pile of papers on the filing cabinet in the study, which is where she found him now.

'Hello, Richard,' she said, closing the door behind her. 'We meet again.' Richard opened his eyes a crack, stood up and turned his back to her. 'I admire his discretion,' her grandfather used to tell people enigmatically if they asked what the appeal of this animal was.

'Well, up yours,' said Molly. She placed the laptop on the desk, pressed play and lay down on the worn Persian rug. She closed her eyes.

A woman's voice came through the speaker. 'Welcome to your Birth World,' she said in a voice that immediately rankled. How could someone sound smug *and* judgemental in five words? How was such a voice supposed to keep her calm and relaxed while she was pushing a baby out of her vagina? This was a mistake. For almost five hundred dollars there really ought to be an alternative to such a self-satisfied smuggo, like with sat nav. Maybe there was a Phoebe Waller-Bridge option. Or Emma Thompson. Molly reached up and pressed pause again.

Richard stared down from the filing cabinet. Not breaking eye contact, he slid a piece of paper off the top with his paw, and they both watched it float down to the floor.

'Don't do that.'

Richard turned away again and with his back feet sent more paper down.

'Richard, you're such a dick.' She gathered the papers and looked at them. They were ancient invoices from her grandfather's work, from the previous decade. She missed him, suddenly and hard. It was Pa who had taught her how to file. As soon as she knew the alphabet he'd shown her how his system worked. He'd shown Naomi and Simon as well, but they were not good at it. Molly had spent hours in there as a little girl, searching for the right client's folder, ordered by surname, then placing documents inside by date. It was, she realised, not dissimilar to the work she did now.

She stood and looked at the first invoice, addressed to Sara Heyward. She opened the top drawer of the filing cabinet, leafing through the folders until she found the hanging file marked *Heyward*, and placed the invoice in the front of the manila folder within. The other invoices were for Maiden, Tory, Kersey, O'Donnell and Bard. All the files were where they should be. This was definitely an improvement on listening to someone telling her to picture her cervix opening like a flower.

The last invoice was for Parikh. Third drawer. She thumbed through the folders until a word caught her eye. Penhaligon. Right-of-Way Ray was Ray Penhaligon. She never knew Pa did any work for him. Why would Ray have used Pa as an accountant when they were, as far as she'd always been led to believe, mortal enemies?

Curious, she removed the file, which was twice as thick as any other, and flicked through the documents inside. They were all letters, handwritten on decorative paper. Some had scalloped edges; some had gilt trim. Many had some sort of floral embellishment printed at the top and bottom. None of them were invoices.

She plucked one out at random. The writing was open and bold, with grandiose looping descenders on the gs and ys. At once it was clear it was a woman's hand, and a young woman's at that. It had none of the cramped scratchiness that comes with age. The letters were round and upright printing, taught after the cursive of her grandmother's generation and before the triangular Foundation Style that Molly and her brother and sister learned.

At the bottom of the page it said: *All my love, I am yours, Heather.*

There were twenty-five letters. They weren't dated, and they were all from Heather Penhaligon, Ray's long-vanished wife. They were love letters. As Molly read them, sitting cross-legged on the floor, she realised she'd never read a love letter before. Not in real life. Outside a book. She'd seen plenty of dick pics, but never a love letter.

The letters began tentatively, flirtation hinting at desire. They developed into outright longing. By the tenth letter Pa was sleeping with Heather, that much was clear. Heather mentioned sharing her bed with Ray after Robert had left it only hours earlier. She longed for Robert's wife to go out more often, and made suggestions for when they might meet again. After twelve letters Molly put the stack down.

What was Pa thinking, leaving these in the file with all his business invoices? Had he forgotten about them before he got too sick to get rid of them? Had the letters been there for forty years? Could anyone have come across them at any time? Could her grandmother have? Her mum? She, as a child, alphabetising accountancy invoices in the summer holidays?

Her stomach turned. She reached for Pa's woven wastepaper basket and retched. Nothing came up, thank god, because what kind of madness was a wicker bin?

She took a deep breath. There were more letters to read. Maybe she should stop. What good could come of this? This was her grandfather's business. Her granny must not have known, nor her mum. Mum, she thought. She remembered her mum talking about Heather, about their friendship. Ray must have mistreated her. That was what Mum always said about why Heather went away. That's what Pa used to say too — *Ray couldn't even keep a wife.*

There was a knock at the door. 'Molly? Are you in there?' It was Simon. 'Can I come in?'

From deep within her came a teenage impulse she hadn't felt for a long time. 'Get a warrant,' she shouted. For years that was how Simon and Molly answered the door to each other. Back before he married Diana, moved to Germany and forgot he even had a little sister. She hadn't thought of it for a decade and that it had burst out of her now was absurd. She started to laugh.

'Are you drunk, arseface?' he called through the door. 'Are you in there getting pissed with your foetus?'

The laughter wouldn't stop. Molly couldn't speak. Tears streamed down her face.

Simon opened the door and came in. He looked at her on the floor, leaning against the filing cabinet, convulsing with laughter and wiping tears away with the hand in which she was still holding a sheaf of Heather's love letters.

'What are you doing?'

She couldn't begin to think where to start. 'Shut the door,' she said. 'I think Pa might have been a bit of a bastard.'

* * *

By the time Simon and Molly finished reading the letters, it was clear their grandfather had been more than a bit of a bastard.

In Heather's thirteenth letter she announced her pregnancy. *It can only be yours*, she wrote. The fourteenth letter revealed that Pa's response had not been what Heather hoped. There would be no running away together. He would not be leaving his wife and child for her. Heather was, understandably, Molly thought, very, very angry.

Heather called him 'Robbie' in her letters, a name Simon and Molly had never known their grandfather to use. He was always Robert to their grandmother. Robert to his colleagues. Dad to Annie, and Pa to them. This man Robbie was a stranger, except for the way in which he seemed to have dealt with the inconvenient consequence of sleeping with his neighbour's young wife. Simon and Molly both recognised their no-nonsense grandfather in Heather's responses. He was a fifty-year-old man — Heather made reference in one early letter to the way he danced with her to 'Concrete and Clay' at his milestone birthday party down at the bowling club. She mentioned his hand on the small of her back, and the way she shivered when he looked at her. The cake Jean had made for the occasion, Heather remarked, was very good.

Heather was half his age — a mere five years older than his daughter.

Simon finished reading and put the letters down. 'Well, who would have fucking thought?'

'Do you think she kept the baby?' Molly asked.

'I don't know,' he said. 'Mum said something about Heather leaving Ray after they had a kid. Was it this kid? Do we know when that was?'

'I don't know. I've never had any reason to ask.'

'Well, we can't ask her now, can we?'

'Why not?'

'Molly, obviously this information isn't going any further than this room, is it?'

'But Mum might have a sibling. She has a right to know that. As much as I mostly hate you, I'm glad I know you exist. And Naomi.'

Simon cast his eyes up. 'Moll, if Mum knows she might have a sibling, then that changes everything.'

'Everything what? What are you talking about?' And then it dawned on her. Money. Of course. The house. Would another child of Pa's be entitled to part of his estate?

Simon saw her realise. 'Do you get it? What happens if this kid was Pa's? She might have to give him half of the house. It would have to be sold. Down the track we'd get barely anything.'

Molly thought about her mother. She couldn't imagine what it would be like, growing up as an only child. She tried to picture her own childhood with Naomi and Simon erased. Her parents' undivided attention. How glorious that would have been. No calm easy-going Naomi to be compared to. No stupid annoying Simon to butt heads with. But she understood that wasn't how everyone's sibling relationships went. Jack was great mates with his sister, Amy.

Footsteps passed the door and they froze. Whoever it was didn't stop, and they heard the heavy front door open and click closed again. Simon crawled over to the window and looked out at the path.

'It's Dad.'

'We should put these away. Until we decide what to do,' Molly said.

'Where? Where can we hide them?'

'I don't know,' she said. 'Maybe the place they have been successfully hidden in plain sight for forty years? I'm pretty sure no one is going to go looking in there. It was a fluke I even found them.'

'Pretty ballsy move,' Simon said admiringly. 'Filing the evidence of an affair in with your business records.'

She stared at him. 'It's not impressive. Don't be impressed by this, Simon. What Pa did was awful. Be horrified. Be appalled. That's what you ought to be feeling about this. Not impressed by his duplicity.'

'I'm not,' he said unconvincingly. 'Anyway, I don't think you should judge Pa too harshly, just based on these.' He waved the letters at her.

'What? Why on earth wouldn't I? He wasn't who we thought he was, Simon. Is that not clear to you?'

'Just because he did something wrong, once, doesn't mean everything we knew about him was a lie.'

'But it *was* all a lie. It was built on lies. Everything everyone did, after this point, was based on people not knowing what he'd done. Granny living with him all those years, Mum coming back and nursing him when he got sick. Simon, they didn't know who he really was.'

There was a tap at the door and Diana's voice interrupted them. 'Simon?'

'Shit.' Molly stuffed the letters back into the filing cabinet and slammed it shut. Richard leaped down, sending the remaining papers flying, and trotted to the door.

Diana knocked again. 'Simon, you have to take the next tray of pfeffernusse out of the oven in five minutes. I'm going to the beach with Naomi and the children.'

Simon clambered to his feet and opened the door. 'Yep, right, no worries, love. Five minutes. Gotcha.'

Diana looked past Simon to where Molly was still sitting. 'Are you all right?'

'Of course. Why wouldn't I be?'

'I don't know. Because you're sitting down on the floor?'

'No, I'm fine.'

'Good.' She closed the door.

'She doesn't like you much, does she?' said Molly.

'Don't be stupid,' he said. 'Of course she likes me.'

'She seems annoyed with you all the time.'

'We're fine,' he said, and he offered her a hand up. 'Oof, you're fucking heavy.'

'I'm nine months pregnant, loser.'

Their momentary connection had slipped away. As she passed him, he put his hand on her arm. 'Molly, remember, not a word.'

She shrugged him off and walked back to her room.

Chapter 11

Patrick Penhaligon sat next door at Ray's kitchen table, counting out tablets for the next day. It was just like his dad to have left it so late to tell him he was dying.

When the email had arrived, Patrick was in Chile, working with a documentary crew filming Humboldt penguins. He'd only read the message five days later when they returned to La Serena, the nearest city. It was the end of the shoot, so two days later he was back in Sydney, where all the roads were impossibly smooth and the faces weirdly pale.

He'd come straight to his dad's house in a taxi, with his backpack, a panic-purchased bottle of duty-free Champagne, a huge Toblerone and a badly screen-printed T-shirt with a picture of penguins on a gravel beach. The perfect gifts, really, with which to say, 'Sorry you've got incurable pancreatic cancer.' Now the two Champagne glasses from the previous night sat upside down on the draining board.

It was five years since he'd been back there. Too long. But in his business, you took the work when it came up, and so for five years he had been everywhere but Sydney. There were no endangered species there. Well, his poor old dad was looking pretty endangered. Weeks to months was what he'd been told when he'd asked the oncologist how long he had left. Patrick thought that was too vague, but the palliative care nurse who had visited that morning said she thought it was more in the days than weeks category. They didn't lie to you, nurses. They were good like that.

His father was sleeping a lot. Patrick wasn't sure if it was the drugs or the illness. It probably didn't matter. Satisfied that he had the medication correct, he filled the kettle and took a mug from the cupboard. His dad wanted tea quite often, but he never managed more than a couple of sips.

A child's voice, surprisingly close, shouted 'Marco!' and a sudden stream of water shot in through the open window, drenching Patrick's shirt and leaving him spluttering. What the hell was that? Excited shrieks and the flash of two small naked bodies past the window answered his question. Those kids next door were loud. He'd asked his dad a few times if their noise bothered him, but he insisted he liked it.

Another shout came along the right of way. 'Be careful with that hose, you'll — oh.' A woman stopped outside the window. She looked up at the dripping Patrick, standing at the sink.

'Sorry,' she said simply, with an apologetic smile. 'I told them not to run with the hose, but they're playing Marco Polo and they're also out-of-control arseholes.' Her face was tanned and her smiling eyes were creased. Her light brown hair hung down to her waist.

'Don't you play Marco Polo in a pool?' Patrick said. 'I thought it was played in a pool.'

'Ideally, it is. But we haven't got a pool, so they just run around with the hose. The one holding the hose has to keep their eyes shut. It's a reasonable substitute. Shocking waste of water, though.' She paused. 'Sorry about your shirt.' She saw him look down and seemed to intuit the large puddle on the lino. 'And your kitchen. Let me come in and mop it up.'

Before he could say that wasn't necessary she was gone, and she reappeared shortly after at the front door, holding a mop and a bucket.

She beamed at him. 'Hello! I'm Naomi, by the way.'

'Patrick,' he said. 'Really, the kitchen is fine. I can mop it up myself.'

'Please,' she said. 'I'd like to. If you're okay with me coming into your space.'

'Um, sure, I guess that's fine.'

'Great!' She walked past him down the hall to the kitchen and began mopping up the water before he was even back in the room. 'This'll take five seconds. There. Done.' She reached into the pocket of her baggy sleeveless smock. It was made of woven fabric the colour of sand. It reminded him of the clothes everyone wore back in the Community in Shropshire. He hadn't seen an outfit like that for almost two decades.

She held up a tiny brown glass bottle. 'Rosemary oil? Can I, while I'm here? If I pop a couple of drops in some water and whiz it over your floor, it'll prevent mould, fungus — any bad bacteria really. It's a wonder herb. Fixes anything.'

'Pancreatic cancer?' He spoke before thinking. 'How is it on terminal pancreatic cancer?' It was the first time he'd said it aloud.

Naomi's bright expression clouded with so much sympathy Patrick had to look away before he began to cry.

'You're so young,' she said.

'My dad, not me.' His voice caught.

'Oh.'

'Yeah,' he said. 'Oh is right.'

'I'm very sorry. Ray's your dad, is he?'

'Yeah.'

'My grandfather lived next door. Robert. He died last week. Heart failure, though, so, you know, we don't have to worry about this being a cancer cluster from power lines or anything.'

Patrick frowned slightly, and didn't speak.

'It's not much of a bright side, is it?' Naomi noticed the mug on the counter. 'Were you making a cuppa? All right if I add one more?'

Patrick couldn't think of any reason not to, so he nodded.

'You sit down,' she said, and started opening cupboards. She opened the one where the mugs lived first. 'Aha. Undefeated. It's my superpower — I instinctively know where things are in people's kitchens. And tea bags will be —' she held her arms out in front of her like she was divining for water '— here!' Her hand landed on the canister marked *Tea*, sitting beside the kettle.

He smiled. She was all right.

* * *

Over tea, Naomi gave Patrick a potted history of her family. He heard about her mum and dad, the musicians, and their friend Brian, who was the third wheel until he slept his way up the ranks. She told him that her brother and his family had come to visit from Germany, and she and her daughter had come down from Byron Bay for the funeral. They'd decided to stay on for a few weeks, despite the overcrowding now her sister and brother-in-law, who were soon to have a baby, had joined the party.

'Because what's Christmas for, if not seeing how long people with fundamentally opposing views on pretty much everything can stand to remain in close quarters?' she mused. 'It's like a breath-holding competition. What are you and your dad going to do for Christmas?'

Patrick looked down into his tea. 'I'm not sure it will still be me and Dad by then.'

Naomi looked shocked. 'Shit, really? That quick? I'm so sorry.'

'It's not your fault. He's not in much pain. Apparently he might not be, even at the end. But I don't know. I've never seen anyone die.'

'You're the right person to be with him.' She gestured to the area around his head. 'Dark red. You're a survivor, and you're grounded.'

'Sorry?'

'I can see auras,' she said simply. 'I know it sounds weird, but I can see colours around people, the quality of their energy. Yours, right now, is a really strong, dark red colour. You're strong. It's a little cloudy, which is normal when there's fear and sadness, or something unresolved, but you're good.'

Patrick didn't know what to say. 'Thanks, I guess?'

Apparently she read his discomfort; she changed the subject. 'Have you got a partner? Where do you live?'

'No partner. I travel most of the time for work. I have a flat in London, and my mate Dipesh shares it with me, but I'm never there. I work on nature documentaries.'

'Like David Attenborough stuff? What a brilliant job.'

'It is. I love it. But occasions like this make you realise your job has become your life. Well, it has for me anyway.'

'What about your mum, is she still around?'

Patrick snorted. 'My mum. Who knows? Last I heard she was in Canada. She's a bit of a one for a commune, my mother. Even the odd cult. The latest one was outside Vancouver. They wear all white.'

'I'd be kicked out of an all-white cult in five seconds,' Naomi said. 'Can't keep anything white with a kid in your life.' She sipped her tea. 'Have you told her about your dad?'

'When he first told me, I emailed her. I thought she should know. I think she's still legally married to him. But I don't know if she even got it. It was an old Hotmail address. She doesn't really stay in touch.'

Naomi didn't say anything, but she kept looking at him. She had a gentle gaze, Patrick thought. Normally people who just stared unnerved him, but she made him feel like he had more to say.

'She raised me in some of the communes. After she left Dad. I don't know why I'm telling you all this.'

'I like to hear people's stories. You can probably sense that. That's why you're telling me yours.'

Mostly people weren't listening the way they pretended to be, but Naomi seemed different — he felt safe, sitting there with her, cradling their cups of tea. He took a deep breath. 'All right then: so she left Dad when I was about one. She wasn't happy. She's not a happy person, though, so that probably wasn't Dad's fault. She took me to a place in the Blue Mountains, and we stayed there for a couple of years. I don't remember any of it.

'After that she joined some people who were leaving that community for one in Spain. We were there until I was seven, when some of them broke off and went to England — Mum and me included. Can you imagine? I hadn't worn shoes until we got to England, I don't think. We lived in a big farmhouse in the country, miles from anywhere. People were naked a lot, but with shoes. I remember that so clearly. All these boobs and penises everywhere, all the time, covered with goose bumps because it was fucking freezing, but then socks and wellington boots. I think they stayed stoned so they wouldn't notice the cold as much.'

'Naturism definitely has its limits,' said Naomi. 'Did you stay in England?'

'Until I was eighteen, then I was out of there. By then ecstasy was a thing, and raves, and Mum was right into all that, dealing and importing and whatever. One of her boyfriends got her started. At least they were back wearing clothes by that stage. That's been her pattern. Meet a bloke, get into whatever he's into, follow him, get bored, meet a new bloke, get into whatever he's into, ditch the first one. And repeat.'

'Good that your dad's always been here then, someone for you to come back to.'

Patrick paused. He drank the cold dregs of his tea. 'I should check on him. He might be awake.'

'And I should go stop those kids wasting water. Thank you for the tea. Can I come again?'

She was so open he could only say yes.

At the door she turned to him. 'I think our mothers were friends, back when they were living here. My mum's called Annie.'

Yeah. His mother used to talk about Annie. Usually when she was off her face. He could remember lying with his head in her lap, listening to her tell stories to help him fall asleep. Always stories about a girl called Annie. Long rambling stories of mountains and angels and dragons: drug-fuelled fairy tales, he knew now. Always about Annie. 'I think she might have mentioned her.'

Naomi stood on the verandah and looked out at the garden. 'You'll need help,' she said, 'with your dad.' It wasn't a question. 'I can help. I'm right next door. I'm good at looking after people.'

'Oh, that's not necessary,' Patrick said. 'I can look after him, and there's a hospice nurse who comes.'

'Then I'll help look after you.' She grabbed his hand and squeezed it, then dropped it just as quickly and jumped down the front steps to the path. 'See you.'

* * *

Jack was parking his car when Naomi came out of Ray's house. It was the hatchback that came with his job, with the words *Dr Paws* painted on it and lots of blue animal silhouettes. She waved to him and waited while he unpacked the boot.

'Grab this would you, Nomes?'

Naomi liked Jack. He was predictable, steady and easy to be around. He was the anti-Molly. She took the bag of dried cat food he held out.

'*Metabolic diet*,' she read. 'Is this for Richard?'

'He's seriously overweight. I reckon your mum's been trying to feed him to death.' Jack loaded himself up with shopping bags and they walked inside. 'Did you have a good day?' he asked.

'I did, yeah, thanks. I've just had a cup of tea with Right-of-Way Ray's son, Patrick. He's back staying with his dad for a bit.'

'Did you? What's he like?'

'Nice. We had a good chat.'

'Excellent.' Jack was very good at minding his own business. Naomi approved of that.

She thought about telling Jack that Ray was dying, and about Patrick's unusual upbringing. He hadn't asked her to keep it to herself, but it wasn't her story to tell. She felt a connection with Patrick. She didn't know quite what it was, but sitting with something was the way to figure it out.

Chapter 12

Molly was on her bed, thinking about her grandfather's love child and practising her pelvic floor exercises. There were some similarities, really. She hadn't known about either until very recently and would have preferred to remain ignorant of both.

What was she meant to do with the knowledge that her mother might have a half-sibling somewhere, and that there was apparently a whole set of muscles she was supposed to be working out so she might remain continent after childbirth? Kegels, the pelvic floor exercises were called. Kegels sounded like something Diana would make involving poppy seeds, but really it was just a fancy name for clenching your undercarriage.

Since learning about Kegels from a pamphlet the midwife gave her, Molly constantly felt guilty for not doing them more. The repercussions could be catastrophic. From what she'd read, her whole person could fall out through her vagina after she gave birth if the pelvic 'sling' of tiny muscles wasn't strong enough to hold everything above it in. It was like filling a sleeping bag cover with rocks and turning it upside down to see if the drawstring would hold. It was deeply unfeminist of nature to do this to her. How were women meant to contend with the glass ceiling when they had to keep thinking about their pelvic floors?

Secret keeping was a different sort of muscle, and hers was very weak. It always had been something of a family joke: they'd called her the Town Crier when she was little because of how frequently she revealed what people were getting for birthday presents, and spoiled the endings of books and movies. She wasn't sure she'd be able to keep Pa's secret to herself, or even if she should.

It was probably too little, too late, anyway, for the Kegels. The baby was so low it felt like with every squeeze of her pelvic muscles she might be giving it brain damage.

Still, she lay there on the bed, staring up at the mattress-ticking ceiling and squeezing and holding. This was just one of many aspects of pregnancy that had been kept secret from her until it was too late. The dark line down the middle of her abdomen — that was another one. That freaked her out. It looked like the 'cut here' line on an individual box of Coco Pops. It made her feel like her body was nothing more than packaging, like the baby would crawl out and she'd just be discarded like the tomato sauce dispensers that come with a meat pie.

Except of course she wouldn't because the baby would need her. She was to become food. She'd tried to avoid looking at her breasts in the final weeks of pregnancy. They no longer felt like hers. They certainly didn't look like hers any more. They were not the same pert B-cups she'd proudly stripped to reveal when she and her best friend, Lou, used to go skinny-dipping. They'd moved on and left her behind.

With a pang, she thought of the last summer before Lou moved to New York, when they were twenty. Molly, between university courses, had still been living at home with her mum, working shifts in the homewares department of David Jones and going to the pub every night, but Lou changed that year. She became obsessed with becoming a writer and was saving all her money to move to New York. Whenever she wasn't working as an usher down at the Opera House, she was writing. It was only when Molly suggested night swims that Lou would agree to do something with her.

Lou was back in Sydney for Christmas. Molly had texted her several times, suggesting they grab dinner, but each time she'd received a variation on the same non-committal *Sorry, so much family stuff, see you at my drinks?* text, adorned with several emojis of stressed-out facial expressions.

Molly reached for her phone, opened Facebook, and clicked onto the Events page. There was Lou, pictured at the top of an event called *Back For a Limited Time Only*. She considered switching her 'going' reply to a 'maybe', but that was probably unnecessarily bitchy.

'Molly?' Her father stuck his head around the door.

'Hi, Dad.'

'Mind if Brian and I come in and relieve you of that piano?'

She put down the phone, propped herself up on her elbows and looked at the piano he was pointing at. It had always been in the sunroom. At the moment it was acting as her dressing table, its top covered in tubes of expensive ointments that were collectively failing to prevent stretch marks on her belly. 'Where's it going?'

'Your mum wants to use it so we're moving it to the living room.'

'Who's moving it?'

'Brian and me.'

'It's a piano, Dad. It's going to take more than you and Brian.'

'No, it'll be fine.' Paul pushed up one sleeve of his T-shirt and flexed the muscles of his pale bicep at her. 'See? We'll just walk it out.'

'It's not like a table. It doesn't have legs. You'll need a dolly or something.'

'A dolly?' Paul raised one eyebrow at his daughter and took a deep breath. Not this, she thought. 'Brian?' he called. 'Apparently we need a dolly.'

'Dad. Don't. Please do not do it. I'm not in the mood.'

But it was too late. Brian dashed in and they launched into a note-perfect a capella version of 'Islands in the Stream', complete with dance moves. Molly should have known better. It was one of their party pieces, and went on for four minutes, including mouth trumpet impressions during the brass interludes. Brian took Kenny Rogers's part and Paul cracked out a stunning falsetto for Dolly Parton's half.

Delighted with themselves, when they finished they grinned at her, awaiting her applause. Her father was fuelled by approval.

'Nice,' she said. 'Are you done? As I was saying, you need a dolly — with wheels — to move a piano.'

'That was good, though, wasn't it?' He wasn't going to let it go.

'It was very impressive. You're very clever. But you're still not strong enough to move a piano.'

'You're probably right. I'll see if Jack and Simon can help.' They left and she wondered whether her mother really did want the piano moved or if it was all just an elaborate set-up to allow them to perform a duet for her. She breathed out and as she relaxed she realised she had been holding her pelvic floor muscles taut the whole way through the song, in reaction to the excruciating embarrassment. That was a plus.

The baby, possibly also reacting to the performance inflicted on it, started to wriggle. Molly could actually see parts of it pushing through her skin. 'Jack!'

'Yeah?'

'Come look.'

Jack appeared, a half-chopped cucumber in one hand and a knife in the other. 'What? Are you all right?'

'The baby. Look.' She pointed at her stomach, which immediately became perfectly still, like a rabbit in the headlights. 'Oh. It was going crazy before. You could see, like, heels and elbows poking out.'

Jack kissed her belly. 'Baby, you are the worst ever at hide and seek. I know you're in there. Stop punching my wife.' Molly admired how easily he talked to the baby. She felt odd when she did it, like the foetus was a prospective client she had to impress.

Jack pressed his ear to her belly and they sat quietly. Molly thought about the letters from Heather and tried to imagine Jack walking away from her and from their child. How could Pa have ignored someone who was having his baby? If she'd stayed with Ray and passed that pregnancy off as his, Heather would have been next door all that time. Pa must've watched his own kid grow, at least for a few months, and never been involved. He mightn't have ever put his hand on Heather's belly or felt the baby kick.

And Heather. Did she ever tell Ray? Did Ray still now think the child was his? Did Heather ever come back? Molly wanted to ask her mother, but surely that would raise suspicion. Which would be the worse situation: to raise a child thinking they were yours, or to know they weren't yours and live with that knowledge, trying not to let it affect how you treated them? It probably didn't matter either way, because Heather ran away with her baby in the end, so neither Pa nor Ray got to see it grow up.

* * *

They had dinner in the garden again that night. Simon arrived home just as the meat was coming off the barbecue. From where,

Molly didn't know. He was going out on his own a lot. Felix had been home all afternoon, roaring about the place with Sunny, and presumably Diana had been there as well, though Molly had managed to avoid her.

Diana waited until they were eating before she cleared her throat. 'Ah, I was wanting to talk to you all about something.'

'What's that, Di?' asked Jack.

'What will we eat for Christmas?' she asked. 'This is my first Australian Christmas, and I was thinking maybe we could incorporate some German foods and traditions? I would be very happy to cook some of the dishes my family always eats, and I would love to see what your family serves.'

Annie and Paul exchanged guilty glances. Molly thought she knew why. As current family elders they should have been able to present their family's Christmas traditions, but, truthfully, neither had ever engaged in the planning of Christmas to any great extent. While Granny was alive, and Paul had still been welcome, they'd always left it to her. It was Granny who would buy a tree from the local Scout troop, decorate it, plan a meal — but even the meal was a movable feast. She liked to watch cooking shows on television, so rarely did they see any dish on the Christmas table twice. Christmases could be remembered not by the calendar year but by the celebrity chef whose latest book the menu was cribbed from.

There was the Naked Chef year, when Jamie Oliver was the New Big Thing and they had roasted poussins wrapped in bacon. There was a Nigella year with a venison pie. Way back there was the Keith Floyd year with the potted shrimp followed by a standing rib roast, and since she was little Molly had heard tell of the last year before the band moved to London when they'd celebrated the Bernard King Christmas, for which Jean had dipped eighty strawberries in chocolate and skewered them to a foam cone in a festive homage to the already festive croquembouche. There had been a Rick Stein, Iain Hewitson, Christine Manfield and Donna Hay Christmas — and the infamous Tetsuya Christmas, where everyone went hungry.

There was the odd year when no one caught Jean's fancy. Then she would default to Margaret Fulton's Guinness-glazed baked ham.

After Paul had left, and they had to celebrate Christmas twice, the Boxing Day meal was sometimes at a fancy hotel buffet in the city, or it was a cold lunch at Brian's mum's house, or a picnic at the beach.

'Maybe we could have a meatless Christmas this year,' ventured Naomi. 'I'll bet there are some wonderful German meatless … Christmas foods.'

The idea fell as flat as the cheese soufflé at the Two Fat Ladies Christmas.

'Or just lots of veggie side dishes,' Naomi said lamely. 'Sides are great. Should we invite Ray and his son?'

Molly froze, her fork halfway to her mouth.

'His son?' echoed Simon and Annie as one.

'Yes. His son is staying. I met him. He's really nice. I reckon they'd come. It could be a good thing to do. An olive branch.'

Molly put down her fork and took a deep breath, overwhelmed with the panic all liars face. How interested should she sound? How interested would a person sound who didn't know what she knew about Ray's son? If she were to feign a complete lack of interest, that would surely arouse even more suspicion than a reasonable polite level of interest. Or would it?

'What's he like, the son?' she asked in a voice she hoped would sound relaxed. It didn't. She heard herself and it sounded like she was in a bad movie playing a character with Something To Hide.

'Nice. His name's Patrick. Remember last night with the Champagne cork, during dinner? That was him. He's back.' Naomi paused. 'For Christmas.' She reached out and served herself another Tofurky sausage. 'He's based in London but he works on nature docos so he travels heaps. He's only a bit older than you, Simon. Maybe four years? I hadn't quite realised how close in age you and Heather were, Mum. So, shall we invite them?'

'I don't think that's what Pa would have wanted,' Simon said. 'You know he didn't like Ray.'

'For no good reason, as far as anyone knows,' said Naomi. 'We could put that to rest now.'

'But ...'

Molly watched Simon run out of ideas.

'If Patrick's come to stay, then Ray might just want Christmas to be the two of them,' said Molly. 'They've probably got plans.'

'Yes, plans,' added Simon, pathetically.

'Hang on, hang on,' said Paul. 'Are you two on the same side? Does it sound to anyone else like Molly and Simon might be on the same side? Brian, hand me my phone, I'm going to call the media. This is worth a newsflash.'

Molly shot him a withering glance. 'There's no such thing as a newsflash any more. Everything that happens gets tweeted or 'grammed and is basically a newsflash. You need to update your references.'

'Fine. Brian, hand me my telephone so I can TikTok the *Herald*.'

* * *

As they carried plates back into the kitchen, Simon nudged Molly with his elbow.

'Garden,' he murmured out the side of his mouth. 'Ten minutes. In the plumbago.'

She rolled her eyes at his cloak and dagger act, but, nonetheless, once the dishwasher was loaded, the children had been taken upstairs by their mothers to have a bath — did Simon ever do any parenting? — and Jack had gone out to the front garden to return a missed call, Molly slipped out the back door and into the darkening garden.

The plumbago was sticky, and the gap to enter was child-sized. Molly crawled through on her hands and knees, her stomach almost grazing the ground. Purple flowers clung to her hair and T-shirt when she emerged into the low clearing in the middle of the shrubbery.

Simon was already there, crouching on the ground.

'You look like you're doing a poo,' she greeted him.

'How is it so muddy in here?' he asked. 'What have they been doing?'

'Dunno,' she said cheerfully. 'Probably having a pissing contest, like we used to.'

'Don't be gross,' he said, wrinkling his nose. 'We never did that.'

'You've repressed the memory because you always lost. We would see who could wee for the longest. Ask Naomi. She'll remember.'

'I'm not here to talk about piss. Didn't you hear what Naomi said at dinner? The baby is back. Next door.'

'He's not a baby.'

'Why is he back? What does he want?'

'It's Christmas. He probably wants to revert to his teenage behaviour, get shit presents, and eat seasonally inappropriate food like everyone else.'

'A week after the man who was his real father dies? That doesn't strike you as suspicious?'

'Do we have any reason to suppose he knows Pa was his real father?'

'We don't know what he knows. Maybe he's always known. Maybe he saw Pa's death notice in the paper and came back to claim his rightful inheritance.'

'It's not *Game of Thrones*, Simon.'

'You've never seen *Game of Thrones*, have you? All I'm saying is we should be careful and maybe not hang around too long deciding what to do.'

'Why do you keep acting like there is anything for us to do? It's not our house.'

'We should at least destroy the letters from Heather. The less evidence that there's even a chance Pa was his dad, the better.'

'I don't know.' Molly didn't share Simon's love of intrigue. 'Maybe we should just tell Mum.'

Simon huffed in exasperation. 'Of course you want to tell Mum. You're the Town Crier.'

'If not Mum, then let's tell Naomi. Bring her in as a tie-breaker. Whatever she reckons, we will do.'

'No way. We know exactly what she'll say. And she's met the baby next door, so she'll —'

'Do what's right? Simon, you know what we should do here. We need to tell Mum and Patrick the truth. Then what happens is up to them.'

'At least let me do some research first — about what the legal situation might be with the house. Two days. Let's sit on this for two more days.'

Molly thought about it. Two days wouldn't make any difference one way or another. And she didn't exactly relish having to reveal to her mum that her beloved father was an adulterer *and* might have abandoned a child. Was it inevitable, letting down your children? Probably, she thought. She'd idolised her father until he'd left her mum and taken up with Brian.

What it comes down to, she thought, is that in an ideal world, children would never have to turn their minds to their parents as sexual beings. That's basically the situation you want to aim for.

Her mum had avoided such a situation, as far as Molly knew, but this discovery was going to change that. Would it be worse for her mother to experience at nearly sixty what had overwhelmed Molly at eight? There was no way of knowing. And a bit more time without that particular domestic grenade going off would be a nice thing. She had another week of work till Tien closed for Christmas and her own maternity leave began. She was starting to wish she and Jack had stayed at the flat.

'All right,' she said. 'Two days. Then we tell at least Naomi and probably Mum.'

Chapter 13

That evening Annie's children and grandchildren scattered to the furthest corners of the house, as was becoming their habit. For a family reunited for the first time in years, they were spending a remarkable amount of time trying to be away from each other.

Annie sat down at the piano, now in the cool living room. This room had been the centre of her childhood home, as far as there was one. She and her parents had sat on the sofa each evening, watching whatever was on the television. This was where she and Brian and Paul had watched *Countdown* on Sunday nights. Her kids had done the same, except it had been *Survivor* and *Buffy* — but now when people wanted to watch something they mostly did it in their rooms, on their private screens, with headphones. It meant everyone was happy, but she mourned the loss of the community that came with several people sitting around hating one person's choice of show.

Her hands moved across the keyboard, quietly playing chords. Something about one progression she played sparked something — a tiny pilot light — and she repeated it. That was quite good. She played a little more, feeding into it the little melody that had been teasing her. That could grow into a song, given the right conditions.

As she went to play it through again, the door from the hall opened and Simon came in.

'Mind if I put the telly on?' he asked. 'I've missed proper Aussie free-to-air. I even miss the ads.'

She closed her eyes in frustration for just a second. 'No, go ahead.'

He sat on the couch and pointed the remote at the TV, flicking through the channels. That there wasn't something in particular he wanted to watch irked her even more.

Escape to the Country filled the screen: a British couple in their seventies were being shown a converted barn in the Devon countryside. Their eyes lit up when they saw the exposed original beams and the woman clapped her hands with joy at the natural light in the kitchen. For god's sake, thought Annie. He wasn't even going to watch an Australian program.

Simon nodded in approval. 'Yes,' he said to no one in particular. 'Yes, good. Dad! Brian!' he shouted. *'Escape to the Country.'*

Bearing glasses of wine and a plate of pfeffernusse, Brian and Paul came to watch. The three men sat lined up on the sofa, engrossed in the real estate journey of a couple they would never know.

Annie hated that show. It was called 'Escape' but the participants were just trapping themselves somewhere new. She wished the producers would make follow-up episodes about all the people who took on falling-apart country houses and hated it, and went mad from the loneliness of rural life, and divorced from the stress.

She watched for a while, sitting on the piano stool, until she could stand it no longer. 'I'll say good night. See you all tomorrow.'

Paul grabbed her hand as she rose. 'But it's so early. Stay and hang out. Don't go up to bed yet.'

'I didn't say I was going to bed.' She slid her feet into her sandals and bent to buckle them up. 'I said I was saying good night.'

'Where are you going?'

'To see a friend.'

Simon looked away from the television. 'What friend?' he demanded. 'Jane?'

'Not Jane,' said Annie, smiling to herself.

'Ah,' said Brian. 'A different sort of friend.'

'What's a "different sort of friend"?' Simon looked suspiciously from his mother to Brian. 'What's going on?'

Paul rolled his eyes. 'For heaven's sake, Simon, your mother has a right to privacy. Stop it with the third degree.'

'I don't mind,' Annie said mildly. 'I have a friend I see in the evenings sometimes. For sex,' she added, because it seemed any amount of subtlety was too much for her firstborn.

Simon recoiled, blinking. 'For ... s— ... for what?'

Annie had had enough. She stood up. 'Sex, Simon. Sex. It's a thing people do before they have children, and then again once their children all leave home.'

'Who is this person? Is it someone I know? Is it serious?'

'The sex? Sometimes it's serious. Sometimes it's very funny.'

'No. Mum. Gross. God. I mean the relationship.'

'I'm not sure I'd call it a relationship, as such.'

'Can we meet him? Or ... her?'

'It's a him. And no. He has no interest in you.'

'Why not? That's a bit weird.'

'Is it? You're a grown adult with a wife and child; you have two perfectly decent parents and a stepfather. My friend is not looking for a grown man to parent.'

'I just mean it's weird he doesn't want to be part of your life,' Simon made giant circling gestures with both arms, 'as a whole.'

Brian pursed his lips together, clearly trying to stop himself saying something. He failed. 'I'd say he's very interested in Annie, as a hole.'

Annie burst out laughing and Simon leaped off the sofa as if he'd been tasered. 'Brian, that's absolutely disgusting and a very wrong thing to say.'

'Calm down, sweetheart.' Annie looked at him, amused.

Paul patted Simon on the arm. 'Come on now. Your mother is a woman. She has —'

'If you say "needs" I swear to god I am going to throw up.'

'Right. Good night everyone,' announced Annie. 'I'll see you in the morning.'

* * *

Annie spent two hours in her lover's bed. They had a very satisfactory arrangement. He was a bit younger — well, a lot younger — and that worked for her. She'd met him through an app, and they'd been sleeping together for six months now. That was all it was, and it was glorious.

Every time they met he fucked her like he couldn't believe his luck. When she told him that he'd laughed. Each time she left him she braced herself for a text breaking things off, but it hadn't come. She was pretty sure he would tire of her eventually, seek out someone closer to his own age. And that would be fine too, but for the moment she revelled in the joy of no-strings-attached sex, with the added post-menopausal benefit that she definitely couldn't get pregnant.

She never stayed the night, and he never asked her to. But they liked each other — there was affection as well as passion, the three evenings a week they saw each other. And there were no demands, which Annie found to be a massive turn-on. He asked for nothing she didn't offer, and he accepted with gratitude whatever she did. They didn't talk about her family, or his life: it had become part of their arrangement. When they talked, Annie loved the freedom of conversing with someone with no preconceived notions about her.

It was midnight when Annie put her clothes back on. He saw her to the door and kissed her.

'Good night, Annie,' he said.

'Good night, Justin.'

* * *

The chords that had been creeping round the periphery of Annie's consciousness solidified in the night, and in the morning she woke and went straight down to the piano, closing the living room door behind her. The house was quiet.

She pressed the keys, gently, cautiously, keeping her foot on the soft pedal. She was nervous: this could stop at any moment. In a second she might realise she was playing a song that already existed. Each choice of note might lead her down a path someone had already trodden, and she almost held her breath.

But she was right — the song was new. And the tiny old thrill she recognised from so long ago sparked inside her: the song was good. She played it through three times, from start to finish, tweaking notes and the timing. She rose briefly to search through the piano stool's storage area for a scrap of paper, and quickly jotted down the chords with a nearly blunt pencil she found in there. But were there words?

They'll be there, she told herself. They'd come after the melody — they always did. Fear crept up on her: she hadn't done this alone. She'd always had Paul and Brian when she wrote actual songs, sitting beside her, throwing around ideas, tossing in rhymes and thoughts. What if she couldn't do it on her own? Maybe she should get the other sides of the triangle involved again. There was nothing to stop her doing that. They'd probably love it.

But in her gut, somewhere deep, something told Annie it was her turn. It wasn't that the guys hadn't pulled their weight when they were all in the band, but … You've always done most of it, Annie told herself. You pretended it was a team but it was always you. And suddenly she was off: her brain shooting from one thought to the next, making leaps, associations, grabbing unrelated ideas by the hand and pulling them up on the stage, not sure why they were useful until she saw how they danced with what was already there. Her brain was crackling with electricity. Nothing had ever made her feel quite like this. It was an intoxicating power, building something from emotions and sounds.

Scribbling and striking through lines and words on the page, linking and disconnecting, she moved ideas around the way her mother used to fiddle with table settings. She glanced up from the page and looked at the dining room table. The memory of her mother at that table was strong. It had baffled her, watching Mum fuss with plates and glasses, cruets of salt and pepper, vases of flowers, candles, napkins and glassware, but maybe that had been to Jean what this process of songwriting was to Annie: she was assembling things into an arrangement that pleased her.

She kept writing, kept pushing out the ideas, pulling at them like tangled wool. When she met a snarl, she picked at it until it came loose and the yarn ran easily again, singing and humming her way past the snags. It was a song of heartbreak and betrayal — about all the lies in her life and none in particular.

Lie with me, lie under me, lie over me like rain,
lie to me, lie through me, lie till I never rise again.

* * *

The sound of the front door opening snapped Annie out of her reverie. She checked her watch. Three hours had passed. From what she could hear, the children had been on an expedition to get a Christmas tree. They must have had an even earlier start than her. She didn't want to stop, though. If she stopped she might never be able to get going again. She remembered that feeling. It was why she had given up writing when the children were small. The interruptions were too painful, and the inevitable stop-start hobbled the process so much it didn't feel worth trying.

'Hold the door right back. No, all the way back, as far as it will go.' Simon had obviously put himself in charge of the Christmas tree transportation.

'It is back as far as it will go,' came Naomi's response.

'It's not flush with the wall: give it a good pull.'

'Simon, there are hats and bags and stuff hanging behind it. I promise this is as far back as I can get it. There's heaps of room to bring it through.'

'Right,' ordered Simon. 'I want everyone under it, here, line up at the back of the car. We're going to carry it like it's a coffin.'

Clearly there was a worse enemy of art than a pram in the hall, Annie thought, remembering an old quote, and that was an entire extended family trying to carry a ten-foot-tall Christmas tree in from the car while you tried to write a song.

With considerable bashing into the walls and swearing, the procession bearing the Douglas fir made it down the hall and, after much back and forth and pivoting, and the loss of several low branches, they entered the living room and Sunny and Felix, who were carrying the light tapered end, leaned it on the arm of the sofa. The adults, ranged along the tree trunk, dropped it to the floor with a thud.

Sunny and Felix quietly sloped off before they were asked to participate in any more helpful Christmas activities.

Annie looked at the tree. 'Why didn't you get one of the ones that comes in a net? To protect it?'

A chorus of groans and a litany of blame followed.

'It was Naomi's fault.'

'She wouldn't let us get the net because it's single-use plastic.'

Naomi was indignant. 'I compromised my beliefs enough to even agree we should buy a cut tree. Is it too much to ask that we don't also pay for something that is basically a murder weapon for sea turtles?'

A cacophonous argument ensued, during which, unexpectedly, Molly and Diana seemed to be on the same side. But everyone was talking too loudly and no one but Annie seemed to notice.

'We are all making compromises,' pointed out Diana, when there was a momentary lull. 'In Germany we don't even put the Christmas tree up until the twenty-fourth of December, but I'm accepting that this is part of my son's heritage too, so we are being cool with it.'

Molly turned on Diana. 'That's very generous of you. How multicultural you are, Diana.'

'You can make fun of me, Molly,' said Diana with a shrug, 'but in my country the Christmas traditions are strong and they are old. I'm not sure why that offends you. But, like I said, I'm here in your country this year so I am happy to do things according to your traditions.'

Ignoring Diana, Molly turned to her mother. 'Did you get the boxes down?'

Annie was still half in her song world and had no idea what Molly was talking about. She felt like she was coming round from an anaesthetic. She struggled to bring herself fully back into the room, to face the demands of all these people. 'Hmmm, what?'

'You said you'd go up into the attic and get the Christmas decorations down.'

'I did, didn't I.'

'Well, were they up there?'

Annie shook her head. 'I haven't looked. I got distracted.'

Molly rolled her eyes. 'Fine. God. I'll get them.'

'Love, I don't think you should go up the ladder. Where are your dad and Brian?'

'We dropped them at the shops to get Christmas lights. They said they'd walk back.'

'Christmas lights? There's no need for more lights. Have they forgotten about Pa's light-up Santas and reindeer and whatnot?'

'No,' said Simon, 'they know about them, but they want more. I told them if they wanted more they could pay for them themselves.'

'They could take them home to London afterwards, I suppose,' said Annie.

'They won't be on the right voltage. They'll have to leave them here for next Christmas.'

'If they leave them here then they belong to the house,' said Molly. 'We should all chip in for them.'

'I'm not chipping in anything. I don't give a shit if there are Christmas lights or not.' Simon was adamant.

'Oh, but you're happy to come here for Christmas and benefit from other people buying them? Nice.'

They thought this was going to go on forever, Annie realised with alarm. Her children thought she was going to stay in this house and grow old, waiting for them to come back each Christmas to restart the same old fights about strings of lights, and take over the TV, and bicker with each other in front of her. Their plan was to do this over and over until she died, then sell up and pocket the money.

It would never occur to them that she might want anything different. She felt a sudden flash of hatred for her offspring. Had they not taken enough of her life? Did they get to keep her forever, as their emotional slave? Surely there was a statute of limitations on parenthood.

She waited for the feeling of guilt — the dark shadow that should follow a mother wanting nothing more to do with her children — but it didn't come. She tuned back in to the conversation in the room, and immediately regretted it. Molly and Simon were niggling each other about the best spot for the Christmas tree. They'd always quarrelled as a hobby. They didn't even notice they were doing it.

'I'm not the one who's moved in for no reason,' Simon was saying. 'There's nothing wrong with your flat.'

'It has concrete cancer.'

'That doesn't mean you needed to move out. Have all your neighbours moved out and gone to live with their mothers?'

'Why do you even care? You're going home in a week. Or aren't you? What was all that "exploring your options" talk the other day?'

'It was none of your bloody business, that's what it was.'

A powerful desire to be somewhere else, far from all of them, took hold of Annie. She put away her notes in the stool, hiding them under the old elementary piano books.

Leaving the room, she headed out to the back garden, collecting her phone from the kitchen bench on the way. She called Paul. When he answered, she asked, 'Are you still at the shops?'

'We are. We've bought all the lights we could find. We almost got into a fight with some guy over multi-coloured icicles that play carols, but we came out on top. Is there something else we should get? Do we need lunch stuff? I could grab a couple of chickens.'

'I'd like some drugs,' she said.

'Sorry? The line went funny, it sounded like you said you'd like some drugs.'

'I did. I would like you to buy some drugs. I want to take drugs.'

'Right. Well. Any specific drugs?'

'What is there nowadays? Not ice. There's enough aggro in this house. Pot? Ecstasy?'

'I'm not sure I know where to buy either of those.'

'You can figure it out. Please.'

'Um, all right. I'll do my best.' He paused. 'Shall I get chicken and chips too?'

'Sure. Thank you.' She ended the call. Chicken and goddamn chips. That had been her father's sole contribution to the catering his whole life. Saturday lunch, he'd buy a barbecued chook and a family size chips. Annie felt like she was going to explode.

She needed to talk to someone. Jane. She'd call Jane. She wasn't certain where Jane stood on drugs, or what her reaction would be, should Paul and Brian actually manage to procure any. Jane liked a few drinks, though — she often expressed disappointment that Annie couldn't really handle her booze any more. It was monstrously unfair the way the fun things turned on you as you aged. She'd have a glass of Champagne on a special occasion, but it usually made her feel sick. Maybe a joint would help.

Chapter 14

It was Jane's idea, proposed several nights later as they lay stoned on the back lawn, looking up at the stars and watching fruit bats skim over their heads, that Annie should perform her new song in public.

'You should stage a comeback. It will be amazing.'

Annie gave a hollow laugh. 'It's not a comeback if no one remembers you were ever there in the first place. Anyway, how would I do that? I don't have any contacts in the industry any more. Everyone I worked with either got out of it or died from it. I might still know some people in advertising, but not actual music. What do you propose I do, just muscle my way onstage at Carols in the Domain?'

'We'll find you an open mike night. You can just play a new song on guitar or the piano and sing it. And a producer will be there, and he'll look like Bradley Cooper, but he'll be less of a terrible alcoholic, and you'll get a record contract and become Lady Gaga but less obsessed with stroking your own nose and more straight-forward hats. And fuck Brian and Paul and, frankly, fuck all your kids too. You have given up enough for them all.'

'Yeah, fuck them all.'

Someone switched on the kitchen light and it spilled out the windows onto the grass, spotlighting them on the lawn and making them raise their forearms up over their eyes.

'Oi,' Annie shouted. 'Light.'

Molly came out. 'I beg your pardon?'

'Sorry.' Annie smiled at her. 'Please, love, would you mind turning off that light? We're communing by starlight.'

'Jesus,' said Molly. 'That stuff stinks. Are you two high?'

'Yes, we are,' said Jane. 'And you are most welcome to join us.'

'I'm thirty-seven weeks pregnant.'

'Smoking for two doesn't mean you can bogart the reefer for twice as long, but here, have some.' Jane held the joint up to Molly, who loomed over her in the darkness.

'Bogart the … reefer? What century do you think this is?'

'Sorry, darling, what's the right word for it these days?' Annie stifled a giggle and coughed out smoke. 'Janey, what do you think the phrase is that makes you sound the most out of touch?'

'"These days",' said Jane without hesitation. 'Definitely "these days".'

'"These Days" is a good name for a song,' Annie said, thinking out loud.

'Do you think?' Molly shot back sarcastically. 'You Am I would probably agree with you.'

'Oh yeah,' Annie said, and she sang the chorus. 'I forgot about that one.'

'It was Powderfinger,' muttered Jane.

Molly ignored her. 'As much as I'd like to hang around inhaling your second-hand drugs, I came to tell you Jack's got to go down to his parents' place early tomorrow. Just for a night or two. His mum's arcing up that we're staying here for Christmas and I'm not doing that drive with him until this baby is out. He's leaving first thing.'

'Are you all right with that? It's quite far. What if you go into labour?'

'I won't. First babies are never early and first births are slow. The midwife told me. Anyway, it can't come early. I haven't done the online thingy to teach me how to have it yet. I'm going to bed now. I've got an early start tomorrow. I'm at a job in the city.'

'Should you still be working?' Annie asked.

'I'm fine, Mum. We need the money. Anyway, I'm nearly done. Tomorrow's my last day.'

Annie looked up at her, sure she was about to come out and say it. 'Oh, and Mum ...' her beautiful entitled daughter would say, like it was no big deal, like she was asking to borrow the car for the evening, 'will you look after the baby for me when I go back to work?' And Annie would say, 'No. I will not.' And in doing so she would break the shackles of emotional servitude and be free.

But Molly turned away and went inside. Saved by the Jane, Annie thought. Molly wouldn't ask when anyone else was around. She'd sense that Jane was her mother's ally, and that Annie would feel strengthened by her friend's presence.

Molly had always been able to find her mother's weakness. Even as a little girl when Annie would cuddle her she would grasp the back of her neck in her little fist and squeeze, digging her nails in until it hurt. Annie had tried to teach her not to, but that was just how Molly hugged — hard and painfully — and you couldn't get her to ease up without hurting her feelings.

'All right then, night night,' Annie said to her child's retreating back.

Molly stopped in the doorway. 'Night. And can you please stop shouting "fuck"? The kids are just up there.' She closed the door behind her and they were again in darkness.

'If you're going to stage a comeback,' said Jane. 'We need to resurrect your profile.'

'I was never that famous,' Annie said. 'We almost were.'

'Rubbish,' shouted Jane, louder than necessary. 'I remember Love Triangle. You were a biggish deal. They played you on the radio. They still play that "Home Is Where Your Heart Is" song on WSFM.'

'Only Lorraine Darmody's version.'

'I think we should start building you again. What social media accounts do you have?'

'Just Facebook,' Annie said. 'That's not very cool, is it?'

'We'll pop you on Twitter and Instagram, and there will be more I don't know about but I'll check with Lily the barista down at the cafe. She's more tattoos than not — she'll know what you should be on. There might be one called Tick Tock.'

'Isn't it a bit tragic, at my age?'

'Fuck tragic. Fuck age. It means nothing. You've got something to say. You have as much right to be heard as anyone else.' Jane had rolled over onto her front and taken out her phone. The glow lit up her face as she propped herself up on her elbows and started typing. 'Look, Love Triangle has a Wikipedia page already — that's a good start.'

'Show me.'

Together they read it. It was a pretty reasonable account of the band's history.

'Who writes Wikipedia entries?' Annie asked.

'Anyone can. By the sounds of this one, I'd say Brian was responsible. See here where it says, "Founded by Brian Pickering with Paul Jones and Annie Thorne"? And then down here where it mentions that Paul was regarded as the heartthrob of the group because of his movie-star looks and charisma?'

'That's Brian's work all right. Click on my name.'

'There's no link — see, it's not blue.'

'But Paul's and Brian's names are blue.'

'Sorry love. They've obviously built themselves individual Wikipedia pages but not one for you. See, look, here's Brian's … blah blah blah, "founding member of Love Triangle, ghostwriter, now resides in London's fashionable Peckham".'

'What does Paul's say? High school music teacher turned occasional model and kept man of ghostwriter Brian Pickering?'

'Not in so many words, but yeah, more or less. It's mostly about his time in the band.'

'And there's just nothing for me. No page at all.'

'We're going to make you a page. We'll figure it out. If Brian and Paul managed then it can't be that hard.'

* * *

Jack was gone when Molly woke the next morning. In the kitchen, Diana was plunging coffee, and Simon, holding a slice of bread in one hand, was pouring cereal into a bowl for Felix. Molly sidled in and slid her bread into the toaster before her brother could. He scowled at her. 'Toast bomber.' Then, as if it had just occurred to him, he said casually, 'Do you remember Justin from school?'

'Justin Wong or Justin Schoolbags?' Molly asked, watching her toast cook.

He threw a scornful look her way. 'Don't call him that.'

'Justin Schoolbags then.'

'Why was he called Justin Schoolbags?' asked Diana, in a voice wary of learning the answer. She poured milk onto Felix's cereal and opened the back door so he could sit out on the grass to eat it.

'He crapped in his schoolbag,' Molly said.

'Molly, you don't know that,' Simon said. 'That was a rumour.'

She ignored him. 'He did, Diana, Amber Gleeson saw him do it.'

'Amber Gleeson was full of shit,' said Simon, before noticing he had lined up his sister's next shot.

Molly paused for a moment to give her brother enough time to think that maybe, just this once, she wouldn't make the stupid easy joke.

As he turned to open the bread bag she landed it. 'Not as full of shit as Justin's schoolbag.'

'You are twelve years old,' he told her. 'The government is going to take your baby away as soon as it's born because you are twelve years old.'

Molly smiled and spread Vegemite on her toast.

'Why did he do the poo in his schoolbag?' asked Diana.

'He didn't — look, can we not discuss it? I'm just trying to say that I ran into him at the service station last night.'

'What, the service station here?' Molly was curious now. 'Does he live up here?'

'Yeah, he's a real estate agent. We had a good chat.'

Her hackles rose. 'About what?'

'This and that. State of the market. He said he could pop round and give us a valuation if we want.'

'Why would we want that? I thought the house was valued already, when Pa was going to change the will.'

'It's good to consider all our options.'

She narrowed her eyes at him. 'Again with the talking about options, Simon. We don't have options. As we have discussed, it's not our house.'

'Yes, it's not our house,' said Diana with a sharp look at Simon.

'House prices are going up,' he argued. 'If Mum knew that now is a good time to sell, then she might put it on the market.'

'What do you get out of this?'

'Nothing. I'm just thinking about Mum.'

'Bullshit. I'm not new here. I know you don't do things that don't benefit you. Do you think she'll give you some of the proceeds?'

'Well, you saw how shocked she was when they read the will. She thought Pa was leaving something to us. I think that's what she wants: to help us all out a bit.'

'Nobody wants to give away a million-dollar house.'

'It'd be worth well over two mill.'

'It's *not our money.*'

Diana shook her head and took her coffee out to the garden.

'I think Mum should stay here,' said Molly. 'Don't you want to be able to keep coming back to visit? Look, we need to tell her about Pa. I said you could have two days to do whatever it was you wanted to do, and that was a week ago. We have to tell Mum.'

Simon looked into the hall, checking for eavesdroppers. 'I need more time. I'm still looking into things.'

'Like the value of the house.'

'We need to know what we're dealing with, asset-wise. That affects what we help Mum decide.'

'Does she know about this valuation?'

He turned away and stared intently at the contents of the fridge. 'Not specifically. I think she's going Christmas shopping in the city today.'

'Which is why you've booked Justin Schoolbags to come now, you sneaky shit.'

Naomi appeared in the doorway carrying a box of cherries balanced on a box of mangoes. 'Simon, please can you get the rest from the car? I've been out to the fruit market. Got there at five when it opened.'

Molly shuddered at the thought, and Simon did what he was told.

Naomi dropped her boxes on the table and sat down. 'Hey, Moll. You good? I thought it would be worth doing a market run because we're going to be so many for Christmas. No point giving the big supermarkets all our money when we can give it straight to the farmers.'

She took her grandmother's ancient slow cooker from under the bench and plugged it in. When Simon appeared with the next boxes, she chopped and threw in an onion, celery, carrots, garlic and parsley, then topped up the cooker with water. How does she know how to do things like that? Molly wondered. She didn't have a recipe out. Simon headed back out to the car for the last load.

'What are you making?' Molly asked her sister.

'Some vegetable soup for Ray.'

'Right-of-Way Ray?'

'Yeah, he's not well.'

'How do you know that?'

'Patrick told me.'

'Oh. Very not well?'

Naomi stopped grinding pepper into the soup and looked at her. 'Why are you asking so many questions?'

'Why do you care how many questions I ask?'

Naomi didn't answer, but turned back to the soup. Molly hated the way her sister had always refused to argue with her. It almost made the last word seem not worth having.

Chapter 15

From her bedroom window, Annie watched Molly leave for work, walking haltingly down the street towards the bus stop. She was really at that lumbering stage now. The baby wasn't going to stay in for much longer. Annie remembered well the purgatory of late pregnancy and she didn't envy Molly.

The heat was rising, the closer they got to Christmas. Still, there was meant to be a cool change that afternoon, and the forecast for the next week or so was mild, with rain. Sometimes Sydney did that at Christmas. It was as if the city looked at people's expectations of it — at their carefully planned seafood menus and ornate Ottolenghi salads, at their halter-neck dresses and fake-tanned legs — and decided to take them down a peg. Goose bumps and cardigans, too wet to send the kids outside — these were not out of the question for Christmas Day in Sydney, and it looked like it might happen again this year. Better than a heatwave and bushfires, though.

Annie felt some sympathy for the weather. She too would like to rebel against the festivities. Today was set aside in her calendar for a bus trip into the city, to battle the crowds in the department stores for gifts and festive bits. She would inevitably end up buying her children books they would probably never read, or shirts that didn't fit. At least the grandchildren had made long and specific wish-lists.

It was pure sentimentality that took her the hour's bus ride to the city, anyway. There were plenty of local shops, both big centres and the small businesses she knew she should support, but the memories of catching the bus with her own mother, drinking a milkshake on the ramp beside Wynyard Station and admiring the decorated windows of David Jones were strong. They seemed to grow stronger every year.

But she liked going into the city less and less. She'd have the memories regardless of whether she took on the hordes in Pitt Street Mall or not. Today, she decided, she'd stay at home, and get the last presents from the local shops. After all, everyone was trekking into town that night anyway to see Carols in the Domain. This way she wouldn't have to carry her shopping around all evening too.

Simon was in the kitchen when she went down to make a cup of tea, leaning against the counter, looking at his phone and frowning. Something was bubbling gently in Jean's old wood-veneer slow cooker. She lifted the lid and peered in: vegetable stock. Naomi's work, she imagined.

'Good morning, love,' she said. 'Everything all right?'

'What? Yep. All good. Coffee?'

She flicked on the kettle. 'No, I'll make a tea. Who's up?'

'Everyone,' he said. 'It's eight thirty. The mums took the kids to the beach. Naomi's already been to the fruit and veg market. Molly's gone to work. Dad and Brian are out the back, doing something garden-related. You off shopping?'

'In a bit.' She took her tea into the living room and sat at the piano.

She went through the songs she'd accumulated over the week. They were good. They were still good. And there was another one coming now. The melody had been in her mind when she woke up. This was extraordinary.

She played the parts of the song she had, but before she could lose herself in it again, Brian and Paul came in from the garden. Brian was carrying a red plastic bucket and stood at the door, tilting it at her so she could see it was filled with passionfruit.

'Fancy making an absolutely massive pavlova?'

'Not even remotely,' she told him. 'But you can. Knock yourself out.' She turned back to the piano and put her hands on the keys.

Paul's voice interrupted her as soon as she played the first notes. 'Where's the recipe?'

Annie scrunched her eyes closed for a few seconds. 'What?'

'Your mum's pav recipe. Have you got it handy?'

She took two slow deep breaths, but there was lava inside her. In a quiet voice, she said, 'Where have you looked so far?'

Paul was confused. 'Nowhere. I thought you'd know where it is.'

'I do know where it is. It's where my mother's recipes have always been. Since you first met her, more than forty years ago. Do you know where that might be?'

'Oh, yes!' Paul was delighted. 'I do know. The wooden box in the cupboard beside the stove. I knew that.'

'Then why did you ask me?' That Annie was shouting came as a surprise to them all, including her.

There was an awkward silence. 'Sorry,' said Paul. 'I didn't realise that was the wrong thing to do.'

She said nothing.

'Is it a bit much, having us all staying with you?' he asked. 'Would it be easier if Brian and I cleared out?'

Annie sighed. 'Paul, no. You're fine. Individually, everyone is fine. On a case-by-case basis, each of you is a perfectly good houseguest and I love you all. It's just that if everyone asks me one unnecessary thing every day — just one thing they could have figured out for themselves — then that's nine times I get interrupted.'

'What are we interrupting?' he asked. 'What are you working on?'

'I don't know. I've written some songs. They're the first I've done in years and years, and I've done them all by myself and I'm a tiny bit excited. I'm also terrified, because obviously I'm a hundred and what am I going to do with a bunch of songs? But I've found … a *flow*, and so when people come and ask me things like where is my mother's pavlova recipe, I sort of want to kill them. Even lovely people like you.'

'Songs for the band?' Paul's face lit up. 'For us?'

She stared at him. 'No. Not for the band. For me.'

* * *

Molly's bus ride into the city was uncomfortable, and surprisingly full for so late in the month. Why hadn't all these people gone on holidays yet? Today her back had started aching more when she stood, but her pelvis hurt when she sat and, although a man had given up his seat for her, there was an old woman on the other side leaving nowhere to put her handbag except wedged between the front of her stomach and the back of the seat in front. She had at least two more weeks of feeling like this to get through and maybe more, although thank Christ definitely no more work and probably no more bus rides.

When Simon called she hung up immediately and texted: *On the bus.*

What about next door? he replied. *Should I go introduce myself to Patrick?*

Typical, that was. Simon asked for more time to figure things out about Patrick, but he had no actual plan of how he was going to go about it.

What could be gained from talking to Patrick? They might figure out whether he knew he was Pa's child. They might discover if he was planning to contest Pa's will. But if he didn't know, Simon was exactly the right person to blunder in and accidentally tell him. She would do some subtle investigation, maybe by introducing herself to Patrick. Simon needed to stick to online research about estate law.

She messaged, *Wait until I get home. Do some googling re wills like you're meant to*, and returned to gazing out the window of the slow-moving bus at people in their cars leaving the city for the holidays. Every vehicle had Christmas presents jammed up against the back windscreen, and pillows, toys, bikes, cases of beer. Missing from her childhood memories of that situation were the little faces staring out of the windows, bored already. Today she saw those faces in profile, staring at screens attached to the headrests of the front seats. Jack said they wouldn't do that when they had kids, and she agreed, in principle, but she was starting to see the appeal now she was looking down the barrel of eighteen years of road trips with a kid.

Being a child these days looked excellent. They had exactly the sort of technology she and her siblings had longed for. She remembered the conversations they used to have: 'Imagine if you could watch TV in the bath.' 'Imagine if you could see where people were on a screen, and, like, track them.' 'Imagine you had every single album in the world, and you could listen to them whenever you wanted.' 'Imagine if you missed your show, and you forgot to set the video, imagine if you could just watch it again any time you liked.'

It had all come true. The world was very cool now. Apart from climate collapse and the incipient fall of democracy, obviously.

Things were better for women now too. No one was expecting Molly to give up her career to have this baby. Which was annoying actually: it would be very convenient to be told to quit her job right now. But still, women started new and better careers when they had babies these days, what with workplaces being so much more flexible. A niggling voice whispered a quiet hope inside her, though, that didn't fit at all with her assessment of the brave new world she would be entering as a mother. Be a boy, she thought.

She sent the telepathic message to the baby, and it squirmed. What did that mean? Was it an affirmative wriggle? It was so stupid to wonder that. It would take one phone call to her GP to learn if the baby was a boy or a girl. The test results from early pregnancy gave that information as a matter of course, but she and Jack had chosen to wait for a surprise. And yet every day she found herself unwittingly sending the same thought to the baby. Please be a boy. Every day she noticed more and more how easy things were for boys, and how hard things were for girls.

It was there at work all the time: the men who hired her to sort out their domestic settings did so with pride. Such work was beneath them, they had the funds to outsource it, so what was there for them to worry about? It was a straightforward transaction. But the women? They also hired her but they apologised endlessly for it, and they flitted about the places where she was trying to work trailing clouds of guilt and shame for needing her services. It was ridiculous.

Today's job would be an easy one, and her last ever, with any luck. She was more and more certain she wasn't going back after the baby was born. She would take a few months off for maternity leave, and then she'd start something new.

Mum would help with the baby. Molly wouldn't actually mind if the work on the flat took longer and they had to stay in Baskerville Road for a while. Things were a bit overcrowded just now, but once Christmas was over and Simon and Naomi and their families and Brian and Dad had all gone home, it would be spacious and peaceful. Her mother would probably actually like them to stay. Maybe they'd rent out their flat and move in for a year, to give her some company.

Back when she first found out she was pregnant, Molly had looked into the daycare situation in her area, but all the centres had been so expensive. If she was going to be starting a new business, they wouldn't have hundreds of dollars a day to spare. Besides, all the good places were full, and had huge wait-lists. Apparently if you hadn't enrolled before the wee on your pregnancy test was dry, you were likely to end up with your only option being two days a week in a family daycare run by crack-addicted murderers with an unfenced pool and a dangerous dog. And they probably wouldn't even be the days you worked. So she hadn't bothered putting the baby on any wait-lists at all.

It would be so much nicer to share the care with her mum. She hadn't actually got round to confirming that with Annie. She couldn't say why. It wasn't as if her mum would say no. She'd be desperate for some purpose now that Pa had died. She really should just ask her and get it sorted.

The apartment she was working in that day was on the twenty-third floor of a luxury building — the five-bedroom home of a man called Pierre Reed and his family. Pierre worked for Google in some high-up capacity, and he spent a lot of time travelling. His wife, Bridget, worked there too, and Molly had only ever seen them wear a uniform of leather trousers and silk shirts, with trainers that looked like box-fresh all-terrain vehicles.

They were an exceedingly cool couple. They worked almost all the time, though the contents of their home suggested they did nothing but buy toys for their two kids. If it weren't for the merciless culls Molly and Tien carried out, the family would have long since disappeared, sucked into a quicksand pit of Shopkins and Pokemon merchandise and Lego.

Neither Bridget, Pierre nor the children were home today. They were in France, on a skiing holiday, and their doorman let Molly into the apartment. Her task was to sort through the children's clothes, culling anything that was too small and making a list she would then use to order replacements from an approved selection of websites.

Work like this was better when the client wasn't around. Bridget wasn't one of the clients who constantly apologised for having hired her, but when she was home she did tend to hang about making loud business calls, as if to make sure Molly knew she was working.

The task was methodical. Without the children there to try on the clothes, she was probably discarding things that still fit, seeing as the sizing varied brand to brand, but she had to follow the brief. It seemed very wasteful. She thought about taking some of the nicer pieces home for her own baby, but it would be years before they fit, she'd have to put them in a box and label them and store them and it seemed too much like more work.

She considered what it would be like to do this for her own child. Her mind whispered a word she pretended not to hear. *Boring.* Shut up. It will be so boring. And you will be so tired. Stop it, she told herself. Then she spoke out loud to the baby: 'I can't wait to meet you.' She wondered how much of what she felt was transferring to it. Could ambivalence flow through the umbilical cord? Was her uncertainty sending negative energy waves through the amniotic fluid?

'How about a kick?' She waited but there was nothing. The baby was quiet today.

'Maybe I'll just text your grandmother,' she told her tummy. 'I'm obviously not doing so well at the in-person conversation, so maybe it's better if I put it to her in writing. She's going to be over the moon to spend time with you. She's probably been dying for me to ask.'

She left the older child's room, where she was shifting his wardrobe from size eight to size nine, and headed back to the open-plan living area where her phone was.

Hi Mum, she typed. *Hope you're having a good day. Are you still* (might as well give the impression she'd already asked) *keen to do a few days a week with the baby when I start working again?* (No need to be specific about what work she would be doing, or when.) *Just trying to get our ducks in a row. Xx M.* She added a line of six duck emojis, sent it, and went back to work.

Chapter 16

Once Annie had explained to Paul and Brian what she was doing at the piano so much, they tried very hard to leave her alone. They managed it for almost half an hour, during which time they bumbled around in the kitchen, separating eggs and whisking the whites, weighing sugar using Annie's mother's old Imperial balance scales, and fiddling with the oven. They were like pantomime actors pretending to be quiet, but their stage-whispered conversations carried through to the living room just as much as their normal voices had.

As if in protest, the song she had been working on lay down like a toddler refusing to walk in a supermarket, and no matter what she did it felt heavy or wriggled away from her.

After an hour she gave up and went into the kitchen. Her phone lay on the table and she picked it up. There was a message from Molly. Opening it, she held her breath. There it was. Exactly like Jane had warned her: a request for a childcare commitment. Shit. She closed the message without replying.

Paul and Brian were reading cookbooks and drinking tea, so she took a mug from the cupboard and joined them, hoping the movements of pouring and sipping would help dissolve the sudden panicked rage she was feeling.

Holding the warm cup with both hands, she considered that a few weeks ago she wouldn't have reacted like this: her whole body flooding with adrenaline, as if she needed to kick her way out of this situation. But that was before the songs had come back. Calm down, she told herself. You are not a hostage. You have options. Money. Rationally she realised it probably wasn't specifically her mother's time Molly wanted here: it was free childcare. And the money from the house, if she chose to sell it, could provide that. She didn't want to respond to Molly now. She needed to think.

Paul and Brian were discussing the relative merits of a chewy versus a foamy pavlova base, when Simon came in, his hair still damp from his post-run shower. He stopped in surprise at the sight of her.

'What are you doing here?' he asked, grabbing a glass and gulping down water.

'I think you'll find I live here at the moment.'

'No, I mean, I thought you were going to the city.'

'I was, but I changed my mind.'

'Oh. Right.'

'Is that a problem? Did you need me out of the house for some reason?'

'Of course not. Not at all. Why would I want you out of the house?'

'Great, then,' she said, and turned back to the cookbook she was leafing through.

Simon was still standing at the sink looking at her. 'It's only that I've got a friend popping in. I didn't want to disturb you.'

She looked at him curiously. 'It won't disturb me if you have a friend over. Is it someone I know?'

'Old mate from school. You won't remember him. He was in a lower year. He's, um, into old houses. Like, architecture and stuff. And we ran into each other and I told him we were staying here and he was keen to have a look. You don't mind, do you?'

'Not in the slightest.'

'Good. Great. We won't disturb you.' He put his glass down on the draining board and headed for the door. 'Right. Better get a move on.'

When he'd gone, Brian said, 'It's not just me, is it? Simon is being weird.'

'Very,' said Paul. 'Annie, any idea what's up?'

'Maybe he's still upset about the will,' she said. 'He was pretty cross Dad didn't leave anything to him and the girls. I imagine this is something to do with that. I had been thinking of putting tenants in here and doing some travelling next year, but maybe I could do that with just the income from my flat and Dad's super, if I sold up here and split the money between the kids. Naomi will never own a home otherwise. And Molly could use the money too.'

'I don't know. You shouldn't have to sell the house unless you want to,' said Paul, and he got up and peered through the oven door at the pavlova. 'Can I open it and look?'

'I wouldn't. It's very humid today. You want it as dry as possible.'

The doorbell rang and they heard Simon open it. Low voices from the hall faded as he and his friend went straight upstairs.

'Have you got a few minutes, a bit later?' asked Paul. 'We've been strategising how to put more Christmas lights up and we reckon two of us on the roof and one person holding the ladder would be the safest. Only if you're not busy. With the songs and stuff.'

Annie thought about saying no, but the song she'd been working on seemed to have taken flight like a startled pigeon, so she nodded. 'I'll be in the back garden. Come grab me whenever you're ready.'

* * *

The garden was quiet. The neighbourhood was emptier than usual: lots of people had gone away now for Christmas. The hot, still air felt heavy and the fragrance of Ray's and Jean's roses mingled across the fence. The forecast said there was a chance of a storm very late tonight.

Annie wandered around, snapping the heads off dead blooms. She went behind the garage again and peered through Ray's fence, but there was no one out in his garden. His roses were beautiful, still.

Would she be sad to leave this house? Could she sell it, hand it over to a new family, walk away and never see it again? The idea was certainly tempting, but on some level did she not owe it to her children to retain the place where they'd all been so happy over the years? She wished, much more now than she had as a child, that she had a sister or brother to share this with. Someone to help her carry the weight of familial responsibility. At least she'd been able to give that to her kids — siblings. Now when she and Paul and Brian were ancient and needed to be locked up in a henhouse, the kids could figure it out together.

Picking up a pair of secateurs someone had left on the ground, she started to prune the brunfelsia. It had almost finished flowering, and the purple, lilac and white flowers had mostly fallen off. Her parents had called this plant Yesterday, Today and Tomorrow. It would be a good name for a song. Someone would have already used it, but she'd play with it anyway.

She could hear voices in the right of way. Simon was attempting to explain to his friend the archaic and unusual land ownership set-up. The other voice sounded familiar, and she placed it just as its owner came round the side of the house and saw her.

She couldn't help smiling. 'Hi, Justin.'

His eyes widened. She'd never seen him in daylight before. He was more handsome. 'Annie?'

She moved towards him, her hands held out, and he took them. 'I didn't know you knew Simon,' she said.

Justin's face reddened, but he kept smiling and looking in her eyes. 'Ah, yes. We went to the same high school. Not the same year. I hadn't put you two together. Jones is a pretty common name.'

'Well, ain't that a kick in the head?'

Simon looked from Annie to Justin. 'Do you know each other?'

Annie raised her eyebrow at Justin, seeking his input on what to say next, and he shrugged.

'Justin is the friend I went to see the other night. Remember, when I went out and you were watching *Escape to the Country* with Brian and Dad?'

The delight she took in her son's discomfort was unkind, but delicious nonetheless. He looked like he wanted to throw up.

'You're … he's … you two are …'

'F—' began Annie, but before she could get a word out, Simon shrieked, 'Don't say fuck buddies.'

She frowned at him. 'I wasn't going to. Good grief, Simon, get a hold of yourself. There's no need to make this awkward. Friends. I was going to say friends.'

Simon was pacing on the spot and running his hands through his hair. 'Right. Cool then. Cool. Yeah, cool. Sorry. Just a shock, that's all. Not a shock, a surprise. That's all. You're adults. I get it. Cool. No worries. None of my business. Shall I go? Leave you to it?'

'To what? Simon, Justin is here as your guest, not mine. I think you should finish showing him around. He can't give you a valuation if he hasn't seen the whole property,' she added with a sly grin.

'Valuation?' Simon blustered. 'What? No. Justin's just interested in the house from an architectural point of view, like I said.'

'I might have been born at night, Simon, but it wasn't last night,' she said. 'Justin is a real estate agent, and I can only assume he's here to give you an estimate on the value of the house. In case I want to sell it. You're very thoughtful, darling.'

With that she kissed Justin lightly on the mouth and went inside. She'd never taken particular pleasure in shocking her elders, but shocking younger people was extremely satisfying. It was probably pathetic, but she found she didn't mind at all. Her smile lingered as she went back to the piano.

No sooner had she played the first chord than Paul appeared at the door.

'Oops, nope,' he said, holding up his hands. 'Sorry. Bad timing.'

'It's all right. What is it?'

'I was going to see if you could help us with the lights. But it's cool. We can do it later.'

'Can Simon help?'

'He and his mate have gone down the road to have a beer. Simon had a face like a smacked arse. Any idea why?'

'None at all.' Annie smiled to herself and closed the piano lid. 'I'm happy to help.'

* * *

Annie stood on the front lawn, holding a ladder that rested in the border full of overgrown agapanthus, while Paul, standing on the top rung, attempted to lash a reindeer made of Christmas lights to the gutter. Brian was up there with him, balancing on the verandah roof with entirely more confidence than the aged corrugated iron he was standing on warranted. He grasped the creature by the antlers and held it steady for Paul.

'I think it needs to come forward a bit,' Brian said.

'Forward where? Towards the street? Or along the gutter?'

'Along the gutter, south.'

'Which way's south? Towards Ray's house or away from Ray's house?'

'How do you not know which way south is?'

'Because I'm not an orienteer.'

'You know which way south is.'

'Well, I'm sure if I think about it for a while I'll figure out which way south is but in the meantime if you just say towards Ray's house or away from Ray's house that would be so helpful, my love.'

Annie tuned them out and started playing with another song idea in her head. The songs weren't stopping. She had bits and pieces of fifteen now. At least five were fully formed. She'd even recorded the piano parts onto her phone, and she was close to understanding how to add her vocal track on top, using her laptop. What on earth she was going to do with them, she hadn't figured out.

Suddenly she was aware of someone nearby. Turning her head, she could see a woman standing by the fence, on the footpath, arms by her sides, just watching her.

'Hello,' Annie said. 'Gorgeous day.'

The woman didn't say anything and Annie wondered if she was all right. She was a big woman, dressed eccentrically in a long paisley wraparound skirt, layered singlets in teal and orange, and a bright gauzy wrap draped over her shoulders. Several bead necklaces disappeared into the chasm of her cleavage, and there were bangles all up her left wrist. She wore shoes made of petals of pale leather gathered with a drawstring, making her feet look like two dumplings, and her hair was flame red, wild and long. Bright red lipstick was applied liberally if inaccurately to her wide mouth, and her eyes were rimmed in smudged black eyeliner. As Annie looked at her eyes, they crinkled into a smile and all at once she knew her. Those eyes. The bluest.

'Heather?' Annie said.

'Hello, gorgeous.' Heather's voice had completely changed. It was rough, like an old metal nail file, and lower than Annie remembered. 'Fancy seeing you here.'

Before Annie could speak, Paul shouted across to Brian, 'Right, ready for the sleigh!'

Heather squinted up at him. 'Is that who I think it is?'

'Most likely,' Annie said.

'God. It's like going back in time. Did you end up with one of them?'

Annie paused. How mortifying, to be there, where she began, with very little to show for the forty years that had passed. She wished she could say no, she hadn't ended up with either man. She had lived a wildly successful, unexpected and unpredictable life. She wished she could say she'd had a dozen fascinating lovers, and that her children had been raised in one, or several, of the great cosmopolitan cities of the world. That she'd allowed nothing, and certainly not her children, to distract her from her life's work, that music had remained her true love and her focus and that she had an award-winning body of work, with wealth, fame and adoring fans to show for it.

'Yep,' she said. 'Paul. I was married to Paul for seventeen years. Three kids. We moved back from London when I was pregnant with the first. Split up almost twenty years ago and he and Brian have been together since then. The Love Triangle turned out to be real. Life imitates art, isn't that what they say?' She was babbling. Heather brought that out in her.

Heather chuckled. 'Brian and Paul. Who'd have thought?' she said in a voice that suggested Blind Freddie could have seen it coming. 'But you all get along? I mean, you're holding their ladder.'

'No point not getting along,' said Annie. 'You have to be practical about these things, especially when there are kids ...' She trailed off, realising it might sound like she was criticising Heather for her own life choices. But if Heather noticed she didn't mention it.

'You still look amazing, Annie. That hair.'

Annie felt a flush of pleasure, and put her hand up to her ash-blonde head. 'It's dyed now.'

Heather made a shocked face. 'No! Well, I'd never have known it if you hadn't said. I always wanted your hair, Annie-Kate.'

Hearing her old nickname cracked Annie wide open. Annie-Kate. Only her dad had called her that. Sometimes her mum would try, but Annie always shunned it from her because it was her special name from her dad. Her eyes filled with tears.

Heather frowned with concern. 'Oh darling, what? What did I say?'

Annie tried to smile as she wiped away her tears, saying, 'Nothing, it's nothing. It's just, well, my dad died, only recently. It's all a bit fresh, and you know, Annie-Kate —'

'Darling, I'm so sorry.'

'It's all right.' Annie sniffed. 'It wasn't sudden — it was a long time coming. I came back here to look after them. Mum first, a few years ago, and I stayed with Dad after that, and now, he's, just a couple of weeks ago, actually, he died too.'

'Really? I'm so sorry, Annie.' Heather came over and hugged her. She smelled like a stall that sold dream catchers and her body

JESSICA DETTMANN

didn't feel familiar at all. Annie kept hold of the ladder with one hand. 'I remember your dad well. He was always nice to me.'

'He liked you.' Annie paused, and then blurted out, 'Where did you go, Heather? And why didn't you say goodbye? My mum always thought Ray had done something to you.'

Heather laughed like a fox barking. 'Ray? Ray wouldn't hurt a fly. I had to leave, Annie. And, honestly, I never thought to say goodbye to your mum. You were the one I was friends with. After you left I was dying here. I wasn't made for suburbia. There was a whole world out there. I didn't think you were made for it either. You inspired me actually, to get up and go. The way you'd just taken off to conquer the world.'

She looked around, taking in the Christmas decorations, Paul and Brian on the roof, now disputing which of the upstairs windows to run the power cord through. Neither of them seemed to have noticed that Annie's past had just strolled down the street from the bus stop. 'Funny to find you came back, and that you were here all along. Maybe I'd have come back sooner if I'd known. Anyway, I'm back now.' She glanced at Ray's house. 'Big family reunion.' She made a face like a naughty schoolgirl.

'I heard Patrick is visiting Ray,' said Annie. 'My daughter met him.'

Heather's shoulders tensed. 'Yes. He emailed me. We're not really in touch that much. Long story. Anyway. Here I am. Ready to face the music.'

'Why?' Annie asked simply. 'Why now?'

'Making amends, Annie-Kate. The time has come. I've got some apologies to make and some bridges to mend.'

That sounded like Alcoholics Anonymous talk to Annie, so she nodded respectfully. 'Will I see you again? Are you staying locally?'

166

'To be honest, I was hoping to stay at Ray's. You know, Christmas and all that. Maybe there'll be room at the inn for me.'

Annie thought that was presumptuous, but she nodded.

'I'll stick my head in,' Heather said. 'Maybe we can get on the Stone's Green Ginger Wine again. For old times' sake.'

For old times' sake. That was one of those phrases Jane collected. The ones that marked you out as ancient. There was such a whiff of desperation about it. Like you wouldn't want to do whatever was being proposed for any other, better reason.

'Sure, I'll be around. Good luck with Ray. Do you think he will forgive you?'

'Maybe. I hope so. It's Christmas, after all. Isn't that what people do? Forgive their prodigal wife and mother?' Heather shrugged and made a face Annie knew would have looked endearing four decades back; now it looked clownish.

A horn sounded and they turned to see Naomi's van pulling up. The sliding door was opened roughly and Sunny and Felix charged out. Their mothers followed from the front seats, pausing to gather their children's discarded wet towels, hats, buckets and drink bottles from the back. Annie frowned. Why did Simon get to go to the pub with Justin while Diana seemed to be permanently on kid duty?

Sunny cartwheeled along the path to her grandmother, stopping to hug her around the waist.

'Hello, sweets,' Annie said. 'How was the beach?

'Really good only I fell on the rocks really hard and scraped my knee and then we found a bluebottle and Felix was about to touch it just when I was about to drop a rock on it and I dropped the rock on his finger and now it's all swollen.'

Felix walked over to confirm his cousin's story, holding up his index finger, which was looking more like a thumb. 'It hurts but I'm putting positive energy into it, like Naomi said.'

'That's the best thing for it,' said Naomi from under a pile of sandy towels as she passed them on the path. 'Hi,' she said to Heather.

Diana followed her, bearing several shopping bags. 'Positive energy will not help it as much as ice.' They disappeared into the house, with Felix tiptoeing after in his sandy bare feet, clutching his finger.

'Well, that all sounds pretty calamitous,' Annie said. 'Shall we have some lunch?'

'We bought pies. Mum's got them. Then she said we could watch a movie before we go to Carols.' Sunny looked up at Heather. 'Hello.'

'Hello to you too,' said Heather. 'Who might you be?'

'This is my eldest grandchild, Sunny,' Annie said. 'Sunny, this is Heather. She used to live next door when I was growing up.'

'Grandchildren! My god, Annie, you were a baby yourself last time I saw you.'

'It's been a long time,' Annie pointed out. It was stating the obvious, but Heather was irritating her, behaving like it was a surprise that after forty years they were now old and had the things old people have, like dyed hair and grandchildren.

'Of course. Now, I'll let you go. I'd better go in and see Ray.' Heather looked up towards the roof. 'Hey, boys. Looking good. And the lights aren't half bad either.' With a wink she turned and headed towards the front steps of Ray's house.

Annie looked up and saw Brian and Paul, staring down, mouths agape.

'Heather Penhaligon,' said Brian. 'As I live and breathe.'

Chapter 17

By one o'clock Molly had finished her job. Emerging onto the city street outside the building she took a deep breath. That was it. She was now officially on maternity leave. She was expecting to feel elated — so much opportunity and excitement lay ahead — but all she felt was dread. Her ducks were not in a row. Her ducks were distinctly scattered. Ahead lay only uncertainty and … and unmanageable ducklings. She felt an almost overwhelming urge to go home, curl up in bed and sleep until she woke up to find she was twelve years old again.

Her phone buzzed with a text and she grabbed it frantically. It wasn't her mum. It was Lou, confirming the location for her drinks get-together. Fuck, thought Molly. Opera Bar. Right in the thick of Christmas party season. Lou had clearly lost her mind in New York.

It wasn't worth heading all the way home and back again, so Molly went to see two movies, one after the other, to pass the time before the drinks. The first was a slow, violent story set in the southwest of America. Everyone was sweaty and bereaved, and the male lead mumbled incomprehensibly. It would win several Oscars: she could tell. After that she saw a very loud superhero movie. It might have made sense if you had seen a lot of other related superhero movies, but she hadn't so she dozed through most of it, jolting awake only when the baby reacted to the explosions.

When she came out of the cinema, blinking in the sunlight she felt should be gone by then, Christmas shoppers were thronging the streets and lunchtime partygoers were leaving restaurants, significantly worse for wear. Red-eyed men with their shirts rolled up at the sleeves staggered four abreast along the footpath, and outside one pub a woman stood rubbing mascara tears from her cheeks as three more girls went in, party dresses on, boobs pushed up and heels threatening their ankles with every step. The heat was punishing and everyone wearing any clothes at all was regretting those of their life choices that had resulted in their being in the city and not at the beach.

If only Jack were coming with her to the party. It was ridiculous, really: these people were her old friends. Her university mates. But she hadn't seen them for ages. They stayed in touch now on social media: everyone was so busy. And since becoming pregnant she probably hadn't been that much fun to hang out with.

She tried to prepare herself. Lou would have changed: that was a given. It was two years since Molly had last seen her. Lou probably thought Molly was an idiot for getting pregnant, living as she was a life that seemed equal parts *Sex and the City* and *When Harry Met Sally*. She was dating enough to provide plenty of fodder for her weekly column on a wildly popular women's website, and she'd hinted a few times that she was writing a novel.

The streets became more crowded the closer Molly got to Circular Quay. Maybe she should just go home. It was too hot and her back hurt. No, she'd go. Once the baby was born this sort of outing might be hard.

Opera Bar was heaving and it took her two complete circuits to figure out where her friends were.

'Molly! We're over here!' It was Lou who finally spotted her and called out. Molly wondered if the pirate 'r' at the end of 'here' was for real or faked for the benefit of her parochial friends, stuck here in Sydney.

Locating the direction of the voice, she spied the group: they had taken over an area behind the DJ, next to the harbour wall. It was a prime position. Behind them the Harbour Bridge arched across the sky, and from where they sat the sails of the Opera House loomed over the mass of beautiful people, drinking and flirting in the dark gold sunshine.

Nudging her way through the crowd, Molly climbed a couple of steps to the level where her friends were. Lou broke away from the group she was talking to and leaned in to hug her, but when Molly's stomach touched hers she reeled back like it was an electric fence.

'Whoa! Oh my god. There is an actual human in there! Shit, Molly!'

Molly dropped her hands to her sides and made a jokey, baffled expression. 'I know, right? It is literally the most insane thing.'

'You still look amazing.' Lou smiled and Molly wanted to tell her how much she had missed her, how she hadn't really thought this whole having a baby plan through very well, how she might have done it because she hated working and didn't know what else to do, and how she was starting to think that possibly wasn't the best idea. Things you couldn't say on WhatsApp or even in the DMs on Instagram, which was mostly where they chatted now. But instead she said, 'Do I? Oh, well, thanks. I mean, I'm massive, but not long to go now.'

'Can I get you a drink?' asked Lou.

'I'd love a mineral water.'

'Coming right up.' Lou moved off to dispatch someone's boyfriend to join the queue at the bar, and she was replaced at once by a girl they'd gone to uni with, India, who teetered on nude patent stilettos and was wearing a dress made from what looked like compression bandages. Her eyes had the unfocussed look of someone who'd had eight glasses of prosecco and only eaten a bowl of olives since breakfast. 'Molly!' she squealed. 'Oh my god! I heard you were pregnant and you are, like, so pregnant! Can I touch it?'

'My belly? I'd sort of prefer — oh, okay, go ahead.' India had already discarded her lipstick-smeared Champagne flute and put both hands on Molly's bump. She crouched slightly and gripped it tightly, as if she were playing Goal Attack in a netball grand final. 'Argh!' she screamed. 'It kicked! I felt it kick! That is the freakiest thing ever. Guys!' she called back to the others. 'Guys, come here. Molly's baby kicks when you squeeze it!'

No one paid her any attention, to Molly's immense relief. She tried to change the subject. 'So, India, what have you been up to?'

India released her grip and stood up again, one hip jutting out to the side. She grabbed a glass from the table. It wasn't the same glass she'd put down, but she didn't seem to notice or care. She took a swig of someone's abandoned red wine. 'Publicity, freelance. I work for various agencies working on various campaigns for various products and events.'

O … kay. 'What are you working on now?'

'Have you heard of Jacques Bambino? The singer?'

'Was he on one of those reality singing shows?'

'He was! He was runner up on *Song and Dance Man*, that Channel Seven one, and now he's going to Eurovision, so we're doing the PR for that.'

'My mum was in Eurovision,' said Molly. 'A long time ago. Well, she almost was. She wrote a song that was in it.'

'Oh my god, no? Really? That is so cool. Imagine if she'd *actually* been in it? Jacques writes and performs his own songs, so he's really the whole package. That's more what people are into now, you know, someone who can write a great song and perform it. No offence to your mum.' Someone yelled India's name and her head snapped around, tonged ombre curls swinging. She held up the now-empty glass and shouted something back, then turned away from Molly, having apparently forgotten they were in the middle of a conversation. Molly was equal parts offended and relieved. The baby shifted and a pain shot down through her pelvis, like someone was trying to hide a sword in her leg.

When Lou returned with her drink, they joined a group of people Molly theoretically considered friends, despite how rarely she saw them. The music was loud and everyone else was drunk, so she shouted the answers to the same questions repeatedly before each conversation partner moved on to someone more interesting. It felt, she thought, like speed dating with people she already knew, in sessions in which they had three minutes to discover how boring she had become since the last time she saw them. And they really did all ask her the same questions. Did she know what sex the baby was? (No, they wanted a surprise.) Where was Jack? (At his parents' house. They were doing Christmas with her family so he'd gone down for a quick visit.) Where was she working? (She name-dropped Tien to universally blank looks.) What were her plans for New Year's Eve? (To that she gave an incredulous look and pointed at her midsection. 'Attempting to squeeze that out through my vagina.')

No one asked how she felt. There was no part of the conversation where she could have reasonably mentioned that her grandfather had died two weeks earlier, or that she'd had to move out of her flat because it was riddled with concrete cancer, or that she'd discovered she probably had a secret uncle because that same beloved grandfather wasn't who he'd pretended to be.

What fascinating things would all these people have to say, she wondered, if they could dispense with the small talk?

Instead everyone reported their wedding plans, engagement stories, trips overseas they were taking before they settled down. Molly zoned out. She couldn't have felt further away from her friends. They were so carefree. The greatest responsibility any of them seemed to have in their lives was for a small dog called Chester, owned by Amelia and Dan, pictures of whom she was shown repeatedly, when Amelia and Dan both called up Chester's Instagram account on their phones. Amelia and Dan seemed devoted to the dog, yet still they were planning a three-month trip to south-east Asia, during which Chester would stay with 'his grandparents'.

One girl, Alyssa, slid over on the bench where she was sitting and gestured for Molly to join her. They hadn't really been friends at school or uni. Alyssa had been an irritating over-achiever, always on the SRC and doing mock trials and debating. But a seat was a seat.

Gratefully, Molly sank down and swapped the back pain for pelvic pain once again. Late pregnancy was an embarrassment of riches when it came to discomfort. She was torn between wanting it to end and the terror of what lay ahead. It felt like being on a seesaw over a pool filled with what were either sharks or dolphins.

Only a few minutes into their chat, it was clear Alyssa wanted to talk to her only because she had decided she too was ready to 'get on the baby train'.

'You don't want to rush into it,' Molly said. 'I mean it's amazing and I can't wait, but, still, it's going to change a few things.'

'A few things?' Alyssa said. 'It's going to change everything. I mean, right now you are sort of a mum and sort of not a mum, if you know what I mean.'

Naomi's liminal space again, Molly thought. The scales were definitely tipping towards the being a mum side, though. She felt invisible and stressed and responsible.

'Are you taking the full year of mat leave?'

'No, just four months, I think.'

'Wow, that's quick. Who's going to look after the baby?'

Molly felt the familiar flash of fury. No one at Jack's work Christmas drinks would have asked him anything like that. Not a chance. 'Probably my mum.' She wanted the conversation to be over.

'What do you do again? Law, was it?'

'Um, no. I'm a home organiser at the moment.'

'Oh!' Alyssa looked shocked. 'So, why can't you take more time off from that? I mean no offence but it's not like an actual profession, right? More a job you can dip in and out of. Which is perfect for mums. I'll have to take a serious break when I have a baby. My job's one of those bloody nightmares that you just have to focus everything on. Kind of wish I'd ended up doing something a bit less intense, to be honest.'

To be honest, I don't think you're being honest, Molly wanted to say to her, because the humblebragging was excruciating.

While Alyssa continued to talk in elaborate detail about her job as a film accountant for Nemasco Pictures, Molly slid into a quiet state of meltdown. She was not even thirty but in three weeks her life as she knew it would end. When the baby came, she would stop being the centre of … anything. She was kidding herself that she'd be able to start something new with a baby in tow. How had this happened? And what was with that expression Alyssa had used: 'ended up doing'? They weren't at the point of their lives where they had ended up doing anything, were they?

Molly wasn't in her 'ended up' job, she was still in one of her 'starting out' jobs. Wasn't everyone? The lawyers and the doctors, sure they were in their 'ended up' jobs, but weren't the rest of them still figuring it out? Or was she supposed to have decided on her 'ending up' job before she had a baby so she could return to it afterwards? Was that what people did? Should she have settled on something already? Would it really be too hard to change with a kid in her life?

She tried to take deep breaths, to not let the panic knock her down. It was all right. She could come back from this. It was just a baby. She wasn't bricking herself into a pyramid. There would be time. What was it Jack was always saying? 'We're adding to our life. Not taking anything away.' He did say that a lot, now she thought about it. Like a mantra you would repeat if you were trying to convince yourself of something.

The sun had begun to set, and as it passed behind a thunderhead that had appeared in the west the light made the sky look like a cover illustration from a Good News Bible. Molly stared at the clouds, watching them spread. They were moving quickly. There was going to be a storm.

Someone ordered bowls of chips, and the smell, strangely, turned her stomach. It was dinnertime, and she hadn't eaten, but she couldn't handle the idea of food. There was just no more room for anything in her body or her mind. She hadn't managed to catch up properly with Lou, but she needed to go home.

The pity everyone would show if she were seen leaving this early would be painful, so Molly asked Alyssa where the toilet was. She grabbed her handbag and headed through the crowd, which was composed entirely of people who refused to move aside. Using her bump like an icebreaker she pushed through, ignoring the looks from people who acted like she was wearing a backpack on a crowded bus.

'Watch it,' said one man, as the froth from his beer splashed onto the ground. Tears welled up in her eyes. This is not a choice, she wanted to tell him. This is my body. I can't make it any smaller right now. Once she was out of sight of the table, she changed direction and headed for the escalators leading up to the boardwalk back to the road. The escalators weren't moving, so she walked up, the peculiar heaviness of trudging up metal stairs that should have been helping but weren't compounding the dragging weight in her pelvis. She wanted to lie down.

At the top she knew she was going to be sick and looked around for a bin. But the bins were designed to stop people stuffing explosives into them and so had only a narrow slot for putting rubbish in. It was beyond Molly to vomit sideways through the small gap, so she rushed to the harbour fence and threw up into the water.

Leaning her elbows on the railing, she wiped her mouth.

'Gross,' declared a passer-by. 'That's disgusting.'

'Yeah, thanks for that,' she replied, and when she stood up the man saw her huge belly and moved on quickly.

She pulled out her phone and ordered an Uber to take her home. It would cost a bomb, but the idea of the bus was more than she could bear. Next she called Jack, but his phone rang out and she didn't leave a message. It's all right, she thought. I've just overdone it a bit. I need to get home and go to bed. She had a sudden yearning for her mother, and for the first time she was grateful for the sequence of events that had led her to her grandfather's house that week. 'I need my mum,' she whispered to no one. 'I'm sorry,' she told her unborn baby. 'I'm not going to be any good at this.'

Chapter 18

When the Uber pulled up, the driver looked alarmed at the state of her. 'Are you all right?'

'I'm fine,' she said, wiping away her tears. 'Just a bit tired. I need to get home.'

'Would you like some music?' he asked.

'No, if that's all right, I think just quiet.'

Five minutes later she changed her mind. 'Excuse me?' she said. 'Do you have Spotify?'

'I do,' he confirmed.

'Can you please put on the theme from *All Creatures Great and Small*?'

'The old TV show?'

'Yes. I think if you just put "All Creatures Great and Small" into your phone … Here, can you give it to me?'

He handed his phone back to her and within seconds she was bathed in the sound of oboes, piano, violins and trumpets that was so familiar, so comforting and so deep inside her that she couldn't do anything but lean her head against the window, close her eyes and let the tears flow. She was little again, curled up on Granny and Pa's sofa next to Naomi and Simon, watching the old program on video on the huge boxy TV. When the music ended, the driver looked at her in the rear-view mirror and pressed repeat.

A crash of thunder sounded and Molly's eyes flew open, as a storm so quintessentially Sydney rolled in that it might as well have been locking you out of a pub at midnight and charging you twenty-six dollars for average fish and chips. The raindrops were fat and heavy at first, and within minutes the windscreen was awash with a torrent the wipers couldn't even begin to stem. The driver turned up the volume so Molly could still hear the music over the pounding water on the car roof.

She texted her mum: *Are you home?*

A baffling two-word reply came straight back: *No, Carlos.*

What? What did that mean? Who the hell was Carlos?

Sometime during the fourth run-through of the song, Molly felt a strange popping sensation and wetness quickly soaked through her knickers. She opened her eyes in panic. What the fuck? Mortified, she stayed silent as the fluid gently trickled out. This couldn't be happening. Not in an Uber. This would *destroy* her star rating.

But it was happening. Trying not to attract the kind driver's attention, she slid her bag under herself. It wasn't going to do anything much, but what else could she use to try to stem the dripping? She sent a text to Jack: *I think my waters have broken.*

When the car arrived at Pa's house, she gingerly climbed out. She vaguely attempted to splash rain onto the little damp patch on the back seat as she did, but she doubted how effective that was. Waving the driver off, she stood at the fence, in the rain, pretending to check the mail until he was out of sight, certain that at any second he would glance into the back seat, see the wetness and come screaming back for vengeance. After a few minutes it was clear he was gone, so she went in. The fluid was coming faster now.

It was hot inside, as though it had been shut up for hours. The temperature outside had dropped about fifteen degrees in five minutes, so she left the front door open to try to cool down the house.

'Hello?' she called out.

Silence.

'Anyone?' She was louder and more panicky now. 'Is anyone home?'

There was a thud and Richard V appeared around the doorway from Pa's study. He curled around her ankles.

'Richard, where is everyone?' Something that could only be a contraction slammed into her and took her breath away. That was not how labour was supposed to begin. The midwife had said it would feel like period pain at first, and it would get gradually worse. There was nothing gradual about whatever had just walloped her. She looked at her phone. Jack hadn't replied so she called his number. It went to voicemail again.

She called her mum next, then Naomi, Simon, her dad and Brian. No one answered. What the fuck? Where were they all? She staggered into the kitchen and leaned on her forearms on the table as another contraction hit. She breathed deeply, which did precisely nothing to alleviate the pain. Looking up, she caught sight of a leaflet on the fridge. It was an ad for Carols in the Domain. Now she remembered. That's where they all were. *Carlos* was a typo.

Lightning flashed through the window as another thunderclap cracked. They couldn't still be at the Carols, could they? Surely it was a complete washout? She just needed to stay calm. Someone would look at their phone soon. They would see all the missed calls. They would listen to her messages. And if she had to, she could call an ambulance, but it wouldn't come to that. She wasn't going to have this baby here, into a laundry basket.

The next contraction came less than two minutes after the previous one subsided. Okay, that was not normal. Molly remembered being told not to go to hospital until the contractions were five minutes apart. These were too close.

Triple 0. She dialled, and when the dispatcher asked whether she wanted Police, Fire or Ambulance, Molly said, politely, uncertainly, 'Um, hi, I think I'm about to have a baby.' Then another contraction hit.

'So, ambulance then,' said the dispatcher, who coaxed the location out of her then passed her on to the ambulance service. Another operator answered and said her name was Sue, which Molly did not care about, and asked several questions, which Molly mostly answered by screaming.

'Is there anyone else in the house with you, Molly?'

'No,' she cried, 'they're at Carols in the Domain.'

'Is there a neighbour you can call?'

'I don't know them; I don't normally live here,' she said, but she struggled into the sunroom and shoved open the window. There was a light on in Ray's kitchen. The rain was still pouring down, and it splashed her arms and face as she leaned out and screamed across the right of way. 'Help me! Please.'

Again and again she called, before turning back to the phone, weeping. 'There's no one home. Oh wait, no! He's there. I can see someone. Help me, please,' she yelled frantically again, as loud as she could, while banging on the window frame.

Patrick, standing at Ray's sink, draining a pot of spaghetti, looked up and saw her. His face became a picture of alarm. He opened his window just as another contraction smashed into her, and when he saw her double over and scream again, he ran from the room.

Then Molly could hear him at the front door, and coming down the hall, and he was in the sunroom with her. He skidded to a halt. 'Oh my god, you're in labour.'

'No shit, Sherlock,' she gasped. Then she couldn't speak.

'Have you called an ambulance?' he asked and she nodded, pointing to the phone lying on the bed. A voice came from the speaker.

'Hello? Molly, is someone with you now?'

Patrick grabbed the phone. 'Yes? I'm here. Patrick. My name's Patrick.'

'Right, Patrick,' said Sue, sounding for all the world like she was about to give instructions to a dim child about where she thought they might find their missing shoes. 'Molly here sounds like she might have a baby in the next little while. An ambulance is on the way, but the rain's making it a bit slow-going out there this evening. I might need your help. Does that sound all right?'

'I don't know anything about babies,' Patrick said, breathing as fast as Molly.

'Well, you're in luck because I do. Now, Molly, how are you going, love?'

Molly replied with a roar, and Sue kicked things up a notch. 'Patrick? Can you get a couple of clean towels without leaving Molly for too long? And can you please make sure the front door to the house is open and any pets are secured?'

'I don't know where the towels are —'

Molly looked up from where she was crouched beside the bed, with her arms stretched forward and her forehead resting on the chenille bedspread, and gasped, 'Under the stairs.'

He returned quickly with an armload of towels.

'Molly,' continued Sue, 'have you got your pants on still?'

Patrick looked her in the eyes and something passed between them. It was an understanding that they were in this together, and despite the fact they'd only just met, they were about to participate in something so huge that it made taking off your knickers in front of a person you've known for two minutes inconsequential. In any case modesty was not why Molly still had her wet knickers on.

'I'm not taking them off,' she said. 'They're all that's keeping the baby in.'

'Molly,' said Sue, 'pop your hand down and tell me if you can feel anything.'

'What?'

'Can you feel the baby's head?'

Molly reached down and burst into tears. 'Yes, I can feel it. Should I just hold it in until the ambulance gets here?'

'No, my love, it's time to let the baby come out. All right then, you push with the contraction — gently, gently, because your body is doing all this for you — and ease off with some little breaths in between.'

'How far away is the ambulance?' Patrick's voice was high and strained.

'Ten minutes, Patrick. You're going to help Molly deliver her baby. Molly, are you in a comfortable position?'

Her wail suggested how far beyond comfort she was.

'Patrick, have you got those towels? What position is Molly in?'

'She's sort of crouching and kneeling, she's leaning on the bed. Is that okay?'

'If she's happy, I'm happy. Patrick, I want you to get in whatever position you need to be in to catch the baby. It might be fast and it will be slippery. Right. Now, Molly: undies off. It's go time.'

Molly struggled to her feet, kicked off her pants and leaned her head out the window, feeling the rain on her face. It was all happening to someone else; she was sure of it. It wasn't her, standing in only a T-shirt and bra in the window of the sunroom at Granny and Pa's, her head in a storm, with a stranger watching her vulva for signs of an emerging human. It couldn't be real. She wasn't really about to give birth with Jack hundreds of kilometres away.

Then she was seized by a force so huge it felt like the whole world was trying to claw its way out of her and she closed her eyes, grasped the flaking paint on the windowsill, and pushed. She was only pain. She was on fire and at the end of this she would be ash.

'There's a head!' yelled Patrick. Molly reached down and felt an entire head, right there, like it had just popped into the room to have a look at what was going on. A person both born and not born. The ultimate liminal space.

There was a moment of silence, a pause, and all Molly could hear was her own breath, before a final contraction swept over her — 'Whoa! Oh my god, I've got it! It's a baby,' cried Patrick — and there was a strange slithering between Molly's legs. She turned around and slid to the floor. Patrick was holding something wet, slippery and furious.

'Patrick,' came Sue's voice, 'I want you to check the cord is away from the baby's neck. Is the baby breathing or crying?'

'Breathing,' said Patrick, and the baby answered with an affronted squawk.

'Lovely. Can you wrap the baby up in a towel, including its head but not its face, and hand it to Molly if she's ready?'

Why would anyone wrap a baby's face? Molly wondered, as Patrick passed her the bleating bundle, wrapped in an ancient faded Ken Done beach towel. She looked at her baby's face. It looked just like Jack, but red and fat and squished.

'Is it a boy?' she asked.

Patrick stared back at her. 'I have no idea,' he said. 'I didn't look.'

Molly unwrapped the towel a bit. 'Nope. Not a boy.'

Sue interrupted to tell them the ambulance was outside, and from sheer relief and shock Molly began to laugh. Her baby had just been delivered by a stranger who might be her uncle. She felt high, like she was floating. She tried to look at the baby but she kept having to look away — it was too overwhelming.

A paramedic with a ponytail came in and crouched down next to Molly. 'Hello, there. My name's Claire. Aren't you a bit of a legend?'

'The baby isn't due yet. Is she all right?'

'Looks pretty good to me. Mind if I take her for a little check? This is Gianni: he's going to have a look at you, make sure everything's okay and help deliver the placenta. Now, who's going to cut the cord? Dad?' Claire looked at Patrick.

'I'm not ... I've just ...' The events of the past ten minutes seemed to suddenly catch up with Patrick and he couldn't get out a clear sentence.

Molly tried to help him. 'Patrick is staying next door. We've only just met. This is my grandparents' house. Everyone's at Carols in the Domain. My husband's away.'

'Shall I cut the cord then?' Claire was unfazed. She laid the baby on the bed and busied herself with a clamp and scissors. 'Are you going to name her after Patrick? People often do in these sorts of situations. I've got a few little Claires running around — but only from when I've got there in time to catch one.'

'Patricia?' Molly suggested dubiously. This was all happening very fast. Were they up to the naming bit? Did she have to decide now? While some man called Gianni was poking away at her groin with his gloved hands? She couldn't imagine anyone naming a baby Patricia. Like polio, the name Patricia had been almost completely eradicated in their part of the world.

'God no,' said Patrick. 'I'd never forgive myself if someone was named Patricia because of me. I'm sure you have a name picked out already.'

Petula, thought Molly suddenly. It was the name her grandmother had wanted to call Annie. Granny had loved Petula Clark. She had played her records and then her cassettes in the kitchen when she was cooking or cleaning or doing the dishes, which seemed to be always, in Molly's memory. Pa had made such fun of her, both for her old-fashioned taste in music and for how she'd wanted to name their daughter Petula. Pa used to tell it as one of his catalogue of funny stories. Imagine, he'd say, just imagine calling a child Petula. It's asking for petulance. And you'd deserve petulance, because what a thing to do to a kid. Calling them a name that only one person has, and that person's a singer of mediocre crowd pleasers. Even Petula Clark wasn't really called Petula, he'd remind them — for goodness' sake, her real name was Sally.

Granny had lost that argument, and they'd named the baby Anne Katherine. It was funny that Annie had gone on to be a singer too. Maybe if she'd changed her name to something more fabulous, like Petula, or Paloma, or Aretha, or Rihanna, maybe she would have had a longer, more successful career. Annie Jones, nee Thorne, wasn't a star's name.

The name Petula had occurred to Molly ages back, but it was clear to her now that it was the right name for this new person, her daughter. Because fuck Pa, she thought. Fuck him for making fun of Granny's taste in music. Fuck him for sleeping with their neighbour. Fuck him for the secrets and the lies, the betrayal and disloyalty. The arrogance and the carelessness with people's hearts.

As the paramedics shifted her off the floor and onto the gurney, and Claire placed a tightly wrapped baby back into her arms, Molly wasn't sure if what she was feeling, what was pulsing through her like a migraine, was love or fury. Suddenly she was searingly angry at her grandfather.

She looked at her child and she knew she was absolutely hooked. No matter what happened, that memory of that tiny person was going to be inside her now, like a piece of shrapnel, for the rest of her life. Who Molly was that day was who she would always have been when her daughter was born. As of that moment, Molly was a mother. And she was not ready.

They wheeled her out through the hall to the front door, past the framed family photos. She looked at the picture of Pa, resplendent in a white dinner jacket on his wedding day, standing beside Granny, who was smiling shyly at the camera as they both held a knife over the top tier of a white cake. Pa's jaw was strong and set, and one eyebrow was slightly cocked. He looked, with the benefit of hindsight, like exactly the sort of man who would go on to father a child extra-maritally and refuse to acknowledge it. Back then, of course, who would have cared? What would anyone have done about it if they had known? Men had been more or less allowed to do that sort of thing.

She looked down at the baby, who was gazing up at her. It was a shock, the intense eye contact. Molly's vision blurred with tears. The responsibility was too much. How could she stop some man — who was currently a baby too, or maybe not even born yet — from trampling all over this girl's heart and dreams, her thoughts and rights? Or what if Jack betrayed her? What if this child's own father was the one who would break her heart, like Paul had Molly's? Like Pa would Annie's, when she found out about Patrick? The world had changed, but how much? And it mightn't even be a man who would make her daughter's life hard. It might be a woman. And it was definitely still a world that would cause her pain, because this child had come into an absolute shitstorm of a civilisation.

'I'm sorry,' she muttered, like someone who hasn't had time to tidy before a visitor arrives, 'everything's a bit of a mess here.' That was an understatement, Molly thought, because actually the world was on fire: it was nothing but melting icecaps, starving polar bears and oppressed minorities dying at the hands of the one per cent. Petula had come into a world of overcrowded feedlots, religious extremism, systemic racism and reality television. Plus she had a mother who hadn't even decided what she wanted to do with her life yet.

'Wait,' called Patrick, from behind her. 'What shall I do? Do you want me to come?'

'No, I'm okay,' she said. 'Can you keep trying to get hold of Jack and my mum? Everyone's numbers are on a list on the fridge.' Granny had put them there years, *years* earlier, and no one had wanted to take the handwritten page down.

'Yes, absolutely. I'll find them.'

It was still pouring outside, so the paramedics borrowed Pa's old golf umbrella from the hall and held it over Petula and Molly as they were wheeled out to the waiting ambulance. Molly wiped a splash off Petula's forehead and wondered if they had any other system for wet-weather patient transportation, or if paramedics always relied on the mortgage broker-branded umbrellas of the recently deceased.

Chapter 19

The thunderstorm had caused an abrupt end to the carols concert. A trio of heavily made-up morning television hosts were belting through 'Jingle Bells' when all at once thunderclaps drowned out the audience applause and hard rain began to pelt down. Thousands of people immediately gathered their sodden picnic blankets, disappointed children and half-eaten pots of hummus, and began to struggle towards bus stops and train stations.

Brian was the first to check his phone, once all eight family members had squeezed, sodden, onto an express bus to the northern beaches.

'Does anyone know this number?' he asked, turning his phone to show the others the source of an alarming twelve missed calls. Droplets of water misted the screen.

'Is it a stranger?' asked Sunny. 'Did a stranger ring you? You shouldn't talk to strangers.'

'It's different on the phone,' said Naomi.

'I don't think so,' Annie said, as she took out her own phone. Nineteen missed calls. Her stomach turned to ice. 'Molly,' she said. She listened to her first voicemail. Molly's voice, sounding nervous, saying something about her waters breaking.

Ringing came from the shopping bag Simon had slung over his shoulder, and he dropped it onto Diana's lap and rifled through the remnants of their picnic until he grasped his phone.

'Hello? Simon speaking?'

The other soggy revellers on the bus listened with interest.

'What? Who? Oh yes, next door. Yes. She's what? Already? Is she? No, yes, good, thanks. Which —? Yep, got it. Thanks. I'll let them know. And thanks. Really, thank you.' He ended the call and breathed out heavily.

'What? Simon, what happened?' Annie could hardly stand it.

'Moll had the baby,' he said, as if reporting that the bins had been collected.

His family erupted into questions.

'When?'

'Where?'

'Is she all right?'

'What did she have?'

'If you shut up I'll tell you.'

They quietened.

'That was Patrick, you know, that bloke staying next door? Ray's kid?'

'But why was he ringing us? Where's Molly?' Annie started up again.

'Mum. Listen. He said Molly was home alone in the house and she went into labour. She called an ambulance, and he heard her and went to help. She's fine, the baby is fine: they're both at the hospital now. It's a girl. She had a girl.'

Annie couldn't speak. She looked up at Paul, who was crushed into the aisle beside her, hanging on to the pole for support. He had tears in his eyes as he bent down and kissed her, hard on the top of her head.

Naomi put her arm around Diana and pulled her in for a hug. 'I knew she'd be fine,' she said happily. 'I had a feeling this baby would join us soon. When I felt Moll's belly the other day I sensed such a longing to be earthside.'

Diana raised one eyebrow at Simon.

* * *

They got off the bus at the hospital, and spent an hour, still damp from the storm and all shivering slightly in the air-conditioned room, paying homage to the new baby. Molly accepted their apologies, flowers — even though they were gerberas — and, despite Naomi's best efforts to talk Felix and Sunny out of it, a balloon in the shape of a Minion.

Annie watched as Paul perched on the edge of the bed and Molly gently placed the baby in his arms. She was relieved to see her daughter smiling proudly, showing her father how to support the baby's little neck, as if he had never held an infant before. Father and daughter, they were so similar in profile, and as they looked down at the baby, beatific half smiles of wonderment on their faces, she was momentarily astonished at their beauty.

Molly looked peaceful and confident handling her child. She was apparently unscathed by the unexpected homebirth. Why had Annie been so worried? Of course Molly was going to manage this perfectly well. The text message with the ducklings — well, Molly had obviously sent that while she was in prelabour. She probably wasn't serious.

'I can't believe Jack missed it,' said Simon. 'Lucky bugger.'

'What do you mean?' asked Naomi. 'Birth is amazing.'

'Yeah, I know that. And I'm glad I was there when Felix was born, but he was a C-section. Can't imagine the other way.' He gave an involuntary shudder.

'I'd be quite pleased if you didn't imagine the other way,' said Molly crossly. 'I'm your sister.'

'I know, it's just, you know, they say it's like watching your favourite pub burn down. Puts some people off ...' He trailed off as he realised they were all staring at him, their expressions running the gamut from disapproving to disgusted.

'Have you spoken to Jack yet?' asked Paul.

'He's on his way,' Molly replied. 'He'll be back in a couple of hours.'

'And, ah, what about old mate next door, Patrick? Was that a bit weird, him coming in when you were having a baby out your —' Simon gave a quick euphemistic whistle.

Annie interrupted her son. 'What are you going to call her? Have you decided?'

'I think so, but I want to tell Jack first.'

They were all agreeing that was sensible when a midwife strode into the room and glared around. 'Eight visitors,' she said, in a fearsome low voice. 'My goodness.'

Paul immediately handed back the baby and stood up. 'We'll see you in the morning.'

Everyone left except Annie, who perched where Paul had been sitting, reached over and tucked a strand of Molly's hair behind her ear. 'I'm so sorry I wasn't there. You must have been frightened.'

Molly smiled. 'I only thought I was going to die for a little bit. It was over so fast.'

'Do you want me to stay with you tonight? I'm happy to.'

Molly shook her head. 'Jack will be here soon. It's all right.' She paused and looked at the baby. 'Mum?'

'Yes?'

A flash of indecision came over Molly's face. 'Do you want to hold her? You haven't held her yet.'

'I'm desperate to cuddle her,' said Annie. 'But I shouldn't before Jack has had a chance to.'

'Dad did,' Molly pointed out.

'Yes,' said Annie. 'But I would feel like I was pushing in. I'll be back first thing tomorrow and then I might not let you get a look-in! I'll come back and hold her and you can tell me how everything happened, but you should rest now.'

The unspoken words hung between them, but Molly nodded.

Annie kissed her and the baby, and left, and walking alone through the quiet corridor to the lift, she hummed one of her new songs to herself.

* * *

Molly woke to a small squeak. She opened her eyes and saw light shining through the beige hospital venetian blinds. Turning her head, she saw Jack sitting in a vinyl armchair. His shirt was buttoned over the baby, who appeared to be mostly naked, if the discarded singlet and little checkered blanket on Jack's knee were anything to go by. As his new daughter unknowingly yanked on his chest hair, he winced in pain, his eyes watering.

'Hey. When did you get here?' she asked.

'A few hours ago. I didn't want to wake you. But Moll! Look what you did!' His eyes shone and his voice cracked. 'She's perfect. I'm so sorry I wasn't there.'

She reached out to touch his arm. 'It's all right. Turns out I didn't need any of those courses. She just shot out of me.'

'Patrick from next door rang. I had a million missed calls from you. I'm really sorry. I was in the pub with my parents.'

Molly remembered now. 'That's right. It was Kara-ho-ho-hoke Night, wasn't it? I should have thought to ring the pub.'

The baby shifted on Jack's front and made a sound like a creaking gate. Jack looked at Molly in alarm. 'What does that mean? Is she haunted?'

Molly frowned. 'I've got no idea. Does she need a feed? I thought she'd wake up properly and cry if she was hungry. I haven't fed her since just after they brought us in.'

'Who do we ask? The midwife?' Jack furrowed his brow and looked around the room.

'Just wait.'

The baby had stopped moving and was sleeping peacefully again.

'What shall we call her?' Jack asked. 'Where's that list we made? Is it in your phone?'

'The list of all the names I like that you said no to?'

'Because they were all dog's names.' Jack took the blanket, wrapped the baby tightly and transferred her to the crook of one elbow so he could pull up the list on Molly's phone. 'Coco. That's a Bichon Frise name. Only golden retrievers are called Pippa. Jessies are all kelpies.'

Molly looked at the baby. 'I don't want any of those names any more anyway. I want to name her Petula.'

Jack blinked. 'You what?'

'Petula. As in Petula Clark. She was my granny's favourite singer. It's a beautiful name.'

'Oh,' said Jack, looking thoughtful. 'I suppose it's all right. It's not a bad name.' He paused.

'What?' Molly asked. 'Say it.'

'It's just, well, the only thing to shorten it to is Pet. Or Tula. Won't kids make fun of her?'

'Kids make fun of all names. What do you want to call her?'

'I don't know. Lucy? After my mum.'

'Lucy's even more of a dog's name than Coco,' said Molly. She took her phone and searched for *popular dog names*. 'Oh. Molly's the number two dog's name. We won't be naming her after me. But look, Lucy is here, and Coco. Petula isn't there.'

'Maybe Lucy is a dog's name. But Mum drove me all the way here last night in our car,' he said. 'When I got all the messages. I was a bit over the limit. That was nice of her, wasn't it?'

'Where did you have to sit?'

'Oh Molly, don't.'

'Go on, where?' The ghost of a smile began to creep across her face.

'The back seat, because Toggle gets carsick and needs to be in the front.'

Molly laughed until she cried. 'Am I going to be a madwoman now too, now that I'm a mother? Do you think I'll go so bonkers that once the baby is grown up I'll have to have something else as my baby, until I die? A dog, or a garden, or you? Maybe I'll treat you like my baby once our real baby is grown up.'

Jack nodded. 'There's every chance.'

'Where's your mum now? Does she want to meet the baby?'

Jack looked uncomfortable. 'She stayed with Aunty Robyn in Mosman and Dad's driven up to collect her this morning. Because of the dogs. And she said you probably wanted to get settled first, before everyone comes crashing in to meet the baby.'

'Hmmm,' said Molly, before whispering, 'you aren't furry enough,' to her daughter.

The baby let out another odd sound, this time like she was trying to lift a very heavy box.

'Here, Jack, give her to me.'

He passed the child over. 'I still don't think she's awake yet. I think that was a sleep grunt.'

Molly cradled the baby and slid her hospital gown from her shoulder, exposing her breast to Jack and the rest of the ward. He got up and closed the curtains around her bed.

She placed the baby's face near her nipple but nothing happened. She looked at Jack helplessly. 'How do I wake her up?'

'Maybe unwrap her?'

Molly removed the swaddling blanket and the baby began to grizzle. Her little mouth nuzzled around for a moment and then she latched on. Molly's eyes widened and her mouth formed a horrified 'O'.

'What?' asked Jack, with a sharp intake of breath.

'Holy shit,' she squeaked. 'Oh my god, that hurts.' Tears sprang to her eyes and her shoulders shot up around her ears. 'Is it meant to feel like this?'

'Like what?'

'Like she has razor blades instead of gums.'

'I don't know. Maybe it will get better?' Jack offered helplessly, and possibly remembering that Molly had given birth at home, in a storm, in an hour, with no pain relief and only a stranger for company, while he was getting drunk with his parents and their neighbours, and undoubtedly winning some alcohol-based prize in a festive singing competition with the Eartha Kitt–inspired version of 'Santa Baby' he trotted out every year, he added, 'I think Petula is a beautiful name.'

Chapter 20

Annie almost didn't go to the open mike night. She'd assumed, when the call had come through that Molly's baby had been born early, at home, in a cataclysmic storm, that there would be no way she'd be able to make it to the city the next evening. She'd need to be at the hospital, or at home getting things ready for Christmas.

But Jane wasn't having it. 'No fucking way you're wriggling out of this,' she said when Annie called her and broached the idea of not going. 'This is the last open mike night for the year, and then as you well know everyone in the entire country gets drunk and has to have a very big lie down until at least February. If you leave it that long, you'll never go. I know you: you don't have that much momentum.'

Annie protested, but she feared Jane was right. She'd lost momentum once before, for almost forty years. She couldn't risk it happening again. After a brief moment of fear that the evening was Yule-themed, Jane confirmed that wasn't the case and Annie gave in. Anyway, Molly didn't seem to need her around. Jack was back now, and that was the way it should be. So she found herself standing in front of her wardrobe, two days before Christmas, staring at its contents with confusion and a nervous feeling not unlike her memories of morning sickness.

Back in the days of Love Triangle they'd worn proper costumes — coordinating outfits in highly flammable fabrics and the kinds of colour combinations you only saw now on the heavily reduced racks at op shops. Clothes used to be fun, she thought. There was more than one tear-away skirt in her past. But after watching numerous videos of open mike nights on YouTube she determined that her best chance of fitting in, of not flagging herself immediately as an ancient throwback, was to wear black skinny jeans and some sort of ironic band T-shirt. It was important to look like she didn't care. She could manage that. She still had original band Ts from Fleetwood Mac, Elton John and Queen. But maybe wearing an original would only emphasise her age?

She pulled on her jeans, turning around with her neck craned to see the reflection of her rear in the mirror. Fine from the front and from the back, but in profile it was apparent that she had old-lady bum — which is to say, it was just gone. Where was it? she wondered. Where did women's bums go? And just when having a bum was really in fashion. She'd heard Molly refer to bubble butts. Hers was more of an Iggy Pop butt. Perhaps she would leave her T-shirt down at the back, and just tuck the front in a bit, in the hope of disguising its absence.

She stared at her face, trying to see what other people saw, to figure out if she was kidding herself. Fifty-eight. How was she fifty-eight? Did she look almost sixty? What did that even look like? Did she look old? She didn't really think so. Justin said she looked late forties. But then Justin would. There were lines around her eyes, and a few on her forehead, but her jaw was still visible. No jowls, and her eyelids were still up where they were meant to be, not hanging down like forgotten blinds over a spare room window. Her hair was okay, more or less. A bit boring.

She'd done her research on the open mike night. Well, Jane had. It was in Surry Hills, and apparently was known for attracting actual music-industry people. The events were held every two months, and there were ten spots each night. It was first in best dressed.

Annie was prepared. She had rehearsed her song, and another as backup — long ago she had learned you never perform without an encore in your pocket — and she'd recorded her five favourite new songs onto her laptop. It was genuinely astonishing how straightforward that was to do these days — there was that phrase again. What used to cost thousands of dollars in studio time and engineers, she'd knocked off in a few afternoons, at home. The hardest part had been finding times when there weren't people arguing or laughing in the background.

Obviously the sound quality wasn't brilliant — you wouldn't record an album like that — but it was absolutely miles ahead of a demo anyone could have recorded by themselves forty years back.

She had five USBs in her handbag now, each loaded up with her five tracks, each tagged with a little typed label bearing her phone number and her name: Annie Thorne. She hadn't written that as her name since she was twenty-three. After the divorce she'd never changed it back: it was easier to keep the same name as the kids. But it was Annie Thorne who had been the almost-successful musician and Annie Jones who had sat quietly caring for others for so many decades she almost dried up and blew away. She briefly considered dropping the Annie part too, and just appearing as Thorne. The androgynous sharpness of that appealed to her. But she wasn't brave enough yet. All you had to do was look at her to know she was an Annie, not a Thorne.

Only Jane knew that Annie was going to the open mike night. The risk of other family members — most worryingly Brian and Paul, with their almost parental levels of enthusiasm — coming along to watch was too high to let them in on the plan. It had crossed her mind to tell Heather about it, but she chided herself.

That was the seventeen year old in her showing off, wanting to impress Heather as she always had.

Jane caught the bus into the city with Annie, and they listened to old songs they loved on the way, sharing a pair of earbuds like Annie saw schoolkids doing all the time. Jane asked once about the new baby, then they didn't mention her again. Annie felt a stab of guilt that she didn't want to gush about her newest grandchild, but it was healed by her gratitude for a friend who didn't want to talk about the baby either. Jane understood that tonight was an exercise in resurrecting a long-dormant version of Annie: the one who wasn't even a mother, let alone a grandmother.

* * *

The pub was quiet when they walked in. She supposed that was to be expected — it was very close to Christmas. It was probably good, for her first time. But she hoped all the producers and A&R people hadn't already gone off on holidays, and that they weren't too busy snorting lines of coke off interns at their Christmas parties.

The main bar was large and seemed proudly scummy. Annie liked it. Most of the pubs in her area had been renovated to bring in lots of light, and rosé drinkers who would order overpriced grilled haloumi. It was comforting being somewhere that still had a floral carpet that stuck to your shoes.

An elfin young woman with pastel pink hair and the sort of short fringe Annie associated with toddlers who have twisted a comb around and around until it's had to be cut out with the good scissors stood at the bar looking at a clipboard.

Annie approached her. 'Hi. Are you where we sign up for the open mike thing?' Why had she called it a thing? It was a night. Not a thing. Her nerves were already failing.

The girl laughed. 'Yeah, why, fancy signing up?'

Annie was confused. 'Well … yes, please.'

The girl stopped laughing. 'Oh, shit, right. Yes, okay. Sorry, I thought you were … never mind. What's your name?'

'Annie Thorne.'

The girl wrote it down on her list.

'And what's your name?' Annie prompted. Why did people never introduce themselves any more?

'Aurora.'

Behind Annie, Jane stifled a laugh.

'Good week to come, Annie,' Aurora said. 'This is the week we get the most people like you.'

'People like me?'

'First-timers. Newbies. New Year's resolutions from last year. Trying to get it in at the last minute. That's you, am I right?'

Jane opened her mouth and puffed herself up, but Annie put her hand on her friend's arm. 'Yes,' she said. 'It's a New Year's resolution.'

'That's great! Never too old to have a go. New tricks and all that! Have you ever performed before?'

'Not for a long time.'

'You'll smash it,' said Aurora, and she gave Annie a patronising smile.

'Is it true that you sometimes get scouts in here from record companies?' asked Annie.

'Yeah, yeah, EMI and Parlophone and a couple others have their offices nearby and sometimes people from there swing in. A couple of our acts have actually ended up being signed.' She paused and added, trying to be polite, 'They've been pretty, um, fresh sorts of artists, if you know what I mean.' Her eyes flicked around, not meeting Annie's as she clarified unnecessarily,

'Younger types.' She smiled. 'But, hey, got to be in it to win it!' she chirped and marched off to welcome a guy with the look of Jesus's anaemic younger brother, who was tuning up his guitar with a pained expression on his face.

Annie secured them a small round table near the makeshift stage area, which was only slightly elevated. Her foot wouldn't stop jiggling, though the stickiness of the floor kept tacking the sole of her sneaker down so she couldn't actually tap her foot. Jane bought them each a vodka soda, and squeezed Annie's hand.

'You're a hundred times the musician anyone else here is.'

'I'm a hundred times older.'

'Nope, we're not doing that. Not the boring age thing. Ignore it. It has no bearing on what you are doing here.'

'All right. Tonight I am ageless. Do you know, I half thought I might not call myself Annie? Do you reckon I could pull off just being Thorne?'

Jane stared at her, chewing her lip thoughtfully. 'Yes,' she said finally, 'but only if you have a fringe. Hair parted like that, with your cheery bright face, you're Annie, one hundred per cent. Thorne needs more mystery.'

'It's a bit late to get a fringe.'

'It's never too late for anything,' said Jane, grinning. 'I'll borrow some scissors and do it for you in the loos if you like.'

'Jane, I'm on stage in about ten minutes.'

'Won't take me more than four.' Jane drained her drink. 'Wait here.'

In moments she was back, brandishing a pair of plastic-handled office scissors. 'These'll do the job. Right, Thorne. Into the ladies'.'

Annie felt dizzy from nerves, but she followed Jane into the toilets and stood, awkwardly leaning over the sink as Jane pulled forward a section of the hair Annie had neatly centre parted, held it between her fingers and with less than no ceremony chopped off a good six inches. Annie gasped as she saw the hair fall into the sink. Jane let the hair drop, tousled it briefly to settle it into place, and let out a horrified gasp.

'What? Oh my god, what have you done?' asked Annie.

Jane burst out laughing. 'I'm only fucking with you. It's amazing. Needs a little bit more off here —' she snipped gently '— and here on the side, to bring it together.'

Turning to look in the mirror, Annie brought her fingers up to her hair in astonishment. 'How did you do that?' It was a transformation on a par with a librarian turning sexy by taking her hair down from its bun and removing her spectacles. Annie the grandmother and the mother was gone. In her place was someone she couldn't quite recognise but who looked a lot more interesting. 'That's so good. I look … I'm not sure. Insouciant.'

Jane stood beside her and they both examined the new reflection. 'You do. Insouciant is exactly right. You look insouciant as fuck. You're Insouciant Sioux and the Banshees. Have you got an eyeliner?'

Annie scrabbled through her bag and produced one. Jane applied it for her in a greater quantity and with more abandon than Annie would have dared to. 'There. Now you're Thorne.'

* * *

Back in the bar, Jane ordered two more drinks, although Annie had hardly dented her first. 'When do you go on? Did Rainbow Brite give you a running order?'

'I'm fifth. Of ten. There was only one other woman on the list.'

'Great. You'll stand out. That's what we want. Get you noticed.'

Annie looked around. It wasn't so empty any more. All the tables were full, and people were standing three deep at the bar. The room hummed with anticipation. She took a deep breath and let it out slowly. You have performed in front of many thousands of people before, she told herself. This is one scummy pub, with a hundred people, maximum. This is nothing.

Aurora stood at the microphone stand and welcomed everyone. She shouted 'Whoo!' at the end of most of her sentences and Annie felt herself frowning. She readjusted her face to a pleasantly neutral expression, and set it there for the first four acts.

Jesus's Anaemic Brother was first up, playing the acoustic guitar, mostly with his eyes shut. The song was called 'Not What I Meant To Say' and it was, in Annie's opinion, execrable. He sounded like a whiny Ed Sheeran, and the song was long and full of blame.

He was followed by three more men who also looked like Jesus. Annie tried to distract herself from her nerves by figuring out appropriate nicknames. The second singer, who played his song on the keyboard like she was about to, was less scruffy than the first one, and the sleeves of his checked shirt had been creased neatly with an iron. He had an air of entitlement and a song called 'Always Be Mine', which he probably thought sounded nostalgic and sweet but actually had more of a stalkery ring to it. The song could equally have been about being broken up with by a girlfriend or being asked to move out of home. 'Head Prefect Jesus', she dubbed him. The next two were Ginger Jesus and Surf Jesus. Of the four, she liked Surf Jesus's song the best.

Suddenly it was Annie's turn.

Aurora came to the mike and said, 'Next up, ladies and gentlemen, we have a bit of a treat for you. For the first time, fulfilling a lifelong dream — this is something she's wanted to do for almost sixty years, people, can you believe it? We have the one, the only, Annie Thorne! Whoo!'

Annie froze. What on earth did the girl say that for? None of that was true. She hadn't wanted to do this for almost sixty years. She hadn't been a newborn with a burning ambition to perform. And then the audience was clapping and whooping, and she wouldn't have thought it was possible to clap and whoop patronisingly but by god that lot was managing it. She wanted nothing more than to turn and run from the pub, into the street, preferably under the nearest bus, but she would not give them the satisfaction.

Jane grabbed Annie by the shoulders and squeezed. 'Fuck them all, Thorne,' she said over the applause. 'Just fucking do it.'

Annie took a last mouthful of her drink and made her way up. Even though it was just a small stage in a pub, there was a spotlight, and when she looked out she couldn't see anyone beyond the front row of tables. That was good. She didn't want to see the looks of encouragement. The good-on-you smiles she was sure were plastered to the faces of those people who were all so young, so confident of their worth in the world, so sure they would have time for everything they wanted to do.

But I have no fear, she thought. I have that over you, at least. I've got nothing to lose. Her nerves had been replaced by a quiet calm. She took a deep breath, placed her hands on the keys, looked up through her new fringe and started to sing.

Chapter 21

At the end of the song, there was applause. It sounded like normal applause. Not rapturous, but neither was it pitying, or polite. There was a bit of whooping. Annie sat back down with Jane and ate a pizza while the remainder of the acts performed. They were less messianic and she liked them all more than the first lot. And the one other woman — a beautiful, shaven-headed creature dressed in the sort of high-waisted, baggy jeans that had been in fashion twenty-five years earlier — was amazing.

The buzz in the room was huge after the last performer finished. People milled around chatting and congratulating each other.

'Go over there,' urged Jane, pointing at the young artists clustered around the bar. 'Go chat with them.'

Emboldened by adrenaline, Annie stood up. 'I will. I think I just will.'

'Do it.' Jane raised her glass to Annie and winked.

At the bar, Annie stood beside the shaven-headed girl, who was ordering a round of drinks.

'I loved your song,' she said.

The girl turned as if she hadn't realised anyone was there. 'Oh, thanks.' She went back to watching the barman adding tonic water to a glass from a soda gun.

Annie tried again. 'Have you performed here before? It was my first time.'

'A few times, yeah. I normally play bigger venues, with my band, but they're away and I thought I'd try a new song tonight, just to run it up the flagpole, yeah?'

'Well, it was great. I really liked it.' Annie waited for the girl to say something about her song. When nothing was forthcoming she added, lamely, 'This is a good pub. I like the … green tiles.'

Now the girl turned to her, holding her tray of drinks. 'It's not bad. They do a karaoke night too. You might enjoy that. Excuse me.' Annie stepped aside and the girl headed over to a table where her friends were waiting.

They thought she was a fun-loving granny. To them she was Susan Boyle. A joke. They hadn't even listened to her song. It only mattered what you looked like. That was what had led to her being kicked out of Eurovision. Maybe that was all that had ever mattered.

Tears stung her eyes and she angrily blinked them back. Her mascara wasn't waterproof and the last thing she needed now was to look like a post-menopausal Alice Cooper.

Jane wasn't alone when Annie returned to the table. Two men were sitting with her. One was very tall and a bit younger than her, and the other looked about mid-forties. That Jane had allowed them to sit and not seen them off at once was reassuring: it meant they had passed a quick and thorough dickhead assessment.

'Got a couple of fans here, Thorne.'

Annie smiled, swallowing down her sadness. 'Hello.'

The tall man held out his hand. 'Such a pleasure,' he said, shaking her hand warmly. His accent was English and he had the rounded vowels of someone with at least one titled godparent. 'I'm Philip and this is Ian. I just loved your song. You were the best by miles tonight. Absolute miles.'

Ian piped up, almost bouncing in his seat. 'You left them in the dust. That song was a knockout. It was a journey, you know? It had power and strength, and it was sad as well as being not just sad.'

'Pathos,' said Philip. 'It had real pathos.'

'But it wasn't depressing.'

'Thank you,' said Annie.

Philip was looking at her intently. 'Is there any chance we've met before? You seem terribly familiar.'

'I don't think so. Where do you live?'

'Shorewood, at the moment, but before that London and a few places in Europe.'

'I lived in London a long time ago,' she said. 'Early eighties.'

'You must have been a child.'

'Not quite. I was in a band then. Maybe you remember me from that?'

His face brightened and transformed as he realised. 'Love Triangle! You were the girl in Love Triangle. I loved you. Had the most tremendous crush. I was horribly bullied about it at school!'

'I'll bet you were,' Annie said, laughing. 'I'm so sorry.'

'Wow,' said Philip, shaking his head in amazement. 'How extraordinary.'

Jane, who seemed to have appointed herself Annie's manager, interrupted. 'Are either of you in the music industry? Annie's been on hiatus for a little while and we're keen to get her back in front of a bigger audience.'

'Jane!' Annie was mortified. 'I haven't decided that. And don't harass them, they're just being nice.'

'I've no objection to their being nice. I'd just prefer them to be nice and give you a record contract.'

'Sorry,' said Ian. 'I'm a private building certifier. I'd give you a record deal if I could. Best I can offer is maybe looking the other way a bit if you want to do something to your house other than what you have council approval for. Add a window or a skylight or something. Maybe even a driveway.'

Philip frowned at him. 'Ian, don't say things like that. You're one of the honest ones. You wouldn't do that.'

'No,' agreed Ian. 'You're right, I wouldn't. Just trying to sound cool. I've never had a cool job.'

'Is this a place where music producers typically come?' asked Philip.

'So we've heard,' said Jane, 'but if they were here they'd be beating a path to Annie's — sorry, Thorne's — door by now.'

'I'm sure that's not how it works,' said Annie. 'No one plays one song and gets signed. It took us a couple of years of gigging really hard last time. It'll be even harder this time.'

'Bullshit. Everything's instant now. The world moves faster. I reckon if the right person sees you, they sign you, then they record and release your work in a couple of weeks, tops. Like that Dancing Monkey girl from Byron.'

Annie wondered if someone had spiked Jane's drink with unjustifiable confidence. 'There's barely even anyone in here old enough to buy alcohol,' she said. 'If these are the people in charge of what music gets signed and released these days, it's not going to happen. I think I've left it too long. No one our age is in charge of anything any more. It's all down to the kids now.'

'No no,' said Philip encouragingly. 'The grownups still run things. I'm not in the music biz but I know one or two people back in England who are. You might say I'm industry adjacent. They're old blokes like me. It's very likely they're the same men who were around when you were starting out. They're still there, up the top of the businesses now. Some of them will remember you, I'm certain of it.'

'That is both mildly encouraging and the most depressing thing I've ever heard,' said Annie.

'I can't promise anything, but I could see if I could get your work in front of the people I know,' said Philip. 'Would that be helpful? I've no doubt you'll be snapped up at the next one of these, of course, but it never hurts to get yourself heard more widely.'

'Thank you,' said Annie. 'I'd be very grateful for that. Here look, I have a USB with some songs I can give you. I just need a pen to fix something on the label.'

Philip produced a fountain pen from the breast pocket of his sports coat. Annie took it. Who carried a fountain pen these days? She unscrewed the lid and carefully struck through the word *Annie* until it was a black ink blot. Now it just read *Thorne*.

'I don't know anyone,' said Ian cheerfully. 'But I'll take one if you have a spare. You never know.'

Annie felt a flicker of hope.

Chapter 22

Molly and Petula spent two days in the hospital, while Molly learned there were ways to breastfeed her child that were less likely to result in screaming pain. There didn't seem to be any completely painless ways, which was a pity, but some positions weren't as bad, and there were tricks to use on Petula to help her get better at it. It seemed insane that both mother and baby needed instruction in breastfeeding. How had the world become so overpopulated when it was this hard to keep a baby alive? Things would improve with time, the nurses assured her.

That the feeding would get easier was just about all the midwives did agree on. There seemed to be no consensus about how best to swaddle Petula, with one nurse telling them the child's arms must be down by her sides before she was tightly wrapped in a blanket, which made her look like an Irish-dancing burrito. Another claimed the arms must first be brought out to the sides, so the top of the blanket could be folded around them before the arms were then crossed in front and lashed down. All the methods left Petula looking like a bald baffled hostage.

'Can't we leave her unwrapped?' ventured Molly to the least terrifying midwife around two o'clock the second morning.

The nurse looked at Molly like she'd suggested they let the baby sleep on the roof of a moving car. 'Of course you can't.

Startle reflex. If you leave her unwrapped, she'll punch herself in the face all night and neither of you will get a wink of sleep.'

Molly didn't know what a startle reflex was. She googled it while the midwife was strapping Petula down and learned that her baby had a deep latent habit of contracting her muscles and flinging out her arms when alarmed. It was an ancient reaction to the perceived loss of support, a survival instinct to help a newborn grab hold of its mother. When was she supposed to have learned all this? Was it something everyone but her knew about? She'd never heard of it. She'd never wondered why babies were wrapped up tightly. She hadn't, to be honest, spent much time around babies — an omission that suddenly felt like it might be a problem.

The nurse was strangely pleased about the extent of Molly's ignorance.

'God, love,' she said, 'it's nice to meet someone who doesn't think they know it all. Most of the new mums we get have read so much about newborns they think they can do my job better than I can.'

Molly thought Toggle the dog would do a better job than she would.

Wrapped or not, after the first twenty-four hours, during which she didn't seem to notice she had been born, Petula wasn't much interested in sleep. But there was no shortage of visitors to hold her while she cried or stared intently into people's eyes, which was all she did apart from feeding. The family seemed to be trying to atone for their conspicuous absence while she was giving birth by maintaining a near permanent vigil at the hospital.

On Sunday morning, Annie had sat at Molly's bedside for hours, cradling Petula in her arms, or dancing her around the ward and up and down the corridors, singing quietly.

Molly didn't mention it — because what on earth would she say? — but after the first flood of maternal adoration and protection had washed over her in the immediate aftermath of birth, she didn't feel very much towards the baby, one way or another. She hoped the detachment was caused by still being in the hospital. After that first night in a private room she'd been moved into a ward, and it was hard to bond in a room of six women — at least one baby was always screaming, and there was usually a mother in tears too. More and more she found herself tuning out the sounds around her. Sometimes she didn't even realise when the crying was coming from Petula in the Perspex cot beside her. But Jack or her mum was usually there to pick up the baby and jiggle her, and everyone kept reassuring Molly that she could just rest now. Rest and feed.

She should take advantage of the help. There would be time to bond later. After all, it wasn't as though she felt anything especially *negative* towards the baby: she just felt so tired, and like she could do with some quiet. And she felt sore. And a bit empty.

The nurses were very keen on people getting up and out of bed as much as possible, but that was completely at odds with what Molly wanted, which was to be horizontal at all times, preferably with her eyes closed. She soon found that if she told them she'd just been for a lovely walk all the way to the end of the corridor, twice, they would leave her alone.

She lay on her side and wondered what she would do when they made her go home. It would be all right. The upside to so many people being in the house was that there would be tons of help. Petula had a father, three grandparents, two aunts, an uncle and a pair of cousins on tap. Molly would sleep until she felt better and then she would tackle this parenting thing. Eventually, she figured, she would wake up and not have forgotten she had a baby.

* * *

In the corridor outside the ward on Monday morning, Jack caught Annie as he went to the kitchen to make Molly a cup of tea. Annie had a sleeping Petula propped up over her shoulder, and she was swaying in front of the picture window that looked out towards the sea.

'Hello, Granny Annie,' he said.

'Naomi and Simon tried to get their kids to call me that. It didn't stick, sadly. I liked it, but they dropped the Granny bit.' Annie turned to show Jack Petula's sleeping face. 'Look, I've just got her off.'

'Thanks. Hey, nice fringe. When did you get that?'

'You're the only one who's mentioned it. I had it done yesterday. Just on a whim. Does it look all right?'

'Yeah,' he said. 'Very cool. Look, I need to pop out to the shops. I sort of assumed Molly was on top of organising all the baby gear but it turns out she hasn't really got much yet.'

'You know what they say about assuming, Jack.'

'It makes you an arsehole?'

'Something like that. What has Molly not got that you need?'

'Well, she actually hasn't got anything. You know Molly: never do today what can be put off until the last minute. It's like she had no idea we were having a baby for the last eight months. We need a car seat for one thing — they won't let her out until we have that. And a cot or something like that, for Petula to sleep in. And clothes. Nappies. A pram. Bottles maybe?'

'If you're going to be at Pa's with us for a while, maybe just get a bassinet for now, rather than a great big cot.'

'Yes, good idea. A bassinet.'

Annie paused in her swaying and looked at her son-in-law. 'It's a basket. For babies to sleep in.'

'I thought that but it's good to be sure.'

'In fact,' Annie remembered, 'I think I still have the one from when my kids were babies, in the attic. I'll get it out. You'll need a new mattress for it.'

Jack looked uncomfortable. 'Annie?' he said. 'Do you think Molly's going all right?'

'How do you mean?'

'Oh, I don't know, it's just, don't new mums normally have all this stuff organised? I mean, I know Petula was early, but shouldn't Molly have put some thought into baby equipment before that?'

Annie looked askance at him. 'How much thought had you put into it?'

'Yeah, fair point,' he admitted. 'Bit sexist of me. It's just … there's something else. It's probably normal. She doesn't seem very connected, or happy, about the baby, you know? I know the pregnancy was a bit of a surprise, but we were excited, and now she seems … disappointed.'

Annie thought about it. Molly had been a bit spaced out, she conceded. And she had been anxious about how she'd adjust … but she was already so good with Petula. 'She's very tired. And the birth was quite a shock. I'm sure she'll feel better once she's home and she's had a bit more time to get used to it all.'

'You're right.' Jack was palpably relieved. 'Silly of me. I was just thinking about these cows on my uncle's farm. Some of them just sniff their calves and wander off. I'm overreacting, aren't I?'

Annie smiled at him. 'Yes, Jack. Molly's not a cow. We're a bit more complicated, human mothers.'

He laughed too, and went red. 'Sure. Yes, of course.'

* * *

That afternoon Jack drove to a local baby megastore. There were two to choose from, and he went with Baby Universe over the more parochial sounding Baby World, assuming its range would be bigger.

The air inside was thick with marital tension. In every aisle were couples engaged in varying levels of discord over devices for keeping their offspring alive. He missed Molly.

'Fine,' he overheard an exasperated man say in the change table aisle. 'So ... not the one we decided on then?'

He passed a woman with a frankly enormous belly, sitting in a beige leather rocking chair, her swollen ankles propped up on the matching footstool. A toddler was sticking his head up her skirt while before her a man was folding the display model of a double stroller and trying to explain how she'd be able to lift it with one hand into the back of a Kia Carnival, but she had the far-off look in her eyes of someone who'd stopped listening to him years before.

Jack spied a shop assistant, a young man in a bright yellow shirt, and after several minutes chasing him round the store, glimpsing him at the ends of aisles and over the tops of displays, managed to corner him.

Unable to escape, the young man, whose nametag read Marco, turned to face Jack. 'Can I help you with anything?' he asked helpfully, as if he hadn't been trying to avoid exactly that for the past five minutes.

'I need a bassinet mattress and a car seat and some other things.'

'Right. Well, here are the mattresses.' Marco gestured vaguely at the area behind him, where assorted baby receptacles were displayed.

'Can you recommend one?'

Marco pretended to know the first thing about them. 'Hmmm. This one is good, I think. It's SIDS-free.'

'What?'

'SIDS-free. It's got no SIDS in the mattress.'

'SIDS, as in Sudden Infant Death Syndrome? What used to be called Cot Death?'

'Is that what it stands for? Well, yeah, I guess. I think the older style of mattress wasn't guaranteed SIDS-free but these new ones, they're made of ti-tree fibres, and they've got no SIDS in them. So, yeah, better for the baby.'

'They would be,' said Jack. 'I'll take one of those.'

'Right you are. And the car seats are up there at the front of the shop.'

'Are they all car-crash-free?'

Marco looked at him like he was crazy. 'What?'

'Never mind,' said Jack. 'I'll just get the second most expensive one.'

Chapter 23

On Jack's return to the hospital, Annie drove home. Molly and the baby would be discharged in a couple of hours, and had been promised a vintage bassinet to hold the brand new SIDS-free mattress. Annie needed to dig it out of the attic, where she assumed it was, somewhere. Jean would have stored it up there, neatly, once Molly herself had outgrown it.

Outside it was cool and overcast, sprinkling with rain, and the roads were quiet. It wasn't looking good for a sunny Christmas Day.

When she opened the front door she was met by the smell of something delicious frying with onions and garlic. It was definitely meat. Naomi must have come to a compromise with Diana. Annie headed straight up the stairs and retrieved from her bedroom the long hook for pulling down the attic ladder. Normally the hook stood in the upstairs hallway, but after an overenthusiastic and unfair jousting match had resulted in a tearful Sunny and a bruised Felix, it had been removed from the children's reach, and the whole house had been searched for other easily weaponised tools.

Annie hooked the ladder, pulled it down and opened the hatch to the attic. The trapped heat coursed out, smelling like dust that was about to catch fire. She climbed up, switched on the light her father had installed, and looked around. Good heavens there was a lot of crap up there. It was crammed with boxes, suitcases, baskets, small pieces of furniture and broken electrical appliances her dad had thought still too good to throw out. It was almost worth bequeathing the house to her children now to make dealing with the detritus of her parents' and grandparents' past someone else's problem.

The sound of footsteps came from the landing, and Naomi appeared halfway up the ladder, her head just visible. 'What are you doing up here? Re-gifting old bits as Christmas presents?'

'I wasn't, but that's not a bad idea. I'm looking for the bassinet. It must be here somewhere.'

Naomi came all the way up and looked around. A box of plastic car tracks was by her feet. She and her siblings had built towns with them in the dining room. She reached in for a piece, which immediately snapped in two, the plastic perished. 'What a shame,' she remarked. 'Felix and Sunny would have been right into that.' She reached for a cardboard box marked *Baby Clothes* in Jean's neat fine handwriting. 'Mum, look. Would these be our old baby clothes or yours? Granny must have packed them away. Molly might like them.'

'Let's have a look,' said Annie, as Naomi passed over the dusty box. 'If they're not all moth-eaten.'

Inside the box were notebooks, not clothes. 'Bummer,' said Naomi. 'Must have been a reused box.' She reached in for a notebook and opened it; turned a few pages. 'Mum, who did these?' She handed over the open book.

Annie looked. It was a drawing of a house: a familiar-looking, single-storey brick house. 'That's the house on the corner. It's the one you look at from the bus stop. This is very good. Look at that detail: you can see the tendrils on that vine growing up the fence. Extraordinary.' She turned the page. It was a drawing of the next house. And the one after that. The book was filled with the houses of Baskerville Road, rendered in intricate detail in what looked like coloured pencil. She flipped back to the front and there, inside the cover, was her mother's name, in her mother's handwriting. *Jean Thorne.*

'Granny did those?' Naomi sounded incredulous.

'She must have. Look.' Annie spotted a pair of tiny initials in the lower right-hand corner of the first picture, and quickly looked at the others again. The initials were present in each. *JT.*

'I didn't know she could draw.' Naomi took out more notebooks filled with more drawings: the houses from the surrounding streets. 'These are really good. They're like, I don't know, the illustrations you'd see for new housing estates. But done in pencil. When was she doing them?'

'They're dated, look there in the corner. This one is '77, that's '74. There's a whole box of them.'

'And you didn't know she did these?'

Annie was embarrassed. She'd never seen her mother draw anything, let alone this near photo-realistic illustrated survey of their entire neighbourhood. 'No.'

'Do you think Pa knew? Look at this one — the detail of those, what are they called, those scalloped wood things?'

'Shingles. Maybe he knew. I don't know.'

'He mustn't have known, or he would have got her to do something with them. Exhibit, or sell them or something.' Naomi spoke with the confidence of an over-encouraged child whose parents, desperate to nurture and facilitate, had pounced on anything creative she and her siblings had shown the slightest aptitude for.

Annie wondered about that. She didn't remember her father ever championing her mother. He'd regarded her highly as chief cook and bottlewasher, he'd praised her pavlova, and he'd loved her, but had he been interested in her? Not really. Annie hadn't either. An ember of shame burned inside her now. And regret. She'd dismissed her mother out of hand without even really bothering to get to know her.

What did the drawings mean? Who had they been for? Why hadn't her mother ever shown them to her?

Mousy and suburban: that's how she had seen Jean. Sweet, but old fashioned. Friendly, sociable, but not someone you could imagine having a really deep conversation with about anything. Mum had just been Mum. She hadn't really been supportive of the idea of Love Triangle moving to England. At the time Annie had seen it as Jean being ultra conservative and thinking Annie had to be a suburban mother too, though perhaps that was just because she was scared of losing her only child to another country. But what else had she been? What parts of her had Annie never looked at? A new image of her mother was emerging, like a slowly shaken Polaroid.

The shame glowed more brightly when Annie considered how she'd used her mother. Every chance she got, she'd dumped Molly, Simon and Naomi on her — though Mum had seemed okay with that. Maybe she had been, but what if she hadn't? She might have just felt there was no way to say no. She might have wanted her daughter's happiness more than she wanted anything for herself.

And what had Annie made of herself? With all that help, all that sacrifice from her mother? She'd produced a few jingles. Nothing more. Not enough to constitute a legacy by any measure.

Was it too late? If she worked extra hard now, could she leave something worthwhile behind? Something that might make Jean's sacrifices for her worth it?

Making her dead mother proud was at best, she realised, a spurious reason for her to pursue her music career again, but like a rock climber, Annie found herself reaching out for any small handhold to help drag herself up the cliff face. It was a stretch, and it wasn't much, but it was enough to hold her for the moment.

She thought of the open mike night and the memory made her burn with embarrassment. But success wasn't meant to be easy. That was part of the deal. Triumph over adversity: that was part of the narrative. Maybe it hadn't been as bad as she thought. Not being signed to a record deal on the spot at her first open mike night didn't mean she had failed. If that was going to be enough to stop her, it was a pretty feeble attempt at a comeback.

The importance of persistence was something she had stressed to her kids when they were growing up. You had to try and try again. Mastery lies atop a mountain of mistakes and all that. Not that you'd know it, from the way they flitted from one thing to another.

'Nomes,' she said, 'remember how I used to write songs, when I was young. Before you guys?'

'Of course.' Naomi smiled at her through the dusty gloom of the attic. 'Love Triangle.' She began to hum the first few bars of 'Home Is Where Your Heart Is', and the phrases drifted into Annie's head and straight back out again without sticking.

'That's right. I've been working on some new songs. Quite a few new songs, actually.'

'That's cool. Are you happy with them?'

'Pretty happy. I even performed at an open mike last night.'

'What? Why didn't you tell us? I'd have come.'

'I didn't want everyone there, making a big deal out of it.'

'Is that why you —' Naomi made a snipping motion near her forehead. 'It looks good. Can you sing something for me? One of the new songs?'

'Now? Up here?'

'Why not? Just quickly. There's not enough oxygen for a long song.'

'All right, let me think.' Annie looked up, furrowed her brow, then closed her eyes. Tapping her foot to count herself in, she sang a funny tune, bouncy and bright.

'What's it called?' asked Naomi.

'I think, "Not the Girl Next Door".' Annie searched her daughter's face, hoping to see a trace of pride.

'Are you sure you wrote that?'

'Yes, I'm sure. What makes you say that?'

'I don't know. It just sounds really … not familiar exactly, but maybe as if it's like something else. But not precisely like anything else. I don't know how to say it.'

'Maybe it's good?' Annie suggested. 'I think good songs make you feel like they were always songs in your soul, and they immediately feel homey and familiar. It's hard to believe you're hearing them for the first time. Like meeting a cousin or something, someone who looks a bit like someone you already know and care about.'

Naomi's face lit up. 'Oh Mum! I know what you should do.'

'What?'

'Kids' songs! What was that old album we had when we were little? With a song about a hippo on it?'

Annie's heart barely had time to register excitement before it thumped back down in her chest like a bag of wet potting mix. 'Anne Murray.'

'Yes! Like that! You should write a whole bunch of songs for kids, and you could record them for Sunny and Felix and Petula. That would be such a sweet thing for them to have.'

Annie forced a smile as her gut clenched with disappointment. It was the open mike night all over again. That was how people saw her. A grandma. Who did she think she was kidding? That was what she was. No one would take her seriously. She hadn't thought this through properly, with a realist's eye. She'd been so caught up in the feeling of freedom, in the joy of creating again after so long, that she'd failed to see the one thing everyone else saw. The only thing most of them would see. She was too old.

She remembered hearing an interview with Pink — on *The Graham Norton Show* she thought it must have been. Pink said when she released an album at the age of thirty-six, her record company had sat her down and told her to prepare for it not being played on the radio, because she was over thirty-five. Annie was more than twenty years older. Even if anyone was interested, did she still have the energy for this fight?

Turning away from Naomi, she shifted more boxes that didn't need moving, blinking away tears. 'That's a good idea,' she said, trying to sound cheerful. 'Maybe I will.' Her fringe tickled her forehead and she blew upwards to shift it. It was annoying. She found the bassinet and passed it to Naomi. 'Here it is. Still in perfectly good nick. Pa bought that. He liked things that were built to last.'

Chapter 24

When the midwives approved Molly's and Petula's release, at five in the afternoon on Christmas Eve, Jack carried the capsule car seat into the hospital room and together they settled Petula into it. They stood back to admire their work. She looked like a doll in a bucket.

'She's too small for it,' said Molly, frowning. 'Didn't it come with more padding?'

'Nope,' said Jack. 'That's it.'

'Are you sure it's for a newborn?'

'It says zero to six months. She's zero months. But, look, we'll bring the straps in more, and there, see? She can't move a muscle. Safe as houses.' He gently pulled on the straps to tighten the harness, and Petula's face crumpled. She started the hiccupping warm-up cry, a little puttering sound they knew already could go one of two ways: either she'd stop, like a lawnmower with a faulty starter, or she'd repeat the sound two or three times, like someone was giving her pull cord a really good yank, and then she'd be off, roaring away.

They both took a small step back and waited to see if their luck would hold. It didn't. Petula began to scream. Molly sighed and gave Jack a look.

He smiled nervously. 'You keep giving me that look. Does it mean you think I know how to make her stop? Because I don't.

I was just trying to make her safer. I didn't know she'd go off. I didn't mean to cut her red wire.'

'It's fine. I'll get her out and feed her again.' Molly picked up the baby, sat back down on the chair by the window and pulled down the front of her top. Petula latched on, Molly bit her lip, and the cries wound down to aggrieved snuffles. Molly stared out the window, astonished by her own power to calm her child. Jack couldn't do that.

'Everyone's so excited to have you both coming home,' Jack ventured.

She didn't answer.

'Moll? At home? Everyone can't wait. It's going to be wonderful to have you back.'

She looked away from the view and focussed on Jack's face. How could he be so blindly optimistic? Surely he didn't actually think things were going to be easy when they got back to Pa's house? His positivity was based on nothing but hope.

'You have no way of knowing that,' she said. 'I'd say there's a good chance it's going to be an absolute nightmare. Sunny and Felix are going to be screaming around the place, Diana's going to be in my face all the time, force-feeding us schnitzel, my brother's trying to sell the house out from under my mum, you're going to need to be working all the time, Dad and Brian will be lighting the place up like lunatic Christmas elves, then they'll go back to London. And if Mum's not at Zumba she'll be playing the piano and being weird. It will be harder at home than in here.'

He looked alarmed, but then he smiled. It was the most patronising thing Molly had ever seen. 'That's hormones,' he said. 'Day three is when your milk comes in properly and sometimes women cry a lot and feel like it's all too much. I read up on it. It's different with animals, I think, though maybe it's not. Maybe they also feel shit on day three but no one notices because they don't cry tears.'

'I'm different from a dog, am I? Thanks for that.'

'That's not what I said.'

'Anyway, I'm not crying.'

She hadn't cried at all. She was oddly calm. All the feelings and thoughts that would make her cry ordinarily were there — all she had said about going home was true — but she felt strong, and on guard.

Looking down she saw Petula had stopped drinking and fallen asleep. Her little face was smooth and peaceful. Molly felt a surge of love so strong she had to restrain herself from crushing her baby in her arms. She wanted to consume her back into her body where she was safe. She raised her daughter against her chest and whispered in her still-unfolding ear, 'I won't let them get you.'

* * *

As they drove home, Jack kept glancing over at Molly, checking she was all right. She hadn't seemed very happy since the birth. He supposed that made sense: it had been pretty traumatic.

But everything was going well now, wasn't it? So why was she so serious all the time? He thought she'd be more relaxed. Molly was always relaxed — that was one of his favourite things about her. The pregnancy had made her a bit grumpier than normal, but generally Molly was cool about things that freaked him out. Too cool, sure, sometimes, like with not getting any baby stuff organised. But overall coolness was a good thing to have in a wife, he reckoned. And Petula was excellent. He couldn't look at her little crumpled face, so much like Molly's, without wanting to laugh. Why wasn't Molly joining him?

People didn't always bond immediately, either with their babies or with the whole concept of motherhood, he knew that, but they usually came good. A midwife had told him so in the middle of the night and he clutched the information now like a lucky coin.

* * *

Molly opened Instagram on her phone. As she scrolled through her feed she was bombarded with images of her contemporaries' carefree twenty-something lives. Few of her friends who lived in Sydney were still home for the summer but many of the expats were back. It was that special time of year, when all the public holidays meant people could cobble together their annual leave to go away for a few weeks, and they'd flown off overseas or piled into vans for road trips to music festivals or to go surfing.

She twisted in her seat to check on Petula, who was now fast asleep in the capsule. A beach camping trip or a week in a hostel in Rome seemed suddenly like someone else's dreams, and she felt like she'd gone from twenty to forty overnight.

* * *

They would be home any minute. Annie went out the front to check there was a car space ready for Molly and Jack. She needn't have worried: the street was almost deserted. She sat down on the front step to wait.

'Little drinky-poo?' came a voice from the direction of Ray's house.

Annie looked up to see Heather on the verandah, waving a distinctive green-labelled bottle at her.

'Green ginger wine? I can't believe they still make that stuff,' she called back, which Heather took as an invitation. She trotted down the steps and crossed the right of way to Annie, two glasses and bottle in hand. Annie must have been wrong about her apology to Ray stemming from recent sobriety.

Heather lowered herself onto the front lawn with a groan. 'God, my knees, Annie. They'll be first against the wall, come the revolution. How are yours?'

'They're not bad,' Annie admitted, not wanting to sound smug. She accepted the glass of amber-coloured liquid and brought it to her nose. The gingery hit was pure nostalgia. 'So, things are okay with Ray?'

'Oh, they're about like you'd expect. He's not my greatest fan, but things could be worse, actually. Ray's mellowed in his old age.'

'I always thought he was mellow. When you left and there were all these rumours he'd been abusive, I was surprised.'

'Were there rumours?' Heather raised an eyebrow. 'That wasn't right. He wasn't abusive. Unless you count being terminally suburban and dull as abuse, which actually I do. I saw what was happening to the women around here. Not you — I could see you were going to get out. But people like your mum. No offence, but they were shrivelling up and turning in on themselves and slowly dying. There was no life. No culture. No art. No drama. No excitement. No joie de vivre. It was a big enough mistake getting married to Ray in the first place. I wasn't going to compound it by *staying* married to him.'

Annie opened her mouth to defend her home and her childhood, and her own mother, but the thought of the notebooks in the attic stopped her. 'Did it work out? Did you get the life you wanted?' she asked instead.

Heather drained her glass and sloshed in more ginger wine. 'On balance, yes. I mean, sure, now I'm in my sixties, and I don't have a home or any money, but my god, the riches, the experiences I've had, Annie-Kate, they'll sustain me forever, in here.' She thumped her chest. 'I followed every path I saw. I slept with every man I wanted to, and some of the women. I showed my kid that there's more to life than going to the same school every day, living in the same house, eating the same old meat and two veg. Patrick got to see the world with me. We were partners in crime. It wasn't the most settled childhood, but, trust me, he had the time of his life.'

'That must have been exciting.'

'You've no idea. God, the things I got up to. I never went to prison, but it wasn't for want of trying. I got mixed up in all sorts of mischief. Here's something I learned, Annie-Kate: the fun men, the sexy men, are the bad men.'

Annie wondered why Heather hadn't learned that the way everyone else had: from reading a Jane Austen book, or *Tess of the D'Urbervilles*. There was no need to drag your child around with you while you slept your way through and had your heart broken repeatedly by the ruffians of the world.

Heather topped up Annie's glass. 'Why are you sitting out here, anyway? Has that lot in there got a bit much?'

Annie felt defensive again. 'No, I'm expecting my daughter back from the hospital with her new baby any minute.' She didn't want Molly's homecoming interrupted by Heather. 'You'll have to come meet her when they get settled.' It was the most low-key version of 'This has been lovely', but it did the trick.

'Aren't you gorgeous. The doting granny,' said Heather as she clambered to her feet. 'You have a merry Christmas, Annie-Kate.' She went back into Ray's house. Annie went back inside too: there was no point sitting out there like a devoted hound.

* * *

'Who is that gypsy person you were drinking with out the front?' asked Simon when Annie entered the kitchen, where everyone seemed to be preparing dinner by getting in each other's way. 'She looked like an RSL Bette Midler impersonator.'

His sister and wife turned, frowning, from opposite sides of the room, reprimanding him like two feminist sphinxes for his casual ageist slandering of a woman he didn't know.

'What?' He laughed. 'She did.'

'Paul,' said Brian, his eyes twinkling. 'She could call her show "Bette Midler: But Only From a Distance".'

'You beat me to it,' said Paul, laughing.

'She's not a Bette Midler impersonator,' Annie said. 'She used to live next door.'

Simon's smile dropped away. 'That was Heather? Next-door Heather?'

'Yes,' said Annie. 'How do you remember her name? She left before you were born.'

'Oh, Pa was always going on about how Right-of-Way Ray drove Heather away. The name must have just stuck in my head.' Simon busied himself emptying clean plates from the dishwasher and stacking them in the cupboard.

It was clear to Annie that he was lying. His ears had gone flaming red, just as they had since he first smeared nappy cream all over the walls of her bedroom at the age of eighteen months before alleging, 'Teddy did it.' She couldn't imagine why he was lying about knowing Heather's name.

'Will she be joining us for Christmas lunch tomorrow?' asked Diana.

Bemused, Annie replied, 'No, I don't imagine so. Why would she?'

'Naomi has invited the man next door, Ray, and his son to lunch. And if Heather is staying with them ...' Diana removed a huge dish of lasagne from the oven and put it on the stovetop more forcefully than she needed to. 'There,' she said disapprovingly. 'Not the most traditional Christmas Eve meal I've ever cooked, but if it's Molly's favourite —'

'Hang on,' said Simon. 'Naomi, you've asked Ray and Patrick for Christmas lunch?'

'Yes. Is that a problem? We talked about this the other night.'

'We didn't decide to do it. We don't even know them.'

'I know them a little,' said Annie. 'And it's a kind gesture.'

'Ray isn't well,' said Naomi. 'I thought it might make things easier.'

'And will Heather come too, now that she's back?' Simon was like a dog with a bone.

Annie turned to him. 'Why is any of this a problem for you, Simon? You're not the one cooking the meal.'

'Well, because it's Christmas. It's a time for family.'

'Don't be silly,' said his mother. 'It will make not the slightest difference if we feed three more people some lunch.'

'It's all right,' agreed Diana. 'We'll have enough. I've done the stuffing, and the chickens are going to be beautiful. Naomi has made shells for the pavlovas.'

'But in the morning we're going to the beach, right? After the presents?' Felix tugged frantically at his mother's arm.

'Yes, we will go to the beach in the morning.' Shaking her head, she continued under her breath, though audibly, 'We will eat lasagne tonight and go to the beach tomorrow. Like it's not even Christmas.'

Felix, apparently well aware of his mother's rising internal pressure, grabbed Sunny's hand and pulled her out into the garden.

Chapter 25

Late that night Annie lay in bed, watching the pattern of flickering coloured lights bounce around her room. It was almost midnight but Brian had begged her not to turn off the illuminated Santa, complete with sleigh and reindeer. He was more excited about Christmas than either of the children in the house. He said he'd switch off all the lights before he went to bed, but as she couldn't hear anyone moving around in the house now she was sure he'd forgotten and turned in for the night, in the matching elf pyjamas he and Paul had bought themselves.

Molly's homecoming had been more subdued than Annie had expected. The family had met her at the door like a litter of puppies, all falling over each other to see the baby. But Molly was distant and quiet, and she hadn't smiled much.

Annie tried to think back to how she had felt coming home with Simon when he was a newborn. She'd been reeling with disappointment about Eurovision, certainly, but Simon had made her so happy. Every time she'd looked at him she'd smiled. She couldn't help it. At least she thought that was what had happened. She'd felt incredibly alive: she remembered that very clearly. There'd been such a huge weight of responsibility on her, to look after Simon, and she remembered feeling like she didn't really know how, but Molly was managing the practical stuff beautifully.

She was so calm you'd have thought Petula was her fifth baby, so confident did she seem in handling, feeding, changing and dressing the baby and putting her to sleep.

Annie had watched Molly at dinner. She'd held the sleeping Petula throughout, even managing to eat with her daughter cradled in the crook of her arm. It wasn't like there was a shortage of people clamouring to hold the baby — everyone offered, at one point or another — but Molly had politely declined each time. The baby was settled, she'd kept saying, no point in waking her up by passing her around.

Was it normal? Annie couldn't tell. Maybe it was just unexpected, Molly apparently mothering with such placid ease. She hoped so.

* * *

Molly lay in bed the next morning, listening to the raucous cackle of a kookaburra in the tree outside, and trying to decide if anything about Christmas mattered any more.

No, she concluded. It didn't. Christmas was nonsensical. Outside her door, she could hear her father and Brian giggling as they arranged presents under the tree. These presents, she assumed, were in addition to those she had heard them bringing downstairs at half past one and stuffing into the kids' stockings, ostensibly from Santa Claus. She didn't remember her dad being this into Christmas when she and Simon and Naomi were young. Had he become a born-again Christmasian when he moved in with Brian? Or was it the advent of grandchildren?

It irritated her the way her father was treating grandparenthood like a second attempt at fatherhood. It was a different job. He couldn't erase having given up on parenting when she was still only little by being the World's Best Granddad.

Did Sunny and Felix even still believe in Santa, anyway? Wasn't six the sort of age where you figured out the ruse?

Jack was still asleep, with one arm flung across his eyes to keep out the bright morning sunshine that was streaming in through the gap between the curtains. When the sounds from the living room had ceased, she eased herself out of bed, gathered up Petula from her bassinet and slipped out. Hearing voices in the kitchen, she padded quietly through the living room and along the hall to the front door.

She walked down the right of way to the seat the boys had left there the night of Pa's wake. That felt like months ago. Back when Pa was alive, he always put the chair back on the patio. He claimed Ray would go berserk if he didn't, because it was technically his land and Pa was only allowed to use it for accessing his garage. Now she wondered if that was true. She'd never heard a peep out of Ray. He didn't seem like a very berserk person.

She settled onto the bench. Petula scrunched her face in her sleep, but didn't wake. Ray's kitchen window was open, and the net curtains were pulled to one side. Why had Pa been so rude to Ray all those years? Was it because Heather, having fallen pregnant, had gone back to Ray, after Pa spurned her? But what else could she have done?

There had to be something missing from this story. It felt like playing Boggle with only fifteen pieces. No matter which way Molly moved things, the story did not make sense. Surely there was something she still didn't know, that would explain why Pa, having slept with Ray's wife and made her pregnant, had gone on to torment Ray, like a low-grade chronic illness, for the rest of his life. If there wasn't, then she could only conclude that Pa had been, in this respect at least, actually a fairly shitty person.

A shriek from inside told her Sunny and Felix were awake. It was followed by the jingling opening strains of 'Santa Claus Is Coming to Town', which she instantly recognised as the first track on the 1987 album *A Very Special Christmas*, the family's festive soundtrack since before her birth. The sun was barely up. It couldn't be much after six o'clock. This was a flagrant violation of the longstanding No Pointer Sisters Before Eight AM On Christmas rule. It was going to be a long day.

* * *

With cups of coffee and croissants, the family gathered in the living room to open their presents. Annie briefly considered suggesting they follow the one-at-a-time, youngest-to-oldest system that had been the tradition when she was a child, but the size of the pile of presents meant they'd be there all day. A free-for-all was the only way. She reached for the record player, flipped over the Christmas album and lowered the needle. Bono began begging his baby to please come home for Christmas, over a background of tortured-sounding backup singers.

Sunny, possessing the unnerving talent of the young for opening the best present first, and thus making all subsequent gift-givers feel inferior, went straight for Paul and Brian's offering: a laser tag set. Felix followed suit, tearing into a child-size metal detector and a rainbow taffeta tutu, also from his grandfathers.

Simon frowned at the skirt, and went off grumbling to locate batteries for the metal detector. To Annie's surprise, Naomi said nothing about the laser tag set: it seemed her ban on toy weapons was relaxed when her father was involved.

Soon there were piles of paper everywhere ('Try to keep it flat, not all scrumbled up,' Naomi beseeched them. 'It's much easier to recycle.') and everyone lost track of who had given what to whom. There had been talk earlier in the week of a Kris Kringle, where everyone just bought one gift, but no one had managed to organise it so there were six or seven presents apiece.

'Who gave me this?' asked Annie, holding up a novel called *Daisy Jones and the Six*.

'We did!' said Paul, beaming. 'It's about a girl who becomes a huge rock star, and her name's Daisy Jones, and your —'

She cut him off. 'Yes, my name's Annie Jones, I get it. That's very sweet. Thank you.' Inside she seethed. Why would she want reminding that her career had gone nowhere? It was clearly so far from Paul's and Brian's minds that she might feel any sadness about this, that they thought nothing of giving her a story about someone who, if the back cover blurb was to be believed, ended up with exactly the life Annie had dreamed of. From anyone else such a gift would have seemed malicious, but she knew it was just carelessness.

None of them except Naomi knew Annie had been to the open mike night. She hadn't even talked to Jane about it since Christmas and family had taken over entirely for them both. And she couldn't expect to hear from that Philip man for ages either. If she ever did. He had probably just been being polite when he took her USB.

She looked around the room. At least the grandchildren were having a good time. Sunny and Felix had both received boogie boards from their parents. Molly was on the sofa with her legs stretched out in front of her, her feet raised on the old leather ottoman and her baby asleep along her thighs. She was gazing at Petula, and hardly seemed aware of anything else going on around her. Brian and Paul were wearing Santa hats and doing the running man to 'Christmas in Hollis'.

The piano called to Annie, but it was trapped: Simon was sitting on the stool and had lined all his gifts up along the closed lid: a multi-tool, a mug that said *Take a Chance on Tea*, a photo of Felix in a picture frame covered liberally in shells and glue, two copies of *The Barefoot Investor*.

Annie took a deep breath. They'd all go to the beach soon. The day was cool, but not enough to put off the kids. She could tidy up, and sit down and play. There was a song that had been knocking on her consciousness since the night Petula was born, and she hadn't had a moment to play with it yet.

* * *

Annie had forgotten that the more people involved in any outing, the longer it takes them to leave the house. Instead of the beach-goers picking up towels and walking out the door, there followed a good forty-five minutes of hunting for swimmers, hats, sunscreen, bags, thongs, water bottles, snacks, and some little plastic models of surfers on boards that Santa had kindly brought and which had disappeared into the strata of wrapping paper that blanketed the living room. Once they were almost out the door, Simon decided to lobby for Diana to join them.

'It's freezing,' she said. 'No.'

'It's barely even cool. How can you say it's freezing? Berlin is freezing,' he argued.

'It feels wrong to swim at Christmas. I just don't want to. Please, Simon. Besides, I need to stay and put the chickens in the oven.'

'We'll only go for an hour,' wheedled Simon. 'Come on, Di. I do all your holiday traditions. This is mine. Please? For Felix?'

Diana sighed heavily. 'All right, all right, I'll go. But someone needs to take the chickens out of the fridge at half past eleven so they can come to room temperature before I cook them. They're stuffed and ready, but they can't go into the oven cold.'

'I'll do it,' Molly said.

'Don't uncover them — you must leave the cling wrap on them. Just take them straight out of the fridge and put them here on the counter, where there's no direct sun.'

Molly bristled. 'I can take a chicken out of a fridge, Diana. I'm not a moron.'

Diana smiled apologetically. 'I know you aren't.' She looked wistfully at Petula, lying with her face on Molly's shoulder. 'I miss that. You should treasure this time, Molly. It all gets harder after this. Now. Where are my sunglasses?'

* * *

When they had gone, Molly changed Petula's nappy, fed her again, and put her back down for another nap. The eat-change-sleep cycle was short and relentless.

Her mother was in the living room, playing the piano. It was so peaceful with everyone out. It felt like the first time in days she'd been able to let her breath out. All she wanted to do was sleep.

At eleven thirty she took the two baking trays of chicken out of the fridge and placed them, as instructed, on the counter, exactly where Diana had shown her. She checked the cling wrap was covering the whole birds completely — it wasn't a hot day but there were still flies around, and eating flyblown chicken was no one's idea of a good Christmas dinner. That done, she went to the sunroom and lay down on the bed.

Almost the moment she closed her eyes she heard the tell-tale squeaks from the bassinet. No. Just half an hour: she sent a silent prayer to her child. Just give me half an hour. But the grizzling gained momentum. Molly lay still, pretending she was back in hospital and the cries were coming from someone else's baby.

Her door opened and Annie tiptoed in. Molly kept her eyes closed, not wanting to interact. Annie gently picked up Petula and crept back out, closing the door quietly behind her.

It all gets harder after this. That's what Diana had said. It was what Molly had feared. This was manageable, with all the help and the immobile baby whom she could protect. But the future was a chasm of darkness, filled with perils she knew about and perils yet to even be invented. Her poor daughter.

Molly began to weep.

* * *

Petula was a baby who liked to be vertical. She reminded Annie of the moo box toy the kids'd had when they were little: a small can that mooed like a cow when it was tilted to its side. Petula too was quiet when she was upright. To that end, Annie propped her up on her shoulder, and danced through the house with her. The screaming eased off to a grizzle.

She sat back down on the piano stool and with her one free hand, played a few chords. They were deep and resonant, and Petula stopped crying altogether, stunned into silence. Annie continued, puzzling out as best she could the ideas that had been building up. She hummed a melody to the baby, whose soft puffs of breath tickled her cheek.

This wasn't something she'd attempted with her babies. She hadn't thought she could manage it. Maybe she should have, she thought now. Would it have worked? Who could say? What if it had been unnecessary to stop her music? But it was too late for that sort of thinking. *All we ever have is the future.* With her left hand, she picked up her pencil and awkwardly jotted those words down on her little pad of lyrics.

* * *

The beach party arrived back at half past twelve, around forty minutes after Richard V had wandered into the empty kitchen, jumped up onto the counter and chewed through the plastic wrap covering the two trays of chicken. It was an aggressive assault. One chicken had been dragged under the table and comprehensively mauled. The other was just nibbled, but a small crowd of flies crawled on each.

Diana made the discovery and her fury echoed through the house. *'Du verdammte Höllenkatze!'* The culprit, who appeared to have no understanding of either right and wrong or German, streaked past her down the hall and out the front door, leaving greasy pawprints in his wake. Everyone followed the trail of destruction to the kitchen.

'That cat!' Diana said, her teeth clenched violently. 'He has ruined Christmas dinner. Now we have nothing!' Her eyes brimmed with tears.

Simon laughed. 'Oh my god, that fucking cat. Never mind, Di, it'll be all right.'

She spun around, holding a tray of chewed chicken, her eyes wide with rage. 'It will be all right? You are laughing? That is your answer to this? After everything, Simon? You still do not care. You do not care about anything if I care about it.'

'Calm down, Di,' he said, as if reading aloud from *The Everyman's Guide to Wrong Moves*.

'I won't calm down! I am only trying to celebrate Christmas, which you place no value on, and now this happens and it is clear to me that you do not even care.'

'The side dishes are fine, we'll just have those.'

'They are side dishes. They go on the side. On the side of what, Simon? On the side of *what*?'

Brian and Paul fled the kitchen and joined Molly, Jack and Annie, who all stood frozen in the living room, as if playing a game of musical statues where they could only move when a German woman was hurling obscenities at a cat or her husband.

They heard someone close the kitchen door, and the argument resumed, muffled now.

'Are the chickens salvageable?' Annie asked.

'Absolutely not,' declared Brian. 'We need a plan B.'

'Nothing will be open,' said Jack, 'it's Christmas Day.'

'KFC,' said Paul triumphantly. 'It's always open. I'll bet it's open today. And it's got chicken. Ladies and gentlemen, thank you very much: I've just saved Christmas!'

'It'll have to do,' said Annie, grudgingly. 'Diana won't be happy.'

'I think there's more than chicken making Diana unhappy,' said Molly.

Chapter 26

The Christmas table was beautiful. By four o'clock, there was red cabbage cooked in butter with onions and apples and simmering resentment, bread dumplings and warm potato salad, and a silver platter was ready to be piled high with an assortment of regular and hot and spicy fried chicken, currently staying warm in its striped red and white boxes in a low oven. Several bottles of wine had been decanted into Granny and Pa's Waterford crystal.

It was still overcast outside, so Annie located a box of creamy tapered candles for the old silver candlesticks, and once she had lit them the room twinkled. It wasn't cool enough for a fire, but other than that, she thought, the day was giving a passable impression of a Northern Hemisphere Christmas. She hoped it would mollify Diana, who was upstairs in her room with the door closed.

The doorbell rang and Sunny and Felix raced to open it. Annie heard Naomi follow them and greet the guests. It sounded like Heather had joined her former husband and son. Brave, thought Annie.

'Come through, come through,' said Naomi, leading them into the living room, where Brian, Jack, Simon and Molly were sitting. Patrick held his father protectively by the elbow. Ray was unsteady on his feet, and very thin. His suit hung off him like a shroud. Heather wore a voluminous red dress with a handkerchief hem, a huge amount of red lipstick and a large fake rose pinned in her hair. Annie didn't remember her dressing so flamboyantly. She looked like an aging Kate Bush groupie. Which she probably was, Annie realised.

Naomi made the introductions. 'I can't remember who's met who, so I'll go round. Ray, Patrick, Heather: this is my brother, Simon, my sister, Molly, and her husband, Jack, and their daughter, Petula — Patrick, you'll remember Petula.'

Patrick gave an awkward nod to Molly and she smiled back uncomfortably. Although Jack had delivered a slab of beer and a case of red wine to Patrick's verandah by way of thanking him for delivering the baby, Molly hadn't seen him since she was wheeled out of the house that night, the baby in her arms.

Jack waved from his seat, and Simon stood to shake hands.

Naomi continued as her father came in, carrying a tray of Champagne glasses. 'This is my father, Paul, and this is his partner, Brian. And my mum, Annie.'

Annie dragged her eyes away from Heather's get-up and shook Patrick's hand. As she did, she looked into his eyes and tried to say hello, but only a dry cough came out. A roaring filled her ears. This man was her father.

Her heart pounded and she tried to take a deep breath. He was not her father. Of course he wasn't her father. Her father was ash now. He was in powdered form in an urn on the mantelpiece in the dining room, overlooking the festive table.

Her eyes flicked to Paul. He had seen it too, she could tell. His mouth hung open like a cartoon character's. The Champagne glasses rattled on the tray he held. Annie let go of Patrick's hand and reached out to steady the tray. Once she had broken eye contact with Patrick her voice returned, overbright. 'Lovely to meet you. Whoops, Paul, hang onto those! I'll get the Champagne.

Is Champagne good for everyone? Molly, do you want a tiny one, or something soft? Heather, Champagne?'

'Champagne'd be gorgeous, darling.' Heather had settled herself into an armchair, while Molly slid over on the sofa to create a space for Ray.

Annie went back to the kitchen. She opened the fridge and stared blankly in.

Behind her, Paul whispered, 'Holy shit. Who was that? Why does he ...?'

Annie didn't want to say it, but not saying it wouldn't make any difference. There was only one way a forty-ish-year-old version of her father could be standing in the living room with Ray and Heather. The knowledge her father had another child flash-flooded her brain and body, washing away everything she thought she knew. Suddenly she felt very tired. She rubbed her face with both hands, digging her knuckles into her closed eyes. The younger man's face remained.

'Why does he look exactly like ...?' Paul didn't finish this question either.

Annie turned to look at him, one eyebrow raised. 'Why do you think?'

Paul stared at her. 'No. Your dad? And Heather? No. Did you know?'

Annie searched her memory for something she'd missed, all those years back, when Heather was her friend.

There must have been something. Her father must have looked at Heather, and Annie must have seen it. He had to have looked at her in a way your father doesn't normally look at the neighbour's wife. Perhaps he did, and stupid adolescent Annie was too naive, too caught up with her own burgeoning romance with Paul, too busy trying to disguise her innocence in her songwriting, to recognise it. Or maybe it didn't start until after Annie had left for London. What had it been between them? A full-blown, years-long affair? One fuck round the back of the garage?

Was there any way she might have been mistaken? No. The cleft in Patrick's chin. The angle of his cheekbones. It was all her father. His eyes. God, even his hand when she'd shaken it. She wished with every part of her for a twinge of doubt, but there was none.

It made sense now: Heather leaving, taking the baby, never to be seen again. Ray and her father's feud. Although that part didn't make complete sense. Her father was awful to Ray for forty years. Why? Did he want Heather to have left Ray for him? She did leave Ray; she went away. Was Robert angry about that?

Annie realised she had been staring at a jar of mayonnaise for several minutes. 'No.' She finally answered Paul's question. 'I didn't know. I guess Dad wasn't exactly who we thought he was. You hear about these things, don't you? I didn't think it would ever be us. I didn't think we were that interesting.'

'I'm sorry.' Paul picked up a tea towel and reached for the spatula.

'You didn't know. It was probably after we left.'

'I know, but could it have started before we went? Did we not see something?'

'That's what I'm wondering. I can't think of anything. I don't remember her ever even being around Dad, really. She and Ray didn't socialise much with my parents. She hung out with me, and that was sort of it. Mum tried to be her friend first, but Heather was so much closer to my age. Dad was usually at work.'

'Do you think he knows?'

'Who?'

'The guy. The son. What's his name?'

'Patrick,' Annie said, and thought back to her mother's last years. 'My mum used to talk about him sometimes, when she was forgetting things, near the end. She said odd things. She thought Patrick and Heather were dead. She was convinced Ray had killed them, because they disappeared and were never heard from again. Well, not by Mum. I suppose this is good news then, that they're not buried under Ray's back patio.'

'There's a bright side,' said Paul. 'No one's going to make a chart-topping podcast about them and drive down the value of your house. Do you think Patrick knows he's your dad's child?'

'I've no idea. Maybe. Could be why he's back. Maybe he wants his inheritance.' She was joking, but it occurred to her that, in fact, that might well be why he was back.

'Would he be entitled to anything?'

Annie was suddenly irritated. 'I don't know, Paul. I'm not a lawyer. How would I know that?' There it was again: Paul expecting her to know things for him. Or to find out things if she didn't know. It had a name now, this constant effort expected of women to keep everything running, to keep all the plates spinning: the mental load. Jane had sent her a cartoon about it. It had shocked her to hear it named. Then she'd been angry that it had taken so long for it to be identified. Of course it had taken that long, though — the people who would benefit from it being identified were all too busy letting the hems down on school uniforms and finding library books and organising the car service and filling up party bags with plastic whistles.

Paul's eyes widened. 'Sorry. I didn't mean anything. You just know lots of things. I thought you might know that.'

'I do know lots of things. Lots of very useless things I wish I didn't know. I know your shirt size and your shoe size, even though I'm not your mother and never have been. I haven't even been your wife for nearly two decades. I know bloody Brian's shoe size. I know all our kids' birth weights. I know our grandchildren's birth weights. I know my parents' medications, still, and their dosages, even though they are dead.' She clenched her fists. 'I tried to convince my father to give this house straight to our kids for lots of reasons, but one was so that I would not have to think about it any more. I don't want to think about which bits are falling off and need sticking back on. I don't want to have to remember to shut fifty-six windows when it rains, and keep track of which ones need towels stuffed around the edges because they leak. I want to empty out some of the damn clutter in my head. I was hoping to make some space for other things. What I really do not need is this sort of complication in my life.' She gestured angrily towards the living room.

Paul sat down at the table and looked at his hands. 'No, I get that. I'll do some research. Or should we talk to him, Patrick, to see what he knows? He may not know about your dad. There might not be a problem.'

Annie sighed. Of course there would be a problem. Bloody secrets. Why did people think they were a good idea? They were never a good idea.

'Annie?' continued Paul tentatively. 'There's something else. I wanted to tell you first, but I think Brian's planning to make an announcement at lunch.'

'You're getting married?'

'Well, yes. We've decided to. I hope that's not, well, you know.'

She smiled ruefully. 'It's fine. It's actually wonderful. You two deserve to be married. I'm glad you can now.'

'You don't feel angry, or sad?'

'Oh Paul, who the fuck knows what I'm feeling? Your engagement, while great, is really the least of my concerns at the moment. Right now I have to figure out how to go back into the dining room, where someone who is apparently my brother is about to eat Kentucky Fried Chicken with us.'

'It's called KFC now.'

'Does that matter?'

'Not very much.'

Chapter 27

Diana came down from her room when lunch was served, but there was a shimmering veil of rage surrounding her, like highly flammable jet fuel fumes. This was not the Christmas dinner she had wanted. It was not even the Christmas dinner she had compromised on.

The others came through to the dining room carrying their Champagne glasses, which had all been refilled several times in the half hour they'd spent making small talk.

Annie was struggling to read the room. The shock of her realisation made her uncertain of her own reactions and unable to tell what other people's behaviour meant and whether any of it was connected to what she'd just discovered.

First there was Heather. Heather knew. She had to. Didn't she? Surely that was why she'd left Ray in the first place: either Ray realised she'd cheated on him and kicked her out, or she left before the baby grew up enough to look like his real father. But maybe she didn't know. Maybe she had been sleeping with Robert and Ray, and hadn't clocked the resemblance between her son and the neighbour she'd had an affair with. That was pretty unlikely. To Annie, the physical likeness between Robert and Patrick was obvious, too obvious to miss.

So Heather probably knew. But did Ray know? Annie looked at the old man. He hadn't said much since they'd arrived. His eyes were watery, and his skin was grey and taut. He was clearly not a well man, but it wouldn't be polite to ask what was wrong. Patrick filled a plate with food for him, and sat beside him at the table, but Ray wasn't eating much. Even lifting the fork looked like an effort.

Annie watched how Ray interacted with Heather in the hope it might provide a clue as to what he knew, but there was precious little to see. Heather paid no more attention to Ray than she did to Petula. In fact, Annie realised as lunch went on, Heather was doing a splendid job of talking about nothing but herself.

She had a tactic, Annie soon figured out, of asking a short question of someone else. They would answer, then politely ask her the same thing. That allowed her to launch into a long and meandering monologue, peppered with rhetorical questions, irrelevant sidebars and an irritating number of characters who were never properly introduced.

'London,' she was saying now to Brian. 'You've been there all this time?'

'Yes, for nearly forty years, give or take,' said Brian. 'Have you spent any time there?'

'Have I spent any time in London? Have I? Brian, darling, I have had more homes in London than you've had hot dinners. I've lived everywhere in London. North, South, the East End, the West End. All the ends. I lived on a canal boat with a very famous artist for a while — I won't name names but he's very, very collectable now — and with Cherry and Kath in a basement flat in Chalk Farm, and when Patrick was young we were in Hampstead Garden Suburb, lodging with Lynn and Graham. Remember Lynn and Graham — they were like grandparents to you, Patrick, do you remember?'

Patrick nodded but didn't say anything.

Heather went on, brandishing a chicken drumstick as if it were a laser pointer and they were a world map projected onto a screen. 'And of course we were in the countryside for a long while, various spots, and since Patrick grew up I've been all over the world, now that I don't need to be so tied down.'

'She sounds as tied down as smoke,' Annie heard Jack murmur to Molly.

Annie looked from Molly to Simon. They were behaving distinctly oddly around the neighbours, and had been all day. Simon had been strange about even inviting them. Had he spotted his grandfather's likeness in Patrick? It was possible, but not probable. In her experience, it was very hard to remember the young face of an old person, and her kids wouldn't have seen many pictures of their grandfather when he was young. There were a couple framed on the wall in the front hall, but no one ever seemed to stop and look at them.

Molly put down her knife and fork — she'd barely touched her lunch, Annie noted — and announced she needed to feed the baby, who was sleeping in her basket in the sunroom.

'Will you rejoin us for dessert?' Diana asked, with a tone of desperation.

'Probably not,' said Molly.

'Molly, love,' said Brian, nervously, 'just before you go, your dad and I have an announcement.'

Molly paused at the door and looked back. She yawned. 'You're getting married?'

'Ah, well, yes. That's what we were going to say. Paul and I are engaged, and we're going to be married.'

Naomi leaped up at once and hugged them both, while the others clapped and said hooray, haphazardly clinking glasses. When she sat back down, Annie saw her elder daughter, ever alert to other people's feelings, glance over at her, worrying how she would take the news. Annie hadn't even been looking at Brian or Paul, but was staring at Simon with her brow furrowed. When she realised she was being watched, she quickly switched her face back to neutral.

'We hoped we might be able to get married here, in the garden,' said Brian.

Annie tuned back in. 'Of course, how gorgeous. That would be perfect.'

Molly kissed her father and Brian and left.

The news of the engagement had surprisingly little impact on the meal. Jack and Patrick went on discussing Tibetan sand foxes — something about a documentary Patrick had worked on, in a remote area of northern India. Brian listened and contributed what he could by shoehorning in anecdotes about the two weeks he and Paul had once spent travelling from five-star-hotel to five-star-hotel in the south of that country. Several times he dropped in the word 'honeymoon', but it was as if their news had been a gold-medal-winning dive from the ten-metre platform, so small were the ripples it created.

Annie looked over at Heather, who had paused her monologue to concentrate on licking clean her chicken bones.

This was impossible, Annie thought. How was she supposed to know who knew what about whom and if they did know how they had found out, and how long they had known for and what they were planning to do with information they may or may not have? This felt like picking up an Agatha Christie novel halfway through. It was a murder mystery, and the victim was Annie's whole history.

She felt sick when she looked at the food on her plate, and ate a few mouthfuls only when she felt Diana's eyes on her. Instead she sipped her wine, an old shiraz that stripped her tongue and tasted of dust. A horrible heaviness was settling upon her, a sense that every decision she had made since she was a teenager had been based on incorrect information.

Her beloved dad had not been a good man. Her idol, her role model of what a man should be: it was all a lie. She had based her family on the model of the one she'd grown up in. Or the one she thought she'd grown up in.

The meal dragged on. Somehow Brian and Heather were getting on like a house on fire while everyone else made only polite conversation, and Annie wondered if the tension was as clear to the others. The children left the table to go play laser tag in the garden, and Diana went to the kitchen to get the dessert.

It occurred to Annie that because she had been focussing on her father's betrayal of her mother, and Heather's horrendous behaviour, she hadn't even begun to address the fact that she now had a brother. A little brother. He was sitting on the same side of the table as Annie, which was probably good, because if she had to look at him she thought she might explode. She cracked open that door a tiny bit but the rush of feelings that begin to fly out was too much and she slammed it shut again. She would deal with that some other time.

Her glass was empty and she reached for the nearest decanter, heavy cut crystal with a wide base and a pointlessly thin neck. You practically had to turn the thing upside down to get anything out. She poured another large glass of red and took a few gulps.

Diana returned and placed a plate of sliced stollen and more spiced biscuits on the table. Naomi presented Jean's crystal trifle bowl, filled with layers of what she announced was a vegan take on the classic, and started passing around bowls filled with enthusiastic helpings of whipped coconut cream, cherries and avocado cacao mousse.

Simon took one mouthful and pronounced it disgusting. 'Thank god it's vegan,' he told her. 'Can you imagine if an animal had suffered for us to eat something that tastes so completely horrible?' He was drunk.

Patrick tasted the trifle and smiled at Naomi. 'It's very nice.'

'Thank you.'

'He's a guest,' said Simon dismissively. 'You can't believe a guest. Guests lie. Trust me, it's objectively not very nice. In fact I would go so far as to say it's pretty yucky.' He made a show of washing the flavour from his mouth with wine.

That meanness, cloaked in attempted humour, seemed familiar. Her son was so like her father, Annie realised with a shock. She remembered occasionally rebuking her dad for small cruel remarks, and how he'd laugh them off. 'Oh, *she* doesn't mind,' he'd say affectionately of his victim, who, now that she thought about it, was often her mother.

'Simon,' she reprimanded him at the same time as Diana.

'*Simon*,' he mimicked them.

'Shall we put on some music?' suggested Brian.

'Oh yes,' said Simon loudly. 'Mum can play some of what she's been diddling around with on the piano lately, can't she? Can't you, Mum?'

They all looked at Annie.

'No, no,' she said. 'Let's put something on the record player. Or Spotify.'

'No, Mum,' Simon spoke louder. 'You play us something. It doesn't have to be new stuff. I like your old stuff better than your new stuff anyway.'

Molly came to the doorway, looking uncomfortable. 'Naomi,' she said with quiet urgency.

'What?' replied Simon, and as he turned his head his eyes followed with a lag. 'What do you want, Molly? We're choosing a set list. Mum's going to do a concert.' He was slurring.

'I just want to talk to Naomi for a second,' she said.

'Why's everything got to be a secret? There are too many secrets. Secrets are bad for families. If it's important, I think you should share it with the whole class.' He gestured expansively around the table, taking out two empty glasses.

Patrick reached out to right them, and Ray grabbed his arm and murmured something in a low voice. Patrick stood and started to help his father up from the table.

'For god's sake, Simon,' said Molly, her voice vibrating. 'I need to wee and your son has been in the upstairs bathroom for twenty minutes and Sunny has been in the downstairs one for the same length of time and they're both doing eternal poos and my pelvic floor frankly isn't up for this so I need someone to go evict one of them right bloody now.' She moved, panicked, from one foot to the other.

Naomi and Diana leaped to their feet and rushed towards the bathrooms, as Patrick, holding Ray's arm, slowly led him towards the hall.

'Oh no, no, no. Shit.' Molly's voice was desperate, and a dark stain appeared on her leggings.

'I'm sorry, I'm sorry,' said Ray, agitated, as the smell of his urine also filled the hallway.

Molly began to cry and she hobbled away towards the stairs, passing Felix on his way down. Naomi pulled Sunny from the downstairs bathroom, hurriedly saying, 'You can wash them in the kitchen, just move,' and Patrick ushered Ray in.

In the dining room Simon swung back on his chair, balancing it on two legs. 'Oh my god. Hands up if you have managed not to wet your pants at dinner this Christmas. I'd have had my money on Petula being the only one who did. Merry Pissmas!'

Heather's cackle rang out and together they roared with laughter.

'I like you,' said Simon. 'You're great fun. Isn't she fun? I can see why Pa liked you so much.'

'Simon.' Annie's voice was a warning. She'd been right: Simon had been behaving oddly. Somehow he knew.

'What? I'm just saying. Fun. She seems fun. I don't remember Granny being this fun. I'm just saying you can't blame Pa.'

'Blame him for what?' Brian asked.

'Simon, don't,' said Annie again.

Simon looked at his mother and squinted. 'Don't what? Don't bring up the whole Ether-hay and Ah-pay's affair-hay?' He chortled. 'Forgot Pig Latin doesn't work on words that begin with a vowel. They're the same, aren't they? I didn't know you knew about it, Mother dearest.'

Heather's eyes darted from Simon to Annie and back again.

'Oh yes,' Simon continued. 'We know, Heather. Or should I call you extra-marital-step-great-Aunt Heather. Or whatever you are.'

'Simon, please,' said Heather, her voice low and strained. 'Not here. Patrick doesn't know. I never told him.'

Simon spluttered. 'Patrick doesn't know? Jesus. What a debacle. You're going to have to tell him if you want him to contest the will, aren't you? Because *you* won't get any money from Pa's estate. He might, because he's Pa's son, but you won't. There's not a provision for mistresses in wills. Were you his mistress or was it a more casual thing?'

Annie stood. 'Simon, that is enough.'

'I don't think it really is enough, Mum. I don't. I think this needs to be brought out into the open because all this hiding stuff is bullshit. And how do you know, anyway? I bet you've always known, haven't you? You and Heather were friends. You would have known she was shagging your dad.'

She couldn't take any more. 'I found out my dad had slept with Heather two hours ago, Simon, when Patrick walked into the living room and I laid eyes on him for the first time ever and I realised he was my brother. Okay? Are you happy? He walked in looking exactly like my dead father. On Christmas Day. Can you imagine for one second what that feels like? My life has been based on a lie. My dad was my hero. I thought he was perfect. Every man I ever met I compared to him. And he was a cheat and a bastard.'

'Annie, I'm sorry,' said Heather. 'But please, please can we stop talking about it before they come back from the loo? I'll tell Patrick, I will, but I need to do it in my own time.'

'There's no need.' Patrick stood in the doorway.

Heather's face fell. 'Patrick, sweetheart —'

He cut her off. 'I've known for over twenty years and I couldn't care less. I'm taking Ray home now. He's not well. Thank you all for a lovely meal. Heather, don't come back next door.'

'But we need to talk, I have to explain.'

'You don't.' His voice was firm and cold. 'Goodbye.'

Heather stood abruptly. 'This,' she said, pointing at Patrick, 'this is why I couldn't stay. All this suburban *drama*. Who needs it?' She pushed past Ray and stormed down the hall and out the front door.

When they heard the door slam, Patrick took Ray's arm and together they walked out.

The front door clicked quietly closed. In the dining room everyone was silent.

Brian looked around and took a deep breath. 'I'm sorry, but what was all that about?'

'Yes,' said Naomi. 'What on earth is going on?'

'Simon?' prompted Annie. 'You were so keen to discuss it. Why don't you fill them in?'

The red wine wind had left Simon's sails. 'Well, um. There were these letters.'

'What letters?' asked Annie.

'In Pa's filing cabinet. Molly found them. They were from Heather. Love letters. They talked about how she and Pa were, you know, doing it. And that she got pregnant.'

'When did you find these letters?' Annie was astonished. 'Why didn't you tell me about them?'

'We didn't want to worry you.'

'Simon.' Annie's voice told him to try answering again, truthfully this time.

'Fine. We found them a couple of days after the funeral and we didn't say anything because we thought if you knew Patrick was Pa's son you might give him half of this house.'

'And you knew I had been encouraging Pa to leave the house straight to the three of you and if I had split it with Patrick you would have only received half as much money.' Annie shook her head. 'Unbelievable. Did it occur to you that maybe I had a right to know I had a brother?'

'It was Molly too. I didn't decide it by myself.' His voice was wheedling. He'd never liked getting into trouble. 'Don't just be angry at me.'

'I'm not angry at you, I'm disappointed.' The old line flew out of Annie's mouth before she could think. 'Actually, no, wait. I am angry. I am *both* angry and disappointed. That seems like very greedy, self-serving behaviour, Simon. Why? You have a job. You have money of your own. You have a house. Why do you need more? Always more and more?'

Simon looked down at his lap. 'I don't have all those things,' he mumbled. 'Not any more.'

'What?' replied Annie. 'Why not?'

Simon looked over at the doorway. Diana stood there, white-lipped.

'I lost my job,' he said quietly.

'You what? Simon, speak up,' Annie ordered.

'I lost my job, okay? They fired me and I lost all our money and we never owned our house in the first place otherwise I would have probably lost that too.' He was shouting now.

'How?' Annie asked simply.

Simon didn't speak.

'Simon, how did this happen?' Paul asked his son, coming over and putting his arm around his shoulder.

'Simon is addicted to gambling.' Diana spoke from the doorway, half in and half out of the room. She sounded tired. 'He plays online poker. Very badly. It got out of control, he spent our savings, then he borrowed some money from his employers. Without their permission. Which is another word for stealing. They fired him. It all happened in a very short time.'

The family sat, the silence heavy with shock.

Naomi pushed back her chair and went to Diana. She put her arm around her shoulder and hugged her. Uncharacteristically, Diana reached up and squeezed her sister-in-law's hand.

Tears were rolling down Simon's cheeks. 'I didn't want you to know.'

Annie went to his side and kneeled down on the carpet. 'Oh, Simo.' Hearing her pet name for him made him sob. She stood and wrapped her arms around him and he buried his face in her chest. 'You silly old duffer. It's all right. It'll be all right.' She looked at Diana, who had tears coursing down her cheeks too. Paul let go of Simon and went to comfort Diana too, wrapping his long arms around his daughter-in-law, who hadn't asked for any of this.

Brian stood and hastily assembled a stack of dirty dishes. Jack followed his lead and they left, past Diana, who watched her husband over his dad's shoulder.

The one candle still alight guttered and flickered, sending dripping wax down the silver and onto the tablecloth. Simon reached out and pressed his finger into the hot wax, wincing, as he cried in his mother's arms.

Chapter 28

That evening the sky was purple as the sun set on Christmas for another year. Naomi flattened the last of the wrapping paper into the recycling bin, and wheeled it down the right of way from the garage to the road. Tough blades of grass poked through the Besser bricks into the soles of her bare feet, but she liked the discomfort. As she wrestled the bin onto the nature strip, she looked over to see Patrick doing the same thing.

She waved at him, tentatively.

He waved back.

'I'd better stop flirting with you now, hadn't I?' she said with a grin. 'Now that I know you're my uncle.'

Patrick looked mortified. 'Flirting? What? Were you …?'

'Oh totally! I thought you were hot. I was fully flirting with you. It's actually a bit problematic that you didn't realise. Only from the point of view of my flirting technique — otherwise it's a good thing. Imagine if something had happened.'

'I knew we were related all along,' he reminded her. 'Nothing could have happened.'

'Oh yeah,' she conceded. 'I forgot you knew. We need a bloody spreadsheet of who knew what. I can't keep it straight. Anyway, the fact we're closely related sort of explains the sexual energy.'

'What?' Patrick was aghast.

'Not in an incesty way, well, not intentionally. But it's quite common for people to be attracted to people they're related to, when they don't know they're related. It's why if you use a sperm donor you should tell your kid, so they don't accidentally hook up with another child from the same sperm donor. Statistically it happens quite often. They mistake the genetic energy connection for sexual energy. Like I did.'

'Can you stop saying sexual energy?'

'Yeah, I can. I just don't want you to feel weird, or uncomfortable. There's a lot of new energy flowing around us all right now — people being born, people dying. It's natural that there will be sexual energy in that mix, and that's okay.'

'Yep,' he said. 'Gotcha.'

She smiled at him. 'You've entered our family in a really amazing way. We're very lucky. What you did for Molly? You literally welcomed your great-niece into the world. That's sacred, you know?' She took his forearm in her hand and squeezed it. 'We're all connected now.'

'We've been connected since my mum slept with your grandfather,' said Patrick, with more than a hint of bitterness. 'None of this is good, Naomi.'

'I don't think that's right,' she said, staring up at the sky. 'Good things come from less good things. Just like bad things come from good things. It's an unpredictable cycle, but there's always something positive. I used to think I fell for the wrong people, but now I think I fall for people who have something to teach me.' They stood in silence for a moment. 'You've taught me a person will get nowhere trying to crack onto their own uncle.' She burst into laughter.

'Oh my god, Naomi,' he said, shaking his head. 'Good night.'

'Night, Uncle Patrick.' She headed back towards the house, still chortling, then stopped and turned back to him, suddenly serious. 'And hey, Patrick? If Ray's worse in the night, if you need any help at all, please text me. I mean it.'

'I know you do,' he said. 'I will.'

* * *

When she finally finished the dishes from lunch and the meal that followed because Sunny and Felix were too young to understand that one meal counts for two on Christmas Day, Annie went out to the garden.

She needed to place all the startling revelations of the day out on the flagstones and examine them, turning them over and getting to know them like she had seen her grandchildren do with their gifts that morning. She hadn't been particularly pleased with the *Daisy Jones* present, but that shone like a beacon of thoughtfulness now, compared to what she'd been given at Christmas lunch.

Should she look at the new information in the order she'd received it, or in order of importance? Was her son's gambling addiction, corporate theft and bankruptcy more important than her father's infidelity and lifetime of deception? It was hard to say.

Both of those were too hard to look at yet, so she turned to the one fact that didn't turn her stomach. She had a brother. Patrick. Twenty years her junior, but still a brother.

Naomi had befriended him. That was nice. Unless she fancied him. That would be bad. But Annie was pretty sure they'd only met once or twice, for tea. They couldn't have swerved quite that fast into Jerry Springer territory. She hoped.

Patrick seemed interesting and funny and most of all kind. The way he looked after Ray warmed Annie's heart. She hoped she'd cared for her mum and dad with the same grace and love.

She thought she had. She had certainly tried not to resent it. Ray was dying, Naomi had told her after everyone left. He didn't have long. Annie could see that. Would Patrick keep Ray's house?

For a moment, Annie indulged in a daydream of living out her life there, with her brother next door. Maybe he would have a family too, and all their children and grandchildren could play and laugh together. They could take down the back fence to make one massive wonderful garden, the wildflowers elbowing their way in among the roses.

She could picture it so clearly, but even as she conjured it up in her imagination she felt the cold pull of dissatisfaction in her stomach. It wasn't what she wanted. She knew that for sure now.

There was no escaping the fact that she was always going to be a mother, eternally needed by three people in one way or another, but she knew now that if she stayed there, tending to their every need, she would not survive. They would eat her alive. The thought, as it sometimes did, sent guilt shooting through her like she'd touched an electric fence. But she held onto the thought this time. Guilt couldn't kill her. Neither would a desperate lack of creative fulfilment, which was the other alternative, but she knew which of the two she could more comfortably live with on a long-term basis.

This house had to be sold. Patrick was probably entitled to half, though she had no idea whether he would go so far as to sue her if she didn't offer it. That meant her children would each get significantly less. The thought didn't bother her. Much as she disliked the phrase, it was a very first-world problem to have. The money would still be enough to cover Molly and Jack's concrete cancer bill, with some over for their mortgage, and it would give Naomi a real start if she wanted to buy some land or a little cottage up north. Simon's share would be enough to pay back what he owed to his former employer, who had, according to Diana, extended some serious largesse to her light-fingered son in the form of not having him charged with theft if he paid them back and sought treatment. They weren't\going to give him his job back, of course, and he wouldn't be hired in that industry in Germany again.

Annie thought they'd probably stay in Australia. Poor Diana would be devastated. Ikea might offer transfers, so she would have that to investigate. And maybe Justin could help Simon get a job. She laughed to herself. That would be the icing on the cake of utter weirdness.

How would she tell Jane all that had happened at Christmas lunch? A phone call or text wouldn't do: her friend's face would be priceless. It would have to wait, though, because Jane and her husband, Alan, were off on a yacht with a couple she only ever referred to as 'Alan's horrible friends'. Jane had been dreading it: she didn't trust the sea and she claimed her only entertainment would be pissing off the horrible friends by wilfully failing to call any part of their vessel by its correct name.

The sound of Petula crying broke the silence, and drifted through the still evening air. Annie heard Jack soothing her in low, calming tones. There was no sound of Molly.

Molly had gone to bed after the unfortunate double bladder incident, which in hindsight was about the least upsetting part of Christmas lunch. Annie had looked in on her before coming outside, but she had the light off.

It occurred to Annie that her plans involved, essentially, trying to buy her freedom from her children. Molly was the only one she wasn't sure would be so easily paid off. Something was different in her now, and it worried Annie. Neither of them had mentioned the text message about childcare. Annie had been waiting to see if Molly would say something, but so far she hadn't. And the way she was constantly holding the baby made it seem like maybe having Annie look after Petula while Molly rushed back to work wasn't what she wanted any more.

* * *

On Boxing Day Annie woke to a gentle tapping on her door. The clouds of Christmas had cleared and sunlight streamed through the window.

'Come in.'

Paul pushed the door open and came in, carrying a tray with three steaming mugs. Behind him Brian had a plate of Vegemite on toast and sliced Christmas cake.

'Morning,' said Brian. 'Can we have brekkie in your bed?'

Annie smiled, rubbing sleep from her eyes. 'Yes, of course. We haven't done that for a while.' She yanked on her new fringe, which had an annoying habit of starting each day standing to attention, like it had woken suddenly from a nightmare. Still, for an impulse haircut executed by an unqualified hairdresser in a pub toilet, she wasn't regretting it half as much as she deserved to.

She tossed two pillows to the foot of the bed and Paul and Brian climbed in, propped the pillows against the footboard, and leaned back against them. Their legs lay alongside hers under the quilt, and they sat quietly, sipping their tea.

'So,' began Paul, in the manner of someone calling a meeting to order. 'Yesterday. Heather. Patrick. Simon. That was ... a lot.'

'That's putting it mildly,' said Annie.

'Are you all right?'

'I'm not sure.' She thought. 'No, I don't think I am. I know this sounds a bit dramatic, but I sort of feel like my whole life has been based on a lie. I thought my dad was a wonderful man. He and I were a team. You remember how much. I feel very stupid not to have seen what was going on. He must have been carrying on with Heather right under our noses.'

'We don't know that. Patrick wasn't born until a fair while after we moved to London,' Brian pointed out. 'Maybe Heather can tell you more.'

'I don't think I ever want to see or speak to Heather again. I don't care what she has to say, and, besides, I'm not sure I'd believe her.'

'What about those letters Simon found? They might shed some light on how it all went down.'

'I thought of that last night, but Simon threw them away. He says he was worried I'd find them.'

'Then why did he blab about it, if he didn't want you to know?'

Annie sighed heavily. 'Why does Simon do anything? Because he lacks self-control. You know that.'

Paul nodded. 'You're right. And about Simon, what are we going to do with him? *Is* there anything we can do?'

All night Annie had wondered how to help Simon, but now she thought about her son's behaviour since his return to Australia and anger surged through her. All he had done was hide and lie. He hadn't been helping his wife deal with the situation he had landed her in, and he hadn't even been helping around the house or spending any time with Felix.

'I don't know about you,' she said, 'but I'm not going to do anything. He's an adult. He got himself into this mess and he can get himself out.'

Paul frowned at her. 'Annie, gambling is an addiction. You wouldn't say that if he were addicted to drugs. You'd want to help him figure out how to get clean.'

'It's not the same. Gambling is a choice. Stealing from your employer is a choice.'

'It isn't a choice. It's the same. It's all addiction. The same chemicals in the brain work the same way whether you're addicted to heroin or porn or hearing people clap for you or playing cards online.'

She sighed. 'I know.' Then more angrily, 'I know. It's just so bloody stupid. How could he be so stupid? He's not a stupid person.'

There was a pause, and then Paul said, 'He is a bit stupid. And he's very greedy.'

Annie laughed so hard she snorted.

Brian looked disapprovingly at them. 'You shouldn't say things like that.'

'Why? It's true.' She was still laughing.

'You're far too nice to my children, darling,' added Paul, brushing off the crumbs that had scattered onto the bed from their toast as they'd laughed. 'But Annie and I can speak the truth. Simon is greedy and sometimes a bit stupid. Molly is as flighty as hell. They're both unbelievably self-involved, though who am I to talk.' He had the grace to look a bit shamefaced, then brightened. 'Naomi's all right, for a mad hippie. One out of three ain't bad, eh, Annie?'

'Not bad at all. If you wrote three songs and one was great, you'd be happy with that. Same goes for kids.'

'And for grandchildren?' asked Brian. 'All three of your kids now have one child each. Do you want them to have two more apiece, so you can guarantee a good one?'

'Simon can't afford more kids, Naomi's on her own, and I can't see her having another, and Molly's only just figuring out how to operate the one she has. I wonder if this'll be another generation of only children, like you, Annie.'

'Ah, but I'm not an only child, am I?' she pointed out. 'I have a little brother.'

'God, of course. And didn't he say that he already knew your dad was actually his dad too?' added Paul.

'Heather seemed to think he didn't know,' Annie said. 'I wonder how he found out.'

'Maybe the same way you did. Maybe he recognised the similarity between him and Robert, physically.'

'But he didn't grow up here. When would he even have seen my father?'

'That's a point. Are you going to talk to him today?'

Annie wasn't sure. What would she say?

'Probably,' she said. 'I guess there are some things we need to sort out.'

Paul patted her comfortingly on the leg, and began to gather up the plates and mugs. He and Brian both disentangled themselves from the bedclothes, stood up and made for the door.

'You'll be fine, Annie. He's lucky to have you as a sister.'

As they walked down the hall Brian began to whistle 'Home Is Where Your Heart Is'. Annie wanted to throw something at him.

Chapter 29

Annie was desperate to talk to Jane about everything that had unfolded on Christmas Day, but Jane was still off on the yacht and her phone kept going straight to voicemail. She wouldn't be back until New Year's Eve. That didn't matter, Annie told herself. She knew her friend well enough to figure out her advice in her absence. What would Jane do in this situation? Jane, she was pretty certain, would simply cross the right of way and knock on Ray's front door. Jane would get to the bottom of everything. Even so, it was almost lunchtime before Annie gathered the courage to go next door.

She wondered if it would be appropriate to take something with her. A gift of some sort. Her mother had never gone anywhere empty-handed. She would have taken a jar of homemade jam or some biscuits, especially if she'd had to go chat to a neighbour about something awkward. But Annie couldn't think of anything to offset the scale of the awkwardness of the conversation she was about to have. Maybe she should take over the entire spare kitchen from the garage.

Her knock on Ray's front door was answered almost immediately — by Naomi.

'Oh,' said Annie. 'Hello, love. I thought you were at home.'

'Ray's had a turn,' said Naomi. 'He's not going to be here in this realm for much longer. I told Patrick I would help him when they reached this point.'

'I'll go then,' said Annie, relieved to have the excuse.

'Don't go. I think Patrick would like to talk to you. He's waited a long time. Ray's asleep now, anyway, and I was just going to make some tea.'

'If you're sure?' Annie was reluctant.

'Please, Mum. Patrick's about to lose — in a corporeal sense, at least — the only real family he's ever known. You're his sister. Come be with him.'

Annie followed her daughter down the hall. Paul was right. There was nothing wrong with Naomi. Annie felt quietly proud of her compassionate, loving daughter. Her siblings could learn a lot from her.

Walking through the house, she was struck by how much lighter and more modern it felt than their place. It was a similar layout, and it hadn't been renovated either, but it was more sparsely furnished. She hadn't quite realised how crowded and cluttered it had been feeling next door, with so many of them living together, their possessions layered over the remnants of her parents' lives. It was like living in a compost heap.

Naomi led the way to the kitchen, where Patrick was sitting at the table, eating a bowl of porridge. He put his spoon down when Annie appeared, and stood up.

'Hi,' he said.

'Hello.' Annie didn't know what to do or say next. Hug him? Shake hands? What was the protocol for surprise brothers?

Naomi couldn't stand the tension. 'Oh, for god's sake, give him a hug, Mum. He's your brother.'

Annie launched herself at Patrick and hugged him tightly. He even felt like her father. Warmth spread through her body and her eyes stung with tears. Letting him go, she rubbed them away.

'Sorry,' she said. 'You're so like him.'

'Just to look at,' said Patrick, tensing up. 'Otherwise I'm more like Ray.'

'Of course, of course you are.' Annie was thrown. Of course he didn't want to be compared to Robert. 'When did you know about my dad?'

'When I was eighteen,' said Patrick. 'You know I was a baby when Heather dragged me off around the world. She wouldn't tell me who my father was. It was like she thought it was some exciting mystery. She never mentioned Ray, or this house, or even Sydney. I knew I was Australian, because I'd seen my passport. And your passport says where you were born, so as soon as I turned eighteen I applied for a copy of my birth certificate. It listed Ray as my dad. So I just looked him up in the phone book and came home to him as soon as I could afford a plane ticket.'

Naomi placed two cups of tea down on the table and pulled out a chair for Annie. 'Sit,' she ordered. 'You've got a lot to catch up on.'

Annie tried to put the years together in her head. 'So, you were eighteen, which means that was what, twenty-two years ago, is that right?' Where had she been? Had it been summer when he'd come back? Had she and the kids been there? Could they have met and uncovered all this twenty-two years ago? What would have happened to her parents if it had come out then?

'Yeah,' he said. 'I didn't stay long. A few weeks that first time. My dad was honest with me, straight away. He told me he wasn't my biological father. Robert was. He told me my mum and Robert had an affair.'

'I like that he was honest with you.'

'I liked that too,' said Patrick. 'I was very angry, though. Not at Ray, but at Heather and Robert. I wanted to go and confront your father. Ray convinced me not to. What would have been the point? Besides, he was so happy to have me back. I couldn't do it to him. He was my father. He'd been looking for us ever since Heather took me away. Biology doesn't mean anything to Ray. It's about who you love, that's what he says. And he loved me for the first two years of my life. "You were mine." That's what he said to me. "You were my little boy." He told me I would always be his boy, if that's what I wanted. It was the first time I ever felt loved. Because I can't imagine Heather was a particularly caring mother when I was a baby. She wasn't for the years I can remember her, so it stands to reason she wasn't much better when I was really little.'

Sadness and rage battled for supremacy inside Annie's head. Her heart broke for poor Ray, who loved his boy so much, and who'd missed out on his whole childhood because Heather was bored by suburban life.

'So when Ray told me the truth, he also told me that as far as he was concerned I had one father and that was him. I said we should at least tell Robert so he could choose to have me in his life or not, but Dad told me Robert already knew. He'd always known. Heather told him when she was pregnant and he didn't care. She asked him to leave his wife — your mum — but he wouldn't. I can see his reasoning, to be honest. Ray's always said your mum was nice, and Heather's a nightmare. Heather hung around for a couple more years, hoping he'd change his mind.'

'But he'd broken it off, dumped her, once she was pregnant?' Annie tried to reconcile this with her own memories of her father.

'More or less. Ray says he sort of strung Heather along. Kept seeing her, on and off. He played with people, your dad. He wasn't kind.'

Annie wanted to throw up. This had to be bullshit. None of it could be right. Not her father. But a horrible recognition was creeping over her, like mould blooming on her memories. It fit. This was true. She hadn't known this particular fact, but she had known her father. What she'd characterised to herself as his casual carelessness with people's feelings hadn't been casual. 'You missed a spot,' he'd always said to her mother. It had been deliberate cruelty. She'd just not wanted to see it because he'd always been good to her.

'Ray said he'd understand if I wanted to confront Robert. But he was right. What would have been the point?'

'I'm sorry,' said Annie, for want of anything better to say.

'You don't need to say that. You had no idea.'

Through the window they heard shouts. Paul was ordering people around in the back garden. Fragments drifted in: 'Right, that's the crease. There. No — there, where the chalk is. You're out if it gets caught on the full or you hit the cat.'

'What's going on?' asked Naomi. 'They're not doing the Boxing Day Test, are they?'

'Sounds like it,' said Annie. 'Why's he resurrecting that? It's been two decades.'

'He'll be doing it because of Pa.'

'I know,' said Annie. 'But he could choose not to. Quite apart from the fact that my dad was a complete arsehole to Paul for nearly twenty years, I mean, read the room: Dad hasn't come out of this week smelling of roses, has he? Perhaps a memorial cricket match in his honour is not the most appropriate choice.'

'Maybe he thinks you want something nice to commemorate him. It was always fun the way we did the Boxing Day Test when we were kids.'

'It wasn't, but I'm glad you remember it fondly. It was only ever fun for about ten minutes and then Pa would half-accuse someone of cheating or something and it would all end in tears.'

Patrick stood and drained his tea. He put his porridge bowl in the sink. 'I'm going back in to sit with Dad,' he said.

'Do you need anything?' Annie asked. 'Is he in pain?'

'No, he's got enough morphine,' said Patrick. 'The palliative care nurse said he could go any time. It seems a bit vague, doesn't it?'

'They told me that too,' said Annie. 'My dad only had a couple of days after they said that. But I know it varies enormously. Is the nurse coming back today?'

'If we need them,' he said. 'At the moment we don't.'

* * *

Annie walked back to the house and went straight to the piano. Outside, the Boxing Day Test raged on, but she ignored it. Once her fingertips were resting on the keys, she felt she could breathe again. How had she gone for so long without writing songs? Now she felt she couldn't stop. The words and the music were flowing like they had never done before. Truly, it was as if she'd picked off a scab and was bleeding songs.

Everything in her life suddenly felt like material, and memories she had closed the door on came drifting back like smoke. She remembered her mother, ten years earlier, beginning to lose herself to dementia, sitting in tears on the sofa one morning, her head in her hands, saying, 'It's like you never knew me' — repeating those words over and over again. Now Annie wrote it down, and sang the line to herself, repeating it like her mother had, until she found a melody to hold its hand, and phrases to put their arms around it.

In an hour the song was fully roughed out, and she moved on to working on 'Not the Girl Next Door'. When she'd started it a few days back, she'd been thinking about Heather, and who she might have become. Now, in the light of what she knew, the song shifted. She altered the perspective: now it was her mother looking at Heather next door. It became a jealous song, with undercurrents of dissatisfaction and rage, and it swept Annie away even as she created it. She didn't know how her mother had seen Heather, whether she had ever known about the affair, but Heather and Robert were such narcissistic, thoughtless people that Annie couldn't imagine they'd been very subtle. Her poor mother. Trapped there, her whole life devoted to her husband and her daughter, and her only creative outlet drawing secret pictures of the houses that made up her suburban prison. Annie felt like smashing something. Instead she kept playing.

Chapter 30

'Mum's having some sort of crisis all over the piano,' whispered Simon, sticking his head into the sunroom where Molly was changing Petula's nappy. 'I need to hide from her and the cricketing maniacs out the back.'

'Get a warrant,' she told him.

He came in anyway, and sat on her bed. 'Phew, open a window.'

'You open a window,' she replied, irritated. 'And leave Mum alone. She's had a pretty shit Christmas.'

'I had a shit Christmas too,' he protested. 'Can you imagine how I felt when everyone found out?'

'Like the thieving idiot you are, I imagine.' Molly snapped Petula's onesie back on and patted her tummy.

'Can I ... have a hold?' Simon asked, tentatively.

Molly paused for a second, then handed the baby to him. 'As long as you support her head. And don't pawn her.' She flopped down on the bed beside them. 'Seriously, though: gambling and stealing from work? What the hell, Simon?'

'I fucked up. Big time. Mum's just not talking about it, and Dad keeps trying to sit me down to have big chats. I think maybe she's told him he has to deal with me because she has to deal with you.'

'You're worse than me. I don't need them. I've got Jack.'

'Well, I've got Di.'

'I don't like your wife, as a general rule, but she's being way nicer to you about this than I would be.'

'Yeah. Honestly, I thought she might leave me when she found out.'

'I would have. For sure.'

'You're an arsehole, though.'

Molly nodded in agreement.

'Diana's angrier than she comes across,' he added. 'We haven't … you know … since it happened.'

'Ew, Simon.' Molly screwed up her face in disgust. 'Priorities.'

'It's only because I found a support group to go to here, and have actually been to it a few times, that she even agreed to come to Sydney, and I haven't been sure she won't piss off back with Felix at any moment. It's horrible, Molly. I've let them down so badly.'

Molly didn't say anything for a while. She pressed her finger into Petula's palm and watched her daughter's fingers instinctively curl over to grasp her.

Finally she spoke. 'What are you going to do?'

'Start again, I suppose. Here. Hopefully Mum will agree to sell up, and I can take my cash and buy a business or something.'

'Jesus, you haven't learned anything, have you? Get a normal job, Simon. Be a dogsbody for a while. Why would Mum give you a massive chunk of cash right now? That's like asking an alcoholic to hold your beer while you go to the loo.'

'But I've stopped. I'm not gambling any more.'

'Might that be because you have no money?'

'No, I've properly stopped. I promise.' He nuzzled Petula's cheek. 'This is a seriously nice baby, Moll.'

'She's all right.' Molly pulled her hand away and turned to fold a pile of her daughter's tiny clothes. Petula was getting through an astonishing number of outfits every day. 'We did the wrong thing, keeping the stuff about Pa and Heather a secret from Mum. That was the worst way she could have found out. And you shouldn't have destroyed the letters.'

Simon nodded. 'I feel bad about that. Do you think it's sent her off the deep end?' With his foot he nudged open the door and a swirl of violent piano chords swept in. He closed it again.

'I don't know. I don't have that passionate artist thing she has. It doesn't make sense to me. Naomi has it too, about her spiritual stuff and her aura-painting bullshit. Have you got something that makes you feel that, I don't know, consumed?'

'Poker makes me feel like that.'

'Oh. You're going to have to take up pottery or making sourdough or something instead now, aren't you?'

Suddenly the music stopped. They heard the piano lid slam shut, then their mother's footsteps racing up the stairs.

'Has she fully lost it?' asked Simon.

They listened again, but all was quiet. 'Maybe. It's got to have been a shock, finding out Pa was a filthy cheater.'

'Yeah, but it's not like she's the first person in the world that's happened to. Our father went off with a bloke and we didn't all lose our tiny minds.'

'Or did we?' Molly replied ruefully.

Footsteps came down the stairs again, and the door was pushed open. Annie stood there, a large cardboard box in her hands, her hair sweaty and dishevelled, her fringe sticking up.

'You need to see these,' she said, and dumped the box on the bed beside Simon.

'What's that?' asked Molly.

'Hopes and dreams. Dissatisfaction, repression, unfulfilled creative ambition.'

A daddy-long-legs crawled out of the box and ambled across the sheet.

'And spiders,' said Simon.

'It's not a joke,' Annie told him. 'I found these the other day. Look at them. Look.' She wrenched open the box and tossed a sketchbook to each of them. 'They were my mother's. She taught herself to draw houses. They're meticulous. Look, perfectly to scale. She had books on draughtsmanship, and grid paper, and for years — decades — she drew all these houses. Every house around here.'

'They're amazing,' said Simon. 'Really good.'

'She never showed them to anyone, as far as I know. She just drew and drew and hid them away because no one gave a shit. That isn't fair, and it isn't good for people. All my mother did was care for everyone else. For Dad, and me, and Paul, Brian, you guys. Her whole life. She even tried to help Heather. And no one — myself included — ever saw her, or actually looked at her as a person, or wondered if she had more to offer the world than free childcare and really good scones.'

Molly and Simon made sorrowful faces and too-bad sounds. Annie looked wildly at them.

'Sorry?' said Simon, uncertain what she wanted from him.

'I do not want that to happen to me,' she said quietly. 'I deserve a chance to be heard and seen, and I'm going to let myself have that chance.' She put the books back into the box, picked it up and walked out.

'That was dramatic,' said Simon, making his eyes wide and clutching at imaginary pearls around his neck. 'Is it The Change, do you reckon?'

'She went through menopause years ago, Simon.'

'Oh. Well, how was I meant to know? And if it's not that, then why's she behaving like this now?'

'You really don't understand humans, do you? She literally just said: she doesn't want to continue her role as a carer. She wants to do something more with her life.'

'What, you don't think she's seriously going to do anything with her music, do you? She's a hundred years old.'

'At least she knows what she wants. It's more than either of us can say.'

* * *

Ray's room was dim, the curtains drawn against the bright summer sun. Patrick offered to open them, but Ray preferred the darkness. It made sense, Patrick thought. Animals went to quiet dark places to die. They sought peace too.

'Howzat!' A shout from next door's cricket match broke the silence, and Ray's eyes flicked open. He looked lost, until his gaze found Patrick.

'I'm sorry, Dad. Are they being too loud? I can go ask them to keep it down.'

'No, don't leave me, Patty. Don't go play cricket with them.' He clutched Patrick's hand in confusion.

'It's all right, I'm not going anywhere.'

'Don't play with Robert. He cheats.'

'Robert's gone, Dad. He died.'

'Good,' said Ray, closing his eyes. 'He was awful.'

Outside, a child squealed with delight.

'I'll just call out and ask them to be a little bit quieter.' Patrick went to stand up.

'No, don't. I like to hear the kids. I missed you, Patrick,' he said, and tears seeped out from under his closed eyelids. 'I missed you all the time.'

'I know, Dad. I missed you too. But I'm here now.'

'Why did those kids next door behave so badly at Christmas?' Ray said. Patrick recognised this was one of his father's brief lucid periods and leaned closer. 'When they realised about you?'

'I think they're worried I'm going to claim half of Robert's house.'

Ray gave a tiny smile. 'Good heavens. What's that house worth? Two million? If someone said it'd cost you a million dollars to not get mixed up with those people, I reckon that'd be a bargain at twice the price. You don't need that house. You don't need that money. This house is yours. Always has been.'

'Thank you, Dad.'

'I've given those people enough,' Ray went on. 'I've spent forty years hating that man. What a waste. Hate's an expensive emotion. It takes more than you think. Don't give them any more of our time, Pat. Don't get mixed up in arguing about that place. Sell this house, take the money and walk away.'

'What if I want to stay? The neighbours aren't so shitty any more.'

'Do what you like, boyo. Just don't feel that you need to stay here on my account.' He coughed, and struggled for breath for a moment. Patrick gave him a sip of water from a cup with a straw.

'Heather,' said Ray.

'I know, she'll try to get your house. I won't let her, Dad.'

'Up to you. But make sure she's all right, Pat. She's your mum.'

'She's a viper,' said Patrick. 'She doesn't deserve anything.'

'She's still your mum.'

They sat in silence for a few minutes, listening to the cricket game, and the pedestal fan whirring and clicking in the corner.

'Patty,' said Ray suddenly. 'I want you to give them the flowers.'

'Who?'

'The boys next door. At Christmas they said they were getting married. The boys from the band.'

'Paul and Brian?'

'Yes. No one was listening but Brian said they wanted to get married in the garden. I want you to cut all my roses and give them to the boys for their wedding. Robert would have hated that so much.' He tried to laugh. 'I'd have liked to arrange them myself. Don't pick them until the night before, at the earliest. Morning of would be better. And you help them, Pat, with the arranging. I have a book about it, on the shelf in the living room. There are lots of good ideas in that. You help make Brian and Paul a beautiful wedding. There's nothing Robert would have liked less than a gay wedding in his precious garden, with flowers by yours truly.'

'That's a very sweet Fuck You, Dad.'

'Kill 'em with kindness, Patty.'

* * *

Simon went back to the cricket match and Molly stayed on her bed, stroking Petula's forehead as she fell asleep, which she somehow managed through the din of Annie thundering on the piano. Something had happened to her mother. Finding those drawings of Granny's had tipped her over the edge, and now she seemed like a stranger. A stranger with a fringe that had appeared out of nowhere while Molly was in the hospital. She'd never replied to Molly's text, with all the little duck emojis, the day she went into labour. Maybe she hadn't seen it, since Molly had followed it with scores of desperate *where are you* messages in the hours that followed.

She needed to ask again. She needed to know there would be some help, a little bit of relief from the relentlessness of this new life. It felt like her mother was drifting away, and Molly couldn't let her. Not now, when she needed her more than she ever had.

The music had stopped. Molly went out to the living room. Her mother was sitting on the piano stool, staring straight ahead.

'Mumma?' Molly hadn't called her that for years.

'Yes?'

'She's asleep.'

'Good.'

'Can we talk?'

Annie sighed. 'About me looking after Petula when you go back to work?'

'Or sooner?' Molly was close to tears. 'It's harder than I thought it would be. When I'm with her I can't stop thinking about all the things that could happen. I get so scared. It's only when she's with someone else that I feel okay. I feel like I can't breathe when she's with me.'

'That's normal,' said Annie. 'But it won't get easier by not being with her. I know you're tired, love, but, honestly, the best thing you can do is spend as much time with Petula as you can. Bond with her. Don't push her away.'

'I'm not pushing her away. I just need some help.'

'I'm happy to help, when I can, but I can't commit to what you say you need from me.'

The words hung in the air.

'Oh,' said Molly. She stood still. 'All right. Why? Are you going to be doing something else?'

'I'm going back to work.'

'What work?'

'Music.'

'You're going to be teaching again? Workshops like you used to do with Dad? That would be after school, wouldn't it? Could you help me with Petula during the day?'

'No,' said Annie. 'Not teaching music. Songwriting. Maybe performing.'

'Can't you do that on the weekends? It doesn't need to be full-time.'

'I *want* it to be full-time. I want to see what happens if I devote time and energy and focus to it. I've managed to finish quite a few songs lately, even with everyone here, and I want to see where it takes me. It might be nowhere, but it might be somewhere and I think I've earned the right to this time. I'm sorry.'

'I understand,' said Molly. 'You need to do your thing.'

'Maybe Dad can help. What if he stayed on for a bit after Brian goes home, and he does some days with Petula?'

Molly wrinkled her nose. 'I don't want Dad. I want you. I sort of don't know him.'

Annie swallowed a sigh of frustration. 'Then get to know him. He loves you just as much as I do. And wouldn't help from him be better than nothing?'

'Knowing and loving are different. But we don't need to go into it. It's fine. I'll be okay. I'll figure it out. I shouldn't have asked.'

'No, you were right to ask. I don't know how to answer you. I want to go away. I want to travel and live overseas for a bit. The last five years, here with my parents, they haven't been easy. I'm exhausted but at the same time I have all this energy I want to use. But I know I do owe you this help. My mother did it for me. I should do it for you.'

'But you don't want to.'

Annie looked her daughter in the eyes. 'No, I don't want to. And if you don't want Dad to do it, then … I don't have a solution.'

Molly looked away, past her mother to the piano. She stared for a moment, then rose. 'I should go move Petula to her basket. She's on the bed.'

'Molly, I'm sorry, I'm so sorry. I just want it to be my turn.'

'It's all right,' Molly said, and she walked away, closing the door quietly behind her.

Annie sat at the piano, and felt like she'd just abandoned her newborn in a basket on the steps of a church.

Chapter 31

When her phone beeped quietly, once, at six o'clock the next morning, Molly woke like a bomb had gone off. She sat bolt upright in bed, looking around wildly. Where was the baby? The room was still dark and she felt around in the bed for Petula, convinced she had fallen asleep while feeding, certain her baby was lost, tangled in the sheets, smothered to death. When she couldn't find her, Molly started to panic.

She shook Jack's shoulder. 'Jack, Jack. She's gone. I can't find her. Where is she? Jack?'

'Mmmm what?' Jack was groggy. He propped himself up on his elbows and looked into the bassinet. 'She's in her basket, Molly. She's fine.'

'What? Oh.' Molly saw the baby's calm sleeping face. 'I thought I'd lost her in the bed.'

'Nup,' said Jack, as he rolled over and went back to sleep.

Molly lay back down, her heart still racing. She reached for her phone and checked it. The beep had been from an app she'd installed the night before. It was supposed to give you little parenting tips and reminders at useful times of the day. After her mum had said she wasn't going to help with Petula, Molly had searched the internet for ways to become a proper mother. There were apps for everything. There had to be one to teach you maternal instincts. She had downloaded eight different apps.

This one — Mum-Ah, it was called — hadn't got off to a great start. The beep that had woken her was for the first reminder, which, despite the fact that Molly had informed the app that she had a five-day-old baby, was *Have you filled your child's cup today?*

What was that supposed to mean? Even read metaphorically, which presumably this was supposed to be, how were you meant to fill a newborn's cup? Molly clicked the link and was treated to six paragraphs telling her how children need their symbolic cups filled with love regularly or they would run low on emotional fuel. Apparently this could be achieved through eye contact or play. But although Petula stared hard when she was awake, Molly wasn't sure that what she could see in her baby's eyes was exactly love. It seemed more like Petula was waiting for something. What, though? What did she want?

Molly's heart wasn't slowing down. She tried some deep breaths, which only made her feel more panicky. The air wouldn't go all the way in. Something was blocking it. She sat up.

Outside. She needed to be outside. She'd been cooped up for days. But her legs were restless now, and even though every muscle in her still hurt from the birth, she rose and pulled on a pair of shorts and her sneakers. Her stomach was still so swollen, and when she bent to tie her laces it squished uncomfortably. It was probably there for good. In the bathroom she changed her pad for a fresh one. These revolting adhesive surfboards were such an indignity: when would the bleeding stop? How could this be normal?

Returning to the sunroom she paused a moment outside the door. Maybe she wouldn't go back in to Petula and Jack right away. Could she go for a walk on her own? All she wanted was to walk out the door — carrying nothing, pushing nothing — and just keep going until she felt better and left behind this heaviness and fear that had wrapped itself around her the day she left the hospital. But Petula would wake again soon and need to be fed. The only way to get out was to take her along.

Molly felt the heaviness grow tighter around her. Now she was trapped, forever. She could never again be herself. She was always part of Petula now too. Quietly she scooped up the baby and tiptoed out.

The pram was on the front verandah. She settled Petula into the bassinet attachment, and slowly, step-by-step, wheel-bounced the whole contraption down the front stairs.

The streets were so quiet. Everyone was away or sleeping off Boxing Day.

She trudged along, pushing the pram and doing her best not to think. But even that was too difficult. Ray's skeletal face kept floating into her mind. He looked so ill. Even her grandfather hadn't looked that bad just before he died. And that woman, Heather. Awful, so awful. Her mother had told her about Heather's life since she'd left Ray. She'd just wandered all over the world, doing exactly as she pleased, giving her kid no stability, or family, or home.

How selfish. How cruel. How entirely heartbreaking to realise that Molly would be judged like that now: the rules had changed. Everything else she had ever been was now eclipsed by her status as mother. 'I'm not ready for this,' she said aloud to the empty streets and the cool morning air. 'I chose wrong.'

* * *

'Morning, all,' said Jack as he wandered into the kitchen, his hair sticking up like a cockatoo's crest. He looked wrecked.

'Morning, love,' said Annie. 'Rough night?'

Jack frowned. 'I don't know. I think it might have been all right. I can't remember too many wake-ups. I might have actually had a few hours in a row.'

Naomi smiled at him. 'Sometimes that makes you feel worse. I remember that. Your body's just getting used to all the waking up and if it gets a taste of sleep you end up feeling like you've got a terrible hangover.'

'That's exactly how I feel,' he said. He reached for the coffee plunger and poured a mug full. 'What time is it?'

Annie checked her phone. 'Nine fifteen.'

'What?' exclaimed Jack. 'How is it so late?'

'Nice of Molly to let you have such a long lie-in,' said Annie.

'She's not here. I thought it was about seven. When did she go?'

'When did who go where?' Annie wasn't following.

'Molly. I just woke up and she and Petula weren't there. I assumed Molly had taken her out for a little walk. But you guys would have seen her go, right? How long have you been up?'

Annie thought. 'I was up at six thirty. I've been reading in the living room. She didn't come out of your room. She must've left before I got up.'

Jack looked concerned. 'Nearly three hours? She can't have been walking for that long.'

Annie looked at Jack. 'I'll give her a buzz. She's probably at the beach or the park, or she might have taken herself out for breakfast.'

She pressed Molly's number and waited.

A ringing sound came from the sunroom. Jack followed it and came back holding Molly's phone. 'She didn't take her phone. She never goes anywhere without her phone.'

'Love,' said Annie, swallowing her own concern to forestall Jack's panic. 'She hasn't slept for five days. She'd forget her head. Don't worry. She'll be back soon, I'm sure.'

Jack sat back down. 'Yeah, you're right. She's fine. They'll be back soon. Probably both asleep under a tree in that park by the beach.'

* * *

Everyone was sluggish that morning. The children were cranky after too much sugar over the preceding days, and even Naomi agreed it would be best for everyone if they were each given an iPad, a charger, some headphones and unrestricted screen time. The adults wanted to be left alone. Simon stayed up in his room: Diana came down at ten to report that he was refusing to get out of bed.

'Leave him there, Di,' advised Annie. 'Let's let the dust settle, and then we can start looking at ways to sort things out.'

Paul and Brian left for a long-planned lunch with friends in the Blue Mountains. At the last minute Annie had a brainwave, and sent Diana off with them. The poor girl deserved some time away from the house, her child, and most of all her wretchedly behaved layabout husband. Annie couldn't undo what Simon had done, but she felt driven to at least try to help Diana in some way.

Brian quietly asked Annie if she needed them at home, but she waved them off. There was so much to think about and sort through, but the days between Christmas and New Year were useless. They felt like a full bar rest in a song: you couldn't skip them but there was nothing to do while you sat through them. There was certainly nothing Paul and Brian could do for the moment. They might as well go drink wine with their friends, celebrate their engagement properly, and get some mileage out of the horror stories from Christmas.

Annie went back to bed. Her room was hot, but there were no bickering children in it, and she wanted to think.

Selling the house and giving the proceeds to the kids would buy her a ticket out of there: she'd never stop being their mum, and she'd always come back, but she wanted that to be because she chose family time, not because it was all she was allowed to have. Annie sat up and reached for her notebook on the bedside table. It was so full now. Song after song, scrawled quickly across its pages. For the first time in a long time, she felt proud. This was her future, on these pages.

She didn't have to look after her children any more. They could manage. Simon had to stick to therapy and Gamblers Anonymous, or whatever group he'd been sneaking off to. He had to rebuild his marriage and learn to act with integrity — illness or no illness. She was pretty sure it was fair enough she'd outsourced those discussions to Paul, seeing as she'd more than done her part on that front and he … hadn't.

Molly would figure out motherhood — everyone did, it wasn't rocket science. She kept reminding herself she wasn't the only option for helping, as Molly seemed to think. There was Jack's family, and now Simon and Diana looked like they were going to be around more. And *Paul*. Not to mention there were so many resources now that Annie and her peers had just done without — counsellors and helplines and books and websites and online forums and parents' groups and all the rest.

Besides, all Annie had said was that she wasn't going to nanny for Molly, not that she wasn't going to take her calls. She wasn't refusing to grandparent altogether. Of course she wanted to be part of Petula's life: just on her own terms, not so Molly and Jack escaped spending money on childcare.

Naomi would go back to leading her own life, her own way. And Annie could fly away.

She reached for her phone and googled *songwriting competitions*. That was the place to start. The search results were loading when there was a loud knock at the front door.

Who had forgotten their keys? Molly, probably. Annie didn't get up. There were at least four people downstairs, closer to the door than her. Let one of them get it.

She heard footsteps in the hall, the door opening, and voices floated up over the verandah and in through her open window. It wasn't Molly. The voices were those of two men. Then there was running on the stairs and a violent knocking on her bedroom door.

'Yes?'

The door burst open and Jack fell in. His face looked stricken.

'Jack?' said Annie. 'What is it? What's happened? Is it Molly?'

'Police.' He could hardly get the word out. 'There are police, Annie. Police. They have the baby.'

'Where's Molly?' Annie was off the bed now, her heart frozen, then painfully starting up at a gallop, and holding Jack's shoulders. 'Jack, where is Molly?'

Jack began to cry. 'They don't know. They found Petula in her pram at the playground at Mona Vale Beach.'

Annie felt her insides turn to ice now. Her knees trembled. She grabbed her phone and her shoes and they ran back downstairs.

In the living room, two uniformed police officers stood in front of the sofa. Annie looked wildly around. 'Where's the baby? Where's Petula?'

'It's all right,' said the older of the two. He was solid and grey-haired. 'The baby is fine. She's down at the station.'

'Why? What happened? *Why didn't you bring her here?*'

'Sorry, madam, and you would be …?'

'Her grandmother. The baby's grandmother. Annie Jones. My daughter Molly Jones is the baby's mother. Where is she?'

'Right. I'm Senior Sergeant Godwin and this is Constable Napier. What we know is that at around eight thirty this morning, your daughter and the baby were at the playground beside Mona Vale Beach. Your daughter approached another woman at the playground, who was there with her small children, and asked if she would keep an eye on the baby for a minute while your daughter went to the public toilet. The woman agreed, and your daughter left the playground. She didn't return. After about fifteen minutes the woman asked someone else in the playground to go check the toilets, but there was no sign of Molly. So she called the police. Your daughter's wallet and keys were in the bag under the pram, and a baby health book containing documents listing this as her current address. She doesn't appear to have taken anything with her. Except possibly her phone. We didn't find one in the pram.'

'It's here,' said Annie, her voice shaky. 'She didn't take her phone with her.' She took a deep shuddering breath. 'Oh god, someone's done something to her. Have you looked for her? Are there people out searching?'

'We've put out an alert for anyone matching her description. That's based on the description the witness at the park gave us. Have you got a recent photo of her?'

'A printed one?' asked Jack. 'No. No one has printed photos. Oh shit. Can you print one if we only have a digital picture?'

'Sure, mate, no worries at all,' said the younger officer. 'Got a snap on your phone there? Give it here and I'll email it through to our desk.'

'Do you have any idea why she would have gone all the way to Mona Vale? Does she have a car?'

'Yes, we have a car but it's outside, here in the street,' said Jack. 'Did she walk to Mona Vale? That would have taken hours.'

'If her car is here, then it's possible she walked. We don't know at this stage. Can you think of anyone who might have driven her? It's important that we find out whether she was alone or if there was anyone else involved.'

'Involved?' Annie was terrified now. 'Involved? In what?'

'Would this be out of character for Molly, to leave the baby?'

'Yes, absolutely,' said Annie immediately. She paused then, and thought. The baby was less than a week old. There hadn't been enough time to know what was in or out of character for Molly as a mother. Molly before having a baby wasn't *unreliable*, as such, but she did get distracted from what she was doing quite easily. But no one goes to the loo and forgets they have a baby. 'Yes,' she said again, firmly. 'It would be very out of character. Molly is a wonderful mother. Please, can we go and get the baby?'

Senior Sergeant Godwin ignored that. 'The baby is quite young: is there any chance that Molly might be suffering from any postnatal symptoms? You know, depression and that?'

'She's very tired,' said Annie, at the same time as Jack said, 'Yes.'

She turned to him. 'What do you mean, yes?'

'I mean, yes, she is probably suffering from postnatal depression,' said Jack angrily. 'She's had a shit of a time in the last week. She hasn't been sleeping. She's weird about the baby. Half the time she won't touch her and the other half she won't let anyone else go near her.'

'That's not postnatal depression,' said Annie. 'Is it? Isn't it far too soon for that? I mean, baby blues, sure. She's exhausted. And who can blame her?' She turned to the sergeant. 'The baby was born early, very quickly, and here at home. Molly was almost on her own. She doesn't know what's hit her.' But she remembered her daughter's words from the day before. How she couldn't breathe when she was with her baby. How she only felt the baby was safe with someone else.

The officers apparently read the expression on her face. Godwin said, 'Look, we'll circulate the photo, and see what we come up with. There's also a fair bit of CCTV in the area, and we can have a look at that. I think it's unlikely she's come to any harm at the hands of someone else. Having said that, I'm not unconcerned for her wellbeing. In these cases it's most likely she's just had a bit of a breakdown — that's not the word they use any more, but that's what it is — and taken herself off for a bit of a think. She's not trying to hide; she didn't harm the child. I reckon we'll spot her quite soon. Can you give us a list of her friends? Anyone she might go see? And we'll take her phone too. Does anyone know her passcode?'

'It's my birthday: 2902,' said Jack, his lip quivering as he handed over the phone.

'You're a leap year birthday?' the constable remarked, as people always did.

'Yeah,' sniffed Jack. 'I'm technically only seven.'

The sergeant patted him on the shoulder. 'We'll find her, mate.'

Annie stood, momentarily unsure what she needed to do next. Call Paul, she thought. Tell him and Brian and Diana to turn the car around and get back to Sydney immediately. And collect

Petula. Take nappies and, what, formula she supposed, down to the station to collect her abandoned granddaughter.

'I'm coming with you,' Annie told the sergeant. 'I'll come get Petula.' She followed him out the door, the sergeant's mention of Molly not having harmed the baby ringing in her ears.

Chapter 32

Molly sat on the beach and stared at the waves. They didn't mind doing the same thing over and over and over forever. Must be nice to be a non-sentient body of water, governed only by the weather and the tides.

How long had it been since she left Petula? Two, maybe three hours, she figured, judging by how much her breasts were starting to hurt. That woman with the little girls would have called the police by now. She'd be thinking Molly was a nutcase. And she'd be right. Who leaves a newborn alone in a playground and walks away? Molly wondered idly if they would send her to prison. Child negligence. That was a crime, surely. Or maybe they'd just lock her up in a mental hospital. Either would be okay. At least she'd be able to sleep. She wouldn't have to figure out what job to do, or how to lead a meaningful life, raising a child and setting a good example for her. They might keep her there forever.

Molly tried to picture what Petula's life would be like without a mother. Her mum would help Jack. She'd have to. Jack would probably stay in Baskerville Road, and maybe Naomi would stay too. Naomi would be a good proxy parent. Better to have a loving aunt than a useless mother.

But they mightn't keep her in a mental hospital forever. They'd let her out eventually. Would she be able to start a new life? No, they'd send her back to her family. They don't give insane mothers new identities because they've decided they don't really want a kid. They give them pills to make them forget they're unhappy, and they try to teach them how to pretend to be better parents. That's what they'd do if she went back. She'd be *given help*.

Was there enough help in the world to fix this, though? Was there a drug she could take to make her stop feeling that this burden was too great and it was all a terrible mistake? Petula deserved better. No one should have to grow up with a mother who regretted having them.

Molly stretched her legs out into the sand. They ached. She'd walked such a long way. She was deeply unfit. An unfit mother in every sense. Now she was so far from home she couldn't even say which beach this was. They all looked the same along here. Huge pine trees, a surf lifesaving club, a fenced playground with primary-coloured plastic climbing frames over squashy soft-fall ground cover. She'd sat for ages that morning in the one where she'd left Petula. It was early but there had been other people. All parents. They'd looked so tired.

She'd wanted to ask them if it was as bad as she feared. But she knew they would lie. You couldn't trust anyone to tell you the truth about having a baby, apparently. It was a huge conspiracy designed to entrap women, and once trapped every last one of them became complicit.

When she was little Simon used to dive straight into swimming pools and then tell her it was warm. 'Nah!' he'd shout. 'It's so nice. It's not cold at all. Come in, Moll!' She'd invariably leap in, only to have the breath knocked out of her by the chill. Cold-pooling someone, they had dubbed it. That's what this felt like. The whole world had cold-pooled her into motherhood.

The tide was coming in. She knew she should get up and shift back on the sand but she couldn't bring herself to move. She wondered where Petula was now. At the thought of her baby, her breasts began to leak. She looked down and saw the darkness spreading across her chest and down. She wasn't even in charge of her own body any more. She'd been hacked.

She watched the waves break, each time the water rolling closer and closer until the foam was splashing onto her sneakers. There still weren't many people on the beach. If she sat there and did nothing — didn't resist, didn't move — would the water pull her out to sea? Maybe. There wasn't much swell, but if she went limp and didn't fight it, she might eventually be dragged out of her depth. Or her mouth would fill with water, then her lungs.

It was funny. She didn't feel suicidal. Well, she didn't think she did. Having never been suicidal she had nothing to compare it with. She didn't actively want to die. She just massively couldn't be bothered. She didn't mind what happened next. She'd like to pause everything, indefinitely. But that was the problem with death: it wasn't indefinite. Would some sort of survival instinct kick in if her life were truly in danger? If someone appeared right now and tried to remove her from the encroaching waves, would she fight them and run into the sea? No, she wouldn't. It would be too embarrassing and, besides, she felt too weak to fight anyone.

The fact she was having such thoughts probably meant she wasn't suicidal. She didn't know what to make of that. At least being suicidal was something. It was a decision. She didn't know what she would do next.

Go home, probably. Home to start her life properly as a mother. She'd take a deep breath and probably a pill and get on with it. She'd put off making a decision. Maybe one day she would, but not today. She'd have to decide soon, though, before Petula was old enough to remember her and miss her.

Molly heard movement and someone sat down on the sand next to her. She looked over. It took her a few moments to place him. 'Justin Schoolbags?'

The man snorted. 'That wasn't actually me — you do realise that?'

'Yes, it was.'

'No, really it wasn't. It was Zac Long. He shat in my bag and told everyone it was me. He was a prick to me all the way through high school, but that really was his piece de resistance.'

'Huh,' said Molly. 'Well, you live and learn.'

They sat and watched the sea.

Justin finally spoke. 'You all right, Molly? Your family are pretty worried.'

Molly looked at him, confused. 'What? How do you know?'

'I'm friends with your mum. She told me they didn't know where you were. The police are looking for you. Jack and Simon are out driving up and down every street, searching.'

'Yeah, I figured they would be. Is the baby okay?'

'She's fine. She's back home with your mum.'

'I knew she'd be all right. I knew that woman in the park would do the right thing. She seemed like a proper mother.'

'What's a proper mother?'

'A mother who actually wants to be a mother. Someone who carries Band-Aids in her handbag. And hand sanitiser. Sultanas.'

'Is that you?'

'No.'

A man appeared with two identical small children covered neck to ankle in neon sun protective clothing. They wore little legionnaire's caps and each carried a plastic bucket and spade. They stumbled their way towards the water, their father righting them each time they fell over, every few steps.

'At least you don't have twins,' said Justin.

'Small mercy,' she agreed.

'Shall I take you home?' he asked.

Molly shook her head.

'Would you like to use my phone? Give them a call?'

Another shake.

'Okay, but I'm going to text them to say you're all right.'

She shrugged. 'All right's putting it a bit strongly.'

'Yeah,' he said. 'But that's what people say.'

Chapter 33

Just after lunchtime, Molly let Justin drive her to Baskerville Road. Her aching chest led her back like an inbuilt homing system. She supposed she could express the milk but she was too tired to figure out the logistics, find a bathroom. It was just easier to go back to the baby. At least for now.

When she walked in through the front door, the house was surprisingly quiet. Everyone must have decided to play it cool.

Jack appeared in the hallway. He wrapped her in his arms and held her so tightly it hurt, but she didn't say anything. It was one of those angry hugs people give you when they want to punish you for scaring them. She hadn't had a hug like that since she was very small. She remembered something about running across a car park. Her non-smacking mother had hugged her so hard Molly thought she might break.

'I'm sorry,' she said.

'I thought you'd done something stupid,' he said into her hair.

The old Sinatra song began to weave through her head. Odd how, when everyone knew 'something stupid' was code for suicide, that song was still re-recorded and released every few years. All *that* 'something stupid' meant was telling someone you loved them too early in a relationship. Those stakes were a fair bit lower than in the current usage.

'No. I just needed to think.'

'What about?'

'I think I've made a mistake.'

'Sweetheart, Petula isn't a mistake. I think … Moll, you might have postnatal depression.'

Which is a term invented for people who realise they have made a mistake in having a baby, thought Molly, because it's not something anyone is allowed to admit to. But she didn't argue.

'Would you like to have a shower, or a sleep?' Jack had released her from his grip and now didn't seem to know what to do with her. He was looking at her like she was a bomb with six red wires.

'I need to feed Petula,' she said. 'My boobs are about to explode.'

'She's had a bottle,' he said nervously. 'I'm sorry: she was hungry. We didn't know what to do. I know you wanted to exclusively breastfeed her …'

'It's all right,' she said, patting his arm as she passed by. She was glad the baby hadn't gone hungry, and she realised she didn't feel strongly one way or the other about whether her baby had breastmilk or formula from a bottle. Only proper mothers had opinions about that.

* * *

Annie hovered outside the living room door while Jack settled Molly on the sofa with Petula and a bottle of water. When he came out to the hall she gave him a querying look.

'Go on in,' he said, and held the door open for her.

Annie sat on the sofa beside her daughter and watched as the baby, her eyes still closed, gulped down the milk. 'She seems happy to have you back.'

Molly didn't answer.

'Moll, I'm so glad you're okay.' Annie's voice was thick with tears. 'I'm so glad you …' She couldn't finish the sentence.

'I'm not suicidal, Mum,' Molly told her firmly. 'I wasn't going to kill myself. I didn't know what to do, but I wasn't going to do that. I'm just not going to be any good at this. And this part is really relatively easy. I mean, I'm tired, and I don't know what I'm doing with her most of the time, but it only gets harder after this. I can see that. I'm not going to be able to deal with it.'

'No, Molly, it gets better, so much better. This is the hard part. The sleeplessness, it's a killer.'

'How can you say that it won't get harder? The sleep deprivation's the easy part,' said Molly. 'At least now I'm awake to watch her. The hard part will be when Petula learns to roll over, and sit up, and then she'll walk and talk and go to school. That's when things can happen. What if she gets away from me in a car park and she's run over? What if I look away from her in the bath and she drowns? What if she chokes on a grape? What if someone abducts her? What if someone drives into the side of our car and she gets a head injury, and never recovers? What if she gets bullied? What if one day I say I feel fat and then she gets an eating disorder? What if she has gender identity issues and I deal with it wrong? What if she ever finds out I went mad and left her in a playground? And what if I don't start enjoying this more? What if I just plod along, hating my life, forever? What if I do nothing but be her mother? What if this feeling never goes away and I always regret having her? And what if she finds out I regret having her?'

'She won't. You won't ever let her know that, even if you continue to feel it, which I am positive you won't.'

'We knew it.'

Annie went cold. 'Knew what?'

'That we fucked up your life, and you regretted having us.'

'You did not fuck up my life,' Annie whispered. 'And anyway, you had no idea until very recently that I was unhappy about any of my life. None of you even remembered I had a career that I gave up when I had children.'

Molly went quiet for a moment. 'Well, you've reminded us now, haven't you? And now we know your career went to shit because you had kids. You put it on hold and then never got it back. I know you regret that. You regret us.'

Annie started to say that wasn't true, but she paused. Was it true? It was a bit true. Lying to Molly wasn't going to help. She blinked hard, trying to stem her tears. 'I regret not trying harder,' she said. 'I look back now and I think I should have tried harder to juggle my music career and being your mother. I don't know if it would have worked. Unfortunately I wanted to be a pop star, and that's a job that doesn't coexist easily with parenting, or at least it didn't. That wasn't your fault. Or mine. It's just what happened. I should have kept writing songs, though. There were things I could have done. I could have written for other people. Plenty of songwriters have great careers writing for other musicians. I think I just threw a very long hissy fit because I couldn't do the job exactly how I'd envisaged it when I was seventeen. Not very sensible, eh? So yes, I regret how I let my dream go, but I never regretted having you and Naomi and Simon.'

'Never?'

'Well, to be honest, at lunch on Christmas Day I did somewhat regret having Simon,' Annie admitted. 'But only for a few minutes.'

Molly smiled.

Annie stroked Petula's head. 'Just don't do nothing. Motherhood asks a lot of you, Moll, but you don't have to give it absolutely everything. It's better for everyone if you don't. Never forget that you are a person before you are a mother and your child has two parents. Being a mother can be a glorious experience, but it can't be everything in your life and it's not fair to ask that of it.'

Molly looked at her mother, her big eyes bright with fear. 'But, Mum, I don't know what else to do. I don't want to tidy people's drawers any more, but I haven't got a passion like you do. A talent. What's my version of your music?'

'You'll find it, darling. It might take you longer, but there will be something you want to do, that drives you and obsesses you. You're so creative. You've always had that. Molly, you can do anything you want: you can sing, you can play music, you can draw, you can write, you can dance.'

'Those things make people demented and miserable,' Molly observed. 'Things can be worth doing even if they're not creative.'

'Of course they can; I never said they couldn't.'

'Yeah, but it's what you think.'

Annie stared at Molly. This child, her last baby, was the sharpest person she'd ever known. She saw through everything and everyone. It was alarming to realise that for twenty-seven years Molly had been watching and observing everything she did. She was correct. Annie did believe creative work was the most important work. But that was normal and right. The whole world was set up to privilege — if not always financially reward — creative work.

'I do think art is special,' she admitted. 'Art is extraordinary. It's what makes us human.'

'No,' said Molly. 'Our brains are what make us human. Language, morality, figuring out how to make fire — that makes us human. Art is icing. And making a living from art — being famous for your art — that's more than icing. That's those completely unnecessary icing roses people make. Or, like, I don't know, fondant Winnie the Pooh figurines.'

Petula was asleep now, Molly's nipple still in her mouth. Her face was relaxed and she snored lightly. Annie and Molly stared at her.

'I once made you a birthday cake with six fondant My Little Ponies on it,' said Annie. 'It took me days.'

'I remember it. Thank you. It was a work of art. No one wanted to eat it.'

'I did lots of that sort of thing. I must have been channelling my creative energy, instead of putting it into my music.'

'You see, we did fuck up your career.'

Annie sighed. 'I just didn't try hard enough.'

'You wanted to be famous, and we buggered up that plan.'

'It wasn't about being famous — it was about the music,' said Annie. 'It was about sharing and communicating what I created with the world.'

Molly raised one eyebrow. 'That's what being famous is. And that's okay. It's all right to have wanted that. But it doesn't mean that wanting to do something that isn't about fame isn't important and valid too.'

'No, of course, you're right.'

Molly tucked her breast back into her bra and pulled her T-shirt back down. Gently she shifted the baby to rest on her thighs. They both stared at Petula, splayed like a starfish, her chest rising and falling.

'What if I'm like Heather?' asked Molly. 'How do you know I won't do what she did, and just be completely selfish, live my life only for myself, and not care how that impacts my kid?'

'Because I know you, Molly, and I know you won't do that. You're a loving person. You're also not usually an anxious person, and feeling like this is freaking you out. But it will be all right. You'll figure out what else you want to do besides mothering. There will be something. There might be lots of things. That's okay too.'

'Will you help me?'

'Figure out what to do? Of course I will. Something will come along that grabs you and gives you purpose.'

'No, will you help me with Petula? Please, will you help me look after her, so I don't lose myself totally and never figure out what else there is for me. Even just a day a week or something? I'm sure you can still do your music too. And not all the time — you can travel as well.'

Annie's pause was short, but it was long enough for Molly.

'Never mind,' she said. 'That wasn't fair. I shouldn't have asked again. You already said no.'

Chapter 34

Finding psychiatric care for a not-quite-emergency patient on the twenty-seventh of December wasn't easy. Annie thought Molly seemed fine, more or less, but she supposed that someone who was actually fine wouldn't have left her tiny baby in the care of a complete stranger, gone wandering up the coast, and been found on the water's edge near an incoming tide.

That afternoon, Brian, Paul and Annie sat at the kitchen table, armed with their mobile phones and laptops, and tried to figure out what to do. The police had advised them to take her to the emergency department of their local hospital for assessment, but that seemed a bit over the top. The ED was going to be full of people having festive breakdowns or nursing injuries inflicted by family members in eggnog-fuelled rages. They didn't think it was a good idea to take Molly and the baby into an environment like that. Annie thought that if they could just stay at home, take care of the baby a bit more, and let her get some sleep, either Molly would be all right in a couple of days or they could find a proper counsellor for her once all the public holidays were done.

They were talking each other into that plan when Diana came in from the backyard, where she had been assembling a totem tennis set Santa had brought so Sunny and Felix could bond by taking turns to hit each other in the face with a tethered tennis ball or hard plastic racquet.

'Have you found a doctor for Molly?' she demanded.

'We think we'll leave it for a few days,' Annie said. 'It's going to do more harm than good, taking her in to the hospital at this time of year.'

'That is the wrong decision,' Diana told them bluntly. 'A mistake.'

'She just needs some sleep.'

'No.' Diana was adamant. 'You don't know that. You are not qualified to make that judgement. Is it worth risking the safety of your daughter and granddaughter?'

'Di,' said Paul jovially, 'she's not psychotic.'

'She needs to see a doctor, Paul,' said Diana. She glared at them each in turn.

'You're probably right,' muttered Paul.

Jack came in, carrying Petula. He closed the door behind him and sat down. 'Moll's asleep.'

'Jack, the police said we should take her to be assessed by a doctor,' Paul began.

'Absolutely,' said Jack. 'As soon as she wakes up we'll go down to the ED.'

'Do you think that's the best idea?' asked Annie. 'Could we wait for her GP to open again? Or even until her hormones level out? Maybe it's the baby blues.'

Jack looked at her, aghast. 'Baby blues is crying when you can't do up the poppers on one of those bloody Wondersuits. Baby blues is not disappearing and abandoning your kid. I can't believe you don't think she needs to see a doctor immediately. It's not like I'm asking you to take her. I'll do it. You just don't want there to be anything wrong with her because it would be inconvenient for you.'

Suddenly Annie was shouting. 'It's not *inconvenient* for me. It's terribly shit and sad and I don't want this to be happening to

Molly. And I realise this makes me the most selfish person alive, but I just want my kids to be well, and safe, and able to take care of themselves for once, because it is time for me to have a fucking break from all this —' she flailed around for the word '— *caring.*' She slammed both hands on the table, rattling the teacups in their saucers. 'All this goddamn *caring.* Why can't they look after themselves? When will they let me go? Jesus, I tried so hard to teach them to be resilient and to stand on their own feet and still they need me. Always.' Tears were coursing down her face.

Finally Diana spoke. 'Annie. You're her mother. That's forever. She'll always need you. Just like Simon will always need you, and Naomi. You're the adult.'

'*I'm* Molly's adult,' Jack interjected. 'It's me now.'

Annie paused and looked at him, frowning. 'Yes, of course, Jack, but I'm still her mother.'

'And Paul is still her father,' he said. 'But I'm her husband and I love her. If you don't want to care about Molly any more, she has me.'

'I didn't say I didn't want to care about her,' said Annie, shamefaced.

'You did.'

'Well, I didn't mean that, exactly. I meant care *for* her.'

'If you want out, if you want to leave Molly to me, then you can,' Jack said, looking her straight in the eyes. 'I've got this.'

Annie held her breath. Jack was offering her an open door. Could she take this chance? Of course not.

'I'd never do that. I'll be here for her. For you both.' Annie slumped back in her chair. She was beaten.

* * *

Paul and Jack took Molly to the hospital that afternoon. When they drove off, Annie went up to her room. She sat at her mother's dressing table and looked at her face in the mirror. Dust motes floated through the air, catching the light as they fell. She looked old and sad. She looked like her mother.

She'd been kidding herself. Her songs were good, but the timing was wrong. Two thirds of her children were not very well. She could not, in good conscience, turn away from them now. She had already had years in which she could have forged on with her music. She should have been doing it all along. Why couldn't she marry the two things? Focus on music *and* her family? Women were meant to be able to multi-task. Why did she have such a one-track mind?

She needed to let go of the music. She'd missed the boat. That ship had sailed. How many more nautical metaphors were there for failure? It was time to ignore the new songs in her head. It would be like stopping breastfeeding. If she stopped letting the songs out, more would stop taking their place. They'd dry up eventually.

At stake now were the futures of Molly's and Simon's families. They had fallen and it was Annie's job to help them up, just as much as it had been when they'd stumbled over their feet as toddlers and come to her to blow the sting from their skinned palms and knees. Jack had said he didn't need her to, but she knew he didn't mean that.

She would stay there, with Molly and Jack. Petula was a gorgeous little thing, and Annie should consider it an honour to be allowed to help with her. It's what lots of people loved doing, minding a grandchild a couple of days a week. Molly desperately needed that help. She would be all right, Annie was fairly sure of that, but this time, this transition from not being a mother to being a mother was challenging, and she could help Molly through it. She owed it to her, after what she had done to her own mother.

Perhaps Simon, Diana and Felix would stay nearby. It would be good to have more family around. Wasn't that what people were always talking about? How wonderful multi-generational living was? Well, that's what they would do. And it would work.

Jane would yell at her when she found out. She would be very disappointed in Annie's lack of backbone. But it wasn't like that. She would explain to Jane how it was actually going to take more backbone to follow this course, not less. This was the road she didn't want to take.

Besides, probably no one wanted Annie's songs. Briefly it crossed her mind that she could keep writing and singing and playing, just for herself, but she dismissed the idea. That would be too painful. She might even go so far as to get rid of the piano. Make a clean break.

A furious disappointment burned inside her. That wasn't helping matters and would need to go. She'd have to figure out some way to extinguish it. Yoga, probably. That must be why women her age became so deeply obsessed with yoga: they needed it to calm their tortured souls, which smouldered with the unfairness of their lives. It was worth a try.

* * *

Late that night, Jack and Paul brought Molly home, armed with a diagnosis of postnatal depression, a prescription for antidepressants, and the number of a psychologist to call in the new year. She also had gained the perspective that only comes from sitting in the waiting room of a public hospital around

Christmas time. She had clutched Petula tightly to her chest as she watched a man having a psychotic episode being wrestled to the floor by two security guards, and she'd looked on while her father had helped an old woman up to the window to present her Medicare card. The woman was alone, and suffering from an ulcerated leg so disgusting Molly couldn't imagine it wouldn't be amputated by the day's end.

* * *

After Molly went to bed, Jack and Paul joined Annie and Brian at the kitchen table, finishing a game of Monopoly they'd started at five o'clock with Sunny and Felix. The children had long since gone to bed, but Annie and Brian had played on, trying to make the game last as long as they could by lending each other money, forgiving debts, and generally behaving in a way that was entirely contrary to the spirit of the game.

'Have the others all turned in?' asked Paul, yawning.

'Naomi's next door with Ray and Patrick, and Simon and Diana are up in their room,' said Brian. 'We invited Simon to play Monopoly with us but he said he wouldn't unless he could be the banker.'

'You're joking.' Paul was aghast.

Brian cracked up. 'Of course I am. Sorry. Too soon for embezzlement jokes?'

'A bit.' Annie was weary. She felt like she hadn't been alone for years. 'Jack,' she said, 'how's Molly feeling?'

'A little bit better, I think. The doctor at the hospital was great. She took her seriously but also made her realise this is very common, and treatable. And we did the right thing by catching it early. Apparently this can slip under the radar really easily. People just soldier on, but they're actually quite sick. So in a way, it's kind of good that Moll fully cracked it and left Petula. We might not have realised otherwise.'

It was a sobering thought. There were ten other people in the house and none of them might have noticed Molly was ill. Not even her own mother, Annie thought, feeling the same heat around her throat that she remembered from the worst months of menopause.

'Yeah, well, it's pretty competitive around here to get your woes noticed. It's got to be high-level drama to register on our family scale right now,' said Paul.

Annie looked up. 'I'm sorry your engagement got completely ignored the other day.'

Brian smiled ruefully. 'It wasn't the best time to have announced it. I feel pretty silly. I didn't know all that Patrick stuff was happening. Or the Simon stuff, obviously.'

'Have you set a date?'

Brian exchanged glances with Paul. 'We sort of hoped we might do it before we go back to London. We only want a small wedding. Do you think … we might be able to do it here, in the backyard?'

Annie vaguely remembered him asking her this on Christmas Day, but the request had been swamped in the breaking waves of revelations about Simon and Patrick. Now she considered it. Her ex-husband marrying her oldest friend in the garden of her parents' home. Her father would have absolutely hated the idea. 'Of course you can. When were you thinking? Isn't there a notice period or something?'

Paul looked sheepish. 'You need to give a month's notice, yes.'

'Are you staying another whole month?' Her heart sank at the thought, then leaped at the idea that maybe Paul was planning to stay on to help Simon and Molly sort themselves out.

'No, we're still booked to fly on New Year's Day, so we thought we'd do it on New Year's Eve! We just won't be able to do the legal part. It'll have to be more a commitment ceremony. We'll do it legally once we get back to the UK.'

'Hang on, hang on,' said Annie. 'You've waited nearly twenty years for marriage equality, and now you're not even going to get legally married at your wedding?'

'Ironic, hey?'

'Very.' Annie looked at the board. 'Brian, your turn.'

'Can I be on your team?' Paul asked Brian.

Brian smiled at him. 'Always.'

Paul rolled the dice, and moved their piece, the top hat, nine spaces. 'Pall Mall. That's yours, Annie. How much?'

'Ten dollars. Do you want help organising the wedding? You haven't got much time.'

Brian and Paul exchanged glances. 'Aren't you going to be busy with your music?' asked Paul.

Annie took a deep breath and let it out. 'No. I've decided to let that be.'

'What do you mean? Not pursue it?'

'Not pursue it. I've got a lot of things on my plate now. I don't have the time or the energy to give the music thing a real go, so I'm going to put it to one side.'

'But you will go back to it, once the kids are sorted?'

'I don't know.'

'But you must,' said Brian. 'It's what you've always wanted.'

'Brian, let it go,' Annie said, her voice small and sad. She rolled the dice and moved her piece five spaces, landing on the corner where a stern police officer ordered her straight into gaol.

'Bummer,' said Paul. 'Do you want to pay fifty bucks now, or try for a double next turn?'

'I'll wait and roll,' she told him. She looked up at her son-in-law. 'Jack?' He was rubbing his eyes.

'Yep?'

'When Molly wakes up, will you please tell her that I'm not going anywhere? Will you say that I would be honoured and delighted to help look after Petula a couple of days a week? And I hope you'll stay here in the house with me for as long as you want to.'

Jack's eyes filled with tears. 'Thanks, Annie. That means a lot. Really.'

She patted his hand. 'Don't mention it.' She turned to Paul and pushed the dice across the board. 'It's your turn.'

* * *

When Ray died just after ten the next morning, Patrick was holding his hand and a gang of rosellas were shouting at each other in the garden. Naomi had dozed on the sofa all night and then, at Patrick's urging, had gone home for a shower and to play with Sunny for a while.

She had told him the end was close, and he could see that. There was more time between each of his father's laboured breaths, and he hadn't opened his eyes for more than twelve hours. It felt to Patrick like watching a spinning top gradually slowing, finally wobbling and toppling.

With each exhalation, Patrick wondered if a breath in would follow, and when at last none did, he sat, holding his own breath, for a long time. His father was gone.

The room was very still, and Patrick felt more alone than he could have imagined. Like a drop of water that had been dangling on the tip of a tap, now he was falling heavily to the ground.

He lowered his head to the mattress and rested his cheek on his father's warm wrist. 'Dad,' he whispered.

After a while, he stood up. He considered pulling the sheet up over his father's face, like you saw on TV, but there didn't seem any good reason to. He was lightheaded and his ears were ringing as he walked from the bedroom, through the kitchen and along the hall to the front door. He didn't know where to go.

Naomi would know.

The neighbours' front door stood open, so he walked inside, down the hall past the photos on the wall, and through to the kitchen. He stood in the doorway for a moment, taking in the scene before anyone noticed him.

Annie was at the counter, whizzing something in the blender. Naomi and Molly sat behind her at the kitchen table, playing with the baby's feet. The baby lay on the table amid discarded cereal bowls and plates of toast crusts.

Patrick cleared his throat when Annie switched off the blender, and they looked up at him.

Naomi knew at once.

'Patrick,' she said, her voice so full of love that he couldn't stand it. He reached for a chair and sat down.

'What happened?' asked Molly quietly.

'He's gone.'

'Oh, love,' said Annie, and she put a tall chocolate milkshake in a metal cup in front of him, adding a stainless steel straw. Patrick removed the straw and drank the milkshake in one go, then put his head on the table and cried, great heaving sobs.

Petula moved her head at the sound and jerked her arms, thumping Patrick as she did so. He looked up, confused. 'Sorry. I shouldn't do this in front of the baby. It'll upset her.'

'She's all right,' Molly said, 'don't stop on her account.' She scooped Petula up and stroked her back.

'Patrick,' said Naomi. 'Have you called anyone? From the list I made you?'

'Oh.' He wiped his eyes and looked worried. 'No, I don't remember where I put it. Who do I ring? Is it the police?'

'No, just his doctor. And then the funeral director. I can do it, if you want.'

'I'll do it. Is it important that it's right now? Is there a rush?'

'No, there's no rush.'

The door from the garden burst open and Sunny tumbled over the threshold. 'Annie, are the milkshakes ready? Can we take them out into the garden?'

'Please,' Annie reminded her.

'Please can we take them out into the garden?' Sunny saw Patrick's teary face. 'Did you hurt yourself?' she demanded. 'Were you running? Was it something sharp?'

Patrick snorted involuntarily with laughter.

Naomi opened her arms to Sunny and took her onto her lap. 'Patrick's dad Ray — remember Ray, from next door? — he's moved on. To another place.'

'Did he say where?' Sunny asked.

'No one really knows where,' said Naomi. 'It's a beautiful mystery. One day we'll all find out.'

Sunny furrowed her brow. 'Sorry, Patrick,' she said. 'Look, if you find out before me, can you tell me where it is, because my dad moved on too. Maybe we can go see them sometime. Mum can take us in her van.'

Annie raised her eyebrows at Naomi. 'I don't think euphemisms are helping here.'

'He's dead, Sunny,' said Molly. 'Ray died.'

'Oh!' Sunny's face brightened. 'Oh, dead. I didn't understand. I thought you meant he went off like my dad did, in the night, when I was a baby.' She paused. 'Wait, did my dad die?'

Naomi shook her head. 'No, your dad really did move on to another place that is also a mystery to me. Sorry, Sunny, I should have been clearer. I didn't mean to freak you out.'

'That's all right. Can we have the milkshakes please?'

'They're on the bench,' said Annie, kissing Sunny's head as she bounced up to get them.

On her way out Sunny stopped and turned back around. 'Patrick,' she said, 'we can bury him in the back here, behind our cubby. Or we can put him in the compost heap. Either's fine.'

The adults began to laugh.

'Can you even imagine?' said Annie. 'My father would turn in his urn.'

Chapter 35

Paul and Brian waited until the car from the funeral directors had been to collect Ray's body, and then for an additional respectful hour and a half after that, before they began their wedding planning in earnest.

They laid out a lunch of smoked salmon and bagels for everyone, and started assigning tasks, which Brian read from a stack of hastily written but nonetheless fairly dictatorial notes. Anyone was welcome to contribute in any way they wanted to, but given the lack of time, if what they wanted to contribute coincided with what he'd allocated them, then so much the better.

Jack had an extra shift to go to, making twenty-five-dollar cocktails at a friend's maritime-themed bar in Manly called the Ship and Steel, so he was excused after agreeing to be in charge of beverages at the wedding. Brian and Paul wanted a signature drink, and they released him from the meeting once he came up with the concept for a twist on the Cosmopolitan called the Suburban, in which the traditional cranberry juice was replaced with Cottee's raspberry cordial.

They would marry at six o'clock on New Year's Eve, in the back garden, on the patio. Diana was in charge of catering and Naomi was the designated Kid-Wrangler-in-Chief. Some suggestion was made that Annie would give one or both of the grooms away, but the logistics and symbolism of that made all their heads ache, and eventually Annie asked if she could please do the flowers instead.

'Don't you want to be in charge of music?' asked Paul. 'We were hoping you'd play a few songs. Maybe something new?'

'Maybe,' said Annie, loath to hurt his feelings, but she couldn't think what song would be appropriate to play at her ex-husband's wedding. Something old, something new, something borrowed, something blue. Well, they had two old grooms, one of whom had been borrowed from her, and she was feeling pretty damn blue. If she wrote them a song that would cover the last of the requirements.

She admonished herself for being so bitter. There was no point. She didn't want Paul. It was fine for him to marry Brian. More than fine. She was genuinely happy for them. But, no, she wouldn't write them a song. There was going to be no more of that. It was the only way to move on.

After the wedding planning meeting was adjourned, Annie went through the house on a mission. She collected all her new songs, scribbled on loose pieces of paper, in old notebooks she'd found on shelves, and even the rough jottings on scraps of envelope, and she put them in a box. Taping it closed, she considered labelling it, then decided there was no point. She taped shut the box of her mother's notebooks too, and carried both boxes up into the attic.

Up there, she breathed in the hot dusty air and looked around at her family's past. There was so much rubbish. Really, she ought to clear it out properly. Now that she was going to be there for a while, helping with the baby, and getting Simon back on his feet, she'd have time for things like this. Having a live-in home organiser would be handy. She pulled aside an old dressmaker's mannequin and shoved the boxes behind it. She didn't want to have to look at them every time she came up there for something.

She switched off the light and climbed back down the ladder.

* * *

Annie avoided the living room as much as possible for the next couple of days. Whenever she had to go in there, the piano seemed to stare reproachfully at her, like a dog she'd given up walking.

'Fuck off,' she muttered to it once, as she passed by to collect an armload of socks and empty glasses that various members of the family had left strewn on the floor in front of the television.

'Sorry?' said Diana, as she went past the hall door.

'Nothing,' said Annie.

Simon had made two more attempts to sit his mother down and convince her to sell the house and give him his share, but Annie had brushed him off each time. 'You can stay here as long as you need to,' she told him by way of consolation, 'but at the moment a place for everyone to live is more useful than a chunk of money for you or the others.'

Apparently feeling (with reason) his mother was treating him like both a child and a criminal, Simon went about in a deep sulk, which had less effect than he would have liked.

* * *

Once Annie had made her decision to Be A Proper Gran, as she couldn't help thinking of it, she took on her new role with gusto. She wore Petula strapped to her chest in a baby carrier whenever she could, watched and discussed *Star Wars*, googled rare Pokemon characters, and turned the kitchen over to Sunny and Felix for the making of slime. She cooked them plain pasta with cheese whenever they requested it, declared Milo a vegetable, and — when Naomi and Diana were out of earshot — decreed it could be eaten straight from the tin with a spoon. If she was going to be a grandmother, she might as well be a fun one.

To her surprise, and as much as she hated to admit it, hanging out with the kids was quite good fun. She wasn't always alone with them, either. Often Diana or Naomi would join in with what they were doing: watching *Big*, or measuring up the garden and counting the chairs in preparation for the wedding.

The music in her head grew quieter, and she found that if she played other people's songs all the time, it was harder for her own to coexist with them. She moved the Bluetooth speaker around wherever she went. She gave the children full control of the music, which meant a lot of Bon Jovi, Taylor Swift and Parry Gripp, and made other adults consider anonymously calling in a noise complaint to the police.

On the second last day of the year, she found herself in the living room with Sunny and Felix, who had dragged in four dining room chairs to build a blanket fort. Annie had advised against it, on account of the ambient temperature having reached the mid-thirties, but they seemed impervious to the heat and had collected several blankets for the walls.

'Is there room for me in there?' she called, on her hands and knees on the carpet.

'Honestly? Not really,' came Sunny's blunt reply.

Felix stuck his face out and gave Annie a sorrowful look. 'Maybe you can be the lookout?' he suggested.

'Great plan,' Annie told him, and clambered up to the piano stool. As much as they seemed to be enjoying her company, she could tell when she was not needed in a game. She lifted the lid of the piano, and for the first time in a couple of days looked at it. Had it really been only days since she packed away her songs? Time was behaving very strangely.

Maybe she'd been a bit rash, forswearing all musical creation forevermore.

Putting one hand back on the keys, she pressed them gently. It responded, the notes familiar and forgiving. She added her other hand and played a sudden storm of chords in vibrant apology for her tantrum. It didn't have to be all or nothing: she could see that now.

'And I thought it was all or nothing,' she sang and stopped. What was a good rhyme for nothing? She bit her lip and thought. What if she switched them around? 'And I thought it was nothing or all.' That was better. 'When I heard your footsteps in the hall.'

From under the blankets came a muffled voice.

'What was that?' she asked.

'What about "fall"?' suggested Sunny.

'That's a good rhyme, did you think of that?'

'No, I did,' said Felix, climbing out. He came to the stool and stood beside Annie. 'I love rhyming.'

'I feared the other shoe would fall,' Annie sang, 'when you walked in.'

'Do "small",' ordered Felix.

'I felt so cold and I felt so small …'

'Wall,' said Sunny.

'I thought the writing was on the wall.'

'"Paul"?'

'Hmmm,' said Annie. 'Shall we put Granddad in our song? Do you think he'd like it?'

'He'd think it was absolutely lovely,' said Sunny with deep certainty, and Annie pulled her in and cuddled her, laughing.

'He probably would. He probably would.'

'If your song is finished, can we do Kiss makeup now, please?' asked Felix. 'Mama said it would be okay to do it this afternoon because we have to have a hair wash tonight anyway before the wedding.'

Annie shut the piano and stood up. 'Let's do it.'

* * *

Simon tapped on Molly's door. There was no answer, but that might have had something to do with the fact that 'I Was Made For Lovin' You' was blasting out through the house. On the patio, he'd just seen his mother carefully painting the outline of a black bat onto his son's face with a small paintbrush.

He knocked harder.

'Yeah?'

'It's me.'

'Get a warrant.'

He opened the door and went in. Molly was lying on the bed, her arm covering her eyes. She had the blinds down and the windows shut.

'You all right?'

She looked at him. 'I'm fine. It's just so fucking loud.'

'Mum's lost it,' he informed her. 'It's like *Lord of the Flies* out there.'

'Have you read *Lord of the Flies*?'

'No one's read *Lord of the Flies*: it's just an expression. Where's your baby?'

'Mum's got her in the pram out in the garden.'

'Oh. Is that good?'

'I guess. Maybe not for Petula's hearing, but I said I wanted help. I asked her for help.'

'Has it made you feel any better? Knowing she's going to look after Petula sometimes?'

Molly shifted irritably on the bed. 'It's only been three days since I failed the multiple choice mothering test at the hospital. I don't know how I feel. I've barely seen Petula since. Mum's been wearing her like a bulletproof vest.' She changed the subject. 'How are you going? Mum was saying you might not go back to Germany.'

Simon twisted the fringe of the chenille bedspread around his fingers. 'Yeah, we might stay here for a bit. Put Felix into school. Stay in the house. How would you feel about that? Us being here with you guys and Mum?'

She thought about it for a minute. 'All right, I guess. I mean, Diana's a lot, isn't she? But she's been nice to me since the baby. And I like Felix. He's a good kid. What will you do for a job?'

'I've been talking to Justin. He might have a position coming up at the real estate agency, helping manage some of the rentals. I've told him the truth. I think there's a chance he'll take me on anyway. You know, because of him and Mum.'

Molly moved her hand away from her face and squinted at him. 'Him and *our* mum?'

'Oh,' said Simon slowly. 'That's another thing. Mum's sleeping with Justin.'

'Our mum is *sleeping* with Justin Schoolbags?' Molly sat up, incredulous.

'Yep.'

'Why? And also, gross.'

'Justin's not that bad.'

'I meant Mum. How did you find that out? And why didn't you tell me?'

'I asked Justin to come round to value the house and she pashed him right in front of me. They weren't even embarrassed. I must have forgotten to tell you. It might have been the day Petula was born. Things got a bit hectic and then there was Christmas and Patrick and Heather, and me blabbing about all my shit and then you went off and everyone freaked. Speaking of which, didn't you wonder why Justin Schoolbags appeared on the beach looking for you that day?'

'Oh.' Molly tried to remember. 'No, I didn't wonder at all. That's quite weird.'

'You were pretty mental.'

'I was only joining the rest of you. This whole family is demented.'

'Molly!' Annie's voice rang down the hall. 'Petula's hungry.' The assessment was backed up by the baby's hiccupping cries, and Annie appeared in the doorway cradling her. Annie's face was painted white, with a large black star obscuring one of her eyes.

'What do you think? Not bad eh? Want me to do yours?' She looked encouragingly at Simon. 'Felix would love it if you joined in.'

'Nope.' Simon stood up. 'I've got to go to the German butcher before it shuts. Diana has ordered enough sausages for a royal wedding.'

'I don't think royals have sausage sizzles at their weddings,' said Molly.

Simon ignored her. 'Mum, you right with the kids for a bit?'

Annie pointed at her face. 'I think we'll be okay. Will you be long?'

'Couple of hours? It's bloody ages away. I don't know why we couldn't get sausages from the butcher three blocks from here, but nobody comes between my wife and a good sausage. Molly, I know what you're going to say and you can just grow up, that is not what I meant, and that is my wife you're about to make a gross joke about.'

'All I was going to say, Simon, is that I imagine you'd come off wurst in that fight,' Molly said, with a smirk.

Simon groaned. 'Puns are the lowest form of wit and puns about wurst are the lowest form of pun.'

'Would you say they're the wurst kind of pun?'

'Stop.'

Molly smiled and leaned back on her pillow. The baby had latched on without hurting her. That was new. It would be all right staying at Pa's house for a bit. Diana wasn't that bad, really. She hadn't picked the easiest life, being married to Simon, let alone the rest of this family, and Molly felt sorry for her. When Dad and Brian flew back to London, and Naomi and Sunny drove back up north to the liminal space between New South Wales and Queensland, things would feel different. Quieter for sure.

With Jack at the bar in the evenings, having the others for company and help with Petula would be good.

And now her mum was going to stay and help. She'd told Molly she wasn't going to go overseas any more. Not that she'd even really had much of a plan for where she was going or what she was going to do. It had been a sort of nebulous theoretical idea about resurrecting her singing career, which hadn't even been that big a deal in the first place. Really, what was there to resurrect? This was good. Good for Molly, good for Petula, and probably good for Annie. So why didn't she feel as relieved as she'd thought she would? Why did she have a nagging sense that she was doing something wrong?

She tried to dismiss the uncomfortable tickle that felt too much like guilt for her liking. No one was forcing her mother to stick around and help. Molly hadn't chained her up in the attic. This was Annie's choice. As the baby drank, Molly picked up her phone and went to the place she knew would inspire enough envy to drown out the guilt: Instagram. She uploaded another picture of Petula and sat back to see how many likes it got.

* * *

Annie's phone was lying out in the garden, deep in the plumbago, when it buzzed with an incoming call. Sunny and Felix had been using it to take photos of the desiccated corpse of a rat they had found in the garage, so old and dried that it didn't even smell. At the sound of the phone, Sunny put down the flower crown she had been making for the dead rat and swiped to answer.

'Hello?' she said cautiously. 'This is Annie's phone but she said we could use it.'

A woman's voice laughed. 'Hello, Annie's phone. I'm looking for Thorne. Have I got the right number?'

'No,' said Sunny. 'This is Annie's phone.'

'What's Annie's last name?' asked the woman.

'Jones,' said Sunny. 'Same as me and Felix.'

'Oh,' said the woman. 'I must have the number wrong. I'm sorry to bother you.'

'That's all right,' said Sunny. 'I like answering phones.'

The woman hung up, and Sunny opened up the camera app. 'Felix,' she instructed, 'prop him up against that bush so he looks like he's dancing, and put this on his head.' She looked critically at the scene. 'That's good. Next, let's get the face paint and we'll make him be in Kiss.'

Chapter 36

By the time Jane returned from sea, Annie was almost dreading seeing her. So much had happened in the short time she'd been away. Her text came the morning of New Year's Eve, announcing that she had mutinied, murdered the captain and sunk the boat. She would be over at midday. *Hope you had a good Christmas*, she signed off.

Annie wasn't sure where she would start. Should she prepare a short digest of events? A briefing paper for her friend. The key points would be: a) Annie's father was a fraud and also the father of the man next door; b) Annie's youngest child had almost immediately developed postnatal depression and attempted to abandon her baby; c) Annie's son was a gambling addict and a thief; and d) which stood for Difficult and Don't Want To Tell Jane This, Annie wasn't going to throw herself body and soul into her music any more, to the exclusion of her family. She knew that was what Jane wanted her to do: sack off everyone, run away after a dream and live for herself. But it wasn't possible. Annie hoped Jane would be mollified by her discovery that maybe writing songs and spending time with her grandchildren needn't be mutually exclusive, but she suspected that wouldn't wash. There would be an addendum explaining that Annie was throwing a wedding for Brian and Paul that night, at her father's house, and that her children had learned she was sleeping with someone they went to school with, and they were horrified.

Jane arrived five minutes before she said she would. The front door was open and she marched straight down the hall to the kitchen. She started talking as soon as she entered the room. 'Thorne, my friend, I have missed you.' Her arms went around Annie and she kept talking. 'Hello, Di, what's all this food for? You lot having a New Year's Eve party? Where's my invitation? If anyone deserves a party it's me. I have been stuck at sea with the worst people you can imagine for eighty days. Well, it felt like eighty days. Christ on a bike, they were the pits. Alan's horrible friends were horrible. Beyond horrible. They were the distilled essence of horrible. If you wanted a horrible-flavoured cake you'd only need a couple of drops of them. And they wore popped-up collars and boat shoes. I've got nothing but hate in me now. Cut me and I bleed hate for those horrible people. Honestly, I kept hoping Billy Zane would show up and *Dead Calm* us all to just make it stop.'

'We're having a wedding. Paul and Brian are getting married.'

Jane pulled back and raised an eyebrow. 'Are they just? Tonight? Right. What can I do to help? Do these need washing, Di?' She seized two lettuces from the table and held them up.

'Sure,' said Diana. 'If you don't mind. I'll be back shortly. The grooms want the kids to do a little run-through.'

'The grooms.' Jane snorted. 'Exactly why are you hosting your ex-husband's wedding?'

Annie shrugged. 'I don't know. It's what they wanted. To do it with all the family together, and that's now, and we're all here, so I thought why not? Dad would have hated it.'

'When did they spring this on you?'

'Christmas Day.'

'For fuck's sake,' said Jane, aggressively tearing leaves off the lettuce and dunking them in the sink of cold water.

'Trust me, that barely made a ripple compared to everything else that happened at Christmas.'

'Oh yeah?'

'This will take a while; are you in a rush to get back to anything?'

'Thorne, I am all ears.'

* * *

The two lettuces were torn to tiny inedible shreds by the time Annie finished her outline of what had gone down while Jane was away.

Jane was pink with fury. 'Never,' she said, her voice shaking, 'ever again, for any reason, am I letting Alan talk me into going anywhere without mobile coverage at Christmas. I cannot believe I missed all this. It's a fucking outrage.'

'It's all right. There wasn't anything you could have done.'

'I know. But I'm your friend. I would have tried to help anyway. I would have, I don't know, kicked that Heather in the shins. I can't believe she was sleeping with your father. My god. The nerve of some people.'

'It was so shocking,' Annie admitted. 'I just never thought of Dad like that. I thought he was one of the good guys.'

There was a pause. 'I have to say, I'm not entirely surprised,' said Jane at last.

'What are you talking about?'

'I only knew him when he was ancient, but he still used to wink at me and pinch my bum.'

'He pinched your bum?'

'Is that so hard to believe?' Jane was affronted. 'I happen to have a very pinchable bum.'

'Why would you tell me that?' Annie demanded. 'What use is it for me to know my father was a geriatric sex pest? Now I'm going to wonder forever if he was always at it. Before you said that, I was hopeful that Heather might have been a one-off.'

Jane looked at her like she was a bit dim. 'Thorne,' she said, 'there's no such thing as a one-off. That's a cover story invented by people who can't stop having it off with people they're not supposed to have it off with.'

Annie got up from the table. She opened the dishwasher, but for once it was empty. A five-kilogram bag of brushed potatoes sat on the counter, so she ran more cold water into the sink, tore open the plastic and let them tumble in. She plunged in her hands and began rubbing the dirt off the potatoes, watching the water turn muddy.

After a while Jane came over and filled the kettle, getting in Annie's way, and set it back in its cradle to boil. She came and stood beside her friend, and reached into the sink for a potato.

'Sorry,' she said. 'That wasn't a helpful comment, about your dad.'

'No.'

'Still —' she nudged Annie with her elbow '— all good material for songs, eh?'

Annie kept scrubbing away at a potato even though it was pretty clean.

'Thorne?'

Annie dropped the potato and stared at her brown hands. 'I'm not Thorne. I'm just Annie.' Her voice wobbled. 'Jane, I've changed my mind. I'm not going to run away from home to be a pop star like we talked about. I don't know what I was thinking. The kids need me here.'

'They bloody don't,' said Jane. 'Thorne, look at me. They are all perfectly able to look after themselves. You're not divorcing them. You'll still be their mother, but you need to pursue this. You need the freedom of knowing you don't have to be home every Tuesday and Wednesday or whatever Molly wants from you. You need to not have to feel like you should be around after school to look after Felix, if his parents get jobs here. Mark my words. Your soul will never forgive you if you don't. If you give up now, it will eat away at you forever. You will regret not taking this chance.'

'What chance?' Annie replied, incredulous. 'There is no chance. This isn't a missed opportunity. This is me trying to pretend anyone gives a shit about an old lady singing her songs. No one called me after the gig. No one cares.' She scratched furiously at a dirty potato eye with her thumbnail.

'For heaven's sake,' said Jane, snatching the potato from her and a peeler from the second drawer down and violently deploying it. 'You played one open mike night. Of course no one called. That's not how it works. You can't expect an immediate break. You'll have to work at it. You're not afraid of a bit of hard work, are you? These things don't happen overnight.'

'But I'm old, Jane, and I'm tired and I *need* things to happen quickly. Otherwise I'm taking myself from the people who actually need me and care about me, here.'

'Which is it? Your family needs you or you aren't up to the challenge? One of them at least is a piss-poor excuse for just not trying. Possibly both.'

Annie sighed and sat down. 'Please don't be angry at me.'

'I'm not angry. I'm just disappointed.' Jane took another peeler from the drawer, handed it to Annie and dropped four soggy, streaky potatoes on the table in front of her.

The pile of peeled potatoes grew. They worked in silence.

Annie wanted to tell her about the previous afternoon, how for the first time ever she had managed to start creating something she thought had promise while in the company of small children, and how it had actually been fun, but Jane wouldn't understand. She'd see it as half-hearted.

Neither of them noticed when Sunny came in from the garden and stood for a moment, taking the measure of the room, then sidled up to the freezer.

'Annie? Please may we have a Calippo?'

Annie didn't answer.

Jane glanced over at Sunny, then at Annie, who seemed to be in another world. 'Thorne? Can the kids have a Calippo?'

'Who's Thorne?' asked Sunny.

'It's what I call your grandma,' Jane said.

'Why?'

'It was her maiden name. You can have a Calippo.'

Sunny extracted two yellow ice blocks from a box and closed the freezer. 'What's a maiden name?'

'It's the last name you were given when you were born. Often it's your father's last name, not your mother's.'

Sunny looked confused. 'But my last name's the same as my mum's. We are both called Jones. So is Annie.'

'Yes, now she is, because your grandfather Paul's name is Jones and when Annie married him she changed her name to his name.'

'Annie's name was Paul?'

'No, just his last name.'

Annie suddenly seemed to notice them. She smiled sadly at Sunny. 'When I was your age my name was Annie Thorne.'

'Huh,' said Sunny, peeling the foil top from her Calippo with her teeth, the other ice block carefully tucked under her arm. 'That's who the woman wanted to talk to.'

'What woman?' Annie asked.

'On your phone. A woman rang your phone when we were doing a photo shoot with Ray.'

'Ray next door? When did you do a photo shoot with Ray?'

'Yesterday. Not Ray next door. Ray the dead rat. We called him that because he was dead. Like Ray next door. We were using your phone to take the pictures. You said we could.'

'All right,' said Annie. 'But who rang my phone?'

Sunny carefully squeezed the base of her Calippo and sucked the top. 'Don't know. She kept asking for Thorne and I said I didn't know anyone called Thorne. But she must have wanted you, Annie.'

'She must have.'

'Bye.' Sunny gave Annie a sticky kiss on the shoulder as she passed, making her way back out to Felix in the sun.

'She should have a hat on,' murmured Annie.

'Fuck hats,' said Jane, almost bouncing in her seat. 'Someone wanted to talk to Thorne.'

'It might not mean anything.' Annie was trying to ignore the flicker of excitement inside her.

'It can't mean nothing. Check your received calls and ring them back.'

'I don't know. I made a decision. It wasn't easy, but I think it was the right thing. This might throw everything up in the air again. I can't keep flip-flopping like this.'

'Christ, Thorne, you don't even know who it was or what they wanted. Just call them back. You can throw yourself off that bridge when you get to it.'

'All right. I'll ring back.'

'Put it on speaker. I'm your manager.'

'You aren't my manager.'

'That's not really up to you, is it? I'll manage you if I want to.'

Annie smiled at her. Why had she only found Jane now? What if she'd had a guardian bully like this when she was twenty-three? Everything might have been very different. They might have conquered the world. 'You can manage me,' she said. 'If there's anything to manage. Just let me make this call on my own first, okay? It's probably nothing.'

She left the room, and as she started up the stairs she heard Jane call after her, 'I'll bet you a hundred thousand bucks it's not nothing.'

Chapter 37

There was only one number in her call log she didn't recognise. They'd called three times the day before, the afternoon of the thirtieth. Sunny probably stopped answering after the first call.

Annie sat down on her bed, holding the phone. Her dress for the wedding hung from the door of the wardrobe. She'd bought it that morning from the only boutique open in the suburb. It was too young for her — too sexy, cut too low in the back — but she'd bought it anyway.

Just call, she told herself. The longer she waited, the more her imagination was going to run away from her, like a metal measuring tape pulled out to its limit. The further out those things were pulled, the more likely they were to slice your hand open when let go. If she called now, the disappointment would be less than if she daydreamed any more about the possibility inherent in this conversation.

She pressed *call*.

The phone rang twice, and a woman's voice said, 'Lizzie Gessle speaking.'

Annie cleared her throat. 'Oh, hello. My name is Annie Thorne. I believe someone on this number tried to call me yesterday?'

The woman responded with a delighted, 'Thorne! Are you Thorne?'

'Yes, I am Thorne,' said Annie, and she felt like someone else was speaking. 'What's this in regard to?'

'I heard your songs. You gave a USB to a man called Philip recently. He said it was at an open mike night? Well, I'm a friend of his girlfriend, Emma, and she listened to your songs and passed the USB on to me and I — how can I say it? I've never heard anything like them.'

Annie held her breath. That could mean anything. It wasn't necessarily a good thing. 'Oh. Right.'

'I loved them. I think you have a real gift.'

'Oh,' said Annie again, and her voice sounded remarkably calm. 'Thank you.'

'Look, I don't know anything about you — I've tried googling you and I found nothing.' She laughed. 'Unless you're the Annie Thorne who wrote "Home Is Where Your Heart Is", back in about eighteen fifty!'

Annie paused.

'Oh,' said Lizzie. 'That is you, isn't it? I am so sorry. That's a brilliant song. A classic. The girl who sang it was pretty annoying, though — what was her name?'

'Lorraine Darmody,' said Annie. 'My band was going to record it, and play it at Eurovision, but I was pregnant and the label recommended we give it to someone else.'

'Weren't those the bad old days? Anyway, these new songs. They're cracking. And my wife and I — we're independent music producers — we're looking for someone to work with a new artist we've signed.'

'Work with them how?' Annie was numb.

'Collaborating on lyrics and music. Is that something you're up for?'

Annie caught her breath. Writing. For someone else. Not performing. For just a moment the disappointment stung like a slap.

But just past the pain, not even very far past, she felt a tingle of something good. Someone liked her songs. Someone who mattered. She could still write. And who could say what an opportunity like this might lead to? It might not have been exactly what she wanted, but it was still an incredible chance and she had to take it.

Gratitude washed over her and she laughed out loud. She couldn't help it. 'Yes!' she wanted to scream down the phone to whoever this Lizzie person was. 'That is everything I am up for. I am entirely up for that. I am up for that so much that you would have to scramble a fleet of fighter jets to shoot me down. Now and forever I am up for that.'

Instead she took a breath and asked, calmly, 'It might be. Can you tell me about the artist?'

'Her name is Juniper Wrenn.'

'Like the bird?'

'Yes but with two ns at the end. She's quite particular about that. She's twenty, and her voice is just something else. Thorne, it's not like anything we've heard before.'

'You can call me Annie. Thorne's my stage name.'

'Right, well, Annie, we've been working on how to describe her, and I guess her voice has elements of Bjork, and Sia, and Lana del Rey. It's really rich, and silvery and taut. It's gravelly sometimes. It sounds like the driveway to a haunted house. But then it can be smooth and it soars and it honestly just mesmerises you to listen to her. She sounds like being two drinks in feels. And she's gorgeous, to look at, I mean. She's most of the whole package. She just can't write songs for shit. She's got no ideas, because she's only a baby. She hasn't lived. She's never been dumped. Never been hurt or rejected, and she hasn't got much imagination. She's had a really nice life so far, you know? Which is great, but you can't sing a song about having an ace time with your mates when your voice sounds like a hangman's noose. It just doesn't gel.'

Annie steeled herself. 'Lizzie, you should know that I am fifty-eight. I am a grandmother of three. I've been working in the office at a school, with a very small sideline in running holiday music workshops for kids, and I've written a few advertising jingles. Nothing very much has happened to me either. I'm not sure I'm what you're after.'

'Yeah, look, I don't really care. Your age isn't relevant. Those songs you gave Philip, are they recent?'

'Extremely. I wrote them all this month.'

'Amazing. They are full of what we want. They have heartbreak and pain. They are clever and wry. Can we get you in a room with Juniper?'

'For what, exactly? To teach her my songs?'

'I want to see if you can write together. I'll buy all the songs of yours that I've heard so far, and if they go on her album you'll get sole credit for them, but I want her to have some co-writes too. Makes her look less manufactured.'

Annie lay back on the bed, staring at the plaster ceiling rose. 'I don't want to ghostwrite. I'll have to have credits on any songs I work on. And if she doesn't contribute, she isn't having a credit on my songs.' Where is this strong voice coming from? she wondered. It felt like Jane had taken over her body.

'Absolutely,' said Lizzie. 'I just have a feeling you can bring out something in her. Your songs and her voice would work, I know it. And I'd love her to learn something from you.'

'Does she have a band?'

'We're putting one together for her. She can play the guitar and the piano, to some extent, but she's going to be a stand-at-the-mike performer. Maybe we'll give her a tambourine. Just for retro kicks, you know? Maybe not. They're harder than they look. She's acting too, and she has a biggish film coming out in April. Annie, this girl is going to be massive. I think you want to get on this train with us.'

Annie thought of something. 'Where would I get in a room with her to write?' She'd been assuming this Juniper girl was Australian, but she hadn't asked. If it was in Sydney it might work. She could do three days with Juniper, and still manage two with Petula, like she'd promised Molly.

'Juniper is LA-based right now. We'd want you out there for a month, to begin with. Would that be possible?'

Annie held her breath. Surely this was a hoax. They'd ask her to send a bunch of money to a Nigerian bank account in a minute.

'Annie? Are you still there?'

'I'm here. Look, this is very flattering. It's just, well, if you'll forgive me for saying so, it sounds too good to be true and frankly I'm wondering if this is some sort of scam.'

'It's not a scam. But I get that. Look, text me your email address, and I'll send you some material about Juniper, and about Celeste and me. We're legit, I promise. You can google us, too. Lizzie Gessle and Celeste Delamotte. Why don't you have a think, and call me back in the morning? Do you have a manager, someone we should discuss money with, or do you do that yourself?'

'I have a manager. I'll have her get in touch with you.' She had no idea if Jane knew the first thing about negotiating a songwriting contract, but if she didn't, Annie was sure she would find someone to teach her pretty swiftly.

'We're keen to move fast, Annie, so don't feel like you have to wait until after the holidays to call. Tomorrow's fine. Might be a pretty cool start to the New Year for all of us?'

'It might be.'

'You doing anything fun tonight?'

'As a matter of fact, the other two members of my old band, Love Triangle, are getting married in my garden in a couple of hours,' Annie said. 'I used to be married to one, Paul, and he fell in love with the other one, Brian.'

Lizzie guffawed. 'If that's what you call nothing much happening in your life, I think you're exactly what Juniper needs. I'm so glad you called me back. Talk soon, Annie. Bye.'

* * *

Molly emerged from her room after having a nap with Petula to find the preparations for the wedding had kicked into high gear. Diana had taken control of operations, and was issuing commands to the others with such authority and speed that Simon couldn't even get a word in edgewise, which was just as well since by the look of him he wanted to make a lame crack about the Germans losing World War II. To her surprise, Simon held his arms out for the baby, so she passed Petula over. He made clucking sounds and started a little bobbing dance, and Molly saw Diana's face soften.

She couldn't see her mother anywhere, but Jane was folding napkins into heart shapes, using a YouTube tutorial. Diana pointed out that it wasn't a sit-down dinner, so the napkins would all have to be thrown into a basket together and they'd come undone, but Jane paid her no attention. She put down the napkin she was working on and came over to admire the baby, giving her an approving frown and a 'Good work, Molly.'

Glancing outside, Molly saw the back garden was festooned with tiny fairy lights and strings of large white lightbulbs. Where had they all come from? Had her dad and Paul been stocking up in preparation for this when they'd been on their Christmas-light bender? All the dining room and kitchen chairs had been assembled for the congregation, and the hall carpet, an old dark red Persian runner, had been moved to the aisle in between the chairs. The afternoon sun shone brightly, and it looked like a clear and warm evening ahead.

The sink was filled with scrubbed potatoes, and someone had made a start at slicing them, so Molly took a knife and continued.

Paul struggled into the kitchen, bowed under the weight of a huge jar of yellowish liquid. Molly paused and made a face at him. 'Toilet too far from your room, Dad?'

'Molly,' came Naomi's reproving voice from behind him. 'He's helping me. The kombucha I've been making is ready and I thought it would be perfect for tonight. It's my gift to Dad and Brian.'

'They might have preferred a toaster,' said Molly.

Paul set the jar on the counter and Naomi took off the lid. She reached in and hauled out a slimy lump that looked like ET's placenta.

'What is that?' Molly asked, horrified. 'Has that been in your room?'

'It's the SCOBY.'

'Answer the question.'

'It's a mixture of yeast and bacteria.'

'I think yeast and bacteria are traditionally the gift for a thirteenth anniversary.'

Paul hugged Naomi. 'I think it's very nice.'

Molly watched them, enviously. Naomi did everything right. Their father had always loved her more. She was so easy-going and accepting. Molly had never been accepting, she knew that. It was a bit late to start now. She put down the knife and walked outside.

In the garden, Jack was using a trestle table as a bar. He'd spread a white cloth over it and was unpacking hired wine glasses from their plastic crate. She stood behind him and watched until he felt her eyes on him and looked around.

'Hey babe. You all right?'

'No,' she said grumpily. 'No one gave me a job. They didn't even think of asking me to contribute something for the wedding. They all think I'm useless. Probably because I am.'

'You can help me.'

'I don't want to.'

'Right,' he answered, confused.

Molly bit her lip. 'It's just, I don't know. What does this wedding mean? Where do we go from here?'

'It means Brian and your dad are spending the rest of their lives together. It's beautiful.'

'It's not beautiful for Mum. Don't you feel like it's disrespectful of them to get married here? It's her home.'

'Annie's okay with it. I think she's been all right with their relationship for a long time. It's you who's struggling.'

She sat down on the grass and stretched her legs out. 'Can you believe we were just a normal family once?'

'What's a normal family?' Jack asked. 'Like one off a detergent ad? Or do you just mean a family without musicians and gay people and depression and Germans and single mothers and problem gamblers and illegitimate secret kids and toyboys and a sister who believes in ghosts and paints auras? The normal family ship has well and truly sailed.'

'I do mean that. Once it was Mum and Dad and us three kids and my grandparents. That was it. Brian was just their friend. I thought my parents were happy — but they can't have been. And my grandparents can't have been either. Is that what being a parent is? Pretending to be happy and normal until your kids are grown up enough for you to let your guard down? Are we going to do that with Petula?'

'I like to think we might actually be happy. Not just pretending.'

'The odds are not in our favour.' She felt dry and hollow. She wished she could cry.

Jack looked at her. 'You'll be back, Molly. The well you. This bit, what you're going through and how you're feeling now, it really is temporary.'

'Maybe,' she said. 'I hope so. But the me at the moment is the one Petula is getting to know, and bonding with. That me is who she'll think I am. That's not what I want. I want to be old me for her. Old me was fun. New me sucks.'

'I know you'll figure it out,' Jack said to her.

Molly tried to think positively. 'Yeah. I will. The pills will kick in. People figure out motherhood. And Mum will help me.'

Jack took a breath — Molly could see him do it. Lord, what was he going to say? 'I don't think we should stay here. I think you'll do better without your mum.'

Molly felt like she'd been slapped. 'What? What's wrong with my mum? I thought you liked her. You said you thought it was a good idea for her to mind Petula.'

'I know. I did think that. And there's nothing wrong with her. I love your mum. But you don't have to do everything like she does. Like she did. Our kid doesn't have to have your childhood. It doesn't mean there was anything wrong with it, but our life isn't her life.'

Molly was still stricken. 'But we don't know what we're doing. We don't know what jobs to do, or where to live. We owe so much money on the flat. The safest thing is to stay here.'

'Do you want to live the safest life? Just because you're scared of making the wrong decision?'

No, of course she didn't. No one was supposed to want that. But maybe she did. 'Yes. I do.'

'I don't think that's true.' His eyes were shining. 'A mortgage like ours is an anchor, and it just leads to bigger heavier anchors. We'll decide the flat is too small, and we'll upsize, and have a bigger mortgage. And that will limit our choices about what we do for work, and how we raise Petula. It's possible that a million-dollar anchor isn't the right thing for us.'

He was speaking aloud all her fears. 'What else can we do?' she asked. 'We need to find proper careers, raise our daughter in a stable home. That's the way it's done.'

'It doesn't have to be. That's what I'm saying.'

Molly began to cry. 'Why haven't we sorted ourselves out yet? We should have decided all this before we had a baby.'

Jack sat on the grass in front of her and cuddled her shaking form. 'My love, this is our life. Remember being a kid, and having no say in anything? Do you remember thinking, "When I'm grown up I'll do whatever I like"? That's now! We're the grownups now. We get to choose. We can go anywhere. Yes, it will be terrifying and hard to move somewhere new and start again, if that's what we decide, and not have family right there to help us all the time. But we can do that. We can do hard things. And if it doesn't work we can come back. No one will care. We could sell the flat, buy a campervan, quit our jobs and travel around Australia.'

She raised her tear-stained face and stroked his cheek. 'Not that. I hate the outback.'

He smiled. 'I know you do. We can move to Mexico. Or Finland. Or Kenya. Or Greece. Wherever we want. We've done the right thing. We got married, got the mortgage, had the baby.

Let's fuck the crappy parts off. Petula is so little and portable. Let's not waste our lives *not choosing* how we want to live.'

Molly pulled him in close and buried her face in his neck. She closed her eyes and tried to picture them somewhere else. Exploring a steep village in Mexico hand in hand with Jack, Petula in a baby carrier on her chest; or watching Petula crawl along a beach in Borneo as the sun set behind her and Molly and Jack sat in the sand with cold beers. The scenes were cheesy, Instagram versions of travel. It wouldn't be quite like that. She was terrified, but she knew his bravery was enough for them both, and inside, for the first time in ages, she felt a tiny bit brighter.

Chapter 38

Annie needed to get out. She didn't know anything else for sure at that moment, except that she couldn't make a decision, or process what had happened in that extremely odd phone call, if she was in the house with everyone in the world who mattered to her, where too much had happened and where she could still feel her parents hovering over her shoulder.

There were only a couple of hours until the wedding, and she should have been helping set up and cook, but she put her sneakers on and crept down the stairs. She waited until the hall was clear before dashing to the front door and down the steps. How ridiculous, she thought. Sneaking out of her own house.

At the gate she turned left, and headed to the end of the block before taking the street on the right that would lead her the rest of the way to the beach. For fifteen minutes she strode along, breathing in the warm afternoon air, and feeling the confetti of her thoughts swirl around until it eventually sank down to stillness. She crossed the main road, and, pulling off her shoes, marched straight down onto the sand. The waves were big, rolling and crashing messily. The lifeguards had knocked off for the day, but they'd left *Beach Closed* signs up, to be on the safe side. As if there would be any stopping the drunken skinny-dippers at midnight.

Annie sank down into the sand and stared at the sea. But the warm wind was stronger than she'd realised, and the sand whipped into her, stinging her shoulders and face. It was not an environment conducive to making big life decisions. Not for the first time, she wondered what people saw in the beach. Yes, she felt in awe of nature, but so often the beach was too hot or too windy, too busy or too rough. Her parents had lived in the house on Baskerville Road because it was where her dad grew up, but had it ever really suited them? Neither of them had been what you'd call beach people. Hardly anyone in the family was. No one could surf. They were all fair and prone to freckling. The little kids enjoyed it, but they'd grow out of that. Allowing thoughts like that into her head felt like pulling down a cobweb, snapping the threads of silk one by one.

A sudden urge to sweep down every cobweb in her life came over Annie, and at once she knew what she was going to do. She would say yes to the music producers. She would close her eyes and step off the cliff. Her body hummed with the thrill of the decision. How it would affect her kids, she still didn't know, but they'd survive. She felt the force of her mother's unlived dreams behind her, and her daughters' and her granddaughters' unrealised futures.

She stood to escape the blowing sand and walked back towards the dunes and the surf club. A woman stood beside the building, sheltering from the wind. Her red hair tangled around her face and she was trying to hold her kaftan down over her legs. Heather.

How long had she been there, watching? Had she followed her? Heather waved. Annie desperately wanted to walk the other way around the club, to avoid her completely, but she heard her mother's voice in her head. 'There's no excuse for rudeness, Annie.' Though she felt fairly certain her mother would have made an exception in this case, Annie approached Heather.

Heather smiled tentatively. 'How are you? I like your new fringe. I meant to say at Christmas, but I didn't get a chance.'

Annie's hand went to her hair and smoothed it. 'I'm wonderful,' she said.

Heather looked as if that wasn't the answer she'd been expecting. 'Oh, good. That's great.' She paused to drag a lock of her own hair out of her mouth. 'I don't know if you've heard, but I'm a widow now. Ray passed away a few days ago.'

'I know. Patrick came to us when it happened. We looked after him.'

Heather's lip curled. 'Oh, well done you. Perfect Annie. Always doing the right thing. Such a good mother. Just like your mum.'

'My mum *was* a good mother.'

'You treated her like dirt, though. All you cared about was your father.'

Annie looked Heather in the eye. 'I'm not proud of that. I was a kid. I didn't know what he was really like.'

'I can tell you what he was like. He was pathetic. He wanted excitement, and great sex, but he didn't want risk. When Ray found out what I was doing, he threatened to tell your mother, to get us to stop. But I knew he wouldn't. He didn't have the guts. He was pathetic too. They were all just sad, trapped, suburban losers.'

A young man walked past carrying a surfboard, a wetsuit pulled down to his waist. He stopped just beyond them, turned on the outdoor shower and rinsed his board. Annie didn't reply, embarrassed to have their heated conversation overheard. Heather used the opportunity to watch the surfer, one eyebrow raised, her mouth in a lascivious pout.

When he moved on, Annie spoke. 'Why didn't you stop the affair once Ray knew?'

Heather shrugged. 'Your dad and I were enjoying ourselves.

I didn't see why we should stop. There was nothing else to do. You were gone. I didn't have any other friends. What was I going to do, eat biscuits and knit things for the op shop like your mum and her cronies? Robbie tried to ditch me, but I kept going back over there and he couldn't resist. Things only changed when I was pregnant. Then he acted like nothing had happened. It made me want to kill him.

'Ray wanted me to leave — he tried to get me to go — but then I got pregnant and he couldn't kick me out. Patrick came and he was besotted. I told him Patrick was his baby. Said the dates didn't work for Robert to be the father.'

'Then why did you leave, and take Patrick?'

'I got too *bored*. I couldn't live in that house for the rest of my life. I didn't want to turn into Jean. At first I wasn't going to take the baby,' she admitted. 'In the end I think I did it to hurt Ray. And because I knew what people thought of women who ditch their kids. And I never told Patrick that Ray wasn't his dad. But he came back and found Ray, when he turned eighteen, and bloody Ray told him he wasn't his real father. Turns out he'd known all along.'

'And Ray had loved Patrick anyway, like he was his own, and you took that away from them, for sixteen years.' Annie spoke like she was passing down a sentence in court.

'Oh boo-hoo,' said Heather. 'Worse things happen. Ray only told him the truth to make me look bad.'

'Maybe he told him the truth because Patrick had a right to know who his father was.'

Heather scoffed. 'Maybe. Anyway, I gave Patrick a way more exciting life. We lived everywhere.'

Annie shook her head. She didn't want to talk about this any more. What was the point? 'Why are you still here, Heather?

Ray's dead. Patrick doesn't want you. Why don't you go lead your exciting life somewhere else?'

Heather smiled. 'I wondered when you'd ask me that. I've decided to challenge Ray's will.'

'What? On what grounds?'

'On the grounds that legally I am still his wife, and he wasn't Patrick's biological father.'

'Did Ray leave the house to Patrick?'

'He left it all to Patrick. But that won't stand up in court. Not once I tell them the truth.'

'I think it costs money to contest a will. Can you afford to do that?'

Heather flicked her hair back confidently. 'I'll borrow it. You've got to spend money to make money. I thought I'd tell you, because you should probably do the right thing and give half of Robert's house to Patrick before he sues you for it. Otherwise he'll be left with nothing. After all, he is your brother.' Heather folded her arms and looked expectantly at Annie.

But Annie just shook her head again in disbelief. 'Heather, I'm going home now. I don't think you'll contest the will. You haven't got the admin skills. I hope you go away and leave Patrick alone. He's better off without you. Some kids are, you know, better off without their mothers, at a certain point.' She turned and walked away, between the dunes, through the car park, over the street and back to Baskerville Road.

* * *

The front door to Ray's house was standing open when Annie got back. She went up the steps and called out. 'Anyone home? Patrick?'

Patrick's voice called back, 'Annie? I'll just be a second. Come in.'

She walked down the cool hall and waited in the kitchen. A large gift-wrapped box sat on the table. Shit, she thought. She hadn't bought Paul and Brian a present. Hosting the wedding and helping Patrick arrange Ray's roses were surely enough, though.

Patrick came in, still drying off his hair with a towel, wearing a pale pink linen shirt and light trousers.

'You look nice,' she told him.

'Thanks. I don't have many clothes with me, so I hope this is fancy enough.'

'Paul and Brian will be overdressed to the nines,' she assured him, 'and they won't care a single bit about what anyone else wears. Anyway, how are you feeling?'

'I'm all right,' he said. 'Better than I thought I'd be. I'm glad he's not in pain. I'm happy he isn't suffering, but I miss him. It probably won't be so bad once the funeral's done and I'm not in his house any more.'

'It'll always be bad some days, and not as bad other days. Grief's weird like that.'

'That's what Naomi said.'

'She knows things, my Naomi,' said Annie. She fiddled with the curled ribbon on the gift. 'I saw Heather. Just now, at the beach. I think she followed me.'

Patrick nodded. 'She was here earlier. She came to tell me she's going to sue me for this house.'

'I don't think she can,' said Annie.

Patrick shook his head. 'I don't care. I'm going to give it to her.'

'Why?' Annie couldn't keep the disdain from her voice.

'She's my mother. Yeah, she's dreadful, and selfish and narcissistic, but she gave me life. I'm grateful.'

'But she also gave you a shitty upbringing. She lied to you and took you away from someone who loved you and would have given you a great childhood.'

'Yeah. But I'm all right. And I can earn money. She can't. She never has, not legally. So I'm going to give her the house. I imagine she'll sell it. You won't have to live next door to her.'

'God, you're a very good person, aren't you? How about my — sorry — our father's will? You should have half the value of his house, by rights.'

'I don't want that. I'm not going to make you sell your family home so I can get the money.'

'I'm probably going to sell anyway. All three of my kids could use a chunk of cash right now. That's more use to them than a house. So I could give you half the proceeds.'

'Annie, you're a good person too.' He looked sadly at her. 'Was our father really a total shit? I hate to think that, because we're not bad.'

Annie smiled ruefully. 'I hope he wasn't. I don't think anyone's a total anything. My dad did some inexcusable things, and I know he could be cruel, but he was also wonderful. He loved me so much. He was the most supportive person in my life.' She began to cry. 'I wish I'd never found out about the other stuff.'

Patrick put his arm around her shoulder. 'Don't let all that eclipse your other memories of him. Everyone makes mistakes.'

Annie sniffed and patted him on the arm. 'You're right. I'm sorry for saying that. You're part of the other stuff and I'm glad I found you. And you're a very generous person. Thank you, Patrick. I'd better get back. I've got an ex-husband to shift.'

Chapter 39

Molly was standing in front of the mirror in the sunroom, attempting in vain to make the straps of her dress cover the thick elastic of her feeding bra. She needed double-sided tape to keep it in place, but heaven only knew where such a thing would be, if there even was any in the house. She satisfied herself by draping a scarf around her shoulders and knotting it behind her. That would have to do. The reflection in the mirror didn't even look like her.

She thought about her own wedding day, almost two years before. They'd had a registry office ceremony, just the immediate families, then a piss-up at a pub with all their mates. It had been so casual it almost didn't feel like a wedding. No bridesmaids, no being given away, just the basics. Maybe they had been a bit embarrassed to be doing it so much earlier than all their contemporaries.

'Molly?' came her father's voice from the doorway. He came in. 'You look beautiful.'

'I don't, but it's okay. Thanks for saying it anyway. You're the one who looks beautiful.' He did too. Paul wore a baby blue three-piece suit over a white shirt and no tie. His collar was open. 'You all ready?'

'Almost,' he said, with a funny look.

'What?'

'Sweetheart, I know when your mum and I split up, you found it harder than Naomi and Simon. You were so much younger. I'm really sorry. And we never really talked about it, did we? Everyone was just so kind to us. But it got to you, I know.'

Molly interrupted him. 'Dad! No, I'm fine with you and Brian. Really. Always have been.'

He took her hand. 'You haven't always been fine, and I get it. It made me sad, because I knew what I did hurt you. But I had to do it. I know it isn't about me being gay, it's just about your parents getting divorced. It was so hard for you. I felt like I'd let you down. I wanted you to admire me, and you didn't any more.'

'I'm sorry,' said Molly.

'You were a kid: you don't need to be sorry. I shouldn't have needed your approval.'

'I'm still sorry. It wasn't ever about you and Brian, Dad. It was that you left. You picked him over us. London. Neither of you made a sacrifice to be with us.'

'I know that now,' Paul said, shaking his head sadly. 'I'm really ashamed. I don't know why I felt like I needed to be out of this city, but I did.'

'People can't always do what they think they need to do,' Molly told him. 'Sometimes you have to do what's right.'

'And sometimes you don't know what the right thing is until you've done the wrong thing,' he said. 'Molly, I'm sorry. I made such a big mistake. I hope we can start to fix it. I hope I can be around more for you now than I used to be. Brian and I have been talking, and we think I should stay on for a bit. We'll go on our honeymoon, but, then, if you want, I can come back here and stay, do a bit of looking after my granddaughter.'

Molly couldn't speak, but she nodded, fighting back tears. She and Jack wouldn't be leaving immediately. Having her dad around more would be really helpful. Even having him offer made her feel stronger.

'And there's one more thing. I want to ask you something, and it's all right if you say no. I won't be offended. There's no pressure. Will you give me away at my wedding?'

'Yes,' said Molly, and the tears rolled down her cheeks.

'Don't,' said Paul, crying too. 'We can't be all red-eyed in the photos.'

Molly laughed and snorted. 'It won't matter. We'll still be the prettiest ones here.'

* * *

Felix and Sunny climbed the ladder to the treehouse to watch the wedding. It was still the aluminium ladder, leaned against the tree. No one had found time to make a new rope one. Earlier in the afternoon they had carefully carried up a battery-operated bubble machine, and it was their responsibility to switch it on when given the signal by the celebrant.

By the time Annie had showered and changed, everyone was assembled out in the garden. Brian stood at the front, resplendent in a mint-coloured suit. Annie hurried along the hall carpet, which now ran across the patio, to the first of two rows of seats, where a chair had a sign on it reading *reserved for Annie* in Felix's best printing. Jane was sitting beside it and she patted the seat. Annie smiled gratefully at her friend and sat.

'What did they say?' Jane asked. 'Did you get on to whoever rang?'

Annie took her hand and squeezed it. 'You've got some work to do, manager. I think I'm going to LA to write some more songs.' She felt like her heart would explode.

Jane didn't even look surprised. She squeezed Annie's hand back. 'Good. Good call, Thorne.'

Annie was about to tell her all about Lizzie and Celeste, and Juniper Wrenn, when the opening chords of the processional rang out from the stereo. The descending piano was as familiar to her as her own name, and she was instantly filled with a deep happiness. Petula Clark. It was her mother's favourite song, 'I Couldn't Live Without Your Love'.

She looked up and saw rose petals falling from the sky, flung down from the treehouse by Sunny and Felix. At the end of the aisle stood Paul, his arm linked with Molly's. Their eyes were red, but they were both giggling as they began to walk towards Brian.

The song finished and the ceremony began. The celebrant, an old friend of Brian's called Kate, spoke thoughtfully and kindly of their love, their long and winding road to this day, and the bright future that lay ahead. Annie could hear in her words the work Brian and Paul had obviously put into making this respectful of her, and their peculiar situation, and she was grateful. Brian and Paul exchanged vows — the traditional ones, she noted, promising to love and honour one another until death — and rings.

Kate smiled. 'Brian and Paul, you have come here today of your own free will, and in the presence of your family and friends have declared your love and commitment to each other. By the power vested in me, I now pronounce you married.'

Brian and Paul kissed, everyone burst into applause and cheers, and, as Felix reached for the on-switch of the bubble machine, he bumped a nail that had been only lightly tapped into the railing around the treehouse. Around the nail Simon had wrapped the end of a string of large lightbulbs, which stretched across from the house, and in that moment the cord slipped, sending the bulbs crashing to the ground, where they smashed along the aisle.

'Mazel Tov!' shouted Jane.

'Fuck,' exclaimed Simon, as others gasped and everyone checked that no one had been hurt.

Naomi looked at the broken glass and nodded calmly. 'That was Pa. I was expecting something. But I think he's done now. He's had his say.'

* * *

After the ceremony and the cleaning up of broken glass, they stood around with glasses of Champagne. The golden summer evening light filtered away the years from their faces. Annie gave Jane a longer explanation of her phone call, and Jane bounced on the spot with excitement.

'This could be a thing, Thorne. An actual thing.'

'It certainly does bear more than a passing resemblance to a thing, Jane,' Annie agreed. 'But it might not be a thing. We'll have to wait and see.'

Jane looked past her and sipped her Champagne. 'Oh, it's a thing all right. I've seen enough things in my time to know a thing when it's in front of me.'

Jack and Simon had moved the chairs and the carpet off the patio and Brian and Paul were getting ready for their first dance, which they wanted to get out of the way before everyone ate Diana's rather heavy dinner, likely as it was to lead more in the direction of somnolence than dancing.

'Bets on their first dance song?' said Jane. 'I'm thinking … "Careless Whisper".'

'No, it'll be something upbeat,' said Annie. 'My money's on "Go West".'

'Village People or Pet Shop Boys?'

'Pet Shop Boys, obviously.'

'Obviously.'

The music started and Annie had to listen for a moment before she could place it. It was from a musical. *Hamilton*. It was 'Helpless'. A strange choice, she thought, but then, as she listened to the lyrics, she understood.

It was a bittersweet tale of two people meeting and falling in love at a ball. It was the story of a love triangle, with a deep undertow of longing.

Annie felt desperately sad. Paul and Brian had loved each other from the beginning: she could see that now. Her whole life, what had become her whole life, was an interruption of someone else's love story. Watching them sway, holding each other close in the twilight, she knew what she'd had with Paul wasn't this. It had never been this.

Jane took Annie's hand again. 'Put it in your songs, Thorne. That's where pain needs to go. If you put it into art it transforms. That's literally the only point of any creative endeavour. It's just fucking misery apart from that. Let's profit from your pain. Let's transcend it. Give me your glass. You need more Champagne.'

After 'Helpless', the next song was indeed 'Go West', and everyone else took to the dance floor. Annie felt vindicated. She knew Brian and Paul so well.

'Dance, Mum?' Simon was at her elbow.

'In a minute,' she said.

'It doesn't have to be with me,' he said. 'Justin's here too.' He gave her a cheeky grin.

'I'm okay for now,' she said. 'Go dance with Diana.' She watched as he awkwardly boogied his way over to his wife, as if attempting a much-needed apology through the medium of interpretive dance.

She felt an arm slip around her waist. 'Hello, Mumma,' said Molly.

Annie's heart fell. She had to tell her. 'Darling.' How could she say it?

'Mum,' said Molly, and her voice shook with nerves. 'I need to tell you something. Jack and I have been talking. We think we might go away. Do some travelling. I think we're going to sell the flat. Which I know is probably a terrible idea, because once you're out of the property market you never get back in, and it will be hard to sell now with the concrete cancer and everything, but we're going to do it anyway. We're still pretty young, and we think it would be cool to show Petula the world. Well, for us to see the world a bit too. I know we'll regret it later, and we won't have a house and all that, but we might take that chance.'

'I think it's a really good idea,' said Annie. 'It's a brave thing to do. You've got to be brave, Molly, it's the only way. Putting off the things you want to do — it doesn't make them go away. Now is a good time for you guys to do this.'

Molly looked surprised. 'I thought you'd be mad. After I made such a fuss about you helping me look after Petula and everything.'

'I'll survive. Maybe I'll try the music idea again.'

'You should,' said Molly encouragingly. 'I don't know how good your songs are, Mum. I don't know if they're objectively better than other people's songs. I like them. But then I like lots of songs. I do get now that it's about the need you have to make them and share them. Maybe one day something will grab me like that. A passion. I'd like it to. Maybe it won't, though. Maybe I'll just be a person who lives a life, and does a job, and tries to have fun with her family and her kids and her friends.'

'And that would be a perfectly wonderful and very worthwhile way to live,' Annie told her firmly. 'Will you dance with me?'

Molly put out her hand and Annie twirled her onto the dance floor. The music was cheesy disco, and she laughed at Paul's and Brian's swing dance moves, and Simon playing air saxophone. Sunny and Felix jumped in time to the music, shouting the word 'together' whenever the lyric required it, and quite often when it didn't. Naomi twisted her body with her eyes half-closed, like she was on acid, and Diana danced with tiny sharp steps, moving her hands like she was describing a box in the air, hinting at a Berlin clubbing past none of them would have imagined she had. Jack stood to the side, bouncing at the knees with Petula in a sling, and Patrick danced an awkward side-to-side shuffle next to him until Jane hauled him into the middle and danced at him in a terrifying fashion, like a little voguing robot.

When the song finished, Annie slipped off the dance floor as 'Can't Take My Eyes Off You', the wedding classic, began. She spotted Justin at the bar and headed over to him.

'You look hot,' he said.

'You don't look half bad yourself.'

'This is pretty great,' he said, gesturing with his glass at the dancers and the lights, the people drinking and laughing.

'I know,' agreed Annie. 'Who even knew they had this many friends in Sydney? Justin, do you fancy selling a house?'

Justin's head whipped around. 'This house?'

She nodded.

'I'd love to,' he said. 'Why?'

'Time to move on. It's been absolutely lovely living here, but it no longer suits the family's needs. I'm going to divide up the money among my kids, so they can go off and sort themselves out in all the various ways they need to.'

'Have you told them?' he asked. 'Is that why everyone's so bloody elated this evening?'

'No,' said Annie. 'I haven't said anything. I think they're all just genuinely happy. How often does that happen?'

Justin leaned over and kissed her. 'I hope you're staying around.'

'I'm heading overseas for a bit. To LA. I'll miss you. We've had a lot of fun, haven't we?'

'We have. I've never met anyone like you.'

'Thank you,' said Annie. 'I hope you do, though — meet someone else like me. Because we're good together, but I'd rather you had someone like me, but twenty years younger. You too could have all this!' She gestured at her family.

'That would make me very happy,' he replied, seriously. 'Your family are quite something.'

'They are, aren't they?' agreed Annie, looking at the three generations in their finery, flinging themselves about on the patio, mimicking each other's dance moves and collapsing with laughter. 'They are quite something.'

Acknowledgements

First things first: this book wouldn't be in your hands if it weren't for the wonder that is Kate O'Donnell. Katie, calling you the editor of this book is like calling Ma Anand Sheela the secretary of Bhagwan Shree Rajneesh. You were the editor, the midwife, the paramedic, the mental health crisis team, the cheerleader, the bartender, the makeup artist, the Jane, the caterer's wife, the spiritual advisor and much more besides. I love you and I thank you from the bottom of the bottom of my heart for your endless hard work, inspiration, help, and friendship.

Now, while Katie chose to be there for me and for the book, there were three people who couldn't escape being present for it. Truckloads of thanks are due to my family for putting up with the writing (and the writer) of this book.

My husband, Drew Truslove, and my children, Teddy and April: you are the reason I write. I mean that in a nice way. Your support of my work, your pride in it, and the love you heap on me – these are things I couldn't do without. I love you the most that anyone ever loved anyone else.

Nor could I manage without your forbearance: the songs that inspired this book have been on constant rotation in our home and car for two years and you have endured more Petula Clark and ABBA than it is reasonable to ask anyone to put up with. I think we're even now, April, for the road-trip when you, at the age of two, made us listen to Feist's song '1234' for six hours in a row.

Jessica Tory, thank you for your love and support. You are an inspiration to me, and so much of what I think and write comes from moments we've spent together. It's time for us to go back to Scandiland, I think.

Thanks to my parents, Nick Dettmann and Carol Dettmann, for their love and support, and thanks for not asking not a word about this book while I was writing, and instead offering up cups of coffee, morning chats, and the use of your home to write in.

Thanks to my brother who reads my books and my brother who doesn't but proofreads the acknowledgements: you know who you are.

Thanks to Kathy Lette, Sally Hepworth and Joanna Nell for their generous cover quotes; to Joshua Dowling for help with questions of police procedure; to Megan Washington for answering my questions about songwriting; and to Richard Cooke for being my occasional study buddy at the State Library of New South Wales.

Sarah Darmody, Ariela Bard, Louise Pounder, Ellie Parker and Amy Maiden: thank you for reading drafts of the book, and for your feedback, encouragement, friendship and food. Amy Kersey, thank you for the food and love.

Thanks to Jo Butler, who sold this book when it was no more than a lie I told about having an idea for a second book. And thanks to Pippa Masson at Curtis Brown Australia for taking me on for the next stage of the journey where I lie about book ideas.

To my publisher, Anna Valdinger: thanks for your patience with me and with the book. Some of these characters needed some serious wrangling and our discussions got me there. And thanks again for believing I could write two books before there was any evidence I could even write one.

The team at HarperCollins Australia operated, as always, like a well-oiled machine. A successful publishing machine, not, like, a jaffle maker. Madeleine James, thanks for your wise and helpful editorial input, and thanks to Pamela Dunne for her keen proofreading eye. Hazel Lam, once again your cover design delighted me and made me so confident to send the book out into the world. My marketing and publicity team, Alice Woods and Kimberley Allsopp: thank you for getting the book in front of the eyes of the right people.

And finally, to everyone who bought, sold, borrowed or stole my first book or this one: thank you. You're all my secret friends now, forever.

Winning
is for losers

How to Be
Second
Best

JESSICA DETTMANN

How to Be Second Best

A hilarious and heartwarming novel that captures the dramas, delights and delirium of modern family life.

Going from one child to two is never easy for a family, but when Emma's husband simultaneously fathers a third child with another woman, things get very tricky, very fast.

Three years later, Emma is no longer trying to be the best wife and mother — now she has to be the best ex-wife, and the best part-time parent to her ex's love child, and that's before she even thinks about adding a new man to the mix.

Set in an upwardly mobile, ultra-competitive suburb, this funny, biting, charming comedy looks at the roles we play, how we compete, and what happens when we dare to strive for second best.

'Sharp and crisp and funny. I was dazzled' — Mia Freedman
'Ultimate summer read' — *Herald Sun*